About the Authors

Sara Orwig lives in Oklahoma and has a deep love of Texas. With a master's degree in English, Sara taught high school English, was Writer-in-Residence at the University of Central Oklahoma and was one of the first inductees into the Oklahoma Professional Writers Hall of Fame. Sara has written mainstream fiction, historical and contemporary romance. Books are beloved treasures that take Sara to magical worlds. She loves both reading and writing them.

As an Air Force officer, **Merline Lovelace** served at bases all over the world. When she hung up her uniform for the last time, she combined her love of adventure with a flare for storytelling. She's now produced more than ninety-five action-packed novels. Over twelve million copies of her works are in print in thirty-five countries. Named Oklahoma's Writer of the Year and Female Veteran of the Year, Merline is also a recipient of Romance Writers of America's prestigious RITA® Award.

Cathy Williams is a great believer in the power of perseverance as she had never written anything before her writing career, and from the starting point of zero has now fulfilled her ambition to pursue this most enjoyable of careers. She would encourage any would-be writer to have faith and go for it! She derives inspiration from the tropical island of Trinidad and from the peaceful countryside of middle England. Cathy lives in

A Surprise Family

July 2020
Against the Odds

August 2020
Proving Their Love

September 2020
Their Perfect Surprise

January 2021
Written in the Stars

February 2021
The Perfect Family

March 2021
Baby Makes Three

Proving
Their Love

SARA ORWIG

MERLINE LOVELACE

CATHY WILLIAMS

MILLS & BOON

First Published in Great Britain 2020
By Mills & Boon, an imprint of HarperCollins*Publishers*
1 London Bridge Street, London, SE1 9GF

A SURPRISE FAMILY: PROVING THEIR LOVE
© 2020 Harlequin Books S.A.

Pregnant by the Texan © 2014 Harlequin Books S.A.
The Diplomat's Pregnant Bride © 2013 Merline Lovelace
The Girl He'd Overlooked © 2012 Cathy Williams

Special thanks and acknowledgement are given to Sara Orwig for her contribution to the *Texas Cattleman's Club: After the Storm* series.

ISBN: 978-0-263-28188-0

MIX
Paper from
responsible sources
FSC™ C007454

This book is produced from independently certified FSC™ paper to ensure responsible forest management.

For more information visit: www.harpercollins.co.uk/green

Printed and bound in Spain
by CPI, Barcelona

PREGNANT BY THE TEXAN

SARA ORWIG

With a big thank you to Stacy Boyd,
Harlequin Desire Senior Editor, and
Charles Griemsman, Harlequin Desire Series
Editorial. Also, with love to my family.

One

Early in December as the private jet came in for a landing, Aaron Nichols looked below. Even though the tornado had hit two months earlier, the west side of Royal, Texas, still looked unrecognizable.

No matter how many times he had gone back and forth between Dallas and Royal, he was shocked by the destruction when he returned to Royal. The cleanup had commenced shortly after the storm, but the devastation had been too massive to get the land cleared yet. Hopefully, he and his partner, Cole Richardson, could find additional ways for R&N Builders to help in the restoration. As he looked at the debris—the broken lumber, bits and pieces of wood and metal, a crumpled car with the front half torn away—he thought of the lives wrecked and changed forever. It was a reminder of his own loss over seven years ago that had hit as suddenly as a storm: a car accident, and then Paula and seventeen-month-old Blake were gone. With time the pain had dulled, but it never went away and in moments like this when he had a sharp reminder, the hurt and memories hit him with a force that sometimes made him afraid his knees would buckle.

Realizing his fists were doubled, his knuckles white, he tried to relax, to shift his thoughts elsewhere. He remembered the day in October when he had met Stella Daniels during the cleanup effort. He thought of their one night together and his desire became a steady flame.

He hoped he would see her on this trip, although since their encounter, he had followed her wishes and refrained from calling her to go out again. The agreement to avoid further contact hadn't stopped him from thinking about her.

At the time he and Stella parted ways, he expected it to be easy. In the seven years since he lost his wife and baby son, women had come and gone in his life, but he had never been close to any of them. Stella had been different because he hadn't been able to walk away and forget her.

He settled in the seat as the plane approached the small Royal airport. Royal was a West Texas town of very wealthy people—yet their wealth hadn't been enough to help them escape the whirlwind.

Almost an hour later he walked into the dining room at the Cozy Inn, his gaze going over the quiet room that was almost empty because of the afternoon hour. He saw the familiar face of Cole Richardson, whose twin, Craig, was one of the storm's fatalities. A woman was seated near Cole. Aaron's heart missed a beat when he saw the brown hair pulled back severely into a bun. He could remember taking down that knot of hair and watching it fall across her bare shoulders, transforming her looks. Stella Daniels was with Cole. Aaron almost whispered "My lucky day" to himself.

Eagerness to see her again quickened his step even though it would get him nowhere with her. He suspected when she decided something, she stuck by her decision and no one could sway her until she was ready to change. Her outfit—white cotton blouse buttoned to her throat and khaki slacks with practical loafers—was as severe and plain as her hairdo. She wore almost no makeup. Few men would look twice at her and he wondered whether she really cared. Watching her, a woman who appeared straitlaced and plain, Aaron couldn't help thinking that the passionate night they'd had almost seemed a figment of his imagination.

As Aaron approached them, Cole stood and Stella glanced over her shoulder. Her gaze met Aaron's and her big blue eyes widened slightly, a look of surprise forming on her face, followed by a slight frown that was gone in a flash.

He reached Cole and held out his hand. "Hi, Cole. Have a seat."

"Aaron, good to see you," Cole said. Looking ready for construction work, he wore one of his T-shirts with the red, white and blue R&N Builders logo printed across the front. "You know Stella Daniels."

Bright, luminous eyes gazed at him as he took her hand in his. Her hand was slender, warm, soft, instantly stirring memories of holding her in his arms.

"Oh, yes," he answered. "Hi, Stella," he said, his voice changing slightly. "We've met, but if we hadn't, anyone who watches television news would recognize you. You're still doing a great job for Royal," he said, and she smiled.

One of the administrative assistants at town hall, Stella had stepped in, taking charge after the storm and trying to help wherever she could. It hadn't taken long for reporters to notice her and start getting her on camera.

Aaron shed his leather jacket and sat across from Cole, aware of Stella to his left. He caught a whiff of the rose-scented perfume she wore, something old-fashioned, but it was uniquely Stella and made him remember holding her close, catching that same scent then.

"I'm glad to have you back in Royal," Cole said. He looked thinner, more solemn, and Aaron was saddened by Cole's loss as well as the losses of so many others in town. He knew from experience how badly it could hurt.

"I know help is needed here, so I'm glad to be back."

"Thanks," Cole said. "I mean it when I say I appreciate

that. When you can, drop by the Texas Cattleman's Club. They're rebuilding now and moving along. They'll be glad to have you here, too."

"Our club friends in Dallas said to tell you and the others hello."

Cole nodded as he glanced at Stella. "Getting to the business at hand, Stella and I were talking about areas where more lumber is needed—all over the west side of town, it seems."

"Each time I see Royal, I can't believe the destruction. It still looks incredible. I've made arrangements to get another couple of our work crews here."

"R&N Builders have helped tremendously," Stella said.

"I'm sure everyone in town thanks you for doing such a great job right from the start, Stella—acquiring generators, getting help to people and directing some of the rescue efforts. When disaster happens unexpectedly like that, usually all hell breaks loose and it takes a calm head to help the recovery," Aaron stated.

"Thanks. I just did what I could. So many people pitched in and we appreciate what R&N Builders, plus you and Cole individually, have donated and done to aid Royal."

"We're glad to. Everyone in the company wanted to help," Cole replied. "So we're adding two more work crews. Stella, you can help coordinate where they should go. I asked men to volunteer for the assignment. They'll be paid by us the same as if they were working on a job at home, but R&N is donating their services to help Royal rebuild."

"That would be a tremendous help," Stella said. "Local companies are booked solid for the next few months. There's so much to be done that it's overwhelming."

"Also, we might be able to get one of the wrecking companies we work with to come in here and pick up debris. I doubt you have enough help now when there's so much to clean up," Aaron said.

"We need that desperately. We have some companies from nearby towns, but we can use more help. There is an incredible amount of debris and it keeps growing as they get the downed trees cut up."

Cole made a note on a legal pad in front of him.

"Right now I wonder if we'll ever get all the debris cleared. It would be great to have more trucks here to help haul things away."

Stella made notes as they discussed possibilities for the next hour. Even as he concentrated on the conversation, Aaron could not keep from having a sharp awareness of Stella so nearby. He wished she had not asked him to back off and forget their night of passion.

He'd done so, but now that he was back in her presence, he found it difficult to keep memories from surfacing and wished he could take her out again, dance with her and kiss her, because it had been an exciting, fun night.

Her long slender fingers thumbed through the notebook she held as she turned to a page of figures. He recalled her soft hands trailing across his bare chest, and looked up to meet her blue-eyed gaze.

She drew a deep breath and her cheeks flushed as she looked down and bent over her open binder. Startled, he realized she had memories, too. The idea that she had been recalling that night stirred him and ignited desire. He wondered how many men paid no attention to her because of her buttoned-up blouses and austere appearance. Her actions that night hadn't been austere. Aware he should get his thinking elsewhere, he tried to focus on what Cole was saying.

At half past three Cole leaned back in his chair. "Sorry to have to break this up. You two can continue and, Aaron, you can fill me in later. I'm going out to a long-time friend Henry Markham's ranch to stay five or six days. He invited me out. He also lost his brother in the storm and he's had a lot of damage, so I'm going to help him. I'll see you both next week and we can continue this."

"Don't forget," Stella said, "I have to leave town for part of the day tomorrow. I'll be back in the afternoon." As Cole nodded, she looked at Aaron. "I'm flying to Austin where my sister lives."

"If you need to stay longer, you should," Cole said.

"I don't think I'll need to stay. Just a short time with her and then I'll be back."

Cole glanced at Aaron. "I'm glad you're here, Aaron. We've got good people running the place in Dallas while we're gone, so everything should be all right."

"It'll be fine. George Wandle is in charge. And if anything comes up he promised he would call one of us."

"Good deal." Cole stood, pulled on a black Western-cut jacket and picked up his broad-brimmed Resistol hat. "Thanks, Stella, for meeting with me."

"All the thanks go to you and Aaron for the help you and your company are giving to Royal. You've been terrific."

"We're glad to help where we can. Aaron, if you need me for anything, I have my phone with me."

"Sure, Cole."

Aaron watched his partner walk through the restaurant and then he turned back to Stella. "It's nice to see you again."

"Thank you. It's nice to see you, too. I really mean it. Your company has done so much to help."

"There's still so much more to do. How's the mayor?"

A slight frown creased her brow as she shook her head at him. "Since the mayor was in the town hall when it sustained a direct hit, he was hurt badly. He was on the critical list a very long time. He's hurt badly with broken bones, internal ruptures and complications after several surgeries. He was in the ICU for so long. With all the problems he's had, he's still a long way from healed."

"That's tough. Tough for him, for you, for all who work for him and for the town. The deputy mayor's death complicated things even more. No one's really in charge. You've sort of stepped into that void, Stella."

"I'm just doing what I can. There are so many things— from destroyed buildings to lost records and displaced pets. Megan Maguire, the animal shelter director, has worked around the clock a lot of the time. It just takes everybody pulling together and it's nice you're back to help."

He smiled at her. "Maybe, sometime, you need a night out to forget about Royal for a few minutes."

"Frankly, that sounds like paradise, but I don't have time right now. Someone texts or calls every other minute. This has been one of the quietest afternoons, but this morning was a stream of calls."

"Royal could manage without you for a couple of hours."

"Don't tempt me, Aaron," she said, smiling at him. "And I won't be here tomorrow."

"I have the feeling that you're working late into the night, too."

"You're right, but every once in a while now, there'll be a lull in the calls or appointments or hospital visits. Lately, I've had some nights to myself. While you're here, let me show you which projects Cole has finished and where we need the work crews next."

She spread a map on the table and he pulled his chair closer to her. Aware of her only inches away now, he once again inhaled a faint scent of her rose perfume. He helped her smooth the map out and leaned close, trying to focus on what she told him but finding it difficult to keep his attention from wandering to her so close beside him.

She showed him where they had repaired houses and finished building a new house. Stella told him about different areas on the west side of town, which had taken the brunt of the storm, the problems, the shortages of supplies, the people in the hospital. The problems seemed staggering, yet she was quietly helping, as were so many others she told him about.

He wondered if she had suffered some deep loss herself and understood their pain. He wouldn't ask, because she probably wouldn't want to talk about it. He didn't want anyone to ask him about his loss and he hadn't reached a point where he could talk about it with others. He didn't think he ever would. The hurt was deep and personal.

"Aaron?"

Startled, he looked at her. "Sorry, I was thinking about some of these people and their terrible losses. Some things you can't ever get back."

"No," she answered, studying him with a solemn expression. "Houses can be rebuilt, but lives lost are gone. Even some material possessions that hold sentimental value or are antiques—there's no replacing them. You can't replace sixty-year-old or older trees—not until you've planted new ones and let them grow sixty or seventy years. It tears you up sometimes." She smiled at him. "Anyway, I'm glad you're here."

"We'll just help where we can. To have a bed and a roof over your head is good and we need to work toward that for everyone."

"Very good. You and Cole are a godsend," she said, smiling at him and patting his hand.

He placed his hand on hers. Her hand was soft, warm,

smooth. He longed to draw her into his arms and his gaze lowered to her mouth as he remembered kissing her before.

She slipped her hand out from under his. "I think they're beginning to set up the dining room for tonight. I wonder if they want us to leave," she said. Her words were slightly breathless and her reaction to him reinforced his determination to spend time with her again.

"We're not in anyone's way and I doubt they want us to leave."

"I didn't realize how long we've talked," she said.

"Have dinner with me. Then I'll give you a ride home tonight."

"I'm still staying here at the inn until the repairs are done on my town house," she said.

"I'm staying here, too, so I'll see you often," he said. She had a faint smile, but he had the feeling that she had put up a barrier. Was she trying to avoid the attraction that had boiled between them the last time they were together? Whatever it was, he wanted to be with her tonight for a time. "Unless you have other plans, since we're both staying here, then, by all means, have dinner with me."

There was a slight hesitation before she nodded. "Thank you," she replied. Even though she accepted his invitation, she had a touch of reluctance in her reply and he had the feeling she was not eager to eat with him.

"Is this headquarters for you?" he asked, his thoughts more on her actions than her words.

"Not at all. I'm not in charge—just another administrative assistant from town hall helping like the others."

"Not quite just another administrative assistant," he said, looking at her big blue eyes and remembering her passionate responses. For one night she had made him forget loss and loneliness. "Should your town house be on our list of places to help with reconstruction?" he asked her.

"Thank you, no. The damage wasn't that extensive, but I was pretty far down on the priorities list. I finally have the work scheduled and some of it has already started. I'm supposed to be back in my place in about a week. Thank goodness. I want to be there before Christmas."

"Good, although I'm glad you're staying here in the hotel because that means we can see each other easily," he said, deciding he would get his suite moved to whatever floor she was on. "They're setting up for tonight and I need to wash up before dinner. Want to meet again in an hour?" he asked her.

"That's a good idea. I've been busy since seven this morning and I'd welcome a chance to freshen up."

As they walked out of the restaurant, he turned to her. "What floor are you on?"

"The sixth floor. I have a suite."

"The same floor I'm on," he said, smiling at her.

"That's quite a coincidence," she said in a skeptical voice.

"It will be when I get my suite moved to the sixth floor, after seeing you to your suite."

She laughed. "I can find my own way to my suite. You go try to finagle a suite on the sixth floor. I don't think you can. It's hopeless. Every available space has been taken because of so many homeless folks having their houses repaired after the storm. People reserved every nook and cranny available in Royal and all the surrounding little towns. Some had to go to Midland, Amarillo and Lubbock. We're packed, so I don't think I'll see you on my floor."

"So you approve if I can get a suite," he said.

"I figure it won't happen," she answered, looking at him intently.

"Not if you don't approve," he said.

"I don't want more complications in my life and you're

a wicked influence, Aaron," she said mischievously, for the first time sounding as if she had let down her guard with him.

"Wicked is more fun and you know you agree," he said softly, standing close in front of her. "I'll show you tonight when we're together."

"Oh, no, you won't. I don't need you to show me one thing. We'll have dinner, talk a little and say good-night. That's the agenda. Got it?"

"Oh, I have an agenda. I had it the moment I walked through the door and saw you sitting there with Cole. One of the goals on my agenda is to get you to take down your hair."

"Amazing. One of my goals is to keep my hair pinned up, so one of us is going to fail completely," she said, her blue eyes twinkling.

Eager to be with her for the whole evening, to flirt and dance and hopefully kiss, he leaned a bit closer. "If I placed my hand on your throat, I'll bet I'd feel your pulse is racing. You want the same thing I do. I'm looking forward to dinner and spending the evening together."

"I'm looking forward to the evening, too, so I can talk to you more about how you and your company can continue to help with the restoration of Royal. You're doing a wonderful job so far, and it's heartwarming to know you're willing to continue to help."

"We'll help, but tonight is a time for you to relax and catch your breath. It's a time for fun and friendship and maybe a kiss or two to take your mind off all the problems, so don't bring them with you. C'mon, I'll walk you to your door," he said, taking her arm and heading to the elevators.

She laughed. "Well now, don't *you* have a take-charge personality."

"It gets things done," he answered lightly as they entered

the elevator and rode to the sixth floor. When they got off, she walked down the hall and put her key card in a slot. As she opened the door, she held the handle and turned to him.

"Thanks, Aaron. I'll meet you in the lobby."

"How's seven?" he asked, placing one hand on the door frame over her head and leaning close. "It's good to see you again. I'm looking forward to the evening."

Her eyes flickered and he saw the change as if she had mentally closed a door between them. "Since I'm leaving town tomorrow, let's make it an early evening, because I have to get up at the crack of dawn. My life has changed since you first met me. I have responsibilities now that I didn't have then."

"Sure, whatever you want," he said, wondering what bothered her. For a few minutes downstairs she had let down that guard. He intended to find out why she was now being distant with him. "See you at seven."

"Bye, Aaron," she said, and stepped inside her suite, closing the door.

As he rode down in the elevator, his thoughts were on her. He knew she had regretted their night of lovemaking. It was uncustomary for her and in the cool light of day, it upset her that she had allowed herself to succumb to passion. Was she still suffering guilt about that night?

He didn't think that was what had brought on the cool demeanor at the door of her suite. Maybe partially, but it had to be more than that. But what else could it be? He intended to find out.

He took the elevator back down and crossed the lobby, determined to get a suite on the sixth floor even if he had to pay far more to do so.

It turned out to be easier than he had thought because someone had just moved out.

My lucky day.

Two

Stella Daniels walked through the living room of the suite in the Cozy Inn without seeing her surroundings. Visions came of Aaron when he had strolled to the table where she sat with Cole. Looking even better than she had remembered, Aaron exuded energy. His short dark blond hair in a neat cut added to his authoritative impression. The warmth in his light brown eyes had caused her heart to miss a beat.

She had a mixture of reactions to seeing him—excitement, desire, dread, regret. She hoped she'd managed to hide her tangled opposing emotions as she smiled and greeted him. Her first thought was how handsome he was. Her second was happiness to see him again, immediately followed by wishing he had stayed in Dallas where the company he shared with Cole was headquartered. His presence complicated her busy life more than he knew.

She'd offered her hand in a business handshake, but the moment his fingers had closed over hers, her heartbeat had jumped and awareness of the physical contact had set every nerve quivering. Memories taunted and tempted, memories that she had tried to forget since the one night she had spent with Aaron in October.

It had been a night she yielded to passion—which was so unlike her. Never before had she done such a thing or even been tempted to, but Aaron had swept her away. He had made her forget worries, principles, consequences, all her usual levelheaded caution, and she had rushed into a blissful night of love with him.

Now she was going to pay a price. As time passed after their encounter, she suspected she might have gotten pregnant. Finally she had purchased a pregnancy kit and the results confirmed her suspicions. The next step would be a doctor. Tomorrow she had an appointment in Austin. Her friends thought she was going there to visit her sister; Stella hadn't actually said as much, but people had jumped to that conclusion and she had not corrected anyone. She did not want to see a doctor in Royal who would know her. She didn't want to see one anywhere in the vicinity who would recognize her from her appearances on television since the storm. If a doctor confirmed her pregnancy, she wanted some time to make decisions and deal with the situation herself before everyone in Royal had the news, particularly Aaron.

Tomorrow she would have an expert opinion. Most of the time she still felt she wasn't pregnant, that something else was going on. It had only been one night, and they'd used protection—pregnancy shouldn't have resulted, regardless of test results or a missed period.

She studied herself in the mirror—her figure hadn't changed. She hoped the pregnancy test was wrong, even though common sense said the test was accurate.

Given all that was going on, she should have turned Aaron down tonight, but she just couldn't do it.

She looked at her hair and thought about what he had said. She would keep it up in a bun as a reminder to stop herself from another night of making love with him. In the meantime, she was going to have dinner with him, work with him and even have fun with him. Harmless fun that would allow them each to say goodbye without emotional ties—just two people who had a good time working together. What harm could there be in that?

Unless it turned out that she was pregnant. Then she couldn't say goodbye.

She showered, took down her hair to redo it and selected a plain pale beige long-sleeved cotton blouse and a dark brown straight wool skirt with practical low-heeled shoes. She brushed, twisted and secured her hair into a bun at the back of her head. She didn't wear makeup. Men usually didn't notice her and she didn't think makeup would make much difference. The times she had worn makeup in high school, boys still hadn't noticed her or wanted to ask her out except when they were looking for help in some course they were taking.

An evening with Aaron. In spite of her promises to herself and her good intentions, the excitement tingled and added to her eagerness.

When it was time to go meet Aaron, she picked up a small purse that only held necessities, including her card key, wallet and a list of temporary numbers that people were using because of the storm. She wouldn't need a coat because they wouldn't be leaving the Cozy Inn.

When she stepped off the elevator, she saw him. She tried to ignore the faster thump of her heart. In an open-neck pale blue shirt and navy slacks, he looked handsome, neat and important. She thought he stood out in the crowd in the lobby with his dark blond hair, his broad shoulders and his air of authority.

Why did she have such an intense response to him? She had from the first moment she met him. He took her breath away and dazzled her without really doing anything except being himself.

He spotted her and her excitement jumped a notch. She felt locked into gazing into his eyes, eyes the color of caramel. She could barely get her breath; realizing how intensely she reacted to him, she made an effort to break the eye contact.

When she looked again, he was still watching her as he approached.

"You look great. No one would ever guess you've been working since before dawn this morning."

"Thank you," she answered, thinking he was just being polite. Nobody ever told her she looked great or gorgeous, or said things she heard guys say to women. She was accustomed to not catching men's attention so she didn't give it much thought.

"I have a table in the dining room," he said, taking her arm. The room had been transformed since they'd left it. Lights had been turned low, the tables covered in white linen tablecloths. Tiny pots wrapped in red foil and tied with bright green satin bows held dwarf red poinsettias sprinkled with glitter, adding to the festive Christmas atmosphere.

A piano player played softly at one end of the room in front of a tiny dance floor where three couples danced to a familiar Christmas song. Near the piano was a fully decorated Christmas tree with twinkling lights.

Aaron held her chair and then sat across from her, moving the poinsettia to one side even though they could both see over it.

"I haven't seen many Christmas trees this season," she said. "It's easy to even forget the holiday season is here when so many are hurting and so much is damaged."

"Will you be with your family for Christmas?"

"No. My parents don't pay any attention to Christmas. They're divorced and Christmas was never a fun time at our house because of the anger between them. It was a relief when they finally ended their marriage."

"Sorry. I know we talked about families before. Earlier today you said you are going to see your sister in Austin tomorrow. Do you see her at Christmas?"

"Some years I spend Christmas at her house. Some years I go back and forth between my parents and my sister. Mom has moved to Fort Worth. She's a high school principal there. After the divorce my dad moved his insurance business to Dallas because he had so many customers in the area. I see him some, but not as much as my mom. My grandmother lives with her and my grandfather is deceased."

"So this year what will you do at Christmastime?"

"I plan to stay here and keep trying to help where I can until the afternoon of Christmas Eve. Then I'll fly to Austin to be at my sister's. I have a feeling the holidays will be extremely difficult here for some people. I'm coming back Christmas afternoon and I've asked people here who are alone to come over that evening—just a casual dinner. So far there are about five people coming."

"That's nice, Stella," Aaron said, sounding sincere with a warmth in his gaze that wrapped her in its glow.

"What about you, Aaron? Where will you spend Christmas? You know more about my family than I do about yours."

For an instant he had a shuttered look that made her feel as if she had intruded with her question. Then he shrugged and looked at her. "My parents moved to Paris and I usually go see them during the holidays. My brother is in Dallas and I'll be with him part of the time, although he's going to Paris this year. I like to ski, and some years I ski. This year I'll see if I can help out around here. You're right. A holiday can hurt badly if someone has lost his home or a loved one. After losing his brother, Cole will need my support. So I'm going to spend the holidays in Royal."

As he spoke quietly, there was a glacial look in his eyes that made her feel shut out. She wondered about his past. More and more she realized how little she knew about him.

Their waiter appeared to take their drink order, and Aaron looked at her, his brown eyes warm and friendly again. "The last time we were together you preferred a glass of red wine. Is that what you'd like now?"

She shook her head. "No, thank you. I would prefer a glass of ice water. Maybe later I'll have something else," she said, surprised that he remembered what she had ordered before. She didn't want to drink anything alcoholic and she also didn't care to do anything to cause him to talk about the last time they were together.

"Very well. Water for the lady, please, and I'll have a beer," he said to the waiter.

As soon as they were alone, Aaron turned to her. "Let's dance at least one time and then we'll come back to place our order. Do you already know what you want? I remember last time it was grilled trout, which is also on this menu here."

"I don't know what I want and I need to read the menu. I'll select something and then we'll dance," she said, trying to postpone being in his arms. If she could gracefully skip dancing, she would, but he knew from the last time that she loved to dance. He was remembering that last time together with surprising clarity. She figured he had other women in his life and had forgotten all about her.

"Let's see what we want. When he brings drinks, we can order dinner. I remember how much you like to dance."

"You have a good memory."

"For what interests me," he said, studying her.

"What?" she asked, curious about the intent way he looked at her.

"You're different from last time. Far more serious."

Her breath caught in her throat. "You notice too much, Aaron. It's the storm and all the problems. There are so many things to do. How can I look or feel or even be the same person after the event that has touched each person who lives here," she said, realizing she needed to lighten the situation a bit so he would stop studying her and trying to guess what had changed and what was wrong.

"C'mon. One dance. You need to get your mind off Royal for just a few minutes at least. We can order dinner after a dance. You're not going to faint on the dance floor from hunger. Let it go for a minute, Stella. You've got the burden of the world on your shoulders."

She laughed and shook her head. "I don't think it's that bad. Very well, you win," she said. By trying to stay remote and all-business, she was drawing more attention instead of less, which wasn't what she wanted.

"That's more like it," he said, smiling. "What time do you leave in the morning?" he asked.

"I'll fly the eight-o'clock commuter plane from here to Dallas and change planes for Austin."

They reached the dance floor as the music changed to an old-time fast beat. She was caught in Aaron's direct look as they danced, and his brown eyes had darkened slightly. Desire was evident in his expression. Her insides clenched while memories of making love with him bombarded her.

His hot gaze raked over her and she could barely get her breath. How could she resist him? He was going to interfere in her work in Royal, interfere in her life, stir up trouble and make her want him. The last part scared her. She didn't want Aaron involved too soon because he was a man who was accustomed to taking charge and to having things his way.

Watching him, she gave herself to dancing around the floor with him, to looking into brown eyes that held desire and a promise of kisses, to doing what he said—having fun and forgetting the problems for just a few minutes. The problems wouldn't go away, but she could close her mind to them long enough to dance with Aaron and have a relaxing evening.

As they danced the beat quickened. Smiling, she shut her mind to everything except dancing and music and a drumming beat that seemed to match her heartbeat. The problems would be waiting, but for a few minutes, she pushed them aside.

Her gaze lowered to Aaron's mouth and her own lips parted. Having him close at hand stirred up memories she had been trying to forget. If only she could go back and undo that night with him, to stop short at kissing him.

The dance ended and when a ballad began he held her hand to draw her closer.

"Aaron, I thought we were going to have one dance and then go order dinner," she said, catching her breath.

"I can't resist this. I've been wanting to dance with you and hold you close."

The words thrilled her, scared her and tormented her. They danced together and she was aware of pressing lightly against him and moving in step with him. Memories of being in his arms became more vivid. His aftershave was faint but she recalled it from before. Too many things about him were etched clearly in her memory, which hadn't faded any in spite of her efforts to try to avoid thinking about him.

The minute the song ended, she stepped away and smiled. "Now, we've danced. Let's go order so we get dinner tonight."

"There, that's good to see you relax a little and laugh and smile. That's more the way I remember you."

"I think you just wanted to get your way."

"No. If I just wanted to get my way, we wouldn't be here right now. We'd be upstairs in my room."

She laughed and shook her head, trying to make light of his flirting and pay no attention to it.

At their table she looked over the menu. She selected grilled salmon this time and sipped her cold water while Aaron drank a beer.

"See, it's good to let go of the problems for at least a brief time. You'll be more help to others if you can view things with a fresh perspective."

"I haven't done much of this. The calls for help have been steady although it's not like it was at first. We've had some really good moments when families found each other. That's a triumph and joy everyone can celebrate. And it's touching when pets and owners are reunited. Those are the good moments. Frankly, I'll be ready to have my peace and quiet back."

Her phone dinged and she took it out. "Excuse me," she said as she read the text message and answered it.

Their dinner came and they talked about the houses that were being rebuilt by his company and the families who would eventually occupy them. With Aaron she had a bubbling excitement that took away her appetite. She didn't want him to notice, so she kept eating small bites slowly. Before she was half-through, she got a call on her phone.

"Aaron—" She shrugged.

"Take the call. I don't mind."

She talked briefly and then ended the call. "That's Mildred Payne. She's elderly and lives alone. Her family lives in Waco. Her best friend was one of the casualties of the storm. She just called me because her little dog got out and is lost. Mildred's crying and phoned me because I've helped her before. I'm sorry, Aaron, but I have to go help her find her dog."

He smiled. "Come on. I'll get the waiter and then I'll take you and we'll find the dog."

"You don't have to."

"I know I don't have to. I want to be with you and maybe I can help."

"I need to run to my suite and get my coat."

"I'll meet you in the lobby near the front door in five minutes."

"Thanks."

"Wouldn't miss a dog hunt with you for anything," he said as they parted.

She laughed and rushed to get her coat. When she came back to the lobby, Aaron was standing by the door. He had on a black leather bomber jacket and once again just the sight of him made her breathless.

His car was waiting outside and a doorman held the door for her as Aaron went around to slide behind the wheel. She told him the address and gave him directions. "You're turning out to be a reliable guy," she said. "I appreciate this."

"You don't know the half about me," he said in an exaggerated drawl, and she smiled.

"To be truthful, I'm glad I don't have to hunt for the dog by myself. I do know the dog. It's a Jack Russell terrier named Dobbin. If you'll stop at a grocery I'll run in and get a bag of treats because he'll come for a doggie treat."

"I'll stop, but if we were home and I was in my own car, we wouldn't have to. My brother has a dog and I keep a bag of treats in the trunk of my car. That dog loves me."

"Well, so do I," she said playfully. "You're willing to hunt for Dobbin."

"When we find Dobbin, we'll go back to the Cozy Inn and I'll show you treats for someone with big blue eyes and long brown hair—"

"Whoa. You just find Dobbin and we'll all be happy,"

she said, laughing. "Seriously, Aaron, I appreciate you volunteering to help. It's cold and it's dark out. I don't relish hunting for a dog, and Dobbin is playful."

"So am I if you'll give me half a chance," he said. She shook her head.

"I'm not giving you a chance at all. Just concentrate on Dobbin."

"I'll only be a minute," he said, pulling into the brightly lit parking lot of a convenience store. He left the engine running with the heater on while he hurried inside. She watched him come out with a bag of treats.

"Thanks again," she said.

"Hopefully, Dobbin will be back home before we get there. You must get calls for all kinds of problems."

"I'm glad to help when I can. I'm lucky that my house didn't have a lot of damage and I wasn't hurt. Mildred had damage to her house. She's already had a new roof put on and windows replaced. She has a back room that has to be rebuilt, but she was one of the fortunate ones who got help from her insurance company and had a construction company she'd worked with on other jobs, so she called them right after the storm."

"That's the best way. Make the insurance call as soon as possible."

"It worked for Mildred." They drove into a neighborhood that had damage but not the massive destruction that had occurred in the western part of Royal. Houses were older, smaller, set back on tree-filled lots. Stella saw the bright beacon of a porch light. "There's her house where the porch light is on. Mildred is in a block where power got restored within days after the storm. Another help. There she is, waiting for us and probably calling Dobbin."

"He could be miles away. It's a cold night and she's elderly. Get her in where it's warm and I'll drive around looking for Dobbin. Hopefully, he loves treats."

When they reached the house, Aaron turned up the narrow drive. A tall, thin woman with a winter coat pulled around her stood on the porch. She held a sack of dog treats in her hand.

"Thanks again, Aaron. You didn't know what you were in for when you asked me to eat dinner with you. I'll get her settled inside and then I'll probably walk around the block and look. She said he hadn't been gone long when she called."

"That's good because a dog can cover a lot of ground. I have my phone with me. My number is 555-4378."

"And mine—"

"Is 555-6294," he said, startling her. "I started to call you a couple of times, but you said you wanted to say goodbye, so I didn't call," he said.

That gave her a bigger surprise. She figured he had all but forgotten the night they were together. It was amazing to learn that not only had he thought about calling her, he even knew her phone number from memory. He had wanted to see her again. The discovery made her heart beat faster.

"Stella—"

Startled, she looked around. He had parked and was letting the motor idle. She was so lost in her thoughts, for a moment she had forgotten her surroundings or why they were there. "I'll see about Mildred," she said, stepping out and hurrying to the porch as Aaron backed out of the drive.

"Hi, Mildred. I came as quickly as I could."

"Thank you, Stella. I just knew you would be willing to help."

"I'm with Aaron Nichols, who is Cole Richardson's partner. They own one of the companies that has helped so much in rebuilding Royal. Aaron will drive around to search for Dobbin."

"I appreciate this. He's little and not accustomed to being out at night."

"Don't worry. We'll find him," Stella said, trying to sound positive and cheerful and hoping they could live up to what she promised. "Let's go inside where it's warm and I'll go look, too. You should get in out of the cold."

"You're such a help to everyone and I didn't know who else to turn to. There was George, my neighbor, but their house is gone now and he and his family are living with his sister."

They went inside a warm living room with lights turned on.

"You get comfortable and let us look for Dobbin. Just stay in where it's warm. May I take the bag of treats with me?"

"Of course. Here it is." Mildred wiped her eyes. "It's cold for him to be out." Gray hair framed her long face. She hung her coat in the hall closet and stepped back into the living room.

"I'm going to walk around the block and see if I can find him. Aaron is looking now. We'll be back in a little while."

Mildred nodded and followed Stella to the door.

"This is nice of you, Stella. Dobbin is such company for me. I don't want to lose him."

"Don't worry." She left, closing the door and hurrying down the porch steps. "Dobbin. Here, Dobbin," she called, rattling the treat sack and feeling silly, thinking Dobbin could be out of Royal by now. She prayed he was close and would come home. No one in Royal needed another loss at a time like this.

"Dobbin?" she called, and whistled, walking past Mildred's and the lot next door where a damaged house stood dark and empty. The roof was half-gone and a large elm had fallen on the front porch. Away from the lights the area was grim and cold. She made a mental note to check tomorrow about Mildred's block because she thought this section of town had already had the fallen trees cleared away.

"Dobbin," she called again, her voice sounding eerie in the silent darkness.

A car came around the corner, headlights bright as it drove toward her. The car slowed when it pulled alongside her and she recognized Aaron's rental car. He held up a terrier. Thrilled, she ran toward the car. "You have Dobbin?"

"Dobbin is my buddy now. He's waiting for another treat."

"Hi, Dobbin," she said, petting the dog. "Aaron, you're a miracle man. I'll meet you on Mildred's porch."

"Get in and ride up the drive with me. I'll hold Dobbin so he doesn't escape."

She laughed, thinking it was becoming more and more difficult to try to keep a wall up between them. All afternoon and this evening he had done things to make her appreciate and like him more.

She climbed into the warm car. "I'll hold Dobbin," she said. When Aaron released the terrier, he jumped into her lap. Aaron drove up the drive and parked.

"Come in and meet Mildred because she'll want to thank you."

"Here, you might as well give Mildred the bag of treats. I'll carry Dobbin until we get to the door," Aaron said, taking the dog from her.

On the porch Aaron rang the bell. In seconds the door opened and Mildred smiled. "You found him. Thank you, thank you." She took the dog from Aaron and the bags of treats from Stella. "Please come in. I'm going to put him in my room and I'll be right back. Please have a seat."

When she came back, Stella introduced everyone. "Mildred, this is Aaron Nichols. Aaron, meet Mildred Payne."

"Nice to meet you, ma'am. Dobbin was in the next block, sitting on a porch of a darkened, vacant home as if waiting for a ride home. I had a bag of treats, so he came right to me."

"Good. He doesn't like everybody."

"Mildred, we're going back. It's been a long day and I still have some things to do."

"I wish you could stay. I have cookies and milk."

"Thanks, but we should go," Stella said. Mildred followed them onto the porch, thanking them as they left and still thanking them when they got into the car.

"Now you've done your good deed for today," Stella said when he backed down the drive. "It was appreciated."

"It was easy. I think you've become essential to this town."

"No. I'm just happy to help where help is needed. And I'm just one of many helping out. The Texas Cattleman's Club has been particularly helpful, and you and Cole have certainly done more than your fair share."

"Your life may have changed forever because of the storm. I'm surprised you haven't had job offers from people who saw you on television."

"Actually, I have from two places. The attorney general's office in San Angelo has an opening for an administrative assistant and another was a mayor's office in Tyler that has a position that would have the title of office manager."

"Are you interested in either one?"

"No, I thanked them and turned them down. My friends are in Royal and I've grown up here so I want to stay. Besides, they need me here now."

"Amen to that. I'm glad you're staying here because

we'll be working together and maybe seeing each other a little more since we're both at the Cozy Inn."

"Did you get your suite changed to the sixth floor?"

"Indeed, I did," he said. "I'll show you."

"I'll take a rain check."

"Oh, well, it's still early. Let's go have a drink and a dance or two."

She hesitated for just a moment, torn between what she should do and what she wanted to do.

"You're having some kind of internal debate, so I'll solve it. You'll come with me and we'll have a drink. There—problem solved. You think you'll be back in Royal tomorrow night?"

"Yes," she said, smiling at him.

When they got back to the hotel, Aaron headed for a booth in the bar. The room was darker and cozier than the dining room. There was a small band playing and a smattering of dancers.

Over a chocolate milk shake, she talked to Aaron. They became enveloped in conversation, first about the town and the storm and then a variety of topics. When he asked her to dance, she put him off until later, relieved that it did not come up again.

"Our Texas Cattleman's Club friends want an update on the progress here. Cole is good about keeping in touch with both groups."

"I think you'll be surprised by how much they have rebuilt and repaired," she replied.

"Good. I'm anxious to see for myself what's been done."

"You'll be surprised by changes all over town."

Later, she glanced at her watch and saw it was almost one, she picked up her purse. "Aaron, I have to fly out early in the morning. I didn't know it was so late. I never intended to stay this late."

"But you were having such a good time you just couldn't tear yourself away," he teased, and she smiled at him.

"Actually, it has been a good time and the first evening in a while that has had nothing to do with the storm."

They headed out to the elevator and rode to the sixth floor. The hallway was empty and quiet as Aaron walked her to her door.

"Let me take you to the airport in the morning and we can get breakfast there."

"No, thank you. It's way too early."

"I'll be up early. It'll save you trouble and we can talk some more. All good reasons—okay?"

She stopped at her door, getting her card from her purse. "I know you'll get your way in this conversation, too, Aaron. See you in the lobby at six o'clock. Thanks for dinner tonight and a million thanks for finding Dobbin. That made Mildred happy."

"It was fun. Mostly it was fun to be with you and see you again. Before we say good-night, there's something I've been wanting to do since the last time we were together."

"Do I dare ask—what have you been wanting to do?"

"Actually, maybe two or three things," he said softly. "First, I want to kiss you again," he said, moving close and slipping his arm around her waist. Her heart thudded as she looked up at him. She should step back, say no, stop him now, but what harm was there in a kiss? She gazed into his light brown eyes and there was no way to stop. Her heartbeat raced and her lips tingled. She leaned closer and then his mouth covered hers. His arms tightened around her and he pulled her against him.

She wrapped her arms around him to return his kiss, wanting more than kisses. She felt on fire, memories of being in his arms and making love tugging at her.

He leaned over her while he kissed her, his tongue going

deep, touching, stroking, building desire. She barely felt his fingers in her hair, but in minutes her hair fell over her shoulders.

She had to stop, to say no. She couldn't have another night like the last one with him.

"Aaron, wait," she whispered.

He looked down at her. His brown eyes had darkened with passion. "I've dreamed of you in my arms, Stella," he whispered. "I want to kiss you and make love."

"Aaron, that night was so unlike me."

"That night was fantastic." He held long strands of her hair in his fingers. "Your hair is pretty."

She shook her head. "I have to go in," she whispered. "Thank you for dinner, and especially for finding the dog."

She opened her door with her card.

"Stella," he said. His voice was hoarse. She paused to look at him.

"I'll meet you in the lobby at six in the morning. I'll take you to the airport."

She nodded. "Thanks," she said, and stepped into her entryway and closed the door. The lock clicked in place. She rested her forehead against the door and took a deep breath. She didn't intend to get entangled with him at this point in time. Not until she had a definite answer about whether she was pregnant.

At six the next morning Aaron stood waiting. He saw her step off the elevator. She wore a gray coat and a knitted gray scarf around her neck. Her hair was back in a bun. She was plain—men didn't turn to look at her as she walked past, yet she stirred desire in him. She was responsive, quick-witted, kind, helpful, reliable. She was bright and capable and—he knew from firsthand experience—sexy.

He drew a deep breath and tried to focus on other things.

But he was already thinking about how long she would be gone and when he would see her again. He hoped that would happen as soon as she returned to Royal. Maybe she would let him pick her up at the airport.

He needed to step back and get a grip. If anyone would be serious in a relationship, it would be Stella. She would want wedding bells, which was reason enough that he should leave her alone. He didn't want a long-term relationship. But she might be one of those women who couldn't deal with a casual affair.

"Good morning," he said as she walked up.

"I'm ready to catch a plane," she said, smiling at him and looking fresh. Beneath the coat he saw a white tailored blouse, tan slacks and brown loafers. Always practical and neat, so what was it about her that made his pulse jump when he saw her?

"You look as if you don't have a care in the world and as if you had a good night's sleep."

"Well, I'm glad I look that way. By the end of some of the days I've spent dealing with all the storm problems, I feel bedraggled."

"I think we can do something about that," he said, flirting with her and wanting to touch her if only just to hold her hand.

"I pass on hearing your suggestions. Let's concentrate on getting to the plane."

"The car is waiting."

As soon as they were headed to the Royal airport, Aaron settled back to drive. "Cole left a list of what we're working on and I have the list we made yesterday of more places where we can help. I'll spend the day visiting the sites, including the Cattleman's Club. When Cole gets back, I want to be able to talk to him about what I can do to help."

"If you have any questions, I'll have my phone, although some of the time it may be turned off."

"I'll manage," he said.

She chuckled. "I'm sure you will."

"You should be able to get away a day without a barrage of phone calls from Royal. Maybe we should think about a weekend away and really give you a break."

She laughed again. "No weekend getaways, Aaron. For more than one reason. You can forget that one. I'll manage without a weekend break."

"Can't blame me for trying," he said, giving her a quick grin. "I'll miss you today," he said.

"No, you won't. You'll be busy. Once people find out who you are and that you're here in Royal, you'll be busy all day long with questions and requests and just listening to problems. I can promise you—get ready to be in high demand."

"Is that the way it's been for Cole? If it has, it probably is good for him because it takes his mind off his loss."

"I'm sure it's what he deals with constantly. We've come a long way, but we still have so far to go to ever recover from all the devastation."

He turned into the small airport and let her out, then parked and came back to join her for breakfast. All too soon she was called to board. He stood watching until she disappeared from sight and then he headed back to town. At least she had agreed to let him pick her up when she returned later today. He was already looking forward to being with her again, something that surprised him. Since losing Paula and Blake, he hadn't been this excited about any woman. Far from it. He felt better staying home by himself than trying to go out with someone and fake having a good time.

That had all changed with Stella—which surprised and puzzled him, because she was so unlike anyone who had ever attracted him before.

Three

Stella left the doctor's office in a daze. The home pregnancy test had been accurate. She was carrying Aaron's baby. Why, oh, why had she gotten into this predicament?

She climbed inside her rental car and locked the doors, relieved to be shut away from everyone else while she tried to adjust to the news.

To make matters worse, now Aaron was not only in Royal, but staying in the neighboring sixth floor suite at the Cozy Inn. He wanted to be with her, to dance with her. She did not want him to know yet. She wished he would go back to Dallas to R&N headquarters and give her time to think things through. She had to decide how much and when she would tell him.

She groaned aloud and put her forehead against the steering wheel. Aaron was a good guy. He had military training, was caring and family oriented, from what little she knew. She could guess his reaction right now. He would instantly propose.

She groaned again and rubbed her temples with her fingertips. "Oh, my," she whispered to the empty car.

She couldn't let Aaron know yet. She would have to get so busy she couldn't go out with him. Her spirits sank lower. He had a suite next to hers—there wasn't going to be any way to avoid him.

He was a take-charge guy and he would definitely want to take charge of her situation.

He would want to marry her. She was as certain of that as she was that she was breathing air and sitting in Austin.

Glancing at her watch, she saw she would be late meeting her sister for lunch. Trying to focus, she started the car and drove to the restaurant they'd agreed on earlier.

At the restaurant, she saw that her sister was already seated. When Stella sat down at the table, her sister's smile faded. "You've had bad news."

"Linda, I just can't believe the truth," Stella said, tears threatening, which was totally unlike her. "I'm pregnant. The test was correct."

"Oh, my, of all people. Stella, I can't believe it. I'll tell you something right now. I know you—you're a wonderful aunt to my children. You're going to love this baby beyond your wildest imaginings. You'll see. I know I'm right."

"That will come, but at the moment this is going to complicate my life. This shouldn't have happened."

"Here comes the waiter."

"I've lost my appetite. There's no way I can eat now."

"Eat something. You'll be sorry later if you don't."

Linda ordered a salad and Stella ordered chicken soup. As soon as they were alone, Linda turned to Stella. "Look, I'll help any way I can, anytime. When the baby is due, you can stay here and I'll be with you."

"Thank you," Stella said, smiling at her sister. "I can't believe this is happening."

"You've said the dad is a nice guy. Tell him."

"I'll have to think about what I'm going to do first and make some decisions. I know I have to tell him eventually, but not yet. The minute he finds out, I'm sure he'll propose."

"That may solve your problem. Marry him. Accept his

proposal. You've already been attracted to each other or you wouldn't be pregnant. There's your solution."

"It's not that simple. Aaron and I are not in love. Look at our parents. That's marriage without love and it was horrible for them and for us. I don't want that. And I feel like there are moments Aaron shuts himself off. He doesn't share much of himself."

"You may be imagining that. Marry him and if he's nice and you've been attracted to each other, you'll probably begin to love him."

"I'm not falling into that trap. Linda, when you married, you and Zane were so in love. That's the way I want it to be if I marry. I couldn't bear to do it otherwise. And it will be a sense of duty for Aaron. He won't give it one second's thought. I'm just sure."

"I'm telling you—if he proposes, marry him. You'll fall in love later."

"Think back to our childhood and the fights that our parents had—the yelling and Mom throwing things and Dad swearing and storming around slamming doors. Oh, no. You can forget the marriage thing. I'll work this out. It's just takes some getting used to and careful planning."

"At least consider what I'm saying. If this man is such a nice guy, that's different from Mom and Dad."

"You know Dad can be a nice guy when he wants to. Mom just goads him. And vice versa. Here comes lunch."

"Try to eat a little. You'll need it."

"It helps to have someone to talk to about it."

"Do you have anyone in Royal?"

"Of course. You should remember Edie. We're close enough that I can talk to her about it. She'll understand, too. Actually, I can probably talk to Lark Taylor."

"I know Lark, but not as well as you do since you're

both the same age. She's not the friendliest person until you get to know her."

"In this storm, believe me, we got to know each other. She and the other nurses from the hospital were out there every day trying to help. So were others that I feel are life-long friends now. Megan Maguire, the shelter director. I feel much closer to some of the people I've worked with since the tornado. I can talk to them if I want."

"Is he good-looking?"

"I think so."

"Well, then you'll have a good-looking baby."

"Frankly, I hope this baby doesn't look *exactly* like him." Stella smiled. "I'm teasing. I'll think about what you've said. Actually, Aaron is in Royal. I'm having dinner with him tonight."

"There," Linda said, sounding satisfied, as if the whole problem was solved. "Go out with him some before you tell him. Give love a chance to happen. You're obviously attracted to each other."

"I might try, Linda. It's a possibility. But that's enough about me. How are the kids?"

They talked about Linda's three children, their parents, progress in rebuilding Royal and finished their lunch.

As they stood in the sunshine on the sidewalk saying their goodbyes, Linda asked, "You're coming for Christmas, aren't you?"

"Yes. I'll fly in late afternoon Christmas Eve and then back home Christmas afternoon."

"Think about what I've said about marrying the dad. That might turn out a lot better than it did for Mom and Dad."

"I'll think about that one. You take care. See you next time." She turned and hurried to the rental car.

She paused to do a search on her phone and located the

nearest bookshop, which was only two blocks away. She
drove over and went inside. It took a few minutes to find
a book on pregnancy and what to expect with a first baby
but before she knew it, she was back in the car, headed to
the airport.

All the way to Dallas on the plane she read her new
book. She would have to find a doctor in Royal. She was
certain Lark could help her there. She knew of two who
were popular with women her age.

When she changed planes for Royal, she tucked her new
book into her purse and tossed away the shopping bag in
the airport.

As she flew to Royal her dread increased by the minute. She felt as if she had gained ten pounds and her waist
had expanded on this trip. She felt uncomfortable in her
own skin.

When she stepped off the plane, Aaron was waiting. He
had on jeans and a navy sweatshirt. There was no way to
stop the warmth that flowed over her at the sight of him
and his big smile. She had mixed reactions just as she always had with him.

"Hi," he said, walking up and draping his arm across
her shoulders to give her a slight hug as they headed for
the main door leading to the parking lot. His brown-eyed
gaze swept over her. He saw too much all the time. How
long did she have before he could tell she was expecting?

"How's your sister?"

"She's fine. I enjoyed seeing her and all is well."

"Good. I hope you had a restful day."

"I did. How was it here?"

"I imagine if you'd been here, you would answer, 'The
usual.' I saw a great deal of the construction and talked
to a lot of people. I've been at the Texas Cattleman's Club
most of the day. Repairs have begun on the clubhouse.

They didn't have total destruction, so it should be done before too long. Actually, I helped some with the work there today." They reached his car and he held the door for her. She watched him walk around the car and slide behind the wheel.

As soon as they were on the freeway, he said, "Let me take you to dinner again. We'll eat at the Cozy Inn if you prefer."

"Thanks, Aaron, I would like that. There's still time for me to go by the hospital this afternoon. By the end of the day, all I'll be up for is the Cozy Inn for dinner. Right now I want to go back to my suite and catch up on emails."

"You may regret doing that. What if you have over a hundred emails waiting? You might have to go look for another lost dog."

She smiled, feeling better.

"I'll tell you one thing," he said, "people are really grateful to you for all you've done. I've had a lot of people out of the blue mention your name. I guess they assume everyone knows who you are and they'll just start talking about 'Stella did this' or 'Stella did that.'"

"I'm always happy to help."

"A lot of people are also talking about Royal needing an acting mayor because it's obvious now that the mayor can't return to work anytime soon. And people I talked to are mentioning your name in the same breath they talk about needing an acting mayor."

"Aaron, I'm an administrative assistant. A lot of us are helping others."

"You've been a big help to lots of people and they appreciate it."

She shook her head and didn't answer him as he pulled to a stop at the front door of the Cozy Inn.

"I'm letting you out here and heading back to the club. I'll see you at seven."

"Let's just meet in the lobby in case I get delayed."

"Sure," he said as a doorman opened her door and she stepped out. She walked into the inn without looking back.

In her room she went straight to her mirror to study her figure. She didn't look one bit different from when she had checked earlier, but she felt different. For one minute she gave herself over to thinking *if only*—if she were married to Aaron this would be one of the most joyous occasions for her.

With a long sigh, she stopped thinking about being married to Aaron and faced the reality that Aaron was in his thirties and still single. She thought back to the night she had met him after the storm. She had been comforting Paige Richardson whose husband, Craig, had died in the tornado. Others had come to call on Paige and someone introduced Stella to Aaron. He was staying in a motel on the edge of Royal, but he offered to take Stella back to the Cozy Inn. They had talked and one thing had led to another until they were in bed together—a rare event to her.

The next morning, when she told Aaron the night was totally uncharacteristic of her and she wanted to avoid further contact, he had agreed to do whatever she wanted and also told her he wasn't in for long-term relationships. She really didn't know much about him. That night they had had fun and lots of laughter, lots of talking, but she was beginning to realize that none of their conversation was about anything serious or important. Last night with him could be described the same way. She knew almost nothing about him and he hadn't questioned her very much about her background. Aaron Nichols would be the father of her child, and it was time she found out more about him. Whether he hated or loved becoming a dad, that was what had happened and they both would have to adjust to the reality of parenthood.

She went to her laptop to read her emails, answering what she needed to, and then left for Royal Memorial Hospital.

The west side of town had taken the brunt of the F4 tornado. Town hall where she had worked was mostly reduced to debris. Almost all three stories of the building had been leveled. The only thing left standing was part of the clock tower—the clock stuck at 4:14 p.m., a permanent reminder of the storm. She couldn't pass it without shivering and getting goose bumps as she recalled the first terrifying moments.

Approaching the hospital, she saw the ripped and shattered west wing. As far as she could tell, rebuilding had not yet begun.

As soon as she went inside the building, outside sounds of traffic and people were shut out. She stepped into an elevator. A nurse had already boarded and Stella realized it was Lark Taylor. They had known each other since childhood, but had become closer in the weeks after the storm. Some accused the ICU nurse of being unfriendly, but Stella couldn't imagine how anyone could feel that way.

"Here to see the mayor's family?" Lark asked.

"Yes. I try to stop by every few days. The changes are slow, but I want to keep up with how he's doing. How's Skye?" As she asked about Lark's sister, Stella gazed into Lark's green eyes and saw her solemn look.

"No change, but thank you for asking about her." Skye had sustained head injuries during the tornado and had been in a medically induced coma ever since. Stella knew Lark was worried about her sister and the baby and it hadn't helped that no one knew who the baby's father was.

"And how's her baby?"

"She's doing well," Lark answered, her voice filling with relief. "I'm so thankful to work here so I can be closer to them."

"I'm glad Skye is doing well," Stella said, happy to hear good news about Skye's tiny baby, who came into the world two months prematurely after her mother was injured during the storm. "Every storm survivor is wonderful," Stella said.

"Right now, we're looking for Jacob Holt." Stella remembered the gossip four years earlier when Jacob had run away with Skye.

"You think he's in Royal?"

"No. If he was here in Royal, I think, in a town this size someone would know. But they're trying to find him. His brother is looking."

"If Keaton doesn't know where Jacob is, I doubt if anyone else does."

"You know so many people—have you heard anything about him?"

"No, nothing. If I do, I'll let you know."

When the elevator stopped on Lark's floor, she stepped into the doorway and turned back.

"If you do hear about him, please let me know. Skye can't tell us anything, and her baby certainly can't. We need to talk to Jacob. With him missing and Skye in a coma, Keaton wants to test the baby's DNA to see if she's a Holt." Lark shook her head. "If you hear anything at all about Jacob, please call me. You have my cell number. Just call or text."

Stella nodded. "I will."

The doors closed and Stella thought about Skye. So many people had been hurt by the storm. But Stella was happy to hear the joy in Lark's voice when she said the little preemie was doing well.

The elevator stopped on Mayor Richard Vance's floor. When she went to the nurse's station, she was told the mayor's wife was in the waiting room.

It was an hour later when Stella left the hospital and hurried to her car. Before she left downtown she stopped at a drugstore to pick up a few things she needed at the Cozy Inn. When she went inside, she recognized the tall, auburn-haired woman she had known for so long because their families were friends. She walked over to say hello to Paige Richardson.

At her greeting Paige turned and briefly smiled. Stella gazed into her friend's gray eyes.

"How are you? How's the Double R, Paige?" she asked about Paige's ranch, which she now had to run without her husband.

"Still picking up the pieces," Paige said. "I heard Aaron Nichols is here again to help. Are you working with Cole and Aaron?"

"A little. A lot of their paperwork comes through the mayor's office. Cole is out at a friend's ranch now—Henry Markham, who lost his brother, too, in the storm."

"His ranch was badly damaged. Cole's probably helping him."

"The storm was hard on everybody. I'm sure you keep busy with the Double R."

"Some days I'm too busy to think about anything else. Is Cole staying very long with Henry?"

"It should be four or five days."

"How's the mayor?" Paige asked. "I'm sure you're keeping up with his condition."

"It's a slow healing process, but each time I check, he's holding his own or getting better."

"It's been nice to talk to you because you have some

good news. Sometimes I dread coming to town because of more bad news," Paige said.

"This week I've gotten some hopeful reports. It's been great to see you, and you take care of yourself."

"Thanks," Paige replied with another faint smile. "You take care of yourself."

Stella left Paige and greeted other people in the store while she got the things she needed, paid for them and left. Outside she ran into two more people she hadn't seen for a few weeks. They talked briefly and she finally started back to the hotel. Her thoughts shifted from the people she had seen to being with Aaron shortly.

At the Cozy Inn, she walked through to her bedroom and went straight to a mirror to study herself and how she looked. So far, she didn't think she showed no matter which way she stood. She felt fine. The baby should be due next summer. Her baby and Aaron's. She felt weak in the knees whenever she thought about having his baby.

Did she want to go out with him, keep quiet and hope they both fell in love before she had to confess that she was pregnant?

She didn't think that was the way it would work out. She pulled out a navy skirt and a white cotton blouse from the dresser, then put on a navy sweater over the blouse. Once again she brushed and pinned up her hair. She saw she just had a few minutes to get to the lobby to meet Aaron.

If anything, when she spotted him standing near the door of the main restaurant, her excited response resonated deeper than it had the night before. At the same time, she had a curl of apprehension. How would she tell him? When would she? How long could she wait until she did?

Wearing a navy sweater, navy slacks and black cowboy boots, he stood near a potted palm while he waited. She crossed the lobby with its ranch-style plank floor scattered with area rugs. Hotel guests sat in clusters and chatted with each other. The piano music from the restaurant drifted into the lobby. So many local hotels had become temporary homes for the folks displaced by the tornado; whole families were staying and becoming friends.

When she approached, she saw a look in Aaron's brown eyes that made her tingle inside. "I've been looking forward to this all day," he said in greeting.

"So have I," she said. "I haven't had many leisurely dinners with a friend since the storm hit and I hope we can have one tonight."

"We're going to try. You know you can turn that phone off."

She shook her head. "This from the man who would never turn down helping someone. There are too many real emergencies. Later, when everyone calms down and is back on an even keel, I'll think about turning it off, but not yet."

Once they had settled at their table and their drinks arrived—water for her and beer for Aaron—she listened to him describe his work at the Cattleman's Club that day.

"How's your sister?" Aaron asked when he was done.

"She's fine. We had a nice time and had lunch together before I left. We don't see each other much, just the two of us."

"Any change with Mayor Vance?"

She shook her head. "No. But his wife told me he's stable. He's had a very rough time. I talked to Lark Taylor briefly. Her sister Skye is still in a medically induced coma, which sounds terrible to me, but I know it's necessary sometimes. I didn't ask further and, of course, she can't tell me details."

"How is Skye's baby? Still in NICU?"

"Yes, but Lark said Skye's baby is doing well."

"That's good," he said. He tilted his head to look at her. "What?" he asked. "You look puzzled."

"Most single men don't have much to say about a preemie baby in NICU."

He gave her that shuttered look he got occasionally. She seemed to have hit a nerve, but she didn't know why. She didn't pry into other's lives. If Aaron wanted to share something with her, he would.

Their dinners came, and once again her appetite fled even though the baked chicken looked delicious.

About halfway through dinner, Aaron noticed. "No appetite?"

"We had a big lunch just before I went to the airport."

She didn't like looking into his probing brown eyes that saw too much. Aaron was perceptive and an excellent listener, so between the two qualities, he guessed or understood things sooner than some people she had known better and longer.

"One thing I didn't mention," she said, to get his attention off her. "Lark said they were searching for Jacob Holt."

"Cole told me something about that. I imagine they are, with Skye in a coma and a new baby no one knows anything about. It's tough. The Holts must be anxious to know if the child is Jacob's."

"You can't blame him. Most people who've lived here long know about the Holt-Taylor feud."

"From what Cole told me, that feud goes back at least fifty years. What I've always heard is that it was over a land dispute."

"There are other things, too. A creek runs across both ranches, so they've fought over water rights," Stella said.

"There's been enough publicity, even nationally, over the tornado, I'd think Jacob Holt would have heard."

"I can't imagine he's anywhere on earth where he wouldn't hear something about it," she said.

"If the baby is Jacob's, she will be both a Taylor and a Holt and it might diminish the feud."

"High time that old feud died. I wonder if Jacob will ever come back to Royal."

"One more of those mysteries raised by the storm." He smiled at her. "Now speaking of the storm—I have a surprise for you."

Startled, she focused intently on him, unable to imagine what kind of surprise he had.

"I have made arrangements for you to speak to a men's group in Lubbock to raise funds for Royal to help in the rebuilding."

Her surprise increased, along with her dread. "Aaron, thank you for setting up an opportunity to raise funds, but I'm not the one to do it. You didn't even ask me. I'm not a public speaker or the type to talk a group of people into giving money for a cause," she said, feeling a momentary panic.

"You've done this countless times since the storm—you've been the town hall spokesperson really. With Mayor Vance critically ill and Deputy Mayor Rothschild killed in the storm, someone had to step forward and you did. You've done a fantastic job getting people to help out and donate. That's all you've been doing since the storm hit," he said, looking at her intently.

"That's so different," she said, wondering why he couldn't see it. "I did those things in an emergency situation. I was talking to people I knew and it was necessary. Someone had to step in. I was helping, not trying to persuade total strangers to donate to a cause. I'm not the person for that job. I'm not a public speaker and I'm not persuasive. I'm no salesperson or entertainer. A group like that will want to be entertained." Her panic grew because what Aaron expected was something she had never done. "Aaron, I can't persuade people to give money."

"I'm not sure I'm hearing right," he said. "You've persuaded, ordered and convinced people to do all sorts of things since the afternoon the storm hit."

"What I've been doing is so different. I told you, I stepped in when someone had to and the mayor couldn't. Of course people listened to me. They were hurt, desperate—what you've set me up to do is to entertain a group of businessmen in a club that meets once a month with a guest speaker. They're used to a fun speaker and then they go back to work. If I'm to walk in and convince them they should contribute money to Royal, I can't do it." Her old fears of public speaking, of having to try to deal with an audience—those qualms came rushing back.

"When you get there, you'll be fine," he said, as if dismissing her concerns as foolish. "When you meet and talk to them, you'll see they're just like people here. I'll go with you. I think once you start, it'll be just like it is when you're here. Relax, Stella, and be yourself. You've done a great job on national television and state and local news." He smiled at her and she could tell he didn't have any idea about her limitations.

"When I had interviews that first afternoon and the day after the tornado, I didn't have time to think about being on national television. I just answered questions and went right back to wherever I was needed."

"This isn't going to be different, Stella. You'll see. You'll be great."

"You may be surprised," she said, feeling glum and scared. "Really, Aaron, I don't know why you think I can do this. So when is this taking place?"

"Day after tomorrow. They have a program that day, so

you're not the only one to talk to them if that makes you feel better."

"It makes me feel infinitely better. Day after tomorrow. Next time run this past me, please, before you commit me to going."

"Sure. Stella, it never occurred to me that you wouldn't want to do this. It'll be so easy for you. I have great faith in you. This will help raise funds for Royal. People will know you're sincere in what you say, which will help."

She shook her head in exasperation. "That's what keeps me from flat-out telling you I refuse. I know it will help Royal. I just think someone else might make a better pitch. Thanks, Aaron, but you just don't get it," she said.

"Sure I do and I'm certain it will be easy for you. But all that is in the future. Right now, in our immediate future, I think it's time to dance," he said, holding out his hand.

She went to the dance floor with him, but her thoughts were on the group in Lubbock. She wanted to ask how many people would be in the audience, but she had already made a big issue of it and she couldn't back out now. It was a chance to raise funds and awareness for Royal, so she had to get over her fears and help. She wanted to help her town so maybe she should start planning what to say.

They danced three fast numbers that relaxed her and made her forget the rest of the week. Next, the piano player began an old ballad and Aaron drew her into his arms.

For a moment she relished just being held so close and dancing with him.

They danced one more song and then sat down and talked. Later, he ordered hot cocoa and they talked longer until she looked at her watch and saw it was after one in the morning.

"Aaron, I lost track of time. I do that too much with

you. I need to go to my suite. It's been a long day. I'm exhausted," she said as she stood up.

"I'm glad you lost track of time," he said, standing and draping his arm across her shoulders to draw her close to him.

When she reached for her purse, it fell out of her hands. As the purse hit the floor, Aaron bent down instantly to pick it up for her. A coin purse, a small box of business cards and a book fell out.

Horrified, she realized she had not taken the book she had bought earlier out of her purse. She tried to grab it, but Aaron had it in his hand and was staring at the cover with its picture of a smiling baby. For a moment her head spun and she felt as if she would faint, because in his hands that tiny book was about to change their future.

Four

Your Pregnancy and Your First Baby. The title jumped out at Aaron. Stella grabbed the book and dropped it into her purse.

When he looked up at her, all color had drained from her face. She stared, round eyed, looking as if disaster had befallen her.

He felt as if a fist slammed into his chest. Was she pregnant from their night together? She couldn't be, because he'd used protection. Gazing into her eyes, he had his answer that the impossible had happened—apparently the protection they'd used wasn't foolproof after all. Her wide blue eyes looked stricken. Shivering, she clutched her purse in both hands.

"I need to go to my suite," she said in almost a whisper. "We can talk tomorrow."

She brushed past him and for one stunned moment he let her go. Then he realized she would be gone in another minute and went after her. He caught up with her at the elevators and stepped on with her. Another couple joined them and they couldn't talk, so they rode in silence to the fourth floor, where the couple got off.

Aaron looked at her profile. Color had come back into her flushed cheeks. She looked panicked. It had to be because she was carrying his child.

Stunned, he couldn't believe what had happened. She might as well shout at him that he had gotten her pregnant. Her stiff demeanor, terrified expression and averted eyes were solid proof.

He felt as cold as ice, chilled to the bone, while his gaze raked over her. Her sweater hid her waist, but he had seen her waist yesterday and she was as tiny as ever, her stomach as flat as when they had met.

He took a deep breath and followed her out of the elevator.

At her door she turned to face him. "Thank you for dinner. Can we talk tomorrow?"

"Are you really going to go into your suite, get in bed and go to sleep right now?" he asked. His own head spun with the discovery, which explained why she had been so cool the other day when she had first seen him again. Shock hit him in waves and just wouldn't stop. She was pregnant with his baby. He would be a father. He had no choice now in the situation. He had made his choice the night he seduced her and he couldn't undo it now. "You're not going in there and going to sleep."

She met his gaze. "No, I guess I'm not," she replied in a whisper. "Come in."

There was only one thing for him to do. She carried his baby. He had gotten her pregnant. He had taken precautions and both of them thought they had been safe when in reality they had not been. It was done and could not be undone. As far as he could see there was no question about what he needed to do.

She unlocked her door and he closed and locked it behind them, following her into a spacious living area with beige-and-white decor that was similar to the suite he had. The entire inn had a homey appearance with maple furniture, old-fashioned pictures, needlepoint-covered throw pillows, rocking chairs in the living areas and fireplaces with gas logs.

"Have a seat, please. Do you want anything to drink?" she asked.

"Oh, yeah. Have any whiskey?"

"No. There's a bottle of wine," she replied, her voice cold and grim.

"That's okay. I'll pass. Have you been to a doctor yet?"

"Yes. That's where I went today," she said, her voice barely above a whisper. "I couldn't go to a doctor here in Royal where I know everybody and they know me. If they don't know me, a lot of people recognize me now from seeing me on television."

She sat perched on the edge of a wing chair that seemed to dwarf her. He studied her in silence and she gazed back. Her hands were knotted together, her knuckles white; once again she had lost her color. He suspected if he touched her she would be ice-cold.

He was in such shock he couldn't even think. This was the last possible thing he thought would happen to him. Actually, he'd thought it was impossible.

"You're certain you're pregnant?"

"Yes, Aaron, I am. There isn't really much to talk about right now. It's probably best you think about it before you start talking to me. I know this is a shock."

He stared at her. She was right in that he needed to think, to adjust to what had happened. It was a huge upheaval, bigger even than the storm, where he had merely come in afterward to try to help. Now he had his own storm in his life and he wondered if he could ever pick up the pieces.

She looked determined. Her chin was tilted up and she had a defiant gleam in her eyes. He realized he had been entirely focused on himself and the shock of discovering that he would be a father. He needed to consider Stella.

He crossed the room and pulled her to her feet, wrapping his arms around her. She stood stiffly in his embrace and gazed up at him.

"Stella, one thing I don't have to think about—I'm here for you. I know it's going to be hard, but let's try to reason this out and avoid worry. First, you're not alone. I want—"

She placed her finger on his lips. "Do not make any kind of commitment tonight. Not even a tiny one. You've had a shock, just as I had, and it takes a bit of time to adjust to this. Don't do something foolish on the spur of the moment. Don't do something foolish because of honor. I know you're a man of honor—Cole has said that and he knows you well. It shows, too, in things you've done to help the people here."

"You've had a head start on thinking about this and the future," he said, listening to her speech. "Stella, I don't have to think about this all night. It seems pretty simple and straightforward. We were drawn to each other enough for a baby to happen."

He took her cold hands in his. Her icy hands indicated her feelings and he wanted to reassure her. He saw no choice here.

"Stella, this is my responsibility. I want to marry you."

She closed her eyes for a moment as if he had given her terrible news. When she opened them to look up at him, she shook her head.

"Thank you, but no, we will not get married. I didn't want you to know until I decided what I would do. I knew you would propose the minute you learned about my pregnancy."

"I don't see anything wrong with that. Some women would be happy to get a proposal," he said, wondering if she was thinking this through. "I'm not exactly repulsive to you or poor husband material, am I?"

"Don't be absurd. There's something huge that's wrong with proposing tonight—within the hour you've discovered you'll be a father. We're not in love, Aaron. Neither one of us has ever said 'I love you' to the other."

"That doesn't mean we can't fall in love."

She frowned and her lips firmed as she stared at him and shook her head. "There was no love between my parents. I don't think there ever was," she said. "They had the most miserable, awful marriage. There was no physical abuse or anything like that. There were just tantrums, constant bickering, tearing each other down verbally. My sister and I grew up in a tense, unhappy household. I don't ever want to be in that situation. I'll have to be wildly in love to marry someone. My sister and her husband are, and it's a joy to be around them. They love each other and have a happy family. I couldn't bear a marriage without love and I don't want you to be in that situation, either. We're not in love. We barely know each other. We'll work this out, but marriage isn't the way."

He pulled her close against him to hold her while they stood there quietly. "Look, Stella, we're not your parents. I can't imagine either one of us treating the other person in such a manner."

She stood stiffly in his arms and he felt he couldn't reach her. He'd had his second shock when she turned down his offer of marriage. It didn't occur to him that she wouldn't marry him. Now there were two shocks tonight that hit him and left him reeling.

"You got pregnant when we were together in October," he said.

"Yes," she whispered.

He tilted her face up to look into her eyes. He caressed her throat, letting his fingers drift down her cheek and around to her nape. He felt the moment she relaxed against him. The stiffness left her and he heard her soft sigh.

"I didn't want you to know yet," she whispered.

"Maybe it's best I do. We'll work through this together," he said.

As he looked into her wide blue eyes, he became more aware of her soft curves pressed against him. His gaze lowered to her lips and his heart beat faster as desire kindled.

"Stella," he whispered, leaning closer. When his lips brushed hers, she closed her eyes.

He wrapped his arms more tightly around her, pulling her closer against him as he kissed her. It started as a tender kiss of reassurance. But then his mouth pressed more firmly against hers as his kiss became passionate. He wound his fingers in the bun at the back of her head and combed it out, letting the pins fall.

He wanted her. As far as he was concerned, their problem had a solution and it would only be a matter of time until she would see it. The moment that thought came to him, he remembered her strength in tough situations. If she said no to him, she might mean it and stick by it no matter what else happened.

She opened her eyes, stepping back. "Aaron, when we make love, I want it to be out of joy, not because of worry and concerns. Tonight's not the night."

Her hair had partially spilled over her shoulders and hung halfway down her back. A few strands were still caught up behind her head. Her lips had reddened from his kisses. Her disheveled appearance appealed to him and he wanted to draw her back into his embrace. Instead, he rested his hands lightly on her shoulders.

"You don't have to be burdened with worry and concerns tonight," he said. "We're in this together."

"Aaron, has anything ever set you back in your life?"

Her question was like a blow to his heart. She still hadn't heard about Paula and Blake, and he still didn't want to talk about them or his loss. Over the years, the pain had dulled, but it would never go away. Everyone had setbacks in life. Why would she think he had never had any? "All right, Stella. You want to be alone. I'll leave you alone," he said, turning to go. He had tried to do the right thing and been rebuffed for it.

"Aaron," she said, catching up with him, "I know you're trying to help me. I appreciate it. A lot of men would not have proposed. You're one of the good guys."

Realizing she needed time to think things through, he gazed at her. "I'm the dad. I'm not proposing just for your sake. It's for mine, too. Stella, this baby coming into my life is a gift, not an obligation," he said.

Her eyes widened with a startled expression and he realized she hadn't looked at it from his perspective, other than to expect him to propose.

"We can do better than this," he said, pulling her into his arms to kiss her again, passionately determined to get past her worries and fears.

For only a few seconds she stood stiffly in his arms and then she wrapped her arms around him, pressing against him and kissing him back until he felt she was more herself again and their problems were falling into a better perspective.

As their kiss deepened, his temperature jumped. He forgot everything except Stella in his arms while desire blazed hotly.

Leaning back slightly, he caressed her throat, his hands sliding down over her cotton blouse. He didn't think she could even feel his touch through the blouse, but she took a deep breath and her eyes closed as she held his forearms. Her reaction made him want to peel away the blouse, but he was certain she would stop him. He slipped his hand to the top button while he caressed her with his other hand. As he twisted the button free, she clutched his wrist.

"Wait, Aaron," she whispered.

He kissed away her protest, which had sounded faint and halfhearted anyway. He ran his fingers through her hair, combing it out, feeling more pins falling as the locks tumbled down her back.

"You look pretty with your hair down," he whispered.

She turned, maybe to answer. Instead, he kissed her and stopped any conversation.

"I want to love you all night. I will soon, Stella. I want to kiss and hold you," he whispered when the kiss subsided.

She moaned softly as he twisted free another button, his hand sliding beneath her blouse to cup her breast.

She gasped, kissing him, clinging to him. He wanted to pick her up, carry her to bed, but he suspected she would end their kisses and tell him good-night.

She finally stepped back. "We were headed to the door."

He combed long strands of brown hair from her face. "I'll go, but sometime soon, you'll want me to stay. I'll see you in the morning." He started out the door and turned back. "Don't worry. If you can't sleep, call me and we'll talk."

She smiled. "Thanks, Aaron. Thanks for being you."

He studied her, wondering about her feelings, wondering where they were headed, because he could imagine her sticking to the decisions she had already made involving their future. "Just don't forget I'm half the parent equation."

"I couldn't possibly forget," she said, standing in the open doorway with him.

"Good night," he said, brushing a light kiss on her lips and going to his suite.

When he got there, he went straight to the kitchen and

poured himself a glass of whiskey. Setting the bottle and his drink on the kitchen table, he pulled out his billfold. As he sat, he took a long drink. He opened the wallet and looked at a picture of Paula holding Blake. Aaron's insides knotted.

"I love you," he whispered. "I miss you. I'm going to be a dad again. I never thought that would happen. It doesn't take away one bit of love from either of you. That's the thing about love—there's always more."

He felt the dull pain that had been a part of him since losing Paula and Blake. "This isn't the way it was supposed to be. I know, if you were here, you'd tell me to snap out of it, to marry her and be the best dad possible." He paused a moment and stared at the photo. "Paula, Blake, I love you both. I miss you."

He dropped his billfold and put his head in his hands, closing his eyes tightly against the hurt. He got a grip on his emotions, wiped his eyes and took a deep breath. He was going to be a dad again. In spite of all the tangled emotions and Stella's rejection of his proposal, he felt a kernel of excitement. He would be a dad—it was a small miracle. A second baby of his own. How would he ever persuade Stella to marry him? She wanted love and marriage.

He could give her marriage. He would have to try to persuade her to settle for that. Just marriage. A lot of women would jump at such a chance. One corner of his mouth lifted in a grin and he held up his drink in a toast to an imaginary companion. "Here's to you, Stella, on sticking to your convictions and placing a premium on old-fashioned love. You'll be a good mother for our child."

So far, in working with her, Stella had proved to be levelheaded, practical and very intelligent. That gave him hope.

He finished his drink and poured one more, capping the bottle. Then he stood up and put it away. He started to pocket his billfold, but he paused to open it and look once more at the picture of his baby son. As always, he felt a hollow emptiness, as if his insides had been ripped out. Now he was going to have another baby—another little child, his child. It was a miracle to him, thrilling.

Stella had to let him be a part of his child's life. It was a chance to be a dad again, to have a little one, a son or daughter to raise. In that moment, he cared. He wanted Stella to marry him or let him into the life of his child in some way. He wasn't giving up a second child of his. One loss was too many. He sure as hell didn't plan to lose the second baby. He would have to court Stella until she just couldn't say no. He had to try to win her love.

As much as he hurt, he still had to smile. Stella wouldn't go for any insincere attempt to fake love or conjure it up where it didn't exist.

He had to make her fall in love with him and that might not be so easy when he didn't know whether he could ever really love her in return.

The next morning Stella was supposed to have breakfast with Aaron, but he called and told her to go ahead because he'd be late. A few minutes after she'd settled in and ordered, she watched him cross the dining room to her table. He was dressed for a day of helping the cleanup effort in jeans, an R&N sweatshirt and cowboy boots. Even in the ordinary clothes, he looked handsome and her heart began racing at her first glimpse of him. The father of her baby. She was beginning to adjust to the idea of being pregnant even though she had slept little last night.

"Sorry. You shouldn't have waited. Did you order from the menu or are you going with the buffet?"

"I've ordered from the menu and I didn't wait," she said, smiling.

"I'll get the buffet and be right back."

While they ate, Aaron sipped his coffee. "So, did you sleep well last night?" he asked.

"Fine," she replied, taking a dainty bite of yellow pineapple.

"Shall I try again? Did you get any sleep last night?"

She stared at him. "How do you know I didn't?"

"You're a scrupulously honest person so prevarication isn't like you. You were a little too upset to sleep well."

"If you must know, I didn't sleep well. Did you?"

"Actually, pretty good after I thought things through."

"I'm glad. By the way, today after work, I'll try to get something together for the presentation in Lubbock tomorrow. Please tell me this is a small group."

"This is a small group," he said, echoing her words.

She wasn't convinced. "Aaron, is this a large or small group?"

"It's what I'd call in-between."

"That's a real help," she said. He grinned and took her hand in his to squeeze it lightly.

"All you need is an opening line and a closing line. You know the stuff in between. You'll be fine. I know what I'm talking about. And so will you, so just relax," he said, his eyes warm and friendly. She would be glad to have his support for the afternoon.

When they finished breakfast and stood to go, she caught him studying her waist. She wore a tan skirt and matching blouse that was tucked in. She knew from looking intently in her mirror before she came down for breakfast, that her pregnancy still didn't show in her waist and that her stomach was as flat as ever.

His gaze flew up to meet hers. "You don't look it," he said quietly.

"Not yet. I will," she replied, and he nodded.

They walked out together and climbed into Aaron's car. He dropped her off at the temporary headquarters for town hall and drove away to go to the Cattleman's Club. Today she would be overseeing the effort to sort records that had been scattered by the storm. She wondered how many months—or worse, years—of vital records they would find. She hoped no one's life changed for the worse because of these lost records.

Stella entered the makeshift office that had been set up for recovered documents. The room held long tables covered with boxes labeled for various types of documents. As Stella put her purse away, Polly Hadley appeared with a box filled with papers that she placed on a cleared space on a desk.

"Good morning, Stella. You're just in time," her fellow administrative assistant said. "Here's another box of papers to sort through. I glanced at a few of these when I found them. What I saw was important," Polly said.

"I'm thankful for each record we find."

"Most of these papers were beneath part of a stockade fence."

"Heaven knows where the fence came from," Stella said.

"I don't want to think about how long we'll be searching for files, papers, records. Some of these were never stored electronically."

"Some records that were stored electronically are destroyed now," Stella stated as she pulled the box closer. "We'll just do the best we can. Thank goodness so many people are helping us."

"I'll be back with more." Polly smiled as she left the makeshift office.

Stella picked up a smudged stack of stapled papers from the top of the pile and looked at them, sighing when she saw they were adoption papers. A chill slithered down her spine as she thought again of important documents they might not ever find. She smoothed the wrinkled papers and placed them in a box of other papers relating to adoptions. She picked up the next set of papers and brushed away smudges of dirt as she read, her thoughts momentarily jumping back to breakfast with Aaron. In some ways it was a relief to have him know the truth. If only he would give her room to make decisions—that was a big worry. As for dinner with him tonight—she just hoped he didn't persist about marriage.

That evening as they ate, she made plans with Aaron to go to Lubbock the next day. She tried to be positive about it, but she had butterflies in her stomach just thinking about it.

She had finished eating and sat talking to Aaron while he sipped a beer when her phone rang. She listened to the caller, then stood up and gave instructions. When she hung up, she turned to Aaron.

"I heard some of that call. Your part," he said.

"We can talk as we walk to the car. That was Leonard Sherman. He's fallen and his daughter is out of town. He can't get up and he needs someone to help him. He hit his head. I told him that I would call an ambulance."

Aaron waited quietly while she made the call. As soon as she finished, she turned to him. "I need to go to his house to lock up for him when the ambulance picks him up. He lives alone near his daughter. He said his neighbor isn't home, either."

"Does everyone in town call you when they have an emergency?"

Smiling, she shook her head. "Of course not, but some of these people have gotten so they feel we're friends and

I'll help, which I'm glad to do. It's nice they feel that way. I'm happy to help when I can."

"I'll take you."

A valet brought Aaron's car to the door of the inn. As they drove away, she finished making her calls.

"You don't need to speed," she said. "I don't think he's hurt badly."

"You wanted to get there before they took him in the ambulance, so we will."

In minutes Aaron pulled into Leonard Sherman's driveway. She stepped out of the car and hurried inside while Aaron locked up and followed.

The ambulance arrived only minutes later and soon they had their patient loaded into the back and ready to go to the hospital. As the paramedics carefully pulled away from the curb, Stella locked up Leonard's house, pocketed the key and walked back to the car with Aaron.

"You don't have to go to the hospital with me. I'll call his daughter and she'll probably want to talk to the doctor. He said she's coming back tonight, so hopefully, she'll be home soon."

"I'll go with you. These evenings are getting interesting."

She laughed. "I told you that you don't have to come."

"You amaze me," Aaron said. "I've never told you any news I get about anyone in Royal that you don't already know. People tell you everything. I'll bet you know all sorts of secrets."

"I'm just friendly and interested."

"People trust you and you're a good listener. They call you for help. Mayor Vance doesn't do all this."

Stella watched him drive, thinking he was one person who didn't tell her everything. She always had a feeling that Aaron held personal things back. There were parts of his life closed to her. A lot of parts. She still knew little about him. She suspected Cole knew much more.

She called Leonard's daughter and, to her relief, heard her answer.

When Stella was done with the call, she turned to Aaron. "I'll go to Memorial Hospital to give her the key to his house, but his daughter is back and she'll be at the hospital, so we don't need to stay."

"Good. You said you wanted to get ready for tomorrow, so now you'll have a chance unless calamity befalls someone else in this town tonight."

"It's not that bad," she said.

"I had other plans for us this evening. We're incredibly off the mark."

"That's probably for the better, Aaron," she said.

"You don't have to do everything for everyone. Learn to delegate, Stella."

"Some things are too personal to delegate. People are frightened and hurting still. I'm happy to help however I can if it makes things even the smallest bit better."

He squeezed her hand. "Remind me to keep you around for emergencies," he said lightly, but she again wondered about what he kept bottled up and how he had been hurt. He might want them to be alone tonight, but she had to respond when someone called.

And she stuck to her guns. When they got back to the hotel, she told Aaron good-night early in the evening so she could get ready to leave for Lubbock with him the next morning.

As soon as she was alone in her suite, she went over her notes for the next day, but her thoughts kept jumping to Aaron. Every hour they spent together bound her a little

more to him, making his friendship a bit more important
to her. Now she was counting on him for moral support
tomorrow.

The next morning, when she went to the lobby to meet
Aaron and head for Lubbock, she saw him the minute she
emerged from the elevator. The sight of him in a flawless
navy suit with a red tie took her breath away and made
her forget her worries about speaking. He looked incredibly handsome, so handsome, she wondered what he saw
in her. She was plain from head to toe. Plain clothes, plain
hair, no makeup. This handsome man wanted to marry her
and she had turned him down. Her insides fluttered and
a cold fear gripped her. Was she willing to let him go and
marry someone else? The answer still came up the same.
She couldn't marry without love. Yet Aaron was special,
so she hoped she wasn't making a big mistake

This baby coming into my life is a gift, not an obligation.
She remembered his words from the night before last. How
many single men who had just been surprised to learn they
would be a dad would have that attitude? Was she rejecting a very special man?

He saw her and she smiled, resisting the temptation to
raise her hand to smooth her hair.

She was aware of her plain brown suit, her skirt ending
midcalf. She wore a tan blouse with a round neck beneath
her jacket. Her low-heeled brown pumps were practical and
her hair was in its usual bun. When she crossed the lobby,
no heads would turn, but she didn't mind because it had
been that way all her life.

When she walked up to him, he took her arm. "The car
is waiting," he said. "You look pretty."

"Thank you. Sometimes I wonder if you need to get
your eyes checked."

He smiled. "The last time I was tested in the air force, I had excellent eyesight," he remarked. "You sell yourself short, Stella. Both on giving this talk and on how you look."

She didn't tell him that men rarely told her she was pretty. They thanked her for her help or asked her about their problems, just as boys had in school, but they didn't tell her how pretty she looked.

In minutes they were on the highway. She pulled out a notebook and a small stack of cards wrapped with a rubber band. "These are my notes. I have a slide presentation. I think the pictures may speak for themselves. People are stunned when they see these."

When she walked into the private meeting room in a country club, her knees felt weak and the butterflies in her stomach changed to ice. The room was filled with men and women in business suits—mostly men. It was a business club and she couldn't imagine talking to them. She glanced at Aaron.

"Aaron, I can't do this."

"Of course you can. Here comes Boyce Johnson, my friend who is president," he said, and she saw a smiling, brown-haired man approaching them. He extended his hand to Aaron, who made introductions that she didn't even hear as she smiled and went through the motions.

All too soon, Boyce called the group to order and someone made an introduction that Aaron must have written, telling about how she had helped after the storm hit Royal. And then she was left facing the forty or so people who filled the room, all looking at her and waiting for her to begin.

Smiling and hoping his presence would reassure her, Aaron sat listening to Stella make her presentation, showing pictures of the devastation in the first few hours after the storm hit Royal. That alone would make people want to contribute. After her slide presentation, Stella talked. She was nervous and it showed. He realized that right after the storm, adrenaline—and the sheer necessity for someone to take charge with Mayor Vance critically injured and the deputy mayor killed—had kept her going. Now that life in Royal was beginning to settle back into a routine, she could do it again, but she had to have faith in herself.

He thought of contacts he had and realized he could help her raise funds for the town. Her slide presentation had been excellent, touching, awesome in showing the storm's fury and giving the facts about the F4 tornado.

He sat looking at her as she talked and realized she might like a makeover in a Dallas salon. She could catch people's attention more. The men today were polite and attentive and she was giving facts that would hold their interest, but if she had a makeover, she might do even better. It should bolster her self-confidence.

She had done interviews and brief appearances almost since the day of the storm. Maybe it was time she had some help. He had statewide contacts, people in Dallas who were good about contributing to worthwhile causes. While she talked, he sent a text to a Dallas Texas Cattleman's Club member. In minutes he got a reply.

He sent a text to a Dallas salon, and shortly after, had an appointment for her.

He hoped she wouldn't balk at changing her hair. She clung to having it up in a bun almost as if she wanted to fade into the background, but hopefully, the makeover in the salon might cause her to be willing to change.

When she finished her speech and opened up the floor to questions, she seemed more poised and relaxed. She gave accurate facts and figures and did a good job of conveying the situation in Royal. Finally, there were no more questions. Boyce thanked her and Aaron for coming. He asked if anyone would like to make a motion to give a check to Stella to take back to Royal now because they seemed to need help as soon as they could possibly get it.

Boyce turned to ask their treasurer how much they had available in their treasury at present and was told there was $6,000.

One of the women made a motion immediately to donate $5,000. It was seconded and passed. A man stood and said he would like to contribute $1,000 in addition to the money from the treasury.

Aaron felt a flash of satisfaction, happy that they could take these donations back to Royal and happy that he had proved to Stella she could get out and lead the recovery effort now, just as she had right after the storm.

By the time the meeting was over, they had several checks totaling $12,000. Stella's cheeks were once again rosy and a sparkle was back in her blue eyes and he felt a warm glow inside because she was happy over the results.

With the help he planned to give her, he expected her to do even better. As he waited while people still talked to her, he received a text from the TCC member he had contacted. Smiling, he read the text swiftly and saw that his friend had made some contacts and it looked hopeful for an interview on a Fort Worth television station. Aaron sent a quick thankyou, hoping if it worked out Stella would accept.

It was almost four when they finally said goodbye and went to his car. When he sat behind the wheel, he turned to her, taking her into his arms. His mouth came down on hers as he kissed her thoroughly. Finally he leaned away a fraction to look at her.

"You did a great job. See, you can do this. You've raised $12,000 for Royal. That's fantastic, Stella."

She smiled. "My knees were shaking. Thank heavens you were there and I could look at your smiling face. They were nice and generous. I couldn't believe they would take all that out of their treasury and donate it at Christmastime."

"It's a Christmas present for Royal, thanks to you. That's what that club does. It's usually to help Lubbock, but Royal is a Texas town that is in desperate need of help. You did a great job and I think I can help you do an even bigger and better one," he said.

She laughed. "Aaron, please don't set me up to talk to another group of businesspeople. I'm an administrative assistant, not the mayor."

"You did fine today and I promise you, I think I can help you do a bit better if you'll let me."

"Of course, I'll let you, but I keep telling you, this is not my deal."

"You're taking $12,000 back to Royal. I think you can make a lot more and help people so much."

"When you put it that way—what do you have in mind?"

"I have lots of contacts in Dallas and across the state. Let me set up some meetings. Not necessarily a group thing like today—what I have in mind is meeting one-on-one or with just two or three company heads who might make some big donations. You can also make presentations to agencies that would be good contacts and can help even more."

"All right."

"Good. After your talk today I went ahead and contacted a close friend in Dallas. Through him you may get a brief interview on a local TV show in Fort Worth. Can I say you'll do it?"

"Yes," she answered, laughing. "You're taking charge again, Aaron."

"Also, if you'll let me contact them, I think I can get meetings in Dallas with oil and gas and TV executives, as well as some storm recovery experts. The television people will help get out the message that Royal needs help. The oil and gas people may actually make monetary donations. How's that sound?"

"Terrifying," she said, and smiled. "Well, maybe not so bad."

"So I can try to set up the meetings with the various executives?"

She stared at him a moment while she seemed to give thought to his question. "Yes. We need all the help we can get for the people at home."

"Good," he said, kissing her lightly.

"Let's take some time and talk about dealing with the press and interviews. We can talk over dinner. The press is important."

"I'll be happy to talk about interviews, but I don't think that I'll be giving many more."

"It's better to be ready just in case," he said, gazing into her wide blue eyes.

"Also I sent a text and asked for a salon makeover in Dallas for you. It's a very nice salon that will really pamper you. Would you object to that?" he asked, thinking he had never known a woman before that would have had to be given a sales pitch to get her to consent to a day at an exclusive Dallas salon.

She laughed. "Aaron, that seems ridiculous. I'm not going into show business. Mercy me. I don't think I need to go to Dallas to have a makeover and then return to Royal to help clean up debris and hunt through rubble for lost documents at town hall. That seems ridiculous."

"Stella, we can raise some money for Royal. A lot more than you did today. Trust me on this," he said, holding back a grin. "I told you that it's a very nice salon."

Shaking her head, she laughed again. "All right, Aaron. I can arrange to get away to go to Dallas. When is this makeover?"

"Someone canceled and they have an opening next Wednesday and I told them to hold it. Or they can take you in January. With the holidays coming, they're booked."

"How long does this take? I'll have to get to Dallas," she said, sounding as if he had asked her to do a task she really didn't relish.

"Cole and I have a company plane. We can fly to Dallas early Tuesday morning and be there in time for you to spend the day. I'll get you to the Fort Worth interview and I'll try to set up a dinner in Dallas that night. Afterward, we can stay at my house. I have lots of room and you can have your own suite there."

She smiled at him. "Very well. I can go to the salon Wednesday and get this over with. Thank you, Aaron," she said politely.

"Good deal," he said, amused at the reluctance clearly in her voice. "Take a dress along to go out to dinner. The next convenient stop, I'm pulling over to text the salon about Wednesday."

"I think this is going to be expensive for you and a waste of your money. People can't change in a few hours with a makeover. I really don't expect to do many more appearances or interviews."

"Just wait and see," he said.

"While we're on the subject of doing something for Royal, I've been thinking about Christmas. There are so many people who lost everything. We've talked about Christmas being tough for some of them. I want to organize a Christmas drive to get gifts for those who lost their homes or have no income because of their business losses. I want to make sure all the little children in those families have presents."

"That's a great idea, Stella. I'll help any way I can."

"I'm sure others will help. I'll call some of the women I

know and get this started. It's late—we should have started before now, but it's not too late to do this."

"Not at all. I think everyone will pitch in on this one. You're doing a great job for Royal."

"Thanks, Aaron. I'd feel better knowing that everyone has presents. We have a list now of all those who were hurt in some way by the storm. It's fairly detailed, so we know who lost homes and who is in the hospital and who lost loved ones or pets—all that sort of thing, and I can use it to compile a list for the Christmas gifts."

With a quick glance he reached over to take her hand. As he looked back at the highway, he squeezed her hand lightly. "Royal is lucky to have you," he said.

She laughed. "And you. And Cole and Lark and Megan and so many other people who are helping." He signaled a turn. "There's a farm road. We're stopping so I can send the text."

As soon as he stopped he unbuckled his seat belt and reached over to wrap his arms around her and pull her toward him.

"Aaron, what are you doing?"

"Kissing you. I think you're great, Stella," he said. As she started to reply, his mouth covered hers. It was as if he had waited years to kiss her. Startled, she didn't move for a second. Then she wrapped her arm around his neck to hold him while she kissed him in return.

What started out fun and rewarding changed as their desire blossomed. She wound her fingers in his hair, suddenly wanting to be in his arms and have all the constraints out of her way. She wanted Aaron with a need that overwhelmed her. The kiss deepened, became more passionate. She wanted to be in his arms, in his bed, making love. Would it give them a chance to fall in love?

She moaned softly, losing herself in their kiss, running

one hand over his muscled shoulder, holding him with her other arm.

She realized how intense this had become and finally leaned away a fraction. Her breathing was ragged. His light brown eyes had darkened with his passion. Desire was blatant in their depths, a hungry look that fanned the fires of her own longing.

"You did well today. You're taking back another check to help people," he said, his gaze drifting over her face. "When we get back we'll go to dinner and celebrate."

"I'm glad you went with me."

He moved away and she watched as he sent a text. He lowered his phone. "I want to wait a minute in case they answer right away."

His phone beeped and he scanned the message. "You're set for Wednesday," he said, putting away his phone. "We'll go home now."

She had a tingling excitement. Part of it was relief that the talk was over and she had been able to raise some money for Royal. Part of it was wanting Aaron and knowing they would be together longer.

They met again for dinner in the dining room at the inn. Both had changed to sweaters and slacks. Throughout dinner Stella still felt bubbly excitement and when Aaron finally escorted her back to her suite, she paused at her door to put her arms around him and kiss him.

For one startled moment he stood still, but then his arm circled her waist and he kissed her in return. Without breaking the kiss, he took her key card from her, unlocked her door and stepped inside. He picked her up and let the door swing shut while she reached out to hit the light switch.

Relishing being in his arms, she let go of all the problems for a few minutes while they kissed. Their kisses were becoming more passionate, demanding. He set her on her feet and then his hands were in her hair. The long locks tumbled down as the pins dropped away. As he kissed her, his hand slipped beneath her sweater to cup her breast and then lightly caress her.

She moaned, clinging to him, on fire with wanting him. He stepped back, pulling her blue sweater over her head and tossing it aside. He unfastened her bra and cupped her full breasts lightly in his hands. "You're soft," he whispered, leaning down to kiss her and stroke her with his tongue.

She gasped with pleasure, clinging to him, wanting him with her whole being but finally stopping him and picking up her sweater to slip it over her head again.

"Aaron, I need to sort things out before we get more deeply involved, and if we make love, I'll be more involved emotionally."

"I think we're in about as deep as it gets without marriage or a permanent commitment," he said solemnly. His voice was hoarse with passion. "You can 'sort' things out. I want you, Stella. I want you in my arms, in my bed. I want to make love all night."

Every word he said made her want to walk back into his arms, but she stood still, trying to take her time the way she should have when she first met him, before she made a physical commitment. Could they fall in love if she just let go and agreed to marry him? Or would she be the only one to fall in love while Aaron still stayed coolly removed from emotional involvement or commitment?

"Aaron, we really don't know a lot about each other," she said, and that shuttered look came over his expression. A muscle worked in his jaw as he stared at her in silence.

"What would you like to know?" he asked stiffly.

"I don't know enough to ask. I just think we should get to really know each other."

He nodded. "All right, Stella. Whatever you want. Let's eat breakfast together. The more we're together, the better we'll know each other."

"I'll see you at breakfast. Thanks again for today. It was nice to raise the money for people here and to have your moral support in Lubbock today."

"Good. See you at seven in the morning."

"Sure," she said, following him to the door. He turned to look at her and she gazed into his eyes, her heart beginning to drum again as her gaze lowered to his mouth. She wanted his kisses, wanted to stop being cautious, but that's how she had gotten pregnant. Now if she let go, she might fall in love when he wouldn't. Yet, was she going to lose a chance on winning his love because of her caution? She couldn't see any future for them the way things were.

Five

The next morning after breakfast with Stella, Aaron sent text messages to three more Texas Cattleman's Club members in Dallas. Stella had given him permission to plan two meetings, so he wanted to get them arranged as soon as possible.

Next, he drove to the temporary office R&N Builders had set up in Royal. It was a flimsy, hastily built building on a back street. He saw Cole's truck already there and was surprised his partner had returned a little earlier than he had planned.

Seated at one of the small tables that served as a desk, Cole was in his usual boots, jeans and R&N Builders T-shirt. His broad-brimmed black Resistol hung on the hat rack along with his jacket.

"How's Henry?" Aaron asked in greeting.

"He's getting along, but he needs help and he still has a lot of repairs to make. He had appointments with insurance people and an attorney about his brother's estate, so I came back here."

"I'm sorry to hear he still has a lot to do. That's tough. In the best of times there's no end to the work on a ranch."

"You got that right. And he's having a tough time about losing his brother. I figure I'm a good one to stay and give him a hand."

"I'm sure he'll appreciate it. I think a lot of people are glad to have you back in Royal. You didn't go home much before the storm."

"I've avoided being here with Craig and Paige since their marriage. I've gone home occasionally for holidays, but never was real comfortable about it since Craig and I both dated Paige in high school," Cole said, gazing into space. Aaron wondered if Cole still had feelings for Paige or if he had been in love with her when she'd married Craig.

"When the folks died, I came even less often." He turned to look at Aaron. "I'm ready to leave for the TCC. Want to ride with me?"

"I'll drive one of the trucks because I'm going to see Stella for lunch. She raised $12,000 from people in Lubbock yesterday afternoon."

"That's good news. Royal needs whatever we can get. There's still so much to be done."

"Cole, she has an idea—she's worried about Christmas and the people who lost everything, the people with little kids who are having a hard time. She wants to have a Christmas drive to get presents."

"She's right. Those people need help. Christmas is going to be tough."

"She's getting some women together to organize it. Meanwhile TCC has its Christmas festival coming up. Sure, you and I are members of the Dallas TCC, so I don't want to come in and start asking for favors, but I'm going to this time. I thought about talking to Gil and Nathan and a few other members. It might be nice to tie this Christmas present drive to the festival and invite all those people and let them pick up their presents then. What do you think?"

"I think that's a great idea. I'd say do it."

"Also, I think we should ask the Dallas TCC to make a

Christmas contribution to Royal. We could invite Dallas members to the Royal TCC Christmas Festival."

"Another good idea. We know some guys who would be willing to help and are usually generous when it's a good cause. I hope the whole town is invited this year. Everyone needs a party."

"I agree. We can talk to Gil."

"I'd be glad to," Cole replied, standing to get his jacket and hat. "I'll see you at the Cattleman's Club."

Aaron waved as he put his phone to his ear to make a call. When he was done, he stuffed some notes into his jacket pocket and locked up to go to the TCC.

When he arrived at the club, he glanced at the damage to the rambling stone and dark wood structure. Part of the slate roof of the main building had been torn off, but that had already been replaced. Trees had fallen on outbuildings, and many windows had to be replaced. A lot of the water damage had been taken care of early while the outbuildings were still in need of repair.

Aaron knew that repairs had started right away. The sound of hammers and chainsaws had become a fixture in Royal as much as the sight of wrecking trucks hauling away debris. As Aaron parked the R&N truck and climbed out, he saw Cole talking to Nathan Battle. Cole motioned to Aaron to join them.

The tall, brown-haired sheriff shook hands with Aaron. "Glad you're here. Work keeps progressing. We have the windows replaced now and that's a relief. You get tired of looking through plastic and hearing it flap in the wind."

"I told Nathan about Stella's idea for the Christmas drive and how it might be nice to combine it with the TCC Christmas festival," Cole said.

"I think it would be great. It'll add to the festivities. The holidays can be hard enough, as both of you know too well," Nathan said. "This will be a nice way to cheer people up."

"When will Gil be here?" Aaron asked.

"He's inside now," Nathan replied. "Let's go find him. We need the president's approval before you take it to a meeting."

Aaron worked through the morning, sitting in one of the empty meeting rooms. He did take time to make some calls to set up more appointments for Stella. He grinned to himself. She might not like all the appointments he planned to get for her, but he was certain she would rise to the occasion and he would help her.

Hopefully, the makeover might help her self-confidence a little. He would talk to her about dealing with the press and interviews and then see what kind of meetings he could help her get with people who would be willing to contribute to rebuilding Royal.

He had heard people mention her for the role of acting mayor if Mayor Vance didn't recover and someone was needed to step in. He wondered whether she had heard those remarks. He suspected if she had, Stella would dismiss them as ridiculous. She had been too busy to take time to realize that she was already fulfilling the position of acting mayor.

He had to admire her in so many ways. And in private— she was about to become a lot more important to him.

He leaned back in his chair, stretching his legs. Stella was going to have his baby. The thought still shocked him. He wanted this baby to be part of his life. He had lost one child. He didn't want to lose this one. And Stella was the mother of his child. He needed to forget shock and do something nice for her right now. Neither of them were in love, but they liked being together. As he thought about it, he was startled to realize she was the first woman he had truly enjoyed being with since his wife.

That was good enough to build a relationship as far as he was concerned, and Stella was a solid, super person who was appealing and intelligent. She deserved better from him. He glanced at his watch, told Cole he was going to run an errand and left the club to head to the shops in town. He intended to do something for Stella soon. Even if he couldn't give her love, he could help her and be there for her.

Stella decided to start with Paige. They agreed to meet briefly in the small café in the Cozy Inn midmorning over coffee. Stella arrived first and waved when she saw Paige step into the wide doorway. Dressed in jeans, a navy sweater, Western boots and a denim jacket, she crossed the room and sat at the small table across from Stella.

"What's up?"

"Thanks for taking time out of your busy day. I want to ask you a favor. I'm concerned about how hard Christmas will be on the people who lost so much in the storm," she said. "Christmas—any holiday—is a tough time when you've lost loved ones, your home, everything. I know you suffered a devastating loss, so if it upsets you to deal with this, Paige, say so and bow out. I'll understand."

"No. The holiday is going to be hard for a lot of people."

"Well, there are some people here who can't afford to have any kind of Christmas after all they lost. It's another hurt on top of a hurt. This is about the people who can't afford to get presents for their kids, for their families, who'll be alone and don't have much, that sort of thing."

"They should have help. What did you have in mind?"

"A Christmas drive with gifts and maybe monetary donations for them so they can buy things."

"Stella, I think that's grand. Thank goodness we can afford to do things at Christmas. But you're right about some of these people who have been hurt in every sort of way including financially. I think a Christmas drive to get presents would be wonderful. I'm so glad you thought about that."

"Well, what I really want— I need a cochair and you would be perfect if you'd do it. I know you're busy—"

Shaking her auburn hair away from her face, Paige smiled. "Stop there. I think it's a good cause so, yes, I'll cochair this project."

"That's so awesome," Stella said, smiling at her friend. "I can always count on you. I'm going to call some others to be on our committee."

"If you need my help, I can ask some friends for you."

"Here's my list. I've already sent a text to Lark and I left a message. I'll call Megan and my friend Edie."

"I can talk to Beth and Julie. I know Amanda Battle and I think she would help."

"I have my lists. We'll have a Christmas tree in the temporary town hall or I can get some of the merchants to take tags and hang them in their windows. We can make little paper ornaments and hang them on merchant's Christmas trees. Each ornament will match up with a person who will receive a gift. The recipients can choose an ornament and take it home. They'll match up with our master list, so we can tell who gets what present and we won't have to use names. So, for instance, the ornament could read, 'Boy—eight years old' plus a number to match our list and suggested gift ideas. We'll need to have gifts for the adults, too."

"Sounds good to me. We'll need to set up a Christmas-drive fund at one of the banks, so people can get tax credit for their donations," Paige said.

"I can deal with that because I'll be going by the bank anyway," Stella said.

"Fine. You take care of setting up the bank account."

"Paige, I appreciate this so much. I talked to Aaron about it and he'll run it past Cole and the TCC guys. I have a list of people who will probably participate in the drive. I'll email it to you."

"Good. I better run."

"Thanks again. I'll walk out with you. I'm going to the office—our temporary one. I think town hall will be one of the last places to get back to normal."

"There are so many places that still need to get fixed, including the Double R," she said.

"How're you doing running that ranch by yourself?"

"I run it in Craig's place, but not by myself. Our hands have been wonderful. They've really pitched in and gone the extra mile."

"I'm glad. See you soon."

They parted and Stella drove to town hall, trying to focus on work there and stop thinking about Aaron.

It was seven when she went down to meet Aaron in the Cozy Inn dining room, which had gotten to be a daily occurrence. She thought about how much she looked forward to being with him as she glanced once more at her reflection in the mirror in the elevator. Her hair was in a neat bun, every hair in place. She wore a thick pale yellow sweater and dark brown slacks with her practical shoes. The night air was chilly, although it was warm in the inn.

She stepped off the elevator and saw him only a few yards away.

Tonight he was in slacks, a thick navy sweater and Western boots. He looked sexy and appealing and she hoped he asked her to dance.

"You're not in your usual spot tonight. I thought maybe you decided not to come," she said.

"Never. And if something ever does interfere with my

meeting you when I said I would, believe me I'll call and let you know unless I've been knocked unconscious."

She laughed. "I hope not. I had a productive day, did you?"

"Oh, yes, I did. Let's get a table and I'll tell you all about it, because a lot of it concerns you. I'll bet they were pleased at town hall with the checks you got yesterday."

"Oh, my, yes. We have three families that are in a desperate situation and need money for a place to stay. Then some of it will go to buy more supplies where needed. Do you want me to keep going down the list?"

"No need." He paused to talk to the maître d', who led them to a table near the fireplace. Mesquite logs had been tossed in with the other logs and the pungent smell was inviting.

Stella ordered ice water again. When they were alone, she smiled at him. "I saw Paige Richardson today. She agreed to cochair my Christmas-drive committee."

"You didn't waste time getting that going."

"No, we need to as soon as possible. Actually, I kept $2,000 of the check from Lubbock to open a fund at the bank for the Christmas drive. She is recruiting some more members for the committee and I have Megan's and Julie's help."

"I talked to Cole about it and then we talked to Gil Addison and Nathan Battle and the TCC is willing to tie the Christmas drive in with their Christmas festival. They'll invite all the families and children to receive their gifts during the festival."

"That's wonderful, Aaron. Thank you. Paige was going to contact Amanda Battle and see if she will be on our committee."

"That's a good person to contact. So you're off to a roaring start there."

"Now tell me more about the Dallas trip."

"Here comes our waiter and then we'll talk."

They ordered and she waited expectantly. "Next week you have one little fifteen-minute spot on the noon news in Fort Worth. This will be your chance to kick off the Christmas drive and maybe get some donations for it."

"I'm looking forward to getting news out about the Christmas drive."

"Good. That night I have the oil and gas executives lined up. We will meet them for dinner and you can talk to them about the storm and what people need. I know you'll reach them emotionally because you have so many touching stories."

"Thank you. I'll be happy to do all of these things but I still say I wasn't meant to be a fund-raiser," she said, suspecting she wasn't changing his mind at all.

"You'll be great. You'll be fine. You've been doing this sort of thing since the storm. I've seen your interviews. I even taped one. You're a natural."

"Aaron, every cell in your body is filled with self-assurance. You can't possibly understand having butterflies or qualms."

"I have to admit, I'm not burdened with being afraid to talk to others about subjects I know."

Smiling, she shook her head. "I don't know everything about my subject."

"You know as much as anybody else in Royal and more about the storm than about ninety-eight percent of the population. You went through it, for heaven's sake. You were at town hall. You were there for all the nightmarish first hours after the storm and you've been there constantly ever since. I heard you crawled under debris and rescued someone. Is that right?"

"Yes. I could hear the cries. She was under a big slab of

concrete that was held up by rubble. Not fun, but we got her out. It was a twenty-year-old woman."

"That's impressive," he said, studying her as if he hadn't ever seen her before. "If you did that, you can talk to people in an interview. After we eat let's go up to your room or mine and go over ways you can handle the interview."

When their tossed green salads came, Aaron continued to talk. She realized he was giving her good advice on things to do and she soaked up every word, feeling she would do better the next appearance she made.

Aaron kept up his advice and encouragement throughout the meal, and when they were through dinner, Stella didn't want him to stop. "Aaron, why don't we go to my room now and you can continue coaching me?"

"Sure, but a couple of dances first," he said, standing and taking her hand. In minutes she was in his arms, moving with him on the dance floor, relishing dancing, being in his arms.

Aaron was becoming important to her. She was falling in love with him, but would he ever let go and fall in love with her? She felt he always held himself back and she still had that feeling with him. There couldn't be any real love between them until all barriers were gone.

Was she making a mistake by rejecting intimacy when Aaron obviously wanted it, as well as wanted to marry her? The question still constantly plagued her.

In the slow dances, their steps were in perfect unison as if they had danced together for years. Sometimes she felt she had known him well and for a long time. Other times she realized what strangers they were to each other. Sometimes when he got that shuttered look and she could feel him withdrawing, she was certain she should tell him goodbye and get him out of her life now. Yet with a baby between them, breaking off from seeing Aaron was impossible.

When the music ended they left and went to her suite. He got the tape of her interview.

"Want something to drink while we watch?" she asked. "Hot chocolate? Beer?"

"Hot chocolate sounds good. Go easy on the chocolate. I'll help."

They sat on the sofa and he put on the tape. While they watched, Aaron gave her pointers and when the tape ended, he talked about dealing with the press. Removing pins from her hair, he talked about doing interviews. As the first locks fell, she looked up at him.

"You don't need to keep your hair up all the time. You surely don't sleep all night this way."

"Of course not. It wouldn't stay thirty minutes."

"So, we'll just take it down a little early tonight," he said. "Now back to the press. Get their cards and get their names, learn their names when you meet them. They have all sorts of contacts and can open doors for you."

As she listened to him talk, she paid attention, but she was also aware of her hair falling over her back and shoulders, of Aaron's warm breath on her nape and his fingers brushing lightly against her. Every touch added a flame to the fires burning inside. Desire was hot, growing more intense the longer she sat with him. She wanted his kiss.

She should learn what he was telling her, but Aaron's kisses seemed more important. When the bun was completely undone, he placed the pins on a nearby table. He parted her hair, placing thick strands of it over each shoulder as he leaned closer to brush light kisses across her nape.

Catching her breath, she inhaled deeply. Desire built, a hungry need to turn and wrap her arms around him, to kiss him.

She felt his tongue on her nape, his kisses trailing on her skin. He picked her up, lifting her to his lap. She gazed into his brown eyes while her heart raced and she could barely get her breath.

"I want you, Aaron. You make me want you," she whispered. She leaned closer to kiss him, her tongue going deep. Her heartbeat raced as she wrapped her arms around his neck.

His hands slipped lightly beneath her sweater, sliding up to cup her breasts. In minutes he cupped each breast in his hands, caressing her. She moaned with pleasure and need, wanting more of him. She wanted to be alone with him. To make love and shut out the world and the future and just know tonight.

Would that bring him closer to her? Her to him? She couldn't marry him without love, but intimacy might be a way to love.

She tightened her arms, pressing against his solid warmth, holding him as they kissed. His fingers moved over her, touching lightly, caressing her, unfastening snaps, unfastening her bra.

His fingers trailed down over her ribs, down to her slacks. While they kissed, she felt his fingers twisting free buttons. Without breaking their kiss, he picked her up and carried her into her bedroom. Light spilled through the doorway from the front room, providing enough illumination to see. He stood her on her feet by the bed and continued to kiss her, leaning over her, holding her against him as his hand slipped down to take off her slacks.

She stepped out of them and kicked off her shoes, looking up at him for a moment as she gasped for breath.

Combing his fingers into her hair on either side of her face, he looked down at her. "I want you. I want to make love to you all night long."

"Aaron—"

He kissed her again, stopping any protest she might have made, but she wasn't protesting. She wanted him, this strong man who had been at her side for so much now, who was willing to do the honorable thing and marry her. She wanted his love. She wanted him with her, loving her. That might not ever happen if she kept pushing him away.

He tugged her sweater up, pulling it over her head and tossing it aside. Her unfastened bra slipped down and she let it fall to the floor. Cupping her breasts again, he trailed light kisses over her while she clung to him and gasped with pleasure. When he tossed away his sweater, she ran her hands across his chest, stroking his hard muscles, caressing him lightly.

Wanting to steal his heart, she kissed him.

It was an impossible, unreasonable fantasy. Yet she could love him until he found it difficult to resist her and impossible to walk away. Would she ensnare her own heart in trying to win his?

He placed his hands on her waist, stepping back to look at her, his gaze a burning brand. "You're beautiful, so soft," he whispered, and leaned forward to trail kisses over her breasts.

Desire continued to build, to be a fire she couldn't control. She wanted him now and there were no arguments about whether she should or shouldn't make love with him. She unfastened his slacks, letting them fall, and then removed his briefs. He pulled her close, their bare bodies pressed together, and even that wasn't enough. Again, he picked her up and turned to place her on the bed, kneeling and then stretching beside her to kiss her while his hands roamed over her to caress her.

She moaned softly, a sound taken by his kisses. Now union seemed necessary, urgent. Her hands drifted over him, down his smooth back, over his hard butt and along a muscled thigh.

He moved, kneeling beside her, looking at her as his hands played over her and then he trailed kisses over her knees, up the inside of her thighs, parting her legs, kissing and stroking her.

Arching beneath his touch, she wanted more of him. Her eyes were shut as he toyed with her, building need. One of his hands was between her thighs, the other tracing her breasts, light touches that drove her wild until she rose to her knees to kiss and stroke him.

His eyes were stormy, dark with desire. Need shook her because of his intensity. His groan was deep in his throat while his fingers locked in her hair and she held and kissed him, her tongue stroking him slowly. He gasped and slipped his hands beneath her arm to raise her.

He kissed her hard, one arm circling her waist, holding her close against him, his other hand running over her, caressing her and building need to a fever pitch.

She clung to him as she kissed him. "Aaron," she whispered. "Let's make love—"

They fell on the bed and he moved over her as she spread her legs for him and arched to meet him, wanting him physically as much as she wanted his love.

He entered her slowly, filling her, taking his time while he lowered himself, moving close to kiss her.

When he partially withdrew, she raised her hips, clinging to him to draw him back.

"Aaron, I want you," she whispered.

He slowly entered her again, and she gasped with pleasure, thrashing beneath him and running her hands over his back. He loved her with slow deliberation, maintaining control, trying to increase her pleasure as she moved beneath him and her need and desire built. Her pulse roared in her ears as his mouth covered hers again in another hungry kiss that increased her need.

Caught in a compelling desire that drove her beyond thought to just react to every stroke and touch and kiss from him, she tugged him closer, moving faster beneath him.

Beaded in sweat, he rocked with her until she reached a pinnacle and burst over it, rapture pouring over her while she moved wildly. When his control ended, he thrust deeply and fast.

Arching against him, she shuddered with another climax. Letting go, she slowed as ecstasy enveloped her.

"Aaron, love," she cried, without realizing what she had said.

Aaron groaned and finally slowed, his weight coming down partially on her. He turned his head to kiss her lightly.

While each gasped for breath, they lay wrapped in each other's arms. Gradually, their breathing slowed until it was deep and regular. He rolled to his side, keeping her with him.

She opened her eyes to look at him and he kissed her lightly again.

"I don't want to let go of you," he whispered.

"I don't want you to," she answered, trailing her fingers over his chest, feeling rock-solid muscles. She kept her mind closed to everything except the present moment and enjoying being in his arms and having made love with him.

"Stella, if you would marry me, we could have this all the time," he whispered, toying with a lock of her long hair.

She didn't feel like talking and she didn't care to argue, so she kept quiet, still stroking him.

They held each other in a silence that was comfortable for her. She suspected it was for him, too. She knew he wasn't asleep because he continued to play with strands of her hair. He had to know she was awake, because she still ran her fingers lightly over him, touching, caressing, loving him.

"Before I commit to marriage, I will have to be deeply in love and so will you. If that happens, we'll both know it and the rest of the world will know it. We're not at that point. We're not in love with each other," she said, the words sounding bleak to her.

"I still say it could come in marriage."

"I don't want to take that chance," she whispered, hoping she wasn't throwing away her future and her baby's future in a few glib sentences that were easy to say when she was being held close to his heart.

"Think about it. We're good together, Stella."

She raised herself slightly on her elbow, propping her head on her hand, and looked down at him. "You think about it. Do you want a marriage without love?"

Again, she got that look from him as if he had closed a door between them. She felt as if he had just gone away from her, almost as if he had left the room even though he was still right here beside her. An ache came to her heart. Aaron had closed himself off. There was a part of his life he wouldn't share, and with time it could become a wedge between them.

She thought about asking him what made him withdraw into a shell, but she suspected that would only make him do so more and make things worse.

"No, I suppose you're right. I don't want that," he answered, and she heard a note of steel in his voice.

"Maybe things will change if we keep seeing each other."

"I want to be in my child's life, so someday we'll have to work out how we're going to share our baby," he said in a different tone of voice. Why had he changed? Only minutes ago he hadn't been this way. She wondered whether they would ever be truly close, much less truly in love.

She lay down beside him again, her hair spreading on his shoulder as he pulled her close against him, leg against leg, thigh against thigh, her head on the indention between his chest and shoulder. He had proposed. He'd helped her. He wanted to be with her and take her out. What had happened in his life to cause him to let it get between him and someone else he would otherwise be close to in a relationship?

Would he ever feel close enough to her to share whatever he held back from her now?

Six

"Hey, why so solemn?" he asked, nuzzling her neck and making her giggle.

"That's better. Let's go shower and see what happens."

"Evidently you have plans," she said, amused and forgetting the serious life-changing decisions that loomed for her.

He stepped out of bed, scooped her up and carried her to the large bathroom, to stand her on her feet in the roomy tiled shower.

They played and splashed beneath the warm water until he looked at her and his smile faded, desire surfacing in his eyes. He reached out to caress her breasts and she inhaled, placing her hands on his hips and closing her eyes.

He was aroused, ready to love again, and she wanted him. She stroked him, stepping closer to kiss him and hold him. His lips were wet, his face wet, his body warm and wet against hers.

He turned off the water and moved from the shower, taking her hand as she stepped out. Aaron picked up a thick towel, shaking it out and lightly drying her in sensuous strokes that heightened desire. She picked up another fresh towel to dry him, excited by the look in his eyes that clearly revealed desire.

She rubbed the thick white towel over sculpted muscles, down over his flat belly, lightly drawing it across his thick staff.

He groaned, dropping his towel and grabbing hers to toss it away. He scooped her into his arms and carried her back to bed as he kissed her. Their legs were still wet, but she barely noticed and didn't care as she clung to him and kissed him.

He shifted between her legs and then rose up slightly, watching her as he entered her again. She cried out, arching to meet him, reaching for him to pull him back down into her embrace.

They made love frantically as if they never had before and she cried out with her climax.

He climaxed soon after, holding her as he pumped, finally lowering his weight and then rolling on his side to hold her against him.

"Fantastic, Aaron," she whispered, floating in euphoria. "Hot kisses and sexy loving."

"I'll have to agree," he said. "I want to hold you all night."

"No arguments from me on that one."

Once again they were silent and she ran her hand over him, thinking she would never tire of touching him. Aaron brought joy, help, fun, excitement, sex into her life. He was giving her his baby. If only he could give her his love.

"This has cut short all your help with giving interviews and dealing with the press."

"I'm still here and we'll continue. Besides, you're a fast learner."

"You don't really know that, but I'm trying. Aaron, when we fly to Dallas on Tuesday, I want to visit with my mom in Fort Worth. I called her and we made plans to have lunch. She's meeting me on her lunch hour and my grandmother has gone to Abilene to stay a week with my aunt. You're welcome to join us for lunch if you want, but you don't have to do that."

"I'll pass because you don't see her real often, so she may want to talk to you alone. I've got a limo for you—"

"A limo? Aaron, that's ridiculous. I can rent a car at the airport."

"No need. Cole and I have a limo service we use and two men who regularly drive for us. Sid will drive you Tuesday. He'll take you to Fort Worth for lunch and the interview and then he'll drive you back to a shop I recommend in Dallas where you can buy some new dresses. He'll either wait or give you a number and you can call him when you're ready to be picked up."

"I'm beginning to feel like your mistress."

Aaron laughed. "This is for Royal. I expect you to get a lot of donations for the town. Just keep thinking about the good we can do. Now if you would like to be my mistress—"

"Forget that one," she said, and he chuckled.

"We'll get back to talking about business tomorrow. Tonight I have other things on my mind. You don't have any morning sickness, do you?"

"Not a bit so far. I just can't eat as much and sometimes I get sleepy about two in the afternoon."

"Why don't you catch a few winks. The world won't stop spinning if you do. You're vital to Royal, Stella. You've done a superb job, but the world will go on without you for the time it takes you to get a good night's sleep."

"Thank you, Dr. Nichols. How much do I owe you for that advice?"

"About two dozen kisses," he said, and she laughed, pushing him on his back and rolling over on top of him.

"I'm going to pay you now."

"Best collection I'll ever make," he said, wrapping his arms around her.

Aaron stirred and rolled over to look at Stella. She lay on her back, one arm flung out, her hair spread over the pillow. She was covered to her chin by the sheet. Even in her sleep she stayed all covered, which amused him.

She continued to fill in for the mayor. It amazed him how people turned to her for help, everyone from the city treasurer to ordinary citizens. He didn't think Stella was even aware of the scope of what she was doing for the citizens of Royal. She was one of the key people in restoring the town and securing assistance for people. She was willing to accept his help and he could introduce her to so many people who would contribute to rebuilding Royal. He liked being with her. He liked making love with her. She excited him, and the more he got to know her, the more he enjoyed her. If she would agree to marriage, he thought, with time they would come to really love each other.

He thought of Paula and Blake, and the dull pain came as it always did.

Along with it came second thoughts. Maybe he was wrong about never being able to love someone else again. And maybe Stella was right—the only time to marry someone would be if he was as wildly in love as he had been with Paula. If he only married to give his baby a father, and wasn't really in love, that wouldn't be fair to Stella and might not ever be a happy arrangement.

He thought the fact that they got along well now and he liked being with her would be enough. The sex was fantastic. But there was more to life than that.

He sighed. He wanted to know this baby of his. He

wanted to be a dad for his child, to watch him or her grow up. Aaron wanted to be a part of that.

If he didn't marry her, she could marry someone else who would take her far away where Aaron wouldn't get to see his son or daughter often. Maybe he needed to contact one of his lawyers and get some advice. The one thing he was certain about—he did not want to lose his second child.

He lifted a strand of Stella's hair. She excited him and he liked being with her. She was levelheaded, practical. If he gave it a little more time and attention, maybe they could fall in love.

He had been a widower for seven years now. How likely was he to change?

If anyone could work a change, it would be Stella. She had already done some miracles in Royal. If Mayor Vance recovered, someone should tell him exactly how much Stella had stepped in and taken over.

Desire stirred. There might not be love, but there was a growing fiery attraction for both of them. He wanted to be with her and he was going to miss her when he returned to Dallas. Right now that wasn't going to happen—without her being beside him—until after the holidays. He would worry about that when it came time for them to part.

He leaned down to brush a kiss on her temple as he pushed the sheet lower to bare her breasts so he could caress her. Then he shifted to reach her so he could trail light kisses over her full breasts. Beneath those buttoned-up blouses she wore, there were some luscious curves.

She stirred, opened her eyes and blinked. Then she smiled and wrapped her arms around his neck, pulling him down so she could kiss him.

Forgetting his worries, Aaron wrapped his arms around her, drawing her close as he kissed her passionately.

* * *

It was Saturday, but still like a workday for her with all that needed to be done in Royal. She glanced at the clock and sat up, yanking the sheet beneath her arms. Alarmed, she glanced at Aaron. "Aaron, it's nine in the morning," she said, horrified how late they had slept. "Aaron."

He opened his eyes and reached up to pull her down. She wriggled away. "Oh, no, you don't. We've got to get out of this bed."

Looking amused, he drew her to him. "No, we don't. It's Saturday. Come here and let me show you the best possible way to start our weekend."

"Aaron, I work on Saturday. Royal needs all sorts of things. I have a list of things to do."

"Any appointments with people?"

"I don't think so, just things to do."

"Like finding Dobbin and locking up Mr. Sherman's house?"

"Maybe so, but I spend Saturdays doing those things. I don't lollygag in bed."

"Let me show you my way of lollygagging in bed." He pulled her closer.

"Aaron, look—"

He kissed away her words, his hand lightly fondling her, caressing her breast while he kissed her thoroughly. He raised up to roll over so he was above her as he kissed her.

She was stiff in his arms for about ten seconds and then she melted against him, knowing she was lost.

It was two hours later when she grabbed the sheet and stepped out of bed. "Aaron, I'm going to shower alone," she said emphatically. "There are things I think I should do today and if someone came looking for either one of us, I would be mortified."

He grinned. "You shouldn't be. First, it's none of anyone

else's business. Second—and most important—you're passing up a chance to spend a day in bed with me."

She had to laugh. "You do tempt me beyond belief, but I know there are things I can get done and sooner or later someone will ask me to help in some manner. I'm going to shower."

She heard him chuckle as she left the room. When she came out of the shower, he was nowhere around. As she looked through the suite, she realized he must have left.

She found a note and picked it up. In scrawling writing, she read, "Meet me in the dining room in twenty minutes."

"Twenty minutes from when?" she said aloud to no one. She shook her head and went to get dressed to go to the dining room and eat with him.

She spent the day running the errands on her list, making calls, going by the hospital again. At dinner she ate with Aaron, and for a short time after he talked to her more about dealing with the press, until she was in his lap, his kisses ending the coaching session on how to deal with the press.

They had grown more intimate, spent more time together, yet he still shut himself and his past off from her.

She could ask someone else about Aaron, but she wanted him to get close enough to her to stop keeping part of himself shut away. Moments still came when she could sense him emotionally withdrawing and at those times, she thought they would never really be close or deeply in love with each other. Not in love enough to marry.

Why was true intimacy so difficult for Aaron when he was so open about other aspects of his life?

The days leading up to the Dallas trip flew by.

Sunday morning Aaron went to church with her. After the service he stood to one side waiting as people greeted her and stopped to talk briefly.

When she finally joined him to go eat Sunday dinner, he smiled at her.

"What are you smiling about?"

"You. How can you lack one degree of confidence about talking to crowds? You had as long a line of people waiting to speak to you as the preacher did."

She laughed. "You're exaggerating. They were just saying good morning."

"Uh-huh. It looked like an earnest conversation three or four times."

"Maybe one or two had problems."

"Sure, Stella. Sometime today or tomorrow I'll bet you do something about those problems."

"Okay, you win. I still say helping people one-on-one is different from talking to a group of people I don't know and trying to get them to donate to the relief effort in Royal."

He grinned and squeezed her arm lightly. "Let's go eat. We missed breakfast."

By midafternoon she was in bed again with Aaron. She felt giddy, happy, and knew she was in love with him. She might have huge regrets later, but right now, she was having the time of her life with him.

Sunday night while she was in his arms in bed, she turned to look at him. "You should either go home now or plan to get up very early because Monday will be a busy day."

"I'll opt for the get-up-early choice," he drawled, toying with locks of her hair. "The more time with you, the better life is."

"I hope you mean that," she said, suddenly serious.

He shifted to hold her closer. "I mean it or I wouldn't have said it." He kissed her and their conversation ended.

Monday, after breakfast with Aaron, she got back on track with appointments and meetings. Later that afternoon, she had another brief meeting with Paige at the Cozy Inn café.

"Paige, we need to have a meeting with everyone who wants to be on this committee. I've talked to Megan Maguire, Gloria Holt, Keaton's mom, Lark Taylor, Edith Simms—they all volunteered to help us. I told Lark that Keaton's mom had volunteered and Lark said she still wanted to be a volunteer. I think it will all be harmonious."

"Great. I have Beth, Amanda Battle and Julie Kingston. This is such a good idea, Stella. It would have been dreadful if we'd ignored these people at this time of year."

"Someone would have thought of it if we hadn't. But it's especially nice to do this in conjunction with the TCC Christmas festival. Also, I intend to raise some money beyond what we'll need for getting presents. It'll be wonderful to have people bring presents for those who lost so much, but I also want them to get cash to spend as they want to. Everyone wants to give their children something they've selected. Donated presents are wonderful, but giving these families a chance to buy and wrap their own gifts is important, too."

"Another good idea, Stella. You're filled with them."

"'Tis the season. I'll be in Dallas tomorrow and gone for the rest of the week. Aaron has made appointments for me to meet people he thinks will be willing and able to help Royal."

"That's good. I'll take care of the Christmas drive while you're gone. You see if you can get some more donations."

"Thanks for all your help," Stella said, giving Paige's hand a squeeze, always sorry for Paige's losses.

After they parted, Stella went to the hospital. Mayor Vance was improving and now he could have visitors. She knocked lightly on the door and his wife called to come in.

The mayor was propped up in bed. His legs were in

casts and he was connected to machines with tubes on both sides of the bed.

"He's sitting up now and he's on the mend," his wife said.

"Mayor Vance, I am so happy to see you," Stella said, walking closer. He had always been thin, but now he was far thinner and pale, his dark brown hair a bigger contrast with his pale complexion. His brown eyes were lively and she was glad he was improving.

"Stella, it's good of you to come by. I've heard you've been a regular and I've heard so many good things about you. I could always count on you at the office."

"Thank you. The whole town has pulled together. Support for Royal has poured in—it amazes me and the donations to the Royal storm recovery fund grow steadily."

"That's so good to hear. It doesn't seem possible the tornado happened more than two months ago. It's almost mid-December and here I am still in the hospital."

"At least you're getting better," she said, smiling at him and his wife.

"I've talked with members of the town council. We need an acting mayor and I hope you'll be willing to do it."

"Mayor Vance, thank you for the vote of confidence, but I think there are more qualified people. I'm sure the town council has others in mind."

"I've heard all the things you've been doing and what you did the first twenty-four hours after the storm hit. You're the one, Stella. I'm pushing for you so don't let me down. From the sound of it, you're already doing the job."

"Well, I'll think about it," she said politely, wanting to avoid arguing with him in her first visit with him since the storm. "We've had so much help from other places that it's really wonderful."

She sat and visited a few more minutes and then left. His wife followed her into the hall.

"Stella, thanks again for coming. You've been good to check on him through all this."

"I'm glad to see he's getting better steadily."

"We're grateful. Come again. Think about what he said about filling in for him. He can't go back for a long time."

"I will," Stella said, maintaining a pleasant expression as she left and promptly dismissing the conversation.

Tuesday morning she flew to Dallas with Aaron. He picked up his car at an agency near the airport and they headed to his house in a gated suburb north of the city.

"We'll leave our things at my house. I've got the limo for you, and Sid will drive you to Fort Worth for lunch with your mother and next, to your interview at the Fort Worth TV station. After that he'll drive you back to Dallas to a dress shop while I go to the office. If you're having a makeover, you should have some new clothes. Get four or five dresses and a couple of suits."

"Seriously?" she asked, laughing. "Have you lost it, Aaron? I don't need one new thing, much less a bunch."

"Yes, you do for the people I'll introduce you to."

"When you tell me things like that, I get butterflies again."

"Ignore them and they'll vanish. Buy some new duds and shoes—the whole thing. This is an investment in Royal. Get something elegant, Stella."

She laughed again. "Aaron, you're talking to me, Stella. I don't need to look elegant to climb over debris in Royal."

"You need to look elegant to raise money so we can get rid of the debris in Royal."

She studied his profile, wondering what he was getting her into and if she could do what he wanted. Would it really help Royal? She thought about the money she had raised in Lubbock and took a deep breath. She would give it a try. "You're changing me," she said, thinking about how that was true in every way possible.

He picked up her hand to brush a kiss across her knuckles while he kept his attention on the highway. "Maybe you're changing me, too," he said.

Startled, she focused more intently on him. How had she made even the tiniest change in his life?

He remained focused on his driving, but he had sounded serious when he spoke. Was she really causing any changes in his life? Continually, ordinary things popped up that reminded her how little she really knew about him, and his last remark was just another one of them.

"Aaron, you and I don't really know each other. You don't talk about yourself much," she said, wondering how many times she had told him the same thing before.

"I think you should be grateful for that one. Also, I think we're getting to know each other rather well. We can work on that when we're home alone tonight."

"I didn't mean physically."

"Whoa—that's a letdown. You got me all excited there," he teased.

"Stop. Your imagination is running away with you," she said, and he grinned.

They finally arrived at his neighborhood and went through the security gate. Tall oaks lined the curving drive and she glimpsed an occasional mansion set back on landscaped lawns through the trees.

"This isn't where I pictured you living."

"I'm not sure I want to ask what you pictured."

"Just not this big." She looked at the immaculate lawns with multicolored flowerbeds. In many ways Aaron's everyday life was far removed from her own. Even so, he was doing so much for her, including all he had set up for today.

"Aaron, thanks for doing all this for me. The appointments, the opportunities to help Royal, the salon visit. I appreciate everything."

With a quick glance, he smiled at her. "I'm happy to help because you've been doing a great job."

"The mayor seemed happy with reports he's had of what's been happening and I'm glad. It would be terrible if he felt pressured to get out of the hospital and back to work."

"I'm sure he's getting good reports. I think he'll get more good reports from what you do today."

"You're an optimist, Aaron."

"It's easy where you're concerned," he said, and she smiled at him. "Earlier, I talked to Cecelia at the dress shop and she'll help you. We're friends and I've known her a long time. Pick several things so you have a choice. It'll go on my bill. You don't even have to take my credit card. If you don't choose something, I will, and I promise you, you won't like that."

She shook her head. "Very well, I won't argue with you, because you won't give up. Don't forget, I'm meeting my mom at half past eleven. You're welcome to join us."

"Thanks, but I have a lot of catching up to do at the office and you and your mom will enjoy being by yourselves. What I will do, if you want me to be there, is meet you at the television station for the interview."

"You don't need to drive to Fort Worth to hold my hand through an interview," she said, smiling. "I can do this one alone. Now tonight, you better join me."

"I'll be with you tonight."

"Buying more clothes and going to a salon will be a

whole new experience," she said. "Aaron, I think I can raise just as much money looking the way I already look."

"Humor me. We'll see. I think you can raise more and you'll be more at ease on television for interviews."

"I don't think clothes will make a bit of difference."

He grinned. "Clothes will make all kinds of difference. You go on television without any and you'll get so much money—"

"Aaron, you know what I mean," she interrupted, and they both laughed. She had fun with him and he was helpful to her. She gazed at him and wished she didn't still feel some kind of barrier between them, because he was growing more important to her daily. And she was falling more in love with him daily while she didn't think his feelings toward her had changed at all.

They passed through another set of iron gates after Aaron entered a code. When he drove up a winding drive to a sprawling three-story house, she was shocked at the size and obvious wealth it represented. "You have a magnificent home."

"I'm in the construction business, remember?"

She rode in silence, looking at the mansion that was far too big for one person. It was just another reminder of how little she knew about Aaron and how closed off he was about himself.

When he parked at the back of the house and came around the car to open the door for her, she stepped out. Stella stood quietly staring at him and he paused.

"What?" he asked. "Something's worrying you."

"I don't even know you."

He studied her a moment and then stepped forward, his arm going around her waist as he pulled her against him and kissed her. For a startled moment she was still and then she wrapped her arms around him to return the kiss.

"I'd say you know me," he said to her when he released her.

As she stepped back, she waved her hand at the house. "This is not what I envisioned."

"You'll get accustomed to it. C'mon, let me show you your room," he said, retrieving their bags from the back.

"We'll take a tour later," he said, walking through a kitchen that was big enough to hold her entire suite at the Cozy Inn. It had dark oak walls and some of the state-of-the-art appliances had a dark wood finish.

She walked beside him down a wide hallway, turning as hallways branched off in opposite directions. He stepped into the first open doorway. "How's this?" he asked, placing her bag on a suitcase stand.

She looked around a spacious, beautiful room with Queen Anne furniture, dark and light blue decor and thick area rugs.

"I'll get my mail and you can meet me in the kitchen. As soon as you're ready, we'll go to town. It'll give you more time to shop and I need to get to the office." He stepped closer, placing his hands on her shoulders and lowering his voice. "There are other things I'd rather do this morning, but with your appointments we better stick to business."

"I agree. You check your mail and I'll meet you."

He nodded and left.

Twenty minutes later, he stood waiting in the kitchen when she returned. "The limo's here. C'mon and I'll introduce you to Sid."

When they stepped outside, a brown-haired man who looked to be in his twenties waited by a white limo. He smiled as they walked up.

"Hi, Sid," Aaron said. "Stella, meet Sid Fryer. Sid, this is Ms. Daniels."

"Glad to meet you, Sid," she said.

"She's going to Cecelia's shop later and you can hang

around or give her a number and she'll call you. She'll be there two hours minimum," Aaron instructed.

Stella was surprised. She couldn't imagine spending that much time picking out dresses.

Sid held the limo door for her and she climbed inside, turning to the window as Aaron stepped away and waved.

Sid climbed behind the wheel and they left. When she glanced back, Aaron was already in his car.

"Sid—?"

He glanced at her in the rearview mirror. "Yes, ma'am?"

"Just call me Stella. Everyone does in my hometown of Royal. I just can't be that formal—we'll be together off and on all day."

She could see him grin in the rearview mirror. "Yes, ma'am. Whatever you say."

When Sid turned out of the gated area where Aaron lived, Stella looked behind them and saw Aaron turning the opposite way.

She met her mother in a coffee shop near the high school where her mother was principal. As Stella approached the booth where her mother sat looking at papers on the table, she realized where she got her plain way of dressing and living. Her mother's hair was in a roll, fastened on the back of her head. She wore a brown blouse and skirt, practical low-heel shoes and no makeup. Stella hadn't told her mother about the pregnancy yet and intended to today, but as she looked at her mother bent over her papers, she decided to wait a bit longer, until she had made more definite plans for raising the child. Her mother would probably want to step in and take charge, although she was deeply wrapped up in her job and, in the past few years, had interacted very little with either Stella or her sister.

Stella greeted her mother, gave her a slight hug and a

light kiss on the cheek and slid into the booth across from her. "How are you?" Stella asked.

"So busy with the end of the semester coming. I can only stay an hour because I have a stack of papers on my desk I have to deal with and three appointments with parents this afternoon. How are things in Royal?"

"Slowly improving."

"I've seen you in television clips. It looks as if you're busy. When will the mayor take over again so you won't have to do his job for him?"

"Mom, he was hurt badly and was on the critical list for a long time. The deputy mayor was killed."

"I'm glad I moved out of Royal. You should give it thought."

"I'll do that," she said, reminded again of why she was so much closer to her sister than her mother.

They talked over salads and then her mother gathered up papers and said she had to get back to her office. Stella kissed her goodbye and waited a few minutes before calling Sid for the limo—something she did not want to have to explain to her mother.

Sid drove her to the television station. Everyone she dealt with welcomed her and was so friendly that she was at ease immediately. A smiling receptionist let the host know Stella had arrived and in minutes a smiling blonde appeared and extended her hand.

"Welcome. I'm Natalia Higgens and we're delighted to have you on the show."

"Thank you," Stella said, shaking the woman's hand and relaxing. "I hope this does some good for my hometown."

"We're happy to have you and sorry about Royal. The tornado was dreadful. I think our viewers will be interested and I think you'll get some support. We'll show a short video one of our reporters made after the storm. I'll have some questions for you. People are responsive when someone has been hurt and you have a town filled with people who have been hurt."

"I really appreciate this opportunity to try to get help for Royal."

"We're glad to air your story. If you'll come with me."

Fifteen minutes later, Natalia Higgens made her brief introduction, looking at the camera. "The F4 tornado struck at 4:14 p.m. on October 6th, a Monday." The camera cut to the video the studio had taken after the storm. As soon as the video ended, Natalia turned to ask Stella about Royal.

From the beginning of the interview, Natalia's friendliness put Stella at ease. She answered questions about the storm and the people in Royal, listing places that were badly damaged, giving facts and figures of families hit, the people who died in the storm and the enormous cost of the cleanup.

"If people would like to help, do you have an address?" Natalia asked.

"Yes," Stella replied, giving the address of the bank in Royal where the account had been set up for donations. "Also, the Texas Cattleman's Club of Royal will have a Christmas festival and we hope to be able to provide toys for all the children of families who were so badly hurt by the storm. Some families lost everything—their homes, their livestock, their livelihoods—and we want to help them have a happy holiday," Stella said, smiling into the camera before turning to Natalia.

Before Stella knew it, her fifteen-minute segment was finished.

When the show ended, Natalia turned to Stella. "Thank you. You gave a wonderful presentation today that should get a big response."

"I enjoyed having a chance to do the show and to tell

about our Christmas festival. I'm very excited about that and the joy it will bring."

"Maybe we can have someone from the Royal and the Dallas TCC be on our show soon to mention it again."

"That would be wonderful," Stella said.

Natalia got a text, which she scanned quickly. "We're getting donations. Your bank will be able to total them up and let you know. Congratulations on getting more help for Royal."

Stella smiled broadly, happy that the interview went well, hoping they did get a big response.

After thanking them, telling them goodbye and making arrangements to get a video of the interview, she was ready to go back to Dallas.

As she left the station, people who worked there stopped to greet her and wish her success in helping her town.

Exhilarated, she saw Sid holding the door of the limo as she emerged from the building.

"I watched your interview in the bar down the block and two guys there said they would send some money to Royal. Way to go," he said, and she laughed, giving Sid a high five, which after one startled moment, he returned.

Sid drove to an upscale shopping area in that city. He parked in front of a redbrick shop with an ornate dark wood front door flanked by two huge white pots of red hibiscus and green sweet potato vines that trailed over the sides of the pots. To one side of the door a large window revealed an interior of subdued lighting and white and red furniture. The only identifying sign was on the window near the door. Small gold letters spelled out the name, Chez Cecilia.

Sid hopped out to open her door. "Here's my number. Just give me a call a few minutes before you want to be picked up and I'll be right here."

"Thanks, Sid," she said, wondering what Aaron had gotten her into. She went inside the shop—which had soft music playing in the background, thick area rugs, contemporary oil paintings on the walls and ornately framed floor-to-ceiling mirrors—and asked for Cecelia.

A tall, slender brunette appeared, smiling and extending her hand. "You must be Stella. I'm happy to meet you. Let me take your coat," she said, taking Stella's jacket and hanging it up. "Aaron has told me about you."

"That surprises me," Stella said, curious how Aaron knew Cecelia and the dress shop but not wanting to pry. She'd rather Aaron would tell her the things he wanted her to know.

"Surprised me, too. Aaron keeps his world to himself. From what he told me, I think I know what we should show you. Let's get you comfortable. I have a few things picked out. He said you have a dinner date tonight with some people who want to hear about Royal and the storm and how they can help."

"You're right."

"Now make yourself comfortable. Can I get you a soft drink? Coffee or tea? Ice water?"

"Ice water please," she said, thinking this whole excursion was ridiculous, a feeling that changed to dismay when Cecilia began to bring clothes out to show her.

"Just tell me what appeals to you and we'll set it aside for you to try on if you'd like."

Within minutes Stella felt in a daze. Nothing Cecilia brought out looked like anything Stella had ever worn. Necklines were lower; hemlines were higher. Skirts were tighter and material was softer. "Cecilia, I can't imagine myself in these," she said, looking at a green dress of clinging material that had a low-cut cowl neckline and a tight, straight skirt with a slit on one side. "These are so unlike me."

"You may be surprised how nice they'll look on you. These are comfortable dresses, too."

Her dazed feeling increased when she tried on the dresses she selected, yet when she looked in the mirror, she couldn't keep from liking them.

When she tried to stop shopping, Cecilia shook her head. "You need to select an elegant dress for evening. You need two suits. You should have a business dress. Aaron made this very clear and he'll come down and pick something out himself if you don't. You will not want him to do that. Aaron is not into shopping for dresses. Our clothing is tasteful and lovely, but he doesn't select what's appropriate for business unless I help him. Fortunately, he'll listen."

Even as Stella laughed, she was surprised and wondered how Cecelia knew this about Aaron. It hinted at more mysteries in his life before she knew him.

Stella tried on a red silk wool sleeveless dress with a low V-neck that she would have to grow accustomed to because she hadn't worn a dress like this one ever. "Cecilia, this isn't me."

"That's the point, Stella. Aaron wants you to have dresses that will help you present a certain image. From what Aaron has said, you're trying to get help for your town. Believe me, that dress will help you get people's attention. It's beautiful on you."

Stella laughed and shook her head. "Thank you. I feel as if I'm only half-dressed."

"Not at all. You look wonderful."

Stella shook her head and studied her image, which she barely recognized.

"Try it," Cecilia urged. "You don't want Aaron shopping for you."

"No, I don't." She sighed. "I'll take this one."

The next two were far too revealing and she refused. "I

would never feel comfortable even though these are beautiful dresses."

The next was a black dress that had a high neck in front, but was backless as well as sleeveless.

She had to agree with Cecilia that she looked pretty in the dress, but she wondered whether she would ever really wear it.

"You should have this. It's lovely on you," Cecilia said. "I know Aaron would definitely like this one."

She felt like telling Cecilia that she was not buying the dresses to please Aaron, but she wondered if she would be fooling herself in saying that. She finally nodded and agreed to take it, because she had to agree that she looked nice in it.

Not until the business suits was she comfortable in the clothes she tried on. The tailored dark blue and black suits were plain and her type of clothing. Until she tried on blouses to go with them. Once again, it was low necklines, soft, clinging material—so different from her usual button-down collars and cotton shirts.

Finally she was finished and had all her purchases bagged and boxed. She was shocked to look at her watch and see that it was almost four.

Sid came in to pick her purchases up and load them into the limo as Stella thanked Cecelia and the two other women who worked in the shop. Finally she climbed into the limo to return to Aaron's to get ready for dinner with the oil and gas executives who were potential donors.

When she arrived, Aaron was waiting on the drive. After she stepped out of the limo, Aaron and Sid carried her purchases into the house.

When Sid left them, Aaron closed the back door and turned to take her into his arms. "We're supposed to meet the people we're having dinner with in less than two hours. These are the oil and gas executives I told you about."

"Thanks, for setting this up, Aaron."

"I'm glad to, and Cole has made some appointments with potential donors, as well. How was your mother?"

"Busy with her own life."

"Have you told her about your pregnancy?"

"No. She was very unhappy to learn she was going to be a grandmother when my sister had her first baby. I think Mom thought it aged her to suddenly become a grandmother. She's not close to her grandchildren and doesn't really like children in general. My mother is in her own world. To her, my news will not be good news."

"Thank heavens you don't take after her. She's missing out on one of the best parts of life," he said, surprising her that a single guy would express it that way.

"It'll take over half an hour to drive to the restaurant," he continued after a pause. "We better start getting ready. I need to shower and shave."

"In other words, I need to start getting ready now," she said, "because I want to shower."

"We can shower together."

"If we don't leave the house tonight," she said.

He smiled. "We can't afford to stand these people up so we'll get ready and shower separately. Maybe tomorrow we can be together. Cecelia said she thinks I'll like what you bought."

"I don't know myself when I look in the mirror. In those dresses the reflection doesn't look like me, but hopefully, we'll achieve the effect you expect. If not, you wasted a lot of money."

"I think it'll be worth every penny."

"So you better run along and let me get ready."

He nodded, his eyes focused intently on her as he looked

at her mouth. She stepped away. "Bye, Aaron. See you shortly."

"Come here," he said, taking her hand and leading her out to the central hall. "See that first open door on the left? When you're ready, meet me there. I'll wait for you in the library."

"The library. Fine," she said.

"See you soon," he said, brushing a light kiss on her lips and leaving her. She went back to shower and dress in the tailored black suit she had bought earlier with an old blouse that had a high collar—an outfit that she could relax in and be comfortable.

When she was ready, she went to the library to meet Aaron, who was already there waiting. Dressed in a brown suit and dark brown tie, he looked as handsome as he always did. His gaze raked over her and he smiled.

"You look pretty," he said, crossing the room to her. "We have to go, but I know what I'd prefer doing."

"I definitely feel the same, but you're right about having to go."

"Before we do, there's something I want you to have," he said, turning to walk to a chair and pick up a gift that she hadn't noticed before. Wrapped in silver paper, it had a blue silk ribbon tied around it and a big silk bow on top. "This is for you."

Surprised, she looked up at him. "It's not my birthday," she said quietly, startled he was giving her a present.

"You're carrying my baby. That's very special and I want to give you something that you'll always have to celebrate the occasion."

"Aaron, that is so sweet," she said, hugging and kissing him. She wondered about the depth of his feelings for her. He had to care to give her such gifts and do so much for her. As quickly as that thought came and went, another occurred to her—that the makeover and clothes benefited Royal. Was she just a means to an end with him? She looked at the present in her hands. This one was purely for her because of the baby—a sweet gesture, but it still didn't mean he had special feelings for her beyond her motherhood.

Finally she raised her head. "Thank you," she whispered.

"Look at your present," he said. "You don't even know what I'm giving you."

Smiling, she untied the bow and carefully peeled away the paper. She raised the lid to find a black velvet box. She removed it from the gift box, opened it and gasped. "Aaron!" she exclaimed as she looked at a necklace made of gold in the shape of small delicate oak leaves, each with a small diamond for a stem. There was a golden leaf and diamond bracelet to match. "These are beautiful." She looked up at him. "These are so gorgeous. Thank you." She stepped forward to kiss him. He held her in one strong arm and kissed her. In seconds the other arm circled her waist and he leaned over her, still kissing her.

"Want to wear them tonight?"

She looked at her suit. "Yes, I'd love to."

"I tried to get something that you can wear whether it's day or night—in other words, all the time."

"I love this necklace and bracelet. I love that you thought of me and wanted to do this," she said, smiling at him.

"Let me put it on you," he said, and she nodded.

In seconds he stepped back. "Hold out your wrist." When she did, he fastened the bracelet on her slender wrist and kissed her lightly. "We'll celebrate more tonight when we get back home. Stella, a baby is precious. It is a celebration and this is just a tiny token."

"It's more than a token and I'll treasure it always, Aaron. It's absolutely beautiful," she said, thrilled that he was that happy about the baby.

"I'm glad you feel that way."

She nodded. Touched, wishing things were different, she felt her emotions getting out of hand. Tears stung her eyes.

"Ready? Sid's waiting."

"Yes," she answered, turning toward the door. She wanted to wipe her eyes but didn't want Aaron to know she was crying. If only he loved her—then his gift would hold a deeper meaning for her.

Seven

That evening, Stella really wowed her dinner companions. She gave a talk similar to the one in Lubbock, showing pictures of the devastation in Royal, which she had on her iPad. By the time the evening was over, it looked promising that the oil and gas executives were going to publicize Royal's need for financial help and make a large donation. As she and Aaron left the restaurant, she breathed a sigh of relief that her efforts for the town were paying off.

Then they went back to Aaron's house to make love through the night. They were in the big bed in the guest bedroom where she was staying. She wore her necklace and bracelet through the night, but in the morning as Aaron held her in his arms, he touched the necklace lightly. "Put your necklace and bracelet away today. Just leave them here instead of taking them to the salon."

"Sure," she answered, smiling at him.

"Sid has the limo waiting," Aaron said. "Tonight, we're meeting television executives from here in Dallas. These people can do a lot, Stella. Tomorrow we'll fly to Austin. You have a lunch, an interview and a dinner there and then we fly back to Dallas for one more interview at noon on Friday."

"Don't say another word. You'll just stir up my nerves more than ever."

"You're doing great. I'll tell you again, relax and enjoy your day at the salon. You better go now. I'm going to the office and I'll see you tonight. It'll take all day at the salon and, afterward, Sid will take you to the restaurant. Just call me when you're on the way. I'll try to get there before you do. That way we'll be ahead of the people we're meeting, so we can just sit and talk until they get there."

"You're getting me into more things," she said, holding a bag with her new dress and clothes that she would wear to dinner. Aaron grinned.

"You'll look back on all of this and be glad. I promise." He took her arm and they left, pausing while he locked up.

When they greeted her at the salon, she couldn't believe her day was turning out this way. It commenced with a massage. As she relaxed, she thought of the contrast with her life the first night after the tornado and how she had fallen into bed about four in the morning and slept two hours to get up and go back to work helping people.

She had her first manicure and first pedicure, which both seemed unnecessary. In the afternoon she had a facial. Following the facial, a salon attendant washed her hair and passed her over to the stylist to cut and blow-dry her hair. By the time she was done, Stella felt like a different woman. Instead of straight brown hair that fell halfway down her back, her hair was now just inches above shoulder length. It fell in a silky curtain that curled under, with slight bangs that were brushed to one side.

Next, a professional did her makeup and took time to show Stella how to apply it herself.

By late afternoon when she looked in the mirror, Stella couldn't recognize herself. She realized that she had so rarely ever tried makeup and then only lipstick that it gave her an entirely different appearance, although the biggest change was her hair.

The salon women gushed over the transformation that was amazing to her. Finally, she dressed for the evening.

"I really don't even know myself," she told the tall blonde named Gretchen at the reception desk.

"You look gorgeous. Perfect. The dress you brought is also perfect. We hope you love everything—your makeup, your hair and your nails."

She smiled at Gretchen. "I'll admit that I do," she said, pleased by the result and wondering what Aaron would think. "I've had the same hairdo since I was in college. It became a habit and it was easy. It's amazing how different I look," she said, turning slightly to look at herself in the mirror. The red silk dress fit her changing waistline; her old clothes were beginning to feel slightly tight in the waist because of her pregnancy.

She still wore her black wool coat and couldn't see any reason for a new coat. When she thanked them and left, Sid smiled at her as he held the limo door.

"You look great," he said appreciatively. "Mr. Nichols isn't going to know you."

"Thanks, Sid. I don't feel quite like me."

"Might as well make the most of it," he said, and grinned. "You'll turn heads tonight."

"You think? Sid, that would be a first," she admitted, laughing as she climbed into the limo and he closed the door.

Midafternoon Aaron went home to shower and change into a charcoal suit, a custom-made white dress shirt and a red tie. He returned to the office to spend the rest of the day catching up on paperwork. Just as he was ready to leave, he was delayed by a phone call. It only took a few minutes, but he guessed he might not get to the restaurant ahead of Stella, so he sent her a text.

He had received a call from the businessmen who'd had dinner with them last night, and they wanted to donate $20,000 to Royal's relief efforts, which he thought would be another boost to Stella's self-confidence. Aaron knew Stella hadn't faced the fact that she was filling in for the mayor as Royal's representative to the outside world even if it wasn't official. She was filling in and getting better at it all the time.

When he arrived at the restaurant, Aaron parked and hurried across the lot. He wanted to see what transformations they had made at the salon. Whatever they had done, he hoped the bun had disappeared for the evening.

The only people in the lobby besides restaurant employees in black uniforms were a couple standing, looking at a picture of a celebrity who had eaten at the restaurant. He didn't see any sign of Stella. The couple consisted of a tall, black-haired man and a beautiful woman half-turned toward him as she looked at the photograph.

He saw the maître d' and motioned to him to ask him about Stella. As the maître d' approached, Aaron glanced again at the woman. The man had walked away, and she was now standing alone. She was stunning in a red dress that ended at her knees, showing shapely long legs and trim ankles in high-heeled red pumps.

"Sir?" the maître d' asked.

"I'm supposed to meet someone here," he said. "Ms. Daniels."

"Aaron?"

He heard Stella's voice and looked up. The woman in red had turned to face him and he almost looked past her before he realized it was Stella. "She's here," he heard himself say to the maître d'. Aaron had expected a change, but not such a transformation that he didn't recognize her. Desire burst with white heat inside him as he walked over to her.

"I didn't even recognize you," he said, astounded and unable to stop staring at her. The temperature around him climbed. He tried to absorb the fact that this was Stella, because she had changed drastically. He was now looking at a stunning beauty.

"I told you long ago you might need to get your eyes checked," she said, smiling at him and making him feel weak in the knees. "Aaron, it's still me."

"You're going to knock them dead with your looks," he said without even thinking about it.

"I hope not," she said, laughing. "Aaron, you're staring."

"Damn straight, I'm staring. I can't recognize you."

"Get used to it. I'm really no different. I take it you like what you see," she prompted.

"Like? I'm bowled over. Stella, do you recognize yourself?"

"I'll admit it's quite a change. I have to get accustomed to my hair."

"You look fantastic. Wait right here," Aaron said and walked back to the maître d' to talk to him. After a moment, Aaron came back to take her arm. "Come with me," he said. The maître d' smiled at them and turned to lead the way.

"Aaron?" she asked, glancing at him.

"Just a moment, you'll see," he answered her unasked question.

The maître d' stopped to motion them through an open door. They entered an office with a desk covered by papers. The maître d' closed the door behind them.

"I asked where I could be alone with you for a few minutes. He's right outside the door should anyone want in this office."

"What on earth are we doing here?"

"I gave you a necklace and bracelet as a token of a celebration because you're carrying my baby, Stella. It's a relatively simple gold necklace and bracelet that you can wear in the daytime and wear often, which is what I wanted. To celebrate our baby, I also want you to have something very special, because this is a unique time in your life and mine. This present you can't wear as often, but you can wear it tonight," he said, handing her a flat package tied in another blue ribbon.

"You've given me a beautiful present. You didn't need to do this." Her blue eyes were wide as she studied him and then accepted the box. She untied the ribbon and opened the velvet box and gasped. "Aaron. Oh, my heavens. This is beautiful. It's magnificent."

He picked up a diamond necklace that sparkled in the light. "Turn around and I'll put it on," he said.

"I've never had anything like this. I feel as if I need a bodyguard to wear it." She turned and he fastened it around her slender throat, brushing a kiss on her nape, catching a scent that was exotic and new for Stella.

"You've got one—me. There," he said after a moment, turning her to face him, his gaze going over her features. Her blue eyes looked bigger than ever with thick lashes framing them. She didn't have on heavy makeup, just enough to alter her looks, but her hair was what had thrown him off.

And now her figure showed in the red dress, which fit a waistline that still was tiny. The diamonds glittered on her slender throat.

"You're beautiful, and that's an inadequate description. *Stunning* is more like it."

"Thank you. I'm glad you're pleased and thank you for doing this for me."

"Do you like the change?"

"After your reaction, yes, I do. It takes some getting used to. I sort of don't recognize myself, either."

They looked at each other and smiled. "I'd kiss you, but it would mess up that makeup."

"Wait until later."

"We better give the guy back his office. I just wanted a private moment to give the necklace to you."

"It's dazzling. I've never had anything like it."

He took her arm and they stepped out. "Thanks," Aaron said, slipping some folded bills to the maître d'. Then he turned to Stella and said, "Let's go meet your public. You'll wow them and get a bundle for Royal."

"Don't make me jittery," she said, but she sounded far more sure of herself than she had on that first drive to Lubbock.

"Also, I didn't tell you. I got a text from the guys last night. They're sending a check to the Royal storm recovery fund for $20,000."

She turned to gaze at him with wide eyes. "Mercy, Aaron. That's a big amount."

"You just wait and see what you can do for your hometown." He glanced at the maître d'. "We're ready for our table now and you can show the others in when they arrive."

Aaron introduced her to two men and a woman, all executives of a television station. Through salads and dinner Stella told them stories of people affected by the storm. Over dessert, and after-dinner drinks for everyone except Stella, she showed them her presentation on her iPad.

"Stella has suggested a Christmas drive," Aaron said, "to get presents for those who lost everything, for families with children and people still in the hospital."

"That's a wonderful idea," the woman, Molly Vandergrift, said. "I think that would be a great general-interest story. Would you like to appear on our news show and talk about this?"

"I'd love to," Stella replied, meaning it, realizing she was losing the butterflies in her stomach. Along with the change in her appearance and the money that she had already raised, she was gaining more confidence in her ability to talk to people about Royal. And tonight, the three television executives were so friendly, enthusiastic and receptive that she felt even better.

"We're going to try to tie it into the Texas Cattleman's Club Christmas festival in Royal this year," she added.

"That'll be good to have on a show. I know Lars West with the Dallas TCC. We could get him to come on, too, with Stella. Are the TCC here doing anything?"

"They will," Aaron replied. "I've just started talking to them."

"I'm sure the sooner you can do this, the better. I'll send a text now," Molly said, "and see if we can get you on the Friday show."

"That would be grand," Stella answered. "Everyone in Royal will appreciate what you're doing to help." She was aware Aaron had been quieter all evening than he had been in Lubbock, letting her do most of the talking. When she glanced at him, he looked pleased.

Excitement hummed in her because she was going to get so much support for Royal. As the evening wore on, she was even more pleased with her makeover, relieved that she could begin to relax talking to people and enjoy meeting them.

They didn't break up until after ten o'clock. She and Aaron told them goodbye outside as valets brought the cars to the door.

Finally she was alone in Aaron's car with him. He drove out of the lot, but on the drive back, he pulled off the road slightly, put the car in Park and turned to kiss and hug her.

Then he leaned away. "You were fantastic tonight. No butterflies either—right?"

"I think they're gone," she said.

"They'll never come back, either. Awesome evening. You did a whiz-bang job. Watch. The television show will be wonderful for Royal."

"I think so, too," she said, feeling bubbly and excited. "Thanks, Aaron, for all you've done for me. And thank you again for this fabulous necklace that I was aware of all evening."

"You're welcome. Stella, you'll be able to do more and more for Royal."

"I hope so." As he drove home they discussed the evening and what they would do Friday.

The minute they were in the kitchen of his house, Aaron turned her. "You take my breath away," he said.

Her heart skipped a beat as she gazed at him. "Thank you again for the diamonds. They're beautiful."

"That's why I didn't want you to take your gold necklace for tonight. I had something else in mind." He slipped his arms around her and kissed her, his tongue thrusting deeply as he held her. After a while he raised his head. "Go with me to the TCC Christmas festival. Will you?"

"I'd be delighted, thank you," she replied.

He kissed her again, picking her up to carry her to the guest bedroom where she was staying. Still kissing her, he stood her on her feet by the bed. "I can't stop looking at you," he whispered. He drew her to him to kiss her. When he released her, he slid the zipper down the back of her dress and pushed it off her shoulders. As it fell around her feet, he leaned back to look at her. "You changed everything," he said.

"I bought the underwear when I purchased the dress," she said as he unfastened the clasp of the lacy red bra that was a wisp of material and so different from her usual practical cotton underwear.

He placed his hands on her hips and inhaled deeply. "You're gorgeous," he whispered, his eyes raking over her lacy panties down to her thigh-high stockings. She was still in her red pumps.

As he looked at her she unfastened the buttons of his shirt and pushed it off his shoulders. Her hands worked to loosen his belt and then his suit trousers and finally they fell away and she pushed down his briefs to free him.

She stroked him lightly and he inhaled, picking her up. She kicked off her pumps, and he placed her on the bed, switching on a small bedside light before kneeling beside her to shower her with kisses.

As she wound her arms around his neck, she rose up slightly, pulling him to her to kiss him. "Aaron, this is so good," she whispered.

He moved over her, kissing her passionately while she clung to him.

Later, she lay in his arms, held closely against him. "Aaron, you're changing my life."

He shifted on his side to face her, toying with locks of her hair. "You're changing mine, too, you know."

"I suppose," she said, gazing solemnly into his eyes. "I hadn't thought about that, but I guess a baby will change both of us. Even just knowing we'll have a baby will bring changes. I was talking about this week and my makeover, my new clothes, meeting so many people and persuading them to help. Of course, I have the pictures and figures to persuade them."

"You're the cause, more than pictures and numbers. The mayor couldn't have had anyone do a better job." Aaron wound his fingers in her hair.

"It's a long time from now, but do you think you'll be present when our baby is born?"

"I want to be and I hope you want me to be there," he said.

"Yes, I do," she answered, hurting, wishing she had his love. "I want you to be there very much."

He hugged her again. "Then that's decided. I'll be there." They became silent and she wondered if he would still feel the same way when their baby came into the world.

"You're beautiful, Stella," Aaron said hoarsely. He drew her closer against him. "I don't want to let you go," he whispered as his arms tightened around her.

Her face was pressed against his chest and she hugged him in return. "I don't want you to let me go ever," she whispered, certain it was so soft, he couldn't hear her. "Tonight we have each other," she said. "Tomorrow we go home and back to the problems."

When they flew back to Royal on Saturday afternoon, she had eight more big checks to deposit in the Royal storm recovery fund. As they sat in the plane, she was aware of Aaron studying her. "What?" she asked. "You're staring."

"I'm thinking about all the changes in you. Now you'll be the talk of Royal with your makeover, plus the money you're bringing in to help everyone."

She laughed. "I'll be the talk of Royal maybe for five minutes. But the checks will last for quite a while. Aaron, I'm so thrilled over the money. People have been really generous. Thank for your introductions."

"Thanks, Stella, for talking to all of them. You're doing a fantastic job. As for the talk of the town—it'll be longer than five minutes. I suspect some guys are going to ask you out. I think I should make my presence known."

She was tempted to fling *What do you care?* at him.

How much did he care? He acted as if he wanted to be with her. He had done so much for her—in the long run, the results had been for Royal, so she didn't know how much of his motivation came from feelings for her or if it was for the town. Even the jewelry had been for her because she was having his baby—not necessarily because he loved her for herself.

She didn't know any more about what he felt now than she had after their first night together.

The sex was fabulous, but did it mean deeper feelings were taking root with Aaron or was it still simply lust and a good time?.

Aaron would talk to Cole Saturday or Sunday and then she would know if the TCC had made any more decisions about the Christmas festival. It could be so much fun for everyone if they opened it up for all to attend.

She hoped to get into her town house soon and have her own little Christmas tree. Each day she was in Royal, she noticed more trees going up in various places in town. Some Christmases they had had a decorated tree on the lawn of the town hall. She wanted to ask about putting up a Christmas tree on the town-hall lawn this year because she hated for the storm to destroy any customs they had.

"You have appointments for us starting Monday with a lunch in Austin and dinner that night. The next day we go to Houston and Wednesday, we have a noon meeting in Dallas. We won't be back to Royal until after lunch Wednesday. No more until after Christmas, Aaron. I need to be in Royal so I can focus on the Christmas gift drive."

"You'll be back Wednesday afternoon. Then you can start catching up."

After landing she ate with Aaron at the Cozy Inn, sitting and talking until after ten. At the door to her suite, she glanced at him as she inserted the card in the slot. "Want to come in?"

"I thought you'd never ask," he said. He held the door for her and she entered.

She turned to face him. "Want something to drink?"

He walked up to her and pulled her close. "No, thank you. I want you in my arms."

She kissed him, wrapping her arms around his narrow waist, holding him, wondering if they were forging any kind of lasting bond at all.

After appearing in Austin for a TV interview on Monday, they flew to Houston on Tuesday. During the flight, Stella turned to Aaron. He was dressed to meet people as soon as they landed. He had shed his navy suit jacket and loosened his matching tie. He sat across from her with his long legs stretched out in the roomy private jet.

She was comfortable in her new navy suit and matching silk blouse. She, too, had shed her suit jacket.

"Still no morning sickness?" he asked.

"Not at all," she said. "Aaron, I've had three job offers this week."

His eyebrows arched. "Oh? Who wants to hire you?"

"The Barlow Group in Houston. They want me for vice president of public relations. It's a prestigious Texas foundation that raises money for good causes."

"I know who you're talking about. I have a friend on their board. Who else has made an offer?" he asked, frowning slightly as he waited.

"A Dallas charity—Thompkins Charities, Ltd. They also want me for director of public relations."

"Another prestigious group that does a lot of good. That's old oil money. I have several friends there."

"The third one is No Hungry Children in Dallas who

want me for a coordinator-of-services position. The only one I'm considering is the Barlow Group in Houston. I'm seriously thinking about taking that job. It pays more than I make now. It would be in Houston, which would be nice. I can help a lot of people—that would be my dream career."

"Congratulations on the offers. Frankly, you're needed in Royal, though."

"Royal is beginning to mend. They can get along without me."

"People have talked to me and I think the whole town wants you to step in and become acting mayor."

"I definitely don't think it's the whole town. The town council would be the ones to select someone and they haven't said a word to me. I can't imagine the town really wanting me for that role."

"Wednesday we're going back to Royal. Are you moving out of the Cozy Inn Friday?"

"Yes. My town house is all fixed up, so I'm going home. Friday or Saturday I'm getting a Christmas tree and decorating it."

"I have appointments Thursday in Royal and Friday I have to go to Dallas. I hate to leave now, but this is a deal I've worked on since before the storm hit. A wealthy family from back east wants to move to Dallas and build a new home. He was a college buddy, so there is a personal interest. I made a bid for R&N on building it. Now they've finally decided to go with R&N Builders. It's a five-million-dollar house, so I have to see them and be there to sign the contract. Cole could, but that would take him away from Royal and this is really something I've dealt with and I know the family."

"Aaron, go to Dallas," she said, smiling. "That's simple enough."

"That's what I have to do. I just wanted you to know

why. I still can move you in early Friday morning before I go to Dallas. Also, I'll help you get a tree on Saturday if you'd like."

"I'd like your help on the tree," she said, smiling at him. "I don't have a lot to move, so I can move home all by myself. Will you stay in Royal through Christmas and New Year's?"

"Yes. Probably about January 3, I'll go back to Dallas for a little while. I'll still be back and forth."

That thought hurt. She would miss him, but she had known that day was inevitable.

Sadness gripped her and she tightened her fist in her lap. "Next week is the TCC Christmas festival. It should be so much fun, Aaron. We're getting lots of presents and I haven't been there this week, but I've had texts from Lark, from Paige and from Megan Maguire."

"You're right—it will be fun. You'll be shocked by the number of presents that are coming into the TCC. That doesn't count the ones dropped off at businesses, fire stations, all over town."

"We have envelopes with checks for individuals and families that are on our list. I'm so grateful we've been able to do this."

"The Christmas drive is a great idea," he said.

She smiled. "Right now I'm excited over the Christmas festival," she said, thinking it would be another chance for her to spend time with Aaron. When January came and he returned to Dallas, it was going to be hard on her without him. She knew that, but she pushed aside her fears. Friday she would move out of the Cozy Inn. She would never again see it without thinking of Aaron.

Their pilot announced they were approaching the Houston area.

"This is exciting, Aaron. I hope we can raise a lot of money and get more help for Royal," she said, slipping into her suit jacket.

By Wednesday afternoon they had finished the interviews, the dinners, the talks to groups, and were flying back to Royal. Aaron knew some money had been sent directly to Royal, some checks had been given to Stella and some to him. He sat with a pen and pad in hand figuring out a rough total. She remained quiet.

When he raised his head, he smiled. "You've done a wonderful job, Stella. As far as the money, the checks that have been promised and the ones we're taking back with us total approximately a quarter of a million dollars. That's tremendous. I don't think the mayor himself could have done any better."

"I'm just astounded by the help we've received. Some of it was from out-of-state people seeing interviews that got picked up and broadcast nationally. I can't believe I've had three more offers to go on television news and local interest shows after the first of the year."

"You look good on camera."

She laughed. "Don't be ridiculous. That isn't why I'm asked."

"I think that's a big part of it."

"I'm sure that it's much more because Royal has some touching stories."

"They do, but it helps to have a pretty lady tell them."

Shaking her head at him, she changed the topic. "I'm hungry and ready to get my feet on the ground in Royal and have dinner."

"That's easy. Where would you like to eat? I'll take you wherever you'd like to go?"

"After being gone this week, I'm happy to eat at the inn."

"That suits me."

"Good," she answered, certain their lives would change and wondering if Aaron would leave hers.

"We'll be on the ground now in about thirty minutes," he said, and she looked out the window, glad to get back to Royal and home.

"It'll be my last two nights in the Cozy Inn," she said, thinking how soon Aaron would be leaving the hotel, too.

"Stella, would you like for me to go with you to a doctor's appointment?"

"I've got to find a doctor in Royal. I went to Houston to my sister's doctor, but I want a doctor here."

"Definitely. I'd like to go with you and meet the doctor."

"I think that would be nice. I'll ask about a pediatrician here, too. I don't want to drive to Dallas each time I need to see the doctor."

"No, you shouldn't. I'll make arrangements for our plane to take you to Dallas when you need to go, but I think you should have a doctor here."

"Thanks, Aaron. I'm glad you're interested."

"Stella, you'd be surprised if you knew how deep my interest runs. You and this baby are important to me," he said in a serious tone and with a somber look in his brown eyes. Her heart skipped. How much did he really mean that? He had included her with the baby. She figured that he had an interest in his child, but she had no idea of the depth of his feelings for her.

How important was she to him?

Stella went by the hospital Thursday. A doctor was with Mayor Vance, so she couldn't see him. She talked briefly with his wife and found out he was still improving, so Stella said she would come back in a few days. She called on others and talked to Lark briefly about the Christmas drive.

Lark smiled at her. "Stella, I really didn't recognize you at first. Your hair is so different and it changes your whole appearance. I saw you on a Dallas TV show. You were great and you took our case to a big audience. It's wonderful for people here to find out about these agencies and how to access them."

"Some of those agencies were new to me. I didn't know all that help was available."

"The shows should do a lot for us. You got in a plug for the Christmas drive also, which was nice. Speaking of the drive, I think there will be some big presents for people this Christmas."

"I hope so. Some of the stores are donating new TV sets for each family on our list. That'll be a fun present. Other stores are sending enough iPads for each family to have one. It makes me feel good to be able to help. I hope Skye and the baby are getting along."

"We just take everything one day at a time for both of them. There's still no word on Jacob Holt. If you hear anything, please call."

"I will, I promise. I'm home to stay now until Christmas Eve day when I'll go to my sister's."

"You just look beautiful. I love your hair."

"Thanks. You're nice."

"I have a feeling your quiet nights at home that you talk about are over," Lark said, smiling at her.

Stella laughed. "I'll keep in touch on the Christmas drive."

As she left the hospital, outside on the sidewalk, she heard someone call her name. She turned to see Cole headed her way.

"Hey, you look great."

"Thanks, Cole." To her surprise, he smiled at her. Since the storm she had rarely seen Cole smile.

"You're doing a bang-up job for the town. Aaron has let me know. Excellent job."

"Thanks. I'm glad to and I'm thrilled by people's generosity and finding specific agencies that can meet people's needs."

"I just wanted to thank you. See you around."

"That's nice, Cole."

He headed toward the hospital entrance and she wondered whom he was going to see. There were still too many in the hospital because of the storm over two months later.

"Stella, wait up."

She turned to see Lance Higgens, a rancher from the next county and someone she had known most of her life. She smiled at him, feeling kindly because the afternoon of the tornado he had come to Royal to help and that night he had made a $1,000 donation to the relief effort.

"I saw you on television yesterday."

"Good. I guess a lot of people caught that show around here."

"I didn't recognize you until they introduced you. You look great and you did a great job getting attention for Royal. I'd guess you'll get some donations."

"We did, Lance," she said. "We received one right away."

"Good. Listen, there's a barn dance at our town center next Saturday night. Would you like to go with me?"

Startled, she smiled at him. "I'm sorry, I'm going to a dinner that night, but thanks for asking me, Lance. That's very nice."

"Sure. Maybe some other time," he said. "Better go. Good to see you, Stella."

"Good to see you, too," she said, wanting to laugh. He had never looked at her twice before, never asked her to anything even though they had gone through high school together.

Her next stop was the drugstore where she ran into Paige. "Stella!" Paige called, and caught up with her.

"You never come to town. What are you doing here again?" Stella asked, smiling at her friend.

"I didn't plan well for anything this week. I saw you on television yesterday. Word went around that you'd be on— probably thanks to Aaron. You look fantastic and you did a great job. I love your makeover except I hardly know you."

"Thanks. It's the same me."

"Actually, I didn't even recognize you at first glimpse."

"Frankly, I barely recognize myself. The makeover has been fun and brought a bit of attention."

Paige's eyes narrowed. "I'll bet you're getting asked out by guys who never have asked you before."

Stella could feel her cheeks grow hot. "A little," she admitted. "I suppose looks are important to guys."

"Stella, most girls come to that conclusion before they're five years old," Paige remarked, and they both laughed. "We need a brief meeting soon for our Christmas drive to figure out how to coordinate the last-minute details. It's almost here."

"If you have a few minutes," Stella said, "we can go across the street to the café and talk about the drive now."

"Sure. Now's as good a time as any," Paige said. "We're running out of time. Christmas is one week away and the TCC festival is next Tuesday."

They walked to Stella's car, where she picked up her notebook. Then they crossed the street to a new café that had opened since the storm. As soon as they were seated, Stella opened the binder with notes and lists.

"Presents and donations are pouring in and I can add to them with checks I brought back from my talks this week."

"That's fantastic. I'll be there that night and I'll check with the others so we can help pass out envelopes with checks and help people get their presents. I'm sure some of the TCC guys will pitch in."

"I really appreciate all you're doing. I think we've contacted everyone we should and there's been enough publicity that no one will be overlooked. We'll have money or gifts for all the people who've lost so much and lost a loved one— I'm sorry, Paige, to bring that up with you," Stella said.

"It's the reality of life. So many of us live with loss. Lark's sister in a coma, Cole's lost his brother, Henry Markham lost a brother—you know the list. Holidays are tough for people with any big loss—that doesn't have to be because of the tornado—people like Aaron. I suppose that's why he's so sympathetic toward Cole."

"Aaron?"

Paige's gray eyes widened. "Aaron's wife and child."

Stella stared at Paige. "Aaron lost a wife and child?" she repeated, not thinking about how shocked she sounded.

"Aaron hasn't told you? You didn't know that?" Paige asked, frowning. "I thought that was general knowledge. It happened years ago. Maybe I know more about Aaron because of his connection to Cole and Craig."

Stella stared into space, stunned by Paige's revelation. "He's never told me," she said, talking more to herself than Paige. She realized Paige had asked her a question and looked at her. "I'm sorry. What did you say?"

"I'm surprised he hasn't told you. I've always known— Cole and I went to the service. A lot of people in Royal knew. I think his baby was a little over a year old. The little boy and Aaron's wife were killed in a traffic accident. It was sudden—one of those really bad things. He's been single since then. It was six or seven years ago. A long time. I don't think he's dated much since, but I know the two of you have been together. I figured that's because of the storm."

"He doesn't talk about his private life or his past and I don't ask. I figure he'll tell me what he wants me to know."

"Men don't talk about private things as much. Aaron may be one of those who doesn't talk at all. I know at one point Craig said Aaron was having a tough time dealing with his loss."

"Paige, I just stayed at his house in Dallas this week. I didn't see any pictures of a wife and child."

"He may not have any. That wouldn't occur to some men."

"Maybe. I also wasn't all over the house. I was just in the back part and the guest bedroom. We didn't even eat there."

"Well, then, it would be easy to not see any pictures. Especially if he has a big house like Cole. Sorry if finding out about his wife and child upset you."

"Oh, don't be silly. It's common knowledge as you said. I'm glad to know. He's just never talked to me about it. It does explain some things about him. Well, back to this Christmas drive—" Stella said, trying for now to put Aaron and his past out of her thoughts and concentrate on working out last-minute details of the event with Paige.

They worked another fifteen minutes before saying goodbye. Stella watched Paige walk away, a slender, willowy figure with sunlight glinting on her auburn hair, highlighting red strands.

Stella sat in the car, still stunned over Aaron's never mentioning his loss. Now she had the explanation for the barrier he kept between himself and others, the door he closed off when conversations or situations became too personal.

No wonder he held back about personal relationships— he was still in love with his late wife. And he'd lost his baby son. That's why babies were so special to him. Stella was unaware of the tears running down her cheeks. She had to stop seeing so much of Aaron. She couldn't cut him out of her life completely because of their baby, but she saw no future in going out with him. She didn't want to keep dating, because she was falling more deeply in love with him all the time while his emotions, love and loyalties were still back with the wife and child he had lost. She was glad he loved them, but he should have leveled with her.

Tears fell on the back of her hand and she realized she was crying. "Aaron, why didn't you tell me?" she whispered. If he really loved her, he would have shared this hurt with her, shared that very private bit of himself. Love didn't cut someone off and shut them out.

She wiped her hand and got a tissue to dry her eyes and her cheeks. Knowing she would have to pay attention to her driving, she focused on the car lot as she turned the key in the ignition.

She drove to the Cozy Inn and stepped out of the car, gathering packages to take inside. She hoped she didn't see Aaron before she reached her suite. She wanted to compose herself, think about what she would say.

She would have to make some decisions about her life with Aaron.

She would see him tonight at dinner. Once again her life was about to change. The sad part was that she would have to start to cut Aaron out of it and see far less of him.

Stella was tempted to confront him with the information she'd learned and ask why he hadn't told her, but instead she wanted him to tell her voluntarily without her asking about it. There was no way she would accept his marriage proposal when he didn't even trust her enough to tell her something that vital. And if he still loved his first wife with all his heart, Stella didn't want to marry him.

Sadly, he wasn't ready to marry again—at least not for love. He had to love his late wife and child enormously still, maybe to the point of being unable to let go and face that they had gone out of his life forever.

Deep inside, her feelings for him crashed and shattered.

Eight

For their dinner tonight, Stella wore one of her new sweaters—a pale blue V-neck—and black slacks. She wore his gold-leaf necklace and bracelet but fought tears when she put the jewelry on.

She went to meet him, her body tingling at the sight of him while eagerness tinged with sadness gripped her as she crossed the Cozy Inn lobby. Aaron was in a black sweater, jeans and boots. She really just wanted to walk into his embrace, but she had to get over even wanting to do so.

"You're gorgeous, Stella. I've missed seeing you all day."

She smiled at him as he took her arm. As soon as they were seated, she picked up a menu.

After they ordered and were alone, he looked at her intently, his gaze slowly traveling over her. "I can't get used to the change in you. I've seen women change hairdos, men shave their heads and grow mustaches, a lot of things that transform appearances, but yours is the biggest change I've ever seen. I never expected you to change this much. It's fabulous."

"Thank you," she said, beginning to wonder if he would lose interest if she returned to looking the way she always had. The minute she thought about it, she remembered that it wouldn't matter because she was going to see him less often.

"Several people have called to thank me for getting you on television because they've found the agency they need for help."

"Good," she said. It was the first bright bit of news since she had sat down to dinner with him.

"Club members have been getting word out that the entire town is invited to the TCC Christmas festival, so I think we will have a big turnout."

"That is wonderful," she said. "It should be a happy time for people," she said. "For a little while that evening, maybe they can all forget their losses and celebrate the season. I know it's fleeting, but it's better than nothing."

"It's a lot better than nothing. It will help people so much and kids will have a great time. Some of the women are beginning to plan games and things they can do for the kids. It'll be an evening to look back on when we all pulled together and had a great time."

"That's good," she said, and then thought of his loss, sorry that Christmas was probably a bad time for Aaron.

She felt responsible for him staying in Royal for the holidays. She didn't think he would be if she hadn't talked about how it would help others if he would stay and do things for people who needed something at holiday time.

She didn't want to deliberately hurt him. But it had ended between them as far as she was concerned. She had to get over him even though she had fallen in love with him.

How long would it take her to get over Aaron?

"Did you buy a dress for the Christmas festival?" he asked.

"Aaron, I already had a dress," she said, beginning to wonder if he was wound up in her new persona and really didn't have that much interest in the former plain Jane that she was. It was a little annoying. Was he not going to like her if she reverted to her former self? She suspected it didn't matter, because after the Christmas festival she didn't expect to continue the intimate relationship they had. She would see him because of their baby, but it would be a parental relationship and not what they had now. She might be with him a lot where their child was concerned, but they wouldn't be having an affair and she wasn't going to marry a man who was still in love with his deceased wife. Aaron couldn't even talk to her about his wife and baby, so he hadn't let go at all.

"I think you should have something new and special," he said, breaking into her thoughts.

"Don't go shopping for a dress for me," she said. "I have a new dress for the festival I got at Cecilia's shop."

Three people stopped by their table to talk to her and tell her what a great job she had done on television Saturday. As the third one walked away, Aaron smiled at her. "I can see the butterflies are completely gone to another home."

"Yes, they are. Thanks to you."

"No, Stella. You did that yourself. You're the one who's developed poise to deal with people. You're the one who's talking to people, telling them what happened, telling people here how to get help. Oh, no. This isn't me. It's you. You have more confidence now and you're handling things with more certainty. You've brought about the changes in yourself. Maybe not hair and makeup, but confidence and self-assurance, making some of the tough decisions that have to be made about who gets help first. No, this is something you've done yourself."

"Thanks for the vote of confidence."

"I've had several people ask me if I would talk to you about stepping in as acting mayor. They're going to have to find someone soon."

"Now *that* position I'm not qualified for," she said firmly.

"Of course, you are. You're already doing the job. Take

a long look at yourself," he said, and his expression was serious, not the cocky friendliness that he usually exhibited.

"I see an administrative assistant."

"Look again, Stella. The administrative assistant disappeared the afternoon of the storm. You're all but doing Mayor Vance's job now. And I checked. The role will end before you have your baby next summer, so that won't be a problem."

She was thinking half about the job and half about Aaron, who looked incredible. How was she going to break things off with him?

All she had to do was remember than he had not recovered from his loss enough to even talk about it. He could not love anyone else and she hadn't changed her views of marrying without love. She wasn't going to do it.

They ate quietly. She listened to him talk about Royal and the things that had happened in the past few days. Finally, he leaned back in his chair, setting down his glass of water while he gazed at her.

"You're quiet. You've hardly said two words through dinner."

"Part of it was simply listening to you and learning what happened while we were in Dallas. I'm worn-out from the whirlwind week coming on top of everything else I've been doing."

"I think it's more than that. You weren't this quiet yesterday."

They stared at each other and she then looked down at her lap. "Aaron, tomorrow I move back to my town house. We have the festival coming up and we're going together. I want to get through that without any big upsets in my life."

"Why do I feel I'm part of what might be a big upset in your life? I don't see how I can be, but I don't think you'd be so quiet with me if I wasn't."

"I think it would be better if we talk when we're upstairs. This really isn't the place."

"I'd say that's incentive to get going," he said. "Are you ready?"

"Yes," she said. When she stood up, he held her arm lightly and led her from the dining room, stopping to say something to the maître d' and then rejoining her.

At her door to her suite, she invited him inside. When they were in the living room, she turned to face him. "What would you like to drink?"

He shook his head as he closed the space between them. He drew her close to kiss her. She melted into his arms, her heart thudding as she kissed him. She wound her arms around him to hold him close, kissing him in return, her resolutions nagging while she ignored them to kiss him.

She ran her fingers in his short, thick hair at the back of his head. She didn't want to stop kissing. She wanted him in her bed all night long. She thought about his loss and knew she couldn't keep spending days and nights with him or she would be so hopelessly in love she would be unable to say no to him.

Finally she stepped back. Both of them were breathing hard. She felt a tight pang and wanted him badly. Just one more night—the thought taunted her. It was tempting to give in, to step back into his arms and kiss him and forget all the problems.

In the long run, it would be better to break it off right now. She wouldn't be hurt as much. She didn't think he would ever love anyone except the first wife. It had been long enough for him to adjust to his loss better than he had. No one ever got over it, they just learned to deal with it and go on with life.

She could imagine how desperately he wanted this baby after losing his first one. She suspected before long he would start showering her with more presents and pressuring her to marry him—and it would be because of their baby.

She would be glad to have him in their baby's life, but that was where it would have to stop. She couldn't go into a loveless marriage just to please Aaron.

She stared at him, making sure she had his attention and he wasn't thinking about kissing her again. "I can't do this, Aaron. We're not wildly in love. I think this is a purely physical relationship. Frankly, it's lust. If we keep it up, I might fall in love with you."

"So what's wrong with that picture," he said, frowning and placing one hand on his hip.

"Because I don't think you're going to fall in love. This is a physically satisfying relationship that you can walk away from at any point in time. Emotionally, you're not in it. I don't want that. I don't want to be in love with a man who isn't in love with me in return."

"I might fall in love and I think we've been good together, and I think I've been good with you and to you, Stella."

"You've been fantastic and so very good to me. I don't want to stop seeing you, I just want to back off and take a breather from the heavy sex. That isn't like me and I can't do that without my emotions getting all entangled."

His frown disappeared and he stepped closer to place one hand lightly on her hip. "I can back off. Are you going to still let me kiss you?"

His question made her feel ridiculous. "As if I could stop you."

"I don't use force," he said as he leaned forward to brush a light kiss on her lips. "Okay, so we don't go to bed together. You'll set the parameters and send me home when you want me to go. In the meantime, kisses are good. Don't cut me off to the point where we don't even have a chance to fall in love," he whispered as he brushed kisses on her throat, her ear, the corner of her mouth.

She should have been more firm with him, but when he started talking, standing so close, his eyes filled with desire, his voice lowering, coaxing—she couldn't say no or tell him to leave. She would have to sometime during the night, but not for a few minutes. There wasn't any point in ending seeing him before Christmas, because they were going to be thrown together constantly and she didn't want a pall hanging over them.

And she couldn't ever end it entirely because of their baby.

His kiss deepened as his arms tightened around her, holding her against him. He was aroused, kissing her passionately, and she stopped thinking and kissed him in return.

Finally he picked her up. She was about to protest when he sat in the closest chair and held her on his lap, but ended up forgetting her protest and wrapping her arms around his neck to continue kissing him. How was she going to protect her heart?

His hand went beneath her sweater to caress her and in minutes he had both hands on her. When he slipped her sweater over her head, she caught his wrists, taking her sweater from him to pull it on again and slide off his lap.

"Aaron, let's say good-night," she said, facing him as she straightened her sweater.

"This is really what you want?" he asked.

"Tonight, it is. I need some space to think and sort out things."

He nodded. "Sure. Maybe you just need some time off. It's been a great week, Stella. You've done so much. You've been a great representative for Royal."

"Thanks. Thanks for everything," she whispered, scared she would cry or tell him to stay for the night or, worse, walk back into his arms, which was what she wanted.

"See you in the morning, hon," he said, brushing a kiss on her cheek and leaving.

She closed the door behind him and touched her cheek with her hand while tears spilled over. She loved him and this was going to be hard. After Christmas she would break up with him. But she wasn't ruining Christmas for either one of them. Suppose she had a little boy who looked like Aaron and was a reminder of his daddy every day of his life?

She had expected Christmas to be so wonderful. Instead, she was beginning to wonder how she would get through it

"Aaron," she whispered, knowing she was in love. He had been so good to her, helping her in multiple ways, changing her life, really. He was a good guy, honorable, loyal, fun to be with, sexy, loving. Was she making a mistake sending him away? Should she live with him and hope that someday he would love her? Was not telling her about his family an oversight—did he think she already knew because so many did?

She doubted it. She thought it was what gave him the shuttered look, what caused him to throw up an invisible barrier. He still had his heart shut away in memories and loss and she couldn't reach it, much less ever have his love.

Aaron lay in bed in the dark, tossing and turning, his thoughts stormy. He missed Stella. He wanted to make love to her, wanted just to be with her. It was obvious something was bothering her. Why wouldn't she just tell him and let them work it out?

Had it been the gifts? Did she want an engagement ring, instead?

He had proposed that first night he learned she was pregnant, but she had turned him down and she would until he declared he loved her and made a commitment to her with his whole heart. Without talking about it, he knew she was bothered and scared she was falling in love and he wouldn't love her in return.

He liked her and maybe there was love up to a point, but he wasn't into making a total commitment to her. He couldn't tell her he loved her with his whole heart and that was what she wanted to hear. They hadn't talked about it, but he felt he was right.

He enjoyed being with her more than any other woman since Paula. It surprised him to realize he wasn't thinking as often of Paula. He would always love her and Blake and always miss them. He knew every time February 5 came around that it would have been Blake's birthday. It always hurt and it always would.

All the more reason he wanted Stella in his life—because this baby was his and he wasn't losing his second child. All he had to do was tell Stella he loved her with his whole heart. But he couldn't; he had to be truthful about it. He was trying to back off and give her room, let her think things through. Why wouldn't she settle for what they had, which was very good. They might fall in love in time and he might be able to handle his loss better. But that wasn't good enough for Stella, because she wouldn't take a chance on falling in love later.

Stella had some strong beliefs and held to them firmly.

Tossing back the covers, he got out of bed. This was his first night away from her for a little while, and he was miserable. What would he feel like in January when they parted for maybe months at a time?

Aaron felt caged in the small suite at the Cozy Inn. At home he would just go to his gym and work out hard enough that he had to concentrate on what he was doing until he was so exhausted he would welcome bed and sleep. Even without her. He couldn't do that here. Knowledge that she was sleeping nearby disturbed him. He could go to her easily, but she would just say no.

Stella was intelligent. He figured at some point she would see they were compatible, the sex was fantastic and she surely would see that, hands down, it would be best for her baby to have a daddy—a daddy who would love him or her and be able to provide well for all of them.

Then he thought about Stella's makeover. He had heard enough talk—guys in Royal had asked her out since she had been back in town after their first trip to Dallas. Trey Kramer had even asked Aaron if they were dating because he wanted to ask her out if she wasn't committed. That didn't thrill him. He had told Trey that he was dating Stella, but when he returned to work in Dallas in January, Aaron expected her to be asked out often by several men.

The thought annoyed him. He didn't want to think about her with other men and he didn't want the mother of his child marrying another man. He realized on the latter point, he was being selfish. If he couldn't make a real commitment to her, he needed to let her go.

He suspected she was going to walk out of his life if he didn't do something. The notion hurt and depressed him.

He paced the suite, hoping he didn't disturb people on the floor below. He tried to do some paperwork, but he couldn't stop thinking about Stella.

It was after four in the morning when he fell asleep. He woke at six when he heard his phone ring, indicating he'd received a text. Instantly awake, Aaron picked up his phone to read the message, which was from Stella.

I have very little to move. Mostly clothes. I've loaded my car and checked out. I won't need any help, but thanks anyway. I'll keep in touch and see you Tuesday evening when we go to the TCC Christmas festival.

She didn't want to see him until Tuesday evening for the party. He had a feeling that she was breaking up with him. The day after the festival would be Christmas Eve when she would fly out of Royal to go to her sister's in Austin. Aaron stared at her message. In effect, she was saying goodbye.

At least as much as she could say goodbye when she was pregnant with his baby. One thing was clear: she had moved on from spending nights with him. No more passion and lovemaking, maybe not even kisses.

He was hurt, but he could understand why she was acting this way. He should accept what she wanted. He needed to go on with his life and adjust to Stella not being a part of it.

He did some additional paperwork, then after a while picked up his phone again to make calls. Soon he had moved his Dallas appointment until later in the day so he didn't have to leave Royal as early. He showered, shaved and dressed, ordering room service for a quick breakfast while he made more calls.

He may have to tell Stella goodbye this week, but before that happened, there was one last thing he could do for her. Hurting, he picked up the phone to make another call.

As soon as the hospital allowed visitors that morning, Aaron went to see Mayor Vance.

After he finished his business in Dallas later that afternoon, Aaron went home to gather some things to take back to Royal with him. He paused to call Stella. He had tried several times during the day, but she had never answered and she didn't now.

He suspected she didn't want to talk to him, because

she kept her phone available constantly in case someone in Royal needed help.

Certain he wouldn't even see her, he decided to stay at home in Dallas Friday night and go back Saturday. He wouldn't have even gone then except he had appointments in Royal all day Saturday to talk to people about the upcoming appointment of an acting mayor.

He already missed Stella and felt as if he had been away from her for a long time when it really wasn't even twenty-four hours yet.

He wondered whether she was thinking seriously about taking the Houston job offer. It would be a good job, but Aaron knew so many people in Royal wanted her to take the acting mayor position—including the mayor, who had now talked to the town council about it.

That night Aaron couldn't get her on her phone. When she didn't answer at one in the morning, he gave up, but he wondered where she was and who she was with. He missed her. She had filled an empty place in his life. He sat thinking about her—beautiful, intelligent, fun to be with, sexy—she was all that he wanted in a woman. Had he fallen in love with her without realizing it?

The idea shook him. He went to his kitchen and got a beer and then walked back to the guest bedroom downstairs where she had stayed when she had been at his house. He thought about being in bed with her, holding her in his arms.

He missed her terribly and he didn't want to tell her goodbye. It shocked him to think about it, and decided that he was in love with her. Why hadn't he seen it before now? He'd wanted to be with her day and night.

When he recognized that he loved Stella, he also saw he might be on the verge of losing her. She was a strong woman with her own standards and views and so far she had turned him down on marriage. Plus, she was considering accepting a very good position in Houston, which was a long way from Dallas.

He was in love with her and she was going to have his baby. He didn't want to lose her. He ran his hand over his short hair while he thought about what he could do to win her love. She'd accused him of proposing out of a sense of duty instead of love, which was exactly what he had done at the time. But he had spent a lot of time with her since then. There had been intimacy between them, hours together. They had worked together regarding Royal, had fun being together.

Why hadn't he seen that his feelings for her were growing stronger? He admired her; he respected and desired her. She was all the things he wanted in a woman. He had to win her love.

While he had never heard a declaration of love from Stella, she had to feel something for him. She acted as if she did. He was certain she would never have gone to bed with him with only casual feelings about him. That would be totally unlike her. Was she in love, too?

Had he already tossed away his chance with her?

He stood and moved impatiently to a window to gaze out at the lit grounds of his estate. If nothing else he would see her Tuesday night when he took her to the TCC Christmas festival. He wished he could move things up or go back to last week, but he couldn't.

He walked down the hall to his office. Crossing the room, he switched on a desk lamp and picked up a picture of his wife and child. "Paula, I've fallen in love. I think you'd approve. You'd like Stella and she would like you."

He realized that the pain of his loss had dulled slightly and he could look at Paula's picture and know that he loved

Stella also. He set the picture on the desk, picked up his beer and walked out of the room, switching off the light.

He wanted to see Stella, to kiss her, to tell her he loved her. This time when he proposed, he would try to do it right. Was she going to turn him down a second time?

Next Tuesday was the TCC Christmas festival, a special time. The town was getting ready to appoint an acting mayor and they wanted Stella, but she just didn't realize how many wanted her and how sincere they were about it.

If he had lost her love, there still was something good that he could do for her.

Saturday morning Stella selected a Christmas tree, getting one slightly taller than usual. As soon as she had set it up on a table by the window across the room from her fireplace, she got out her decorations. Her phone chimed and she glanced at it to see a call from Aaron. She didn't take it. She would talk to him soon enough Tuesday night; right now she still felt on a rocky edge. Aaron could get to her too easily. She wanted to be firm when she was with him. After Tuesday night, she really didn't expect to go out with him again except in the new year when she had to talk to him about their baby.

She placed her hand on her tummy, which was still flat. Her clothes had gotten just the slightest bit tighter in the waist, but otherwise, she was having an easy pregnancy so far.

She was excited about the Christmas drive, which was going even better than she had expected. The presents were piling up at the TCC. Paige had told her that each day now, TCC members picked up presents from drop-off points around town and took them to the club to place around the big Christmas tree.

She tried to avoid thinking about Aaron, but that was

impossible. She wasn't sleeping well, which wasn't good since she was pregnant. After Tuesday, maybe it would be easier to adjust because they wouldn't be in each other's lives as much.

She talked to her sister and learned their mother would be in Austin Christmas Eve, too. Stella checked again on her flight, scheduled to leave Christmas Eve and come back Christmas afternoon.

Aaron finally stopped calling on Monday and she heard nothing from him Tuesday. He must have caught on that she didn't want contact with him. She assumed he would still pick her up, but if he didn't show by six-thirty, she would go on her own. According to their earlier plans, he would come by for her at 6:15 p.m., which was early because the celebration did not begin until six-thirty. Her anticipation had dropped since she had parted with Aaron. She just wanted to get through the evening, leave the next day for Austin and try to pick up her life without Aaron.

For the first time in her life, Stella had her hair done at the Saint Tropez Salon. The salon was on the east side of town, which had escaped most of the storm damage.

As she dressed, a glimmer of the enthusiasm she had originally experienced for the night returned. It was exciting to have a party and to know it would be so good for so many people who had been hurt in the storm. It cheered her to know that all the families would have presents and money and hope for a nice Christmas.

On a personal level, she hoped things weren't tense all evening with Aaron, but she thought both of them would have enough friends around that they could set their worries aside and enjoy the party. And Aaron might not care as much as she did that they would be saying goodbye.

She guessed Aaron would ask about her job offers. She

still had not accepted the job offer in Houston. Every time she reached for the phone to talk to them, she pulled back.

Getting ready, she paused in front of the full-length mirror to look at herself. She wore the red dress she had worn before. One other new dress still hung in the closet, but the red dress was a Christmas color and it should be fine for the evening. When she put it on, the waist felt tighter. It was still comfortable, but she thought this was the last time she would wear the red dress until next winter.

Thinking it would be more appropriate for this party and also draw less attention, she wore the gold and diamond necklace. Once again, she wondered if Aaron was more interested in the person she had become after the makeover and all that had happened since, or the plain person she really was.

She made up her face as they had taught her at the salon, but when she started to put something on her lips, she stared at herself and put away the makeup, leaving her lips without any. She studied herself and was satisfied with her appearance.

She heard the buzzer and went to the door to meet Aaron. When sadness threatened to overwhelm her, she took a deep breath, thought of all the gifts people would be receiving tonight and opened the door with the certainty that this was the last time she would go out with Aaron Nichols.

Nine

Looking every inch the military man in civilian clothes, ready for a semiformal party, Aaron stood straight, handsome and neat with his short dark blond hair. Wearing a flawless navy suit and tie and a white shirt with gold cuff links, he made her heart beat faster.

"I've missed you," he said.

Her lips firmed and she tried to hang on to her emotions. "This is a night we've both looked forward to for a long time. Come in and I'll get my purse and coat."

"You're stunning, Stella," he said as he stepped inside and closed the door behind him. "I'm glad you wore your necklace."

"It's lovely, Aaron."

He studied her intently and she tilted her head, puzzled by his expression.

"So what are you thinking?"

"That you're the most gorgeous woman in the state of Texas."

His remark made her want to laugh and made her want to cry. It was a reminder of one of the reasons it was going to hurt so much to tell him goodbye. "A wee exaggeration, but thank you. I'm glad you think so."

"Tonight should be fun," he said. "Let's go enjoy the evening."

"We're early, but there may be things to do."

He pulled her close. "I don't want to mess up your makeup so I won't kiss you now, but I'm going to make up for it later."

She pulled his head down to kiss him for just a minute and then released him. "Nothing on my lips—see. I'm not messed up."

"No, you're hot, beautiful and I want you in my arms, Stella," he said in a husky voice with a solemn expression that might indicate he expected her to tell him goodbye tonight.

"C'mon, Aaron. We have a party to go to." He held her coat and then took her arm to go to his car.

When they arrived at the Texas Cattleman's Club, she was amazed to see the cars that had already filled the lot and were parked along the long drive all the way back down to the street.

"Aaron, it looks like most of the people in Royal are here. Wasn't this scheduled to start at six-thirty tonight?"

"It was. I can't believe they already have such a huge turnout."

"I never would have imagined it," she said. "I know the TCC invited everyone in Royal, but I never dreamed they would all come. Did you?"

"The town's pulled together since the storm—neighbor helping neighbor. I think everyone is interested."

"I'm surprised. This isn't what I expected."

"It's what I expected and hoped for." A valet opened the door for her and she stepped out. Aaron came around to take her arm. Once inside the clubhouse, she glanced around at the rich, dark wood, the animal heads that had been mounted long ago when it was strictly a men's club. Now women were members and there was a children's center that had a reputation for being one of the finest in Texas. They paused by a coatroom where Aaron checked their coats and then he turned to take her arm again.

They headed for the great room that served for parties, events, dances and other club-wide activities. The sound of voices grew louder as they walked down the hall.

When they stepped inside the great room, a cheer went up, followed by thunderous applause. Stunned, Stella froze, staring at the smiling crowd. Everywhere she looked, people held signs that read, Stella for Acting Mayor, We Want Stella, and Thanks, Stella.

The TCC president, Gil Addison, appeared at her side. "Welcome, Stella."

Dazed, she tried to fathom what this was all about. She looked at Gil.

"This little surprise is to show you the support you have from the entire town of Royal. We all want you to accept the position of acting mayor until an election can be held and a new mayor chosen."

"I'm speechless," she said, smiling and waving at people.

"Stella, I have a letter from the mayor that I want to read to you and to all," Gil said. "Let's go up to the front."

"Did you know about this?" she asked, turning to Aaron. He grinned and gave her a hug.

"A little," he said, and she realized that Aaron might have been behind organizing this gathering of townspeople.

Gil smiled. "Aaron, you come with us," Gil said, and led the way. There was an aisle cleared to the stage at the front of the room.

As she approached the stage, people greeted her and shook her hand and she smiled, thanking them. Dazed, she couldn't quell her surprise.

At the front as she climbed the three steps to the stage,

more people greeted her. She shook hands with the town council and other city dignitaries. The sheriff greeted her, and the heads of different agencies in town crowded around to say hello.

"Stella, Stella, Stella," several people in the audience began chanting and in seconds, the entire room was chanting her name. She saw her friends Paige and Edie in the front row, smiling and waving.

"Mercy, Aaron, what is all this?" Dazed, embarrassed, she turned to Gil. "Gil—" She gave up trying to talk with all the chanting. Smiling, she waved at everyone.

Gil stepped forward and held up his hands for quiet. "Thanks to all of you for coming out tonight. The Texas Cattleman's Club is happy to have nearly everyone in Royal come celebrate the Christmas season and the holidays. We have a bit of business we wanted to discuss before the partying begins."

The crowd had become silent and Gil had a lapel mike so it was easy to hear him. "We have some people onstage—I imagine everyone here knows them, but in case they don't, I want to briefly tell you who is here. Please save your applause until I finish. I'll start with our sheriff, Nathan Battle." Gil ran through the list, reeling off the names of the town council members and heads of various agencies, and when he was done, the audience applauded.

"Now as you know, Mayor Vance was critically injured by the tornado. He is off the critical list—" Gil paused while people clapped. "He is still in the hospital and unable to join us tonight, but he has sent a letter for me to read, which I will do now.

'To the residents of Royal,
I am still recovering from the storm and most deeply

grateful to be alive and that my family survived. My deepest sympathy goes out to those who lost their loved ones, their homes, their herds or crops. We were hurt in so many ways, but from the first moment after the storm, people have helped each other.

It was with deep regret that I learned that Deputy Mayor Max Rothschild was also killed by the tornado. Since I will not be able to return to this job for a few more months, Royal will temporarily need an acting mayor. I have talked to our city officials, agency heads and concerned citizens, and one name comes up often and we are all in agreement. I hope we can persuade Ms. Stella Daniels to accept this position.'"

Gil paused to let people applaud and cheer. The noise was making her ears ring. Just then, Aaron leaned close to whisper in her ear, "I told you everyone wants you."

She smiled and threw kisses and waved, then put her hand down, hoping Gil could calm the crowd. She was stunned by the turnout and the crowd's enthusiastic support—for the first time in her life, she felt accepted by everyone. She glanced at Aaron, who smiled and winked at her, and she was certain he was the one behind this crowd that had gathered.

Gil raised his hand for quiet. "Folks, there's more from Mayor Vance.

'Please persuade Ms. Stella Daniels to accept this position. Since the first moments after the storm Stella has been doing my job. Now that I have recovered enough to read the mail I receive, I have had texts, emails, letters and cards that mention Stella and all she is doing for Royal and its citizens. I urge

Stella to accept this position and I am heartily supported by the town council, other officials of Royal and by its citizens.

Merry Christmas. Best wishes for your holiday,

The Honorable Richard Vance, Mayor of Royal, Texas.'"

There was another round of cheers and applause and Gil motioned for quiet. "At this point, I'm turning the meeting over to Nathan Battle."

Nathan received applause and motioned for quiet. "Thanks. I volunteered to do this part of the program. Royal needs an acting mayor." Nathan turned to Stella. "Stella, I think you can see that Mayor Vance, the town council and the whole town of Royal would like you to accept this position that will end in a few months when Mayor Vance can return to work. Will you be acting mayor of Royal?"

Feeling even more dazed, she looked up at Nathan Battle's dark brown eyes. Taking a deep breath, she smiled at him. "Yes, I'll accept the job of acting mayor until Mayor Vance gets back to work."

Her last words were drowned out by cheers and applause. Nathan shook her hand as he smiled. "Congratulations," he shouted. He stepped back and applauded as she turned and Aaron gave her a brief hug.

Everyone onstage shook her hand and tried to say a few words to her. The audience still cheered so she waved her hands for quiet.

"I want to thank all of you for this show of support. I'm stunned and amazed. I'll try my best to do what I can for Royal, as so many of you are doing. Let's all work together and, hopefully, we can get this town back in shape far sooner than anyone expected. Thank you so very much."

As the crowd applauded, Gil stepped forward and motioned for quiet again. "One more thing at this time. We can go from here to the dining hall. There's a buffet with lots of tables of food. Everyone can eat and during dessert we'll have Stella perform her first task as acting mayor and make presentations of gifts. There will be singing of Christmas carols in the dining room and then dancing back in this room, games in other rooms and the children's center will be open for the little ones. We have staff to take care of the babies. Now let's adjourn to the dining hall."

They applauded and Stella started down the steps to shake hands with people and talk to them. She lost track of Aaron until he showed up at her side and handed her a glass of ice water.

Gratefully, she sipped it and continued moving through the crowd toward the dining room. "You did this," she said to him.

"All I did was tell people we would do this tonight. No one would have come tonight if they hadn't wanted you for acting mayor and hadn't wanted to thank and support you."

"Aaron, I don't know what to say. I'm still reeling in shock."

"Congratulations. Now you'll get paid a little more for what you've been doing anyway. That's the thing, Stella. You're already doing this job and you have been for the past two months."

"If people know I'm pregnant, they might not want me for the job."

"It's most likely only for a couple more months and you're doing great so far."

"How many more surprises do you have in store tonight, Aaron?"

"I'm working on that one," he said, and she rolled her

eyes. "The band is coming in now. Let's head to the dining room and nibble on something while they set up."

"I don't know how long I'm going to feel dazed."

"It'll wear off and life will go right back to normal. You'll see."

Cole suddenly appeared in front of her. "Congratulations, Stella. You deserve to have the official title since you're doing all the work that goes with it."

"Thank you for coming tonight, Cole. I appreciate everyone showing their support. I had no idea."

"Well, Aaron organized this and I'm glad to be here because you should have this position. Just keep up what you're doing," he said, smiling at her.

"Thanks so much," she said.

"I'm touched you came tonight, Cole. I'm really amazed."

"I wouldn't have missed this."

As they moved on, she leaned closer to Aaron. "I'll remember this night all my life. I'll go see Mayor Vance tomorrow and thank him. But I suppose my biggest thanks goes to you. You must have been really busy talking to everyone."

"It didn't take any persuasion on my part. Everyone thought you'd be the best person for the job."

"Well, I'm amazed and touched by that, too. I just did what needed to be done, like hundreds of other people in Royal."

Gil Addison appeared again. "Stella. As acting mayor you should take charge of the next event on tonight's schedule. We'd like to tell people to pick up their envelopes and their presents whenever they want. Some families have little children and they won't want to stay long. Also, as acting mayor, you really should be at the head of the food line."

"I don't want to cut in front of people," she said, laughing and shaking her head. "I'll just get in line."

"Enjoy the few little perks you get with this job," Gil said. "There won't be many."

As they headed toward the dining room, people continued to stop and congratulate her. Paige walked up while the Battles talked to Aaron.

"You look gorgeous," she said. "Your necklace and bracelet are beautiful."

"Thank you. Aaron gave them to me."

"Aaron? I'm surprised, but glad Aaron is coming out of his shell. All our lives are changing, some in major ways, some in tiny ones, but the storm was a major upheaval for all of us. At least it looks as if we're all pulling together."

"I'm astounded, but oh, so thrilled. Thanks, Paige, for your part in this evening."

"Whatever I can do, I'm glad to. After I eat, I'll be at the table with the envelopes we're giving out. Members of the TCC will help us and we're doing this in shifts."

"Great, thanks."

Paige moved on and Aaron took Stella's arm to walk to the dining room. Enticing smells of hot bread, turkey and ham filled the air, and the dining room had three lines of long tables laden with food. The rest of the room was filled with tables covered in red or green paper where people could sit. At the back of the room was a huge decorated Christmas tree. Presents surrounded it, spilling out in front of it, lining the wall behind it. There appeared to be hundreds of wrapped presents. Paige, Lark, Edie, Megan and four TCC members sat at two tables to hand out envelopes of money some families would be receiving.

Gil appeared again. "Stella, you're the guest of honor—you get to go to the head of the line."

"I feel ridiculous doing that."

"We need you to go anyway so you can make the announcement about the gifts. Aaron, you go with her. Everyone's waiting for you to start."

Aaron took her arm as they followed Gil to the head of a line.

She had little appetite, but she ate some of the catered food that was there in abundance—turkey, dressing, mashed potatoes and cream gravy, ham, roasts, barbecued ribs, hot biscuits, thick golden corn bread, pickled peaches, an endless variety.

When they finished, Gil excused himself and left the table. He was back in minutes to sit and lean closer to talk to Stella. "We're ready to start matching people up with their gifts. People can pick up their things all evening long until eleven-thirty. The volunteers will change shifts at regular intervals so no one has to spend the whole evening handing out presents. If you're ready, I'll announce you. Aaron, go onstage. You'll be next about the Dallas TCC."

"Sure," she said. "Excuse me," she said to Nathan Battle, who sat beside her.

At the front of the room, Gil called for everyone's attention. "As I think all of you know, some people in Royal lost everything in the storm. A good number of Royal residents have been badly hit. So many of us wanted to do something about that. This was Stella's idea and I'll let her tell you more about it—" He handed a mike to Stella.

"As you all know," Stella began, "we decided to do a Christmas drive to provide presents and support for the people who need it most. All the Texas Cattleman Club's members, along with the ladies from the Christmas-drive committee volunteered to help. Those who could do so, both from Royal and other parts of Texas have contributed generously so everyone in Royal can have a wonderful holiday.

"Each family receiving gifts tonight has been assigned a number. First, go over to the table where the volunteers are seated near the west wall and pick up the envelope that matches your number. That envelope is for you and your family. Also, there are gifts that correspond to those numbers under the Christmas tree and along the back wall. Just go see a volunteer, who will help you. You get both an envelope plus the wrapped gifts that correspond to your number.

"We want to give a huge thanks to all who contributed money, time and effort to this drive to make sure everyone has a merry Christmas. Thank you."

People applauded and Stella started to sit, but Gil appeared and motioned her to wait. He took the mike. "I have one more important announcement—some really good news for us. Aaron Nichols and Cole Richardson are members of the Dallas, Texas, Cattleman's Club, but they are spending so much time and money in Royal trying to help us rebuild the town that the Texas Cattleman's Club of Royal invited them to join, which they did. Aaron Nichols and Cole will tell you about the rest. Aaron," Gil said, and handed the mike to Aaron while everyone applauded.

"Thanks. We're glad to help. This is Cole's hometown and I feel like it's mine now, too, because I've been here so much and everyone is so friendly. We've talked to some of our TCC friends in Dallas. I'll let Cole finish this." Aaron handed the mike to Cole, who received applause.

"It's good to be home again." He received more applause and waved his hand for quiet as he smiled. "We have friends here tonight from the Dallas TCC. They told us today that they wanted to make a presentation tonight. I want to introduce Lars West, Sam Thompkins and Rod

Jenkins. C'mon, guys," he said as each man waved and smiled at the audience.

Tall with thick brown hair, Lars West stepped forward. "Thanks, Cole. We know the TCC suffered damage along with so much of Royal. We talked to our Dallas TCC and we want to present a check to the TCC here in Royal," he said, turning to Gil Addison. "We'd like the Royal TCC to have a check for two million dollars to use for Royal storm aid however the TCC here sees fit."

The last of his words were drowned out by applause as the audience came to their feet and gave him a standing ovation.

Aaron motioned to Stella to join him and he introduced her to the men from Dallas. "Thank you," she said. "That's an incredibly generous gift and will do so much good for Royal."

"We hope so. We wanted to do something," Sam said.

They talked a few more minutes and then left the stage while Cole lingered and turned to Stella.

"I was about to go home," Cole said. "I thought Aaron could do this by himself, but he talked me into staying for the presentation. There are other Dallas TCC members here for a fun night. These three guys insist on going back to Dallas tonight, so we're all leaving now," Cole told them as Gil shook hands and thanked the Dallas TCC members.

"Cole, again, thanks so much for coming out," Stella said.

"I want to thank you, too," Aaron added.

"I hope all of this tonight brightened everybody's Christmas," Cole said. He left the stage to join the TCC Dallas members, moving through the crowd. He passed near Paige Richardson, speaking to her, and she smiled, speaking in return, both of them looking cordial as they passed each other.

Gil left to put the check in a safe place. Aaron took Stella's arm to go back to the great room where a band played and people danced. People stopped to congratulate Stella, to thank her. Some thanked Aaron for the TCC Dallas contribution.

"I'm going to dance with you before we leave here," Aaron said.

"I just hope we didn't miss anyone tonight in terms of the presents and money we're giving to families."

"Everyone could sign up who felt the need and some people signed up friends who wouldn't come in and sign up themselves. I don't think anyone got overlooked, but there's no way to really know," he said. "And with that, let's close this chapter on Royal's recovery for tonight and concentrate on you and me."

Startled, Stella looked up at him.

"Let's dance," he said, taking her into his arms. "We can't leave early, Stella. All these people came for you and they'll expect you to stay and have a good time. They'll want to speak to you."

"Aaron, in some ways," she said as she danced with him, "all my life I've felt sort of like an outsider. I've always been plain—I grew up that way and my mother is that way. For the first time tonight, I feel really accepted by everyone."

"You're accepted, believe me. Stella, people are so grateful to you. I've talked to them, and they're grateful for all you've done. And as for plain—just look in the mirror."

"You did that for me," she said solemnly, thinking the evening would have been so wonderful if she'd had Aaron's love. It was a subject she had shut out of her mind over and over since their arrival at the club tonight. Tears threatened again and she no longer felt like dancing.

"Aaron, I need a moment," she said, stepping away from him. She knew the clubhouse from being there with members for various events and she hurried off the dance floor and out of the room, heading for one of the small clubrooms that would be empty on a night like this. Tears stung her eyes and she tried to control them, wiping them off her cheeks.

A hand closed on her arm and Aaron stopped her. He saw her tears and frowned.

"C'mon," he said, holding her arm and walking down the hall to enter a darkened meeting room. Hanging a sign, Meeting in Progress, on the outside knob and switching on a small lamp, he closed the door.

She wiped her eyes frantically and took deep breaths.

He turned to face her, walking to her and placing his hands on his hips. "I was going to wait until we went home tonight to talk to you, but I think we better talk right now. What started out to be a great, fun evening for you has turned sour in a big way."

"Aaron, we can't talk here."

"Yes, we can." He stepped close and slipped one arm around her waist. His other hand tilted her chin up as he gazed into her eyes. "This is long overdue, but as the old saying goes, sometimes you can't see the forest for the trees. I've missed you and I've been miserable without you. I love you, Stella."

Startled, she frowned as she stared at him. "You're saying that—I don't think you mean it. It's one of those nice and honorable things you do."

"No. I'm not saying it to be nice and not out of honor. It's out of love. After I lost Paula and Blake, I didn't think I would ever love again. I didn't think I could. I was wrong, because there's always room in the heart for love. I just couldn't even see that I had fallen in love with you."

Shocked, she stared at him. "Aaron, I didn't know about your wife and son until this past week."

He frowned. "I thought everyone around here knew that. I just didn't talk about it."

"That's been a barrier between us, hasn't it?"

"It was, but it's not now. I'm in love with you. I want to marry you and if you'd found out today that you're not really pregnant, I would still tell you the same thing. I love you. When I lost Paula and Blake, I didn't want to live, either. I hurt every minute of every day for so long. When I finally did go out with a woman, I think it was three or four years later and after the date, I just wanted to go home and be alone."

She hurt for him, but she remained silent because Aaron was opening himself up completely to her and gone was the shuttered look and the feeling that a wall had come between them.

"I finally began to socialize, but I just never got close to anyone until you came along. I soon realized that you were the first woman I'd enjoyed being around since Paula. I also noticed I didn't hurt as much and I didn't think about her as much.

"Stella, I will always love Paula and Blake. There's room in my heart for more love—for you, for our baby. I love you and I have been miserable without you and it's my own fault for shutting you out, but I just didn't even realize I was falling in love with you."

"Aaron," she said, her happiness spilling over.

He pulled her close, leaning down to kiss her, a hungry, passionate kiss as if he had been waiting years to do this.

Joyously she clung to him and kissed him. "I love you, Aaron. I missed you, but I want your love. I just want you to be able to share the good and the bad, the hurts, the happiness, everything in your life with me and me with you. That's love, Aaron."

He held her so tightly she could barely breathe. "You mean everything to me. I just couldn't even recognize what I felt until I saw I was losing you. Thank goodness I haven't."

"No, you haven't. You have my heart. I love you, Aaron. I've loved you almost from the very first."

"Stella, wait." He knelt on one knee and held her hand. "Stella Daniels, will you marry me?" he asked, pulling a box from his jacket pocket and holding it out to her.

"Aaron." She laughed, feeling giddy and bubbly. "Yes, I'll marry you, Aaron Nichols. For goodness' sake, get up," she said, taking the box from him. "What is this, Aaron?"

She opened the box and gasped. Aaron took out the ten-carat-diamond-and-emerald ring he had bought. He held her hand and slipped the ring onto her finger. "Perfect," he said, looking into her eyes. "Everything is perfect, Stella. I will tell you I love you so many times each day you'll grow tired of hearing it."

"Impossible," she said, looking at the dazzling ring. "Oh, Aaron, I'm overwhelmed. This is the most beautiful ring. I can't believe it's mine."

"It is definitely yours. Stella, I love you. Also, I'm going to love our baby so very much. This child is a gift and a blessing for me. The loss of my first child—I can't tell you how badly that hurt and I never dreamed I'd marry and have another baby."

"We'll both be blessed by this child. I'm so glad. From the first moment, I thought this would be the biggest thrill in my life if I had your love when I found out we would have a baby."

"You have my love," he said, hugging her and then kissing her. After a few minutes, he leaned away. "C'mon. I think it's time for an announcement."

She laughed again. "Aaron, I'm used to staying in the background, being quiet and unnoticed. My life is undergoing every kind of transformation. I don't even know myself anymore in so many ways.

"I'm announcing this engagement to keep the guys away from you. I've even had them ask me if I cared if they asked you out. Yes, I cared. I wanted to punch one of them."

She laughed, shaking her head as he took her hand.

"C'mon. I'm making an announcement and then all those guys will stay away from my fiancée."

When he said *my fiancée*, joy bubbled in her as she hurried beside him.

"Stella, let's get married soon."

"You need to meet my family. I should meet yours."

"You will. I'll take you to Paris soon to meet them. Either before or after the wedding, whichever you want."

"You're changing my life in every way."

In the great room, when the band stopped between pieces, Aaron found Gil. Stella couldn't believe what was happening, but Gil motioned to the band and hurried to talk to them.

He turned to the dancers and people seated at small tables around the edge of the room. There was a roll from the drummer and people became quiet. "Ladies and gentlemen," Gil said. "May I have your attention? We have a brief announcement."

Stella shook her head. "Aaron, you started this," she said, and he grinned.

Aaron stepped forward, but Stella moved quickly to take the mike from a surprised Gil. "Folks," she said, smiling at Aaron as he took her hand. "I'd like to make my first announcement as acting mayor. I'd like to announce my engagement to Aaron Nichols," she proclaimed, laughing and looking at Aaron.

As everyone applauded and cheered, Aaron turned to slip his arm around her and kiss her briefly, causing more applause and whistles.

When he released her, he took the mike. "Now we can all go back to partying! Merry Christmas, everybody!"

There was another round of applause as the band began to play.

"Thanks, Gil," Aaron said, handing back the mike. "Let's go dance," he said to Stella. "Two dances and then we start calling family."

It was a fast piece and she danced with Aaron, having a wonderful time. She wanted him and was certain they would go home and make love. When the number ended, people crowded around them to congratulate her and look at her ring. She left the dance floor to let them and remained talking to friends until Aaron rescued her a whole number later.

"Instead of dancing some more, how about going to your place?"

"I'll beat you to the door," she said, teasing him, and he laughed. "I have to get my purse and start thanking people."

"Everybody is partying. Save the thank-you for one you can write on a Christmas card or wedding announcement or something."

"You're right about everyone partying," she said. "You win. Let's go."

He took her hand and she got her purse. They stopped

to get their coats and then at the door they waited while a valet brought Aaron's car.

Everybody who passed them congratulated her on becoming acting mayor and on her engagement.

When they drove away from the club, she turned toward him slightly. It was quiet and cozy in his car. "Aaron, this has been the most wonderful night of my life," she said. "Thanks to you."

"I'm glad. Let's have this wedding soon."

"That's what I'd like."

"I don't care whether we have a large or small one."

"My parents will want no part of a large wedding. I got my plain way of life from my mother."

"If you prefer a large wedding, have it. I'll pay for it and help you."

She squeezed his knee lightly. "Thank you. That's very nice. What about you?"

"I don't care. Mom and Dad will do whatever we want. So will my brother."

"Probably a small wedding and maybe a large reception. After tonight, I feel I have to invite the entire town of Royal to the reception."

"I agree. That was nice of everyone. All the people I talked to were enthused, everybody wanted you to be acting mayor. Stella, I didn't find anyone who didn't want you. Mayor Vance definitely wanted you."

"That makes me feel so good. I can't tell you. In high school I was sort of left out of things socially. I guess I always have been."

"Not now. You'll never be left out of anything with me."

"I think you're speeding. I'd hate for the new acting mayor to get pulled over the first few hours I have the job."

"I want to get home to be alone with you," he said as he slowed.

In minutes they reached her town house. "My trunk is filled with Christmas gifts. I'm not carrying them in tonight. I'll get them in the morning," he said.

"I have to go shopping tomorrow. I've been so busy I haven't gotten all my presents and I don't have any for you yet. I really didn't expect to be with you Christmas."

"But now you will be if I can talk you into it. How disappointed will your sister be if you don't come this year and we spend Christmas here, just the two of us?"

"With three kids, she won't care. We can go sometime during the holidays. We can call her."

"We sure can, but later. I have other plans when I close the door."

"Do you really?" she teased.

He parked where she directed him to and came around to open her door. As soon as they stepped into her entryway, Aaron closed the door behind him and turned to pull her into his embrace, giving a kiss that was filled with love and longing.

Later Stella lay in his arms while he toyed with her hair. The covers were pulled up under her arms.

Aaron stretched out his arm to pick up his phone and get a calendar. "Let's set a date now."

"Aaron," she said, trailing her fingers along his jaw, "since I just accepted the job of acting mayor, I feel a responsibility for Royal. I'll have to live here until I'm no longer acting mayor."

"I'm here all the time anyway. I'll work from here and go to Dallas when I feel I need to. We can build a house here if you want. Remember, that is my business."

"Whatever you'd like. When my job ends, I don't mind moving to Dallas."

"We'll work it all out. I just want to be with you."

"Our honeymoon may have to come after baby is here," she said.

"Baby is here," he echoed. "Stella, I've told you before and I'll tell you again—I'm overjoyed about the baby. I lost Blake and he was one of the big loves of my life. I have a second chance here to be a dad. I'm thrilled and I hope you are."

"I am. Do you particularly want another little boy?"

"No, I don't care," he said, and she smiled, relieved and happy that he didn't have his heart set on having a boy.

"Just a baby. I can't tell you." His voice had gotten deep and she realized he was emotional about the baby he'd lost. She hugged him and rose up to kiss him, tasting a salty tear. His hurt caused her heart to ache. "Aaron, I'm so glad about this baby. And we can have more."

He pulled her down to kiss her hard. When he released her, she saw he had a better grip on his emotions. "For a tough, military-type guy, you're very tenderhearted," she said.

"I am thrilled beyond words to be a dad. That's why I got those necklaces for you. I love you, Stella."

"I love you," she responded.

"Now let's set a date for a wedding. How about a wedding between Christmas and New Year's? That's a quiet time. January won't be."

"You're right. I'd say a very quiet wedding after Christmas. Can you do that, Mr. Nichols?"

"I can. Want to fly to Dallas next week to get a wedding dress from Cecilia? That'll be a Christmas present to you."

She smiled. "Your love is my Christmas present. Your

love, your baby, this fabulous ring. Aaron, I love you with all my heart. I give you my love for Christmas." Joy filled her while she looked into his brown eyes.

"Merry, merry Christmas, darling," he said as he wrapped his arms around her and pulled her close to kiss her.

Happiness filled her heart and after a moment she looked up at him. "Your love is the best Christmas gift possible." She felt joyous to be in Aaron's strong arms and to know she had his love always.

* * * * *

THE DIPLOMAT'S
PREGNANT BRIDE

MERLINE LOVELACE

To my gorgeous niece Cori and Jane and the rest of the crew at Clayton on the Park, in Scottsdale. Thanks for the inside look at the ups and downs of an event coordinator's life!

Prologue

I could not have asked for two more beautiful or loving granddaughters. From the first day they came to live with me—one so young and frightened, the other still in diapers—they filled the empty spaces in my heart with light and joy. Now Sarah, my quiet, elegant Sarah, is about to marry her handsome Dev. The wedding takes place in a few hours, and I ache with happiness for her.

And with such worry for her sister. My darling Eugenia has waltzed through life, brightening even the sourest dispositions with her sparkling smile and care-free, careless joie de vivre. Now, quite suddenly that carelessness has caught up with her. She's come face-to-face with reality, and I can only pray the strength and spirit I know she possesses will help her through the difficult days ahead.

Enough of this. I must dress for the wedding. Then it's off to the Plaza, which has been the scene of so many significant events in my life. But none to match the delight of this one!

From the diary of Charlotte,
Grand Duchess of Karlenburgh

One

Gina St. Sebastian forced a smile to hide her gritted teeth. "Good Lord, you're stubborn, Jack."

"*I'm* stubborn?"

The irate male standing before her snapped his sun-bleached brows together. Ambassador John Harris Mason III was tanned, tawny-haired and a trim, athletic six-one. He was also used to being in charge. The fact that he couldn't control Gina or the situation they now found themselves in irritated him no end.

"You're pregnant with my child, dammit. Yet you refuse to even discuss marriage."

"Oh, for...! Trumpet the news to the whole world, why don't you?"

Scowling, Gina craned her neck to peer around the bank of gardenias shielding her and Jack from the other guests in the Terrace Room of New York City's venerable Plaza Hotel. With its exquisitely restored Italian Renaissance ceiling and crystal chandeliers modeled after those in the Palace of Versailles, it made a fabulous venue for a wedding.

A wedding put together on extremely short notice! They'd had less than two weeks to pull it off. The groom's billions had eased the time crunch considerably, as had the miracle worker Dev Hunter employed as his executive assistant. Gina had done all the planning, though, and she would not allow the man she'd spent one wild weekend with to disrupt her sister's wedding day.

Luckily no one seemed to have heard his caustic comment. The band was currently pulsing out the last bars of a lively merengue. Sarah and Dev were on the dance floor, along with the St. Sebastians' longtime housekeeper, Maria, and most of the guests invited to the elegant affair.

Gina's glance shot from the dancers to the lace-clad woman sitting ramrod-straight in her chair, hands crossed on the ebony head of her cane. The duchess was out of earshot, too, thank God! Hearing her younger granddaughter's pregnancy broadcast to the world at large wouldn't have fit with her notions of proper behavior.

Relieved, Gina swung back to Jack. "I won't have you spoil my sister's wedding with another argument. Please lower your voice."

He took the hint and cranked down the decibels, if not his temper. "We haven't had ten minutes alone to talk about this since you got back from Switzerland."

As if she needed the reminder! She'd flown to Switzerland exactly one day after she'd peed on a purple stick and felt her world come crashing down around her. She'd had to get away from L.A., had to breathe in the sharp, clean air of the snow-capped Alps surrounding Lake Lucerne while trying to decide what to do. After a day and a night of painful soul-searching, she'd walked into one of Lucerne's ultramodern clinics. Ten minutes later, she'd turned around and walked out again. But not before making two near-hysterical calls. The first was to Sarah—her sister, her protector, her dearest friend. The second, unfortunately, was to the handsome, charismatic and thoroughly annoying diplomat now confronting her.

By the time Sarah had made the frantic dash from Paris in response to her sister's call, Gina's jagged nerves had smoothed a little. Her hard-won poise shattered once again, however, when Jack Mason showed up on the scene. She hadn't expected him to jump a plane, much less express such fierce satisfaction over her decision to have their child.

Actually, the decision had surprised Gina as much as it had Jack. She was the flighty, irresponsible sister. The good-time girl, always up for a weekend skiing in Biarritz or a sail through the blue-green waters of the Caribbean. Raised by their grandmother, she and Sarah had been given the education and sophisticated lifestyle the duchess insisted was their birthright. Only recently had the sisters learned how deeply Grandmama had gone into debt to provide that lifestyle. Since then, Gina had made a determined effort to support herself. A good number of efforts, actually. Sadly, none of the careers she'd dabbled in had held her mercurial interest for very long.

Modeling had turned out to be a drag. All those hot lights and temperamental photographers snapping orders like constipated drill sergeants. Escorting small, select tour groups to the dazzling capitals of Europe was even more of a bore. How in the world could she have imagined she'd want to make a career of chasing down lost luggage or shuffling room assignments to placate a whiny guest who didn't like the view in hers?

Gina had even tried to translate her brief sojourn at Italy's famed cooking school, the Academia Barilla, into a career as a catering chef. That misguided attempt had barely lasted a week. But when her exasperated boss booted her out of the kitchen and into the front office, she'd discovered her apparently one real talent. She was far better at planning parties than cooking for them. Especially when clients walked in waving a checkbook and orders to pull out all the stops for their big event.

She was so good, in fact, that she intended to support herself and her child by coordinating soirees for the rich and famous. But first she had to convince her baby's father that she neither needed nor wanted the loveless marriage he was offering.

"I appreciate your concern, Jack, but..."

"Concern?"

The handsome, charismatic ambassador kept his voice down as she'd requested, but looked as though he wanted let loose with both barrels. His shoulders were taut under his hand-tailored tux. Below his neatly trimmed caramel-colored hair, his brown eyes drilled into her.

Gina couldn't help but remember how those eyes had snared hers across a crowded conference room six weeks ago and signaled instant, electric attraction. How his oh-so-skilled mouth had plundered her throat and her breasts and her belly. How...

Oh, for pity's sake! Why remember the heat that had sizzled so hot and fast between them? That spontaneous combustion wouldn't happen again. Not now. Not with everything else that was going on in their lives.

"But," she continued with a forced smile, "you have to agree a wedding reception is hardly the time or place for a discussion like this."

"Name the time," he challenged. "And the place."

"All right! Tomorrow. Twelve noon." Cornered, she named the first place she could think of. "The Boathouse in Central Park."

"I'll be there."

"Fine. We'll get a table in a quiet corner and discuss this like the mature adults we are."

"Like the mature adult at least one of us is."

Gina hid a wince. The biting sarcasm stung, but she had to admit it wasn't far off the mark. The truth was she'd pretty much flitted through life, laughing at its absurdities, always counting on Sarah or Grandmama to bail her out of trouble every time she tumbled into it. All that changed about ten minutes after she peed on that damned stick. Her flitting days were over. It was time to take responsibility for herself and her baby.

Which she would.

She would!

"I'll see you tomorrow."

Chin high, she swept around the bank of gardenias.

Jack let her go. She was right. This wasn't the time or the place to hammer some sense into her. Not that he held much hope his calm, rational arguments would penetrate that thick mane of silvery blond curls or spark a glimmer of understanding in those baby-doll blue eyes.

He'd now spent a total of five days—one long, wild weekend and two frustrating days in Switzerland—in Gina St. Sebastian's company. More than enough time to confirm the woman constituted a walking, talking bundle of contradictions. She was jaw-droppingly gorgeous and so sensual she made grown men go weak at the knees, but also friendly and playful as a kitten. Well-educated, yet in many ways naive beyond belief. And almost completely oblivious to the world around her unless it directly impacted her, her sister or her dragon lady of a grandmother.

Pretty much his exact opposite, Jack thought grimly as he tracked her progress across the crowded room. He came from a long line of coolheaded, clear-thinking Virginians who believed their vast wealth brought with it equally great responsibility. Jack's father and grandfather had served as advisors to presidents in times of national crisis. He himself had served in several diplomatic posts before being appointed the State Department's ambassador-at-large for counterterrorism at the ripe old age of thirty-two. As such, he'd traveled to some of the most volatile, violent trouble spots in the world. Recently he'd returned to State Department headquarters in Washington, D.C., to translate his hard-won field knowledge into policies and procedures that would improve the security of U.S. diplomatic personnel around the world.

His job demanded long days and long nights. Stress rode on his shoulders like hundred-pound weights. Yet he couldn't remember any issue, any recalcitrant bureaucrat or political pundit, who frustrated him as much as Gina St. Sebastian. She was pregnant with his child, dammit! The child he was determined would carry his name.

The child he and Catherine had tried so hard to have.

The familiar pain knifed into him. The feeling wasn't as vicious as it had once been, but was still ferocious enough to carve up his insides. The lively conversation around him faded. The flower-bedecked room blurred. He could almost see her, almost hear her Boston Brahman accent. Catherine—brilliant, politically savvy Catherine—would have grasped the irony in his present situation at once. She would have…

"You look like you could use a drink, Mason."

With an immense effort of will, Jack blanked the memory of his dead wife and turned to the new groom. Dev Hunter held a crystal tumbler in one hand and offered one to Jack with the other.

"Scotch, straight up," he said dryly. "I saw you talking to Gina and figured you could use it."

"You figured right."

Jack took the tumbler and tipped it toward the man who might soon become his brother-in-law. Not might, he amended grimly as they clinked glasses, would.

"To the St. Sebastian sisters," Hunter said, his gaze shifting to the two women standing with their heads together across the room. "It took some convincing, but I got mine to the altar. Good luck getting yours there."

The Scotch went down with a well-mannered bite. Jack savored its smoky tang and eyed the sisters. They were a study in contrasts. Dark-haired Sarah was impossibly elegant in a clinging ivory gown with feathered clasps at each shoulder and glowed with the incandescent beauty of a bride. Blonde, bubbly Gina was barely six weeks pregnant and showed no signs of a baby bump. She was still slender but more generously endowed than her sister. Her flame-colored, body-hugging, strapless and backless sheath outlined her seductive curves to perfection.

Jack's fingers tightened on the tumbler. Six weeks after the fact and he could still remember how he'd positioned those seductive hips under his. How he'd buried his hands in her silky hair and lost himself in that lush body and those laughing blue eyes.

They'd used protection that weekend. Went through a whole damned box of it, as he recalled. So much for playing the odds.

"I'll get her to the altar," he vowed. "One way or another."

Hunter raised a brow but refrained from comment as his bride smiled and crooked a finger. "I'm being summoned. I'll talk to you again when Sarah and I get back from our honeymoon."

He handed his empty tumbler to a passing waiter and started for his wife, then turned back. "Just for the record, Mason, my money's on Gina. She's got more of the duchess in her than she realizes. And speaking of the duchess..."

Jack followed his glance and saw the silver-haired St. Sebastian matriarch thumping her way toward them. A long-sleeve, high-necked dress of ecru lace draped her slight frame. A trio of rings decorated her arthritic fingers. Leaning heavily on her cane with her left hand, Charlotte dismissed her new grandson-in-law with an imperious wave of the right.

"Gina says it's time for you and Sarah to change out of your wedding finery. You only have an hour to get to the airport."

"It's my plane, Charlotte. I don't think it'll leave without us."

"I should hope not." Her ringed fingers flapped again. "Do go away, Devon. I want to talk to Ambassador Mason."

Jack didn't consciously go into a brace but he could feel

his shoulders squaring as he faced Gina's diminutive, indomitable grandmother.

He knew all about her. He should. He'd dug up the file the State Department had compiled on Charlotte St. Sebastian, once Grand Duchess of the tiny principality of Karlenburgh, when she fled her Communist-overrun country more than five decades ago. After being forced to witness her husband's brutal execution, she'd escaped with the clothes on her back, her infant daughter in her arms and a fortune in jewels hidden inside the baby's teddy bear.

She'd eventually settled in New York City and become an icon of the social and literary scenes. Few of the duchess's wealthy, erudite friends were aware this stiff-spined aristocrat had pawned her jewels over the years to support herself and the two young granddaughters who'd come to live with her after the tragic death of their parents. Jack knew only because Dev Hunter had hinted that he should tread carefully where Charlotte and her granddaughters' financial situation were concerned.

Very carefully. Jack's one previous encounter with the duchess made it clear her reduced circumstances had not diminished either her haughty air or the fierce protectiveness she exhibited toward her granddaughters. That protectiveness blazed in her face now.

"I just spoke with Gina. She says you're still trying to convince her to marry you."

"Yes, I am."

"Why?"

Jack was tempted to fall back on Gina's excuse and suggest that a wedding reception was hardly the proper place for this discussion. The steely look in the duchess's faded blue eyes killed that craven impulse.

"I think the reason would be obvious, ma'am. Your granddaughter's carrying my child. I want to give her and the baby the protection of my name."

The reply came coated with ice. "The St. Sebastian name

provides more than enough cachet for my granddaughter and her child."

Well, hell! And he called himself a diplomat! Jack was delivering a mental swift kick when the duchess raised her cane and jabbed the tip into his starched shirt front.

"Tell me one thing, Mr. Ambassador. Do you honestly believe the baby is yours?"

He didn't hesitate. "Yes, ma'am, I do."

The cane took another sharp jab at his sternum.

"Why?"

For two reasons, one of which Jack wasn't about to share. He was still pissed that his father had reacted to the news that he would be a grandfather by hiring a private investigator. With ruthless efficiency the P.I. had dug into every nook and cranny of Gina St. Sebastian's life for the past three months. The report he submitted painted a portrait of a woman who bounced from job to job and man to man with seeming insouciance. Yet despite his best efforts, the detective hadn't been able to turn up a single lover in Gina's recent past except John Harris Mason III.

Furious, Jack had informed his father that he didn't need any damned report. He'd known the baby was his from the moment Gina called from Switzerland, sobbing and nearly incoherent. He now tried to convey that same conviction to the ferocious woman about to skewer him with her cane.

"As I've discovered in our brief time together, Duchess, your granddaughter has her share of faults. So do I. Neither of us have tried to deceive the other about those faults, however."

"What you mean," she countered with withering scorn, "is that neither of you made any protestations of eternal love or devotion before you jumped into bed together."

Jack refused to look away, but damned if he didn't feel heat crawling up the back of his neck. Wisely, he sidestepped the jumping-into-bed issue. "I'll admit I have a lot to learn yet about your granddaughter but my sense is she doesn't lie. At least not about something this important," he added with more frankness than tact.

To his relief, the duchess lowered the cane and leaned on it with both hands. "You're correct in that assessment. Gina doesn't lie."

She hesitated, and a look that combined both pride and exasperation crossed her aristocratic features. "If anything, the girl is too honest. She tends to let her feelings just pour out, along with whatever she happens to be thinking at the time."

"So I noticed," Jack said, straight-faced.

Actually, Gina's exuberance and utter lack of pretense had delighted him almost as much as her luscious body during their weekend together. Looking back, Jack could admit he'd shucked a half-dozen layers of his sober, responsible self during that brief interlude. They hadn't stayed shucked, of course. Once he'd returned to Washington, he'd been engulfed in one crisis after another. Right up until that call from Switzerland.

The duchess reclaimed his attention with a regal toss of her head. "I will say this once, young man, and I suggest you take heed. My granddaughter's happiness is my first—my *only*—concern. Whatever Eugenia decides regarding you and the baby, she has my complete support."

"I wouldn't expect anything less, ma'am."

"Hrrrmph." She studied him with pursed lips for a moment before delivering an abrupt non sequitur. "I knew your grandfather."

"You did?"

"He was a member of President Kennedy's cabinet at the time. Rather stiff and pompous, as I recall."

Jack had to grin. "That sounds like him."

"I invited him and your grandmother to a reception I hosted for the Sultan of Oman right here, in these very rooms. The Kennedys attended. So did the Rockefellers."

A distant look came into her eyes. A smile hovered at the corners of her mouth.

"I wore my pearls," she murmured, as much to herself as to her listener. "They roped around my neck three times before draping almost to my waist. Jackie was quite envious."

He bet she was. Watching the duchess's face, listening to her cultured speech with its faint trace of an accent, Jack nursed the hope that marriage to her younger granddaughter might not be such a disaster, after all.

With time and a little guidance on his part, Gina could learn to curb some of her impulsiveness. Maybe even learn to think before she blurted out whatever came into her mind. Not that he wanted to dim her sparkling personality. Just rein it in a bit so she'd feel comfortable in the restrained diplomatic circles she'd be marrying into.

Then, of course, there was the sex.

Jack kept his expression politely attentive. His diplomatic training and years of field experience wouldn't allow him to do otherwise. Yet every muscle in his body went taut as all-too-vivid images from his weekend with Gina once again grabbed him.

He hadn't been a saint since his wife died, but neither had he tomcatted around. Five women in six years didn't exactly constitute a world record. Yet the hours he'd spent in that Beverly Hills penthouse suite with Gina St. Sebastian made him come alive in ways he hadn't felt since...

Since Catherine.

Shaking off the twinge of guilt that thought brought, Jack addressed the woman just coming out of her reverie of presidents and pearls.

"Please believe me, Duchess. I want very much to do right by both your granddaughter and our child."

Those shrewd, pale eyes measured him for long, uncomfortable moments. Jack had faced cold-blooded dictators whose stares didn't slice anywhere as close to the bone as this white-haired, seemingly frail woman's did.

"You may as well call me Charlotte," she said finally. "I

suspect we may be seeing a good deal of each other in the weeks ahead."

"I suspect we may."

"Now, if you'll excuse me, I must help Sarah prepare to depart for her honeymoon."

Two

After Sarah changed and left for the airport with Dev, Gina escorted her grandmother and Maria down to the limo she'd ordered for them.

"I'll be a while," she warned as the elevator opened onto the Plaza's elegant lobby. "I want to make sure Dev's family is set for their trip home tomorrow."

"I should think that clever, clever man Dev employs as his executive assistant has the family's travel arrangements well in hand."

"He does. He's also going to take care of shipping the wedding gifts back to L.A., thank goodness. But I need to verify the final head count and see he has a complete list of the bills to expect."

The duchess stiffened, and Gina gave herself a swift mental kick. Dang it! She shouldn't have mentioned those bills. As she and Sarah knew all too well, covering the cost of the wedding had come dangerously close to a major point of contention between Dev and the duchess. Charlotte had insisted on taking care of the expenses traditionally paid by the bride's family. It was a real tribute to Dev's negotiating skills that he and Grandmama had reached an agreement that didn't totally destroy her pride.

And now Gina had to bring up the sensitive subject again! It was Jack's fault, she thought in disgust. Their confrontation had thrown her off stride. Was still throwing her off. Why the heck had she agreed to meet him for lunch tomorrow?

She was still trying to figure that one out when the limo pulled up to the Plaza's stately front entrance. The driver got out to open the door but before his two passengers slid into the backseat, the duchess issued a stern warning.

"Don't overtax yourself, Eugenia. Pregnancy saps a woman's strength, especially during the first few months. You'll find you're more fatigued than usual."

"Fatigue hasn't been a problem yet. Or morning sickness, knock on..."

She glanced around for some wood to rap. She settled for wiggling a branch of one of the massive topiary trees guarding the front entrance.

"My breasts are swollen up like water balloons, though. And my nipples ache like you wouldn't believe." Grimacing, she rolled her shoulders to ease the constriction of her tight bodice. "They want *out* of this gown."

"For pity's sake, Eugenia!" The duchess shot a glance at the stony-faced limo driver. "Let's continue this discussion tomorrow, shall we?"

Nodding, Gina bent to kiss her grandmother's cheek and breathed in the faint, oh-so-familiar scent of lavender and lace. "Make sure you take your medicine before you go to bed."

"I'm not senile, young lady. I think I can manage to remember to take two little pills."

"Yes, ma'am."

Trying to look properly chastised, she helped the duchess into the limo and turned to the Honduran native who'd become a second mother to her and Sarah. "You'll stay with her, Maria? I shouldn't be more than another hour or two. I'll have a car take you home."

"Take as long as you need. *La duquesa* and I, we'll put our feet up and talk about what a fine job you did organizing such a beautiful wedding."

"It did come off well, didn't it?"

Maria beamed a wide smile. "*Sí, chica,* it did."

Buoyed by the compliment, Gina returned to the reception room. Most of the guests had departed. Including, she saw after a quick sweep, a certain obnoxious ambassador who'd shown up unexpectedly. She should have had him escorted out when he first walked in. Being summarily ejected from the wedding would have put a dent in the man's ego. Or maybe not. For a career diplomat, he seemed as impervious to Gina's snubs as to her adamant refusal to marry him.

He didn't understand why she wouldn't even consider it for their baby's sake. Neither did the duchess. Although Grandmama and Sarah both supported Gina's decision to go it alone, she knew they wondered at her vehemence. On the surface, John Harris Mason III certainly made excellent husband material. He was rich, handsome and charming as the devil when he wanted to be.

It was what lurked below the surface that held Gina back. Every story, every bio printed about the charismatic diplomat, hinted that Jack had buried his heart with the young wife he'd first dated in high school and married the day they both graduated from Harvard. From all reports, Catherine Mason had been every bit as smart, athletic and politically involved as her husband.

Gina knew in her heart she couldn't compete with the ghost of his lost love. Not because she lacked her own set of credentials. The Duchy of Karlenburgh might now be little more than an obscure footnote in history books, but Grandmama could still hold her own with presidents and kings. What's more, she'd insisted her granddaughters be educated in accordance with their heritage. Gina had actually graduated from Barnard with a semi-decent grade point average.

She'd pretty much majored in partying, though, and to this day had zero interest in politics.

She might have cultivated an interest for Jack. Had actually toyed with the idea during that crazy weekend. For all her seemingly casual approach to life and love, she'd never met anyone as fascinating and entertaining and just plain hot as Jack Mason.

Any thoughts of fitting into the mold of a diplomat's wife went poof when Gina discovered she was pregnant. There was no way she could dive into politics *and* marriage *and* motherhood at the same time. She already felt as though she were on an emotional roller coaster. All she could think about right now, all she would *allow* herself to think about, was proving she could take care of herself and her baby.

"You put on a helluva party, lady."

Smiling, she turned to Dev's gravel-voiced buddy from his air force days. Patrick Donovan now served as Dev's executive assistant and pretty much ruled his vast empire with an iron fist.

"Thanks, Pat."

Tall and lanky and looking completely at home in his Armani tux, Donovan winked at her. "You decide you want to come back to L.A., you let me know. We could use someone with your organizational skills in our protocol office. Seems like we're hosting some bigwig industrialists from China or Germany or Australia every other week."

"I appreciate the offer but I'm going to try to break into the event-planning business here in New York. Plus, I'm thinking about moving in with Grandmama for the next eight months or so."

If the duchess would have her. They'd all been so busy these past few weeks with Sarah's wedding, Gina hadn't found the right time to broach the subject. Her sister heartily endorsed the plan, though. Both she and Gina hated the thought of the duchess living alone now that Sarah was moving out.

Okay! All right! So Gina needed a place to stay until she landed a job and became self-supporting. Despite her determination to prove herself, she had to have a base to build on. Grandmama wouldn't object to letting her move in. Probably.

"I've got some pretty good contacts in New York," Patrick was saying. "You want me to make a few calls? Grease the skids a little?"

"I need to do this on my own, Pat. But thanks for the offer."

"It stays on the table," he said with a shrug as he wrapped an arm around her shoulders and gave her a squeeze. "Call me if you change your mind. Or better yet, let your new brother-in-law know. Dev is complete mush right now. He'd set you up with your own agency if you so much as hint that's what you want. And let me know if you want me to close up your apartment in L.A. and have your things shipped here."

"I will. Thanks again."

Gina climbed out of a cab some two hours later. The Dakota's red sandstone turrets poked against the darkening night sky, welcoming her to the castlelike apartment complex that was one of New York City's most prestigious addresses. The duchess had bought an apartment here shortly after arriving in New York City. The purchase had put a serious dent in her cache of jewels, but careful investments during those first years, along with the discreet sale of a diamond bracelet here, a ruby necklace there, had allowed Charlotte to maintain the apartment and an elegant lifestyle over the decades.

Keeping up the facade had become much tougher in recent years. The jewels were gone. So were most of the haute couture gowns and designer suits that once filled her grandmother's closet. With her love of the classic retro look, Sarah had salvaged a number of the outfits and saved money by not splurging on new clothes for herself, but she'd had to struggle to cover the bills from her own salary.

Dev, bless him, wanted to make things easier for his wife's grandmother. But like the wedding expenses, taking over the duchess's financial affairs involved delicate negotiations that had yet to reach a satisfactory conclusion. Which put the burden on Gina's shoulders. She couldn't just move in and expect her grandmother to support her. She had to pay her own way.

On that determined note, she thanked Maria for staying so late and told her to sleep in the next morning. "I'll make breakfast for Grandmama."

The Honduran looked dubious. "Are you sure, *chica? La duquesa*, she likes her egg poached just so."

"I know. It has to sit for exactly four minutes after the heat's turned off."

"And her tea. It must be…"

"The Twinings English Black. I've got it covered. The car's waiting for you. Go home and get some rest."

Maria obviously had her doubts but gathered her suitcase-sized purse. "I'll see you tomorrow."

Gina was up and waiting when her grandmother walked into the kitchen just after eight-thirty the next morning. The duchess was impeccably dressed as always in a calf-length black skirt and lavender silk overblouse. Her hair formed its usual, neat snowy crown atop her head, but Gina saw with a quick dart of concern that she was leaning more heavily than she normally did on her cane.

"Good morning," she said, masking her worry behind a cheerful smile. "I got a text from Sarah a while ago. She says it's balmy and beautiful in Majorca."

"I expect it is. Are you doing breakfast?"

"I am. Sit, and I'll bring your tea."

Surprised and just a little wary, the duchess seated herself in the sunny breakfast room off the kitchen. Its ivy-sprigged wallpaper, green seat cushions and windows overlooking

Central Park seemed to bring the bright May spring right into the room.

Gina poured hot water over the leaves she'd measured into her grandmother's favorite Wedgwood teapot and placed the pot on the table. While the Twinings Black steeped, she popped some wheat bread in the toaster and brought a saucepan of water back to a boil before easing two raw eggs out of their shells. The sight of the yolks gave her a moment's qualm, but it passed. Still no twinge of morning nausea, thank God! With any luck, she'd escape that scourge altogether.

"Here we are."

She hadn't kept the yolks from breaking and going all runny, but the duchess thanked her with a smile and buttered her toast. Sensing there was something behind this special effort, she munched delicately on a corner of toast and waited patiently.

Gina pulled in a deep breath and took the plunge. "I was wondering, Grandmama…"

Dang! Admitting she was a screwup and needed to come live with her grandmother until she got her life in order was harder than she'd anticipated.

"I thought perhaps I might stay with you until I get a job. If you don't mind, that is."

"Oh, Eugenia!" Charlotte's reaction came swift and straight from the heart. "Of course I don't mind, my darling girl. This is your home. You must stay for as long as you wish. You and the baby."

Gina wasn't crying. She really wasn't. The tears just sort of leaked through her smile. "Thanks, Grandmama."

Her own lips a little wobbly, the duchess reached for her granddaughter's hand. "I admit I wasn't looking forward to rattling around this place by myself now that Sarah's moving out. I'm delighted you want to stay here. Will you need to fly back to L.A. to pack up your things?"

"Dev's assistant, Patrick, said he would take care of that if I decided to stay in New York."

"Good!" Charlotte gave her hand a quick squeeze and picked up her fork. "Now, what's this Sarah told me about you wanting to go into the catering business?"

"Not catering. Event planning. I did a little of it in L.A. Just enough to know I'm better at organizing and throwing parties than..." She managed a watery chuckle. "Than everything else I've tried."

"Well, you certainly did an excellent job with the wedding."

The praise sent Gina's spirits winging. "I did, didn't I?" She preened for a moment, her tears forgotten. "And the photographer from Sarah's magazine shot some amazing video and stills. He gave me a disk with enough material to put together a portfolio. I just emailed it to the woman I'm interviewing with this afternoon."

Her grandmother paused with her fork halfway to her lips. "You have an interview this afternoon?"

"I do. With Nicole Tremayne, head of the Tremayne Group. TTG operates a dozen different event venues, three right here in the city."

"Hmm. I knew a Nicholas Tremayne some years ago. Quite well, actually." Her thoughts seemed to go inward for a moment. Shaking them off, she lowered her fork. "This Nicole must be his daughter. If so, I'll call him and..."

"No, Grandmama, please don't."

The urgent plea brought a look of surprise. "Why ever not?"

"I want to do this on my own."

"That sentiment does you justice, Eugenia, but..."

"You don't have to say it. I know my track record doesn't suggest I'll make a very reliable employee. When you add the fact that I'm pregnant, it'll be a miracle if I land any job. I want to try, though, Grandmama. I really do."

"Very well. I'll refrain from interfering."

"Thank you. Dev and Patrick made the same promise. And I'll get Jack to do the same when I meet him for lunch today."

The duchess tilted her head. Sudden interest gleamed in her faded blue eyes. "You're having lunch with Jack? Why? I thought you'd said all you have to say to him."

"I did. Several times! The man won't take no for an answer."

"So again I ask, why are you having lunch with him?"

"He badgered me into it," Gina admitted in disgust. "You can see why I don't want to marry him."

The duchess took her time replying. When she did, she chose her words carefully.

"Are you sure, Eugenia? I treasure every moment I had with your mother and with you and Sarah, but I speak from experience when I say raising a child on your own can be quite terrifying at times."

"Oh, Grandmama!"

Her eyes misted again. Blinking furiously, Gina bared her soul. "I'm scared out my gourd. I admit it! The only thing that makes me even think I can do this is you, and the love you lavished on Sarah and me. You filled our lives with such joy, such grand adventures. You still do. I can give that to my child. I know I can."

A smile started in her grandmother's eyes and spread to Gina's heart.

"I know you can, too."

Gina had intended to spend the rest of the morning prepping for her interview with Nicole Tremayne. To her annoyance, her thoughts kept slipping away from party planning and instead landed on Jack Mason.

Her irritation increased even more when she found herself scowling at the few outfits she'd brought to New York with her. They were all flashy, all playful. Thigh-skimming skirts in bold prints. Tights in eye-popping colors. Spangled,

midriff-baring T-shirts. Reflective of her personality, maybe,
but not the image she wanted to project to Ms. Tremayne.
Or to a certain ambassador-at-large.

Abandoning the meager offering, she went next door to
Sarah's room and rummaged through the designer classics
her sister had salvaged from their grandmother's closet.
After much debate and a pile of discards strewn across the
bed, Gina decided on wide-legged black slacks. She topped
them with a summer silk Valentino jacket in pearl gray that
boasted a flower in the same fabric on one lapel. The jacket
strained a bit at the bust but gave her the mature, responsible air she was aiming for. A wad of cotton stuffed into the
toes of a pair of sensible black pumps added to the look. As
a final touch, she went light on the makeup and wrestled her
waterfall of platinum-blond curls into a French twist. When
she studied the final result in the mirror, she gulped.

"Oh, God. I look like Grandmama."

If the duchess recognized herself, she mercifully refrained
from saying so. But Gina caught the slightly stunned look
she exchanged with Maria as her new, subdued granddaughter departed for her lunch meeting.

If Gina had needed further evidence of her transformation, she got it mere moments after walking into the Boathouse. A favorite gathering place of tourists and locals alike,
the restaurant's floor-to-ceiling windows gave unimpeded
views of the rowboats and gondolas gliding across Central
Park's Reservoir Lake. Both the lake and the trees surrounding it were showcased against the dramatic backdrop of the
Manhattan skyline.

The Boathouse's casual bar and restaurant buzzed with a
crowd dressed in everything from business to smart casual
to just plain comfortable. Despite the logjam, Gina spotted
Jack immediately. As promised, he'd secured a table tucked
in a quiet corner that still gave an unobstructed view of the
lake. She stood for a moment at the top of the short flight of

steps leading down to the dining area and put a hand on the railing to steady herself.

Oh, Lord! Her hormones must be cartwheeling again. Why else would her knees get all wobbly at the way the sunlight streaked his tawny hair? Or her lungs wheeze like an old accordion at the sight of his strong, tanned hands holding up a menu? In the tux he'd worn to the wedding yesterday, Jack had wreaked havoc on her emotions. In a crisply starched pale blue shirt with the cuffs rolled up on muscled forearms lightly sprinkled with gold fuzz, he almost opened the floodgates.

She was still clinging to the wooden rail when he glanced up. His gaze swept the entrance area from left to right. Passed over her. Jerked back. He was too polished a diplomat to reveal more than a flash of surprise, but that brief glimpse gave Gina the shot in the arm she needed. Channeling the duchess at her most regal, she smiled at the head waiter, who hurried over to assist her.

"May I show you to a table?"

"Thank you, but I see the party I'm meeting."

She tipped her chin toward Jack, now rising from his chair. The waiter followed her gaze and offered a hand.

"Yes, of course. Please, watch your step."

Jack had recovered from his momentary surprise. Gina wasn't sure she liked the amusement that replaced it.

"I almost didn't recognize you," he admitted. "Are you going for a new look?"

"As a matter of fact, I am."

She took the seat next to him and considered how much to share of her plans. After a swift internal debate, she decided it might be good to let him know that she did, in fact, have plans.

"I'm also going for a new career. I have a job interview this afternoon with the head of the Tremayne Group. TTG is one of the biggest event-coordinating companies in the business, with venues in New York, Washington and Chicago."

The change in Jack was so subtle she almost missed it. Just a slight stiffening of his shoulders. She bristled, thinking he was going to object to her making a foray into the professional party world while carrying his child. Instead, he responded quietly, calmly.

"TTG also has a venue in Boston. My wife used them to coordinate our wedding."

Three

"Oh, Jack!"

Gina's soft heart turned instantly to mush. She didn't want to marry this man but neither did she want to hurt him. Ignoring the obvious inconsistency in that thought, she dug in her purse for her cell phone.

"I'm sorry. I didn't know you had that connection to TTG. I'll call and cancel my interview."

"Wait." Frowning, he put a hand on her arm. "I'll admit I would prefer not to see you pursue a career here in New York. Or anywhere else, for that matter. But..."

"But?"

Still frowning, he searched her face. "Are you really dead set against marriage, Gina?"

Her gaze dropped to his hand, so strong and tan against the paler skin of her forearm. The stress and confusion of the past weeks made a jumble of her reply.

"Sort of."

"What does that mean?"

She looked up and met his serious brown eyes. "I like you, Jack. When you're not coming on all huffy and autocratic, that is. And God knows we were fantastic together in bed."

So fantastic she had to slam the door on the images that thought conjured up.

"But I think…I know we both want more in a marriage."

He was silent, and Gina gathered her courage.

"Tell me about your wife. What was she like?"

He sat back, withdrawing his hand in the process. Withdrawing himself, as well. His glance shifted to the rowboats circling the lake. The ripples from their oars distorted the reflected images of the high-rises peeking above Central Park's leafy green tree line. The buildings seemed to sway on the lake's blue-green surface.

"Catherine was funny and smart and had a killer serve," he said finally, turning back to Gina. "She cleaned my clock every time we got on a tennis court. She might have turned pro if she hadn't lived, breathed and slept politics."

The waiter appeared at that moment. Gina ordered decaffeinated mango tea, Jack a refill of his coffee. They listened to the specials and let the menus sit on the table after the waiter withdrew. She was afraid the interruption had broken the thread of a conversation she knew had to be painful, but Jack picked it up again.

"Catherine and another campaign worker were going door-to-door to canvas unregistered voters for the presidential campaign. She suffered a brain aneurysm and collapsed. The docs say she was dead before she hit the sidewalk."

"I'm so sorry."

"We didn't learn until after the autopsy that she had Ehlers-Danlos syndrome. It's a rare, inherited condition that can cause the walls of your blood vessels to rupture. Which," he said as he eased a leather portfolio out from under his menu, "is why I prepared this."

"This" turned out to be a set of stapled papers. For a wild moment Gina thought they might be a prenup. Or a copy of a will, naming the baby as his heir if he should die as unexpectedly as Catherine had. Or…

"Your obstetrician will want a complete medical history

of both parents," he said calmly. "As far as I know, I haven't inherited any rare diseases but my father and grandfather both suffer from chronic high blood pressure and my mother is a breast cancer survivor. Who's your doctor, by the way?"

"I don't have one yet."

The frown came back. "Why the delay? You should've had your first prenatal checkup by now."

"It's on my list, right after getting resettled in New York and finding a job."

"Move the obstetrician to the top of the list," he ordered, switching into his usual take-charge mode. "I'll cover your medical expenses until you land a job."

"No, Mr. Ambassador, you won't."

"Oh, for…!"

He dropped the papers, closed his eyes for a moment and adopted a calm, soothing tone that made Gina want to hiss.

"Let's just talk this through. You're currently unemployed. I assume you have no health insurance. Few obstetricians will take you on as a patient unless there's some guarantee you can pay for their services."

"I. Will. Find. A. Job."

"Okay, okay." He held up a placating hand. "Even if you do land a job in the next few days or weeks, health benefits probably won't kick in for at least six months. And then they may not cover preexisting conditions."

Well, crap! Gina hadn't considered that. Her throat closed as her carefully constructed house of cards seemed to teeter and topple right before her eyes.

No! No, dammit! Hormones or no hormones, she would not break down and bawl in front of Jack.

He must have sensed her fierce struggle for control. His expression softened, and he dropped the grating, let's-be-reasonable tone. "This is my baby, too, Gina. Let me help however I can."

She could handle autocratic and obnoxious. Nice was

harder to manager. Shoving back her chair, she pushed away from the table.

"I have to go to the bathroom."

After some serious soul-searching, she returned from the ladies' room to find the waiter had delivered their drinks. Gina dumped artificial sweetener in her tea and took a fortifying sip before acknowledging the unpalatable truth.

"I guess I didn't think this whole insurance thing through. If it turns out I can't get medical benefits in time to cover my appointments with an obstetrician, I would appreciate your help."

"You've got it." He hesitated a moment before extending another offer. "Finding a good doctor isn't easy, especially with everything else you have going on right now. Why don't I call my chief of staff and have him email you a list of the top OB docs in the city? He can also verify that they're accepting new patients."

And coordinate the payment process, Gina guessed. Swallowing her pride, she nodded. "I'd appreciate that."

"Just call me when you decide on a doctor. Or call Dale Vickers, my chief of staff. He'll make sure your appointments get on my schedule."

"Your schedule?"

"I'll fly up from D.C. to go with you, of course. Assuming I'm in the country."

"Oh. Of course."

The sense that she could do this on her own was rapidly slipping away. Trying desperately to hang on to her composure, Gina picked up her menu.

"We'd better order. My appointment at the Tremayne Group is at two-thirty."

Jack's hand hovered over his menu. "This might sound a little crass but between Catherine's family and mine, we spent an obscene amount of money on our wedding. I could make a call and..."

"No!"

Gina gritted her teeth. Was she the only person in the whole friggin' universe who didn't have an inside connection at TTG? And the only fool who refused to exploit that connection? Sheer stubbornness had her shaking her head.

"No calls. No pulling strings. No playing the big ambassadorial cheese. I have to do this myself."

He lifted a tawny brow but didn't press the point. After signaling the waiter over to take their orders, he steered the conversation into more neutral channels.

The awkwardness of the situation eased, and Gina's spirits took an upward swing. Jack soon had her laughing at some of his more humorous exploits in the field and realizing once again how charming he could be when he wanted to.

And sexy. So damned sexy. She savored the lump crab cake she'd ordered for lunch and couldn't help admiring the way the tanned skin at the corners of his eyes crinkled when he smiled. And how the light reflecting off the lake added glints to the sun-streaked gold of his hair. When he leaned forward, Gina caught the ripple of muscle under his starched shirt. She found herself remembering how she'd run her palms over all that hard muscle. That tight butt. Those iron thighs. The bunched biceps and...

"Gina?"

She almost choked on a lump of crab. "Sorry. What were you saying?"

"I was asking if you'd consider coming down to D.C. for a short visit. I'd like to show you my home and introduce you to my parents."

The request was reasonable. Naturally Jack's parents would want to meet the mother of their grandchild. From the little he'd let drop about his staunchly conservative father, though, Gina suspected John Harris Mason II probably wouldn't greet her with open arms.

"Let's talk about that later," she hedged. "After I get settled and find a job."

They finished lunch and lingered a few minutes over tea and coffee refills. Gina's nerves had started to get jittery by the time they exited the Boathouse. Jack walked with her through the park now filled with bicyclers and in-line skaters and sun worshippers sprawled on benches with eyes closed and faces tilted to the sky.

A group of Japanese tourists had congregated at Bethesda Fountain and were busy snapping photos of each other with the bronze statue of the *Angel of the Waters* towering over them. At the shy request of one of the younger members of the group, Jack obligingly stopped to take a picture of the whole party. Everyone wanted a copy on their own camera so Gina ended up acting as a runner, passing him ten or twelve cameras before they were done. By the time they reached Fifth Avenue and Jack hailed a cab to take her to her interview, she was feeling the pressure of time.

"Keep your fingers crossed," she said without thinking as the cab pulled over to the curb.

Only as he reached to open the door for her did she remember that he would prefer she didn't land this—or any job—in New York. He made no secret of the fact that he wanted to put a ring on her finger and take care of her and their child. To his credit, he buried those feelings behind an easy smile.

"I'll do better than that. Here's a kiss for luck."

He kept it light. Just a brush of his lips over hers. On the first pass, at least.

Afterward Gina could never say for sure who initiated the second pass. All she knew was that Jack hooked a hand behind her nape, she went up on tiptoe and what had started as a friendly good-luck token got real deep and real hungry.

When he finally raised his head, she saw herself reflected in his eyes. "I...I have to go!"

He stepped back and gave her room to make an escape. She slid into the cab and spent the short drive to the Tremayne Group's headquarters trying desperately to remember all the reasons why she wanted—no, needed!—this job.

* * *

At three-ten, she was reiterating that same grim list. She'd been sitting in Nicole Tremayne's ultramodern outer office for more than half an hour while a harried receptionist fielded phone calls and a succession of subordinates rushed in and out of the boss's office. Any other time Gina would have walked out after the first fifteen or twenty minutes. She didn't have that luxury now.

Instead, she'd used the time to reread the information she'd found on Google about the Tremayne Group. She also studied every page in the slick, glossy brochure given out to prospective clients. Even then she had to unlock her jaw and force a smile when the receptionist finally ushered her into the inner sanctum.

Stunned, Gina stopped dead. This dark cavern was the command center of a company that hosted more than two thousand events a year at a dozen different venues? And this tiny whirlwind erupting from behind her marble slab of a desk was the famed Nicole Tremayne?

She couldn't have been more than five-one, and she owed at least four of those inches to her needle-heeled ankle boots. Gina was still trying to marry the bloodred ankle boots to her salt-and-pepper corkscrew curls when Nicole thrust out a hand.

"Sorry to keep you waiting. You're Eugenia, right? Eugenia St. Sebastian?"

"Yes, I…"

"My father had a thing for your grandmother. I was just a kid at the time, but I remember he talked about leaving my mother for her."

"Oh. Well, uh…"

"He should have. My mother was a world-class ball-breaker." Swooping a thick book of fabric swatches off one of the chairs in front of her desk, Tremayne dumped it on the floor. "Sit, sit."

Still slightly stunned, Gina sat. Nicole cleared the chair

next to hers and perched on its edge with the nervous energy of a hummingbird.

"I looked at the digital portfolio of your sister's wedding. Classy job. You did all the arrangements?"

"With some help."

"Who from?"

"Andrew, at the Plaza. And Patrick Donovan. He's…"

"Dev Hunter's right-hand man. I know. We coordinated a major charity event for Hunter's corporation last year. Three thousand attendees at two thousand a pop. So when can you start?"

"Excuse me?"

"One of the assistant event planners at our midtown venue just got busted for possession. She's out on bail, but I can't have a user working for TTG." Her bird-bright eyes narrowed on Gina. "You don't do dope, do you?"

"No."

"I'd better not find out otherwise."

"You won't."

Tremayne nodded. "Here's the thing. You have a lousy work record but a terrific pedigree. If you inherited half your grandmother's class and a quarter of her smarts, you should be able to handle this job."

Gina wasn't sure whether she'd just been complimented or insulted. She was still trying to decide when her prospective boss continued briskly.

"You also grew up here in the city. You know your way around and you know how to interact with the kind of customers we attract. Plus, the classy digital portfolio you sent me shows you've got a flair for design and know computers. Whether you can handle vendors and show yourself as a team player remains to be seen, but I'm willing to give you a shot. When can you start?"

Tomorrow!

The joyous reply was almost out before Gina caught it. Gulping, she throttled back her exhilaration.

"I can start anytime but there's something I need to tell you before we go any further."

"What's that?"

"I'm pregnant."

"And I'm Episcopalian. So?"

Could it really be this easy? Gina didn't think so. Suspicion wormed through her elation.

"Did my grandmother call you?" she asked. "Or Pat Donovan?"

"No."

Her jaw locked. Dammit! It had to have been Jack.

"Then I assume you talked to the ambassador," she said stiffly.

"What ambassador?"

"Jack Mason."

"Jack Mason." Tremayne tapped her chin with a nail shellacked the same red as her ankle boots. "Why do I know that name?"

Gina didn't mention that TTG had coordinated Jack's wedding. For reasons she would have to sort out later, that cut too close to the bone.

"Who is he," Tremayne asked, "and why would he call me?"

"He's a friend." That was the best she could come up with. "I told him about our interview and…and thought he might have called to weigh in."

"Well, it certainly never hurts to have an ambassador in your corner, but no, he didn't call me. So what's the deal here? Do you want the job or not?"

There were probably a dozen different questions she should ask before jumping into the fray. Like how much the job paid, for one. And what her hours would be. And whether the position came with benefits. At the moment, though, Gina was too jazzed to voice any of the questions buzzing around in her head.

"Yes, ma'am, I do."

"Good. Have my assistant direct you to the woman who handles our personnel matters. You can fill out all the necessary forms there. And call me Nikki," she added as her new employee sprang out of her chair to shake on the deal.

Gina left the Tremayne Group's personnel office thirty or forty forms later. The salary was less than she'd hoped for but the description of her duties made her grin. As assistant events coordinator she would be involved in all phases of operation for TTG's midtown venue. Scheduling parties and banquets and trade shows. Devising themes to fit the clients' desires. Creating menus. Contracting with vendors to supply food and decorations and bar stock. Arranging for limos, for security, for parking.

Even better, the personnel officer had stressed that there was plenty of room for advancement within TTG. The tantalizing prospect of a promotion danced before Gina's eyes as she exited the high-rise housing the company's headquarters. When she hit the still glorious May sunshine, she had to tell someone her news. Her first, almost instinctive, impulse was to call Jack. She actually had her iPhone in hand before she stopped to wonder why.

Simple answer. She wanted to crow a little.

Not so simple answer. She wanted to prove she wasn't all fun and fluff.

With a wry grimace, she acknowledged that she should probably wait until she'd actually performed in her new position for a few weeks or months before she made that claim. She decided to text Sarah instead. The message was short and sweet.

I'm now a working mom-to-be. Call when you and Dev come up for air.

She took a cab back to the Upper West Side and popped out at a deli a few blocks from the Dakota. Osterman's had occupied the same choice corner location since the Great Depression. Gina and Sarah had developed their passion for corned beef at the deli's tiny, six-table eating area. The sisters still indulged whenever they were in the city, but Gina's target tonight was the case displaying Osterman's world famous cheesecakes. With unerring accuracy, she went for a selection that included her own, her grandmother's and Maria's favorites.

"One slice each of the white chocolate raspberry truffle, the key lime and the Dutch apple caramel, please. And one pineapple upside down," she added on an afterthought.

The boxed cheesecake wedges in hand, she plucked a bottle of chilled champagne from the cooler in the wine corner. She had to search for a nonalcoholic counterpart but finally found it in with the fruit juices. Driven by the urge to celebrate, she added a wedge of aged brie and a loaf of crusty bread to her basket. On her way to check out she passed a shelf containing the deli's selection of caviars.

The sticker price of a four-ounce jar of Caspian Sea Osetra made her gasp. Drawing in a steadying breath, she reminded herself it was Grandmama's caviar of choice. The duchess considered Beluga too salty and Sevruga too fishy. Gina made a quick calculation and decided her credit card would cover the cost of one jar. Maybe.

"Oh, what the hell."

To her relief, she got out of Osterman's without having the credit card confiscated. A block and a half later she approached the Dakota with all her purchases.

"Let me help you with those!"

The doorman who'd held his post for as long as she could remember leaped forward. Although she would never say so to his face, Gina suspected Jerome assumed his present duties about the same time Osterman's opened its doors.

"You should have called a cab, Lady Eugenia."

Sarah and Gina had spent most of their adult years trying to get Jerome to drop their empty titles. They'd finally agreed it was a wasted effort.

"I'm okay," Gina protested as he tried to relieve her of her burdens. "Except for this."

She sorted through her purchases and fished out a wedge-shaped box. Jerome peeked inside and broke into a grin.

"Pineapple upside down! Trust you to remember my favorite."

Gina's emotions jumped on the roller coaster again as she thought about his devoted loyalty to her and Grandmama over the years.

"How could I forget?" she said with a suspicious catch to her voice. "You slipped me an extra few dollars every time I said I was going to Osterman's."

For a moment she thought the embarrassed doorman would pat her on the head as he'd done so many times when she was a child. He controlled the impulse and commented instead on the bottles poking out of her bag.

"Still celebrating Lady Sarah's wedding?"

"Nope. This celebration is in my honor."

Riding her emotional roller coaster to its gravity-defying apex, she poured out her news.

"I'm moving back to New York, Jerome."

"Lady Eugenia! That's wonderful news. I admit I was a bit worried about the duchess."

"There's more. I've got a job."

"Good for you."

"Oh," she added over her shoulder as she made for the lobby. "I'm also pregnant."

Four

Gina walked into the Tremayne Group's midtown venue at 9:30 a.m. the next morning. She didn't drag out again until well past midnight.

Her first impression was *wow!* What had once been a crumbling brick warehouse overlooking the East River was now a glass-fronted, ultra-high-rent complex of offices, restaurants and entertainment venues. TTG occupied a slightly recessed four-story suite smack in the center of the complex. The primo location allowed into a private ground-floor courtyard with bubbling fountains and a top-floor terrace that had to offer magnificent views of the river.

A young woman with wings of blue in her otherwise lipstick-red hair sat at a curved glass reception desk and fielded phone calls. Gina waited until she finished with one caller and put two others on hold to introduce herself.

"I'm Gina St. Sebastian. I'm the new…"

"Assistant coordinator. Thank God you're here! I'm Kallie. Samuel's in the banquet hall. He said to send you right up. Third floor. The elevators are to your right."

Gina used the ride to do a quick check in mirrored panels. She'd left her hair down today but confined the silky curls behind a wide fuchsia headband studded with crystals. A belt in the same hot pink circled the waist of her apple-green J. Crew tunic. Since this was her first day on the job she'd gone with sedate black tights instead of the colorful prints she preferred. She made a quick swipe with her lip gloss and drew in a deep, steadying breath. Then the elevator door glided open and she stepped out into a vortex of sound and fury.

What looked like a small army of workers in blue overalls was yanking folded chairs from metal-sided carrier racks, popping them open and thumping them around a room full of circluar tables. Another crew, this one in black pants and white shirts, scurried after the first. They draped each chair in shimmering green, the tables in cloth of gold. Right behind them came yet another crew rattling down place settings of china and crystal. The *rat-tat-tat* of staple guns fired by intent set designers erecting a fantastic Emerald City added to the barrage of noise, while the heady scent of magnolias wafted from dozens of tall topiaries stacked on carts waiting to be rolled to the tables.

Soaking up the energy like a sponge, Gina wove her way through the tables to a wild-haired broomstick with a clipboard in one hand, a walkie-talkie in the other and a Bluetooth headset hooked over one ear. "Not *The Wizard of Oz*," he was shouting into the headset. "Christ, who does Judy Garland anymore? This is the new movie. *Oz the... Oz the...*"

Scowling, he snapped his fingers at Gina.

"Oz the Great and Powerful," she dutifully asserted.

"Right. *Oz the Great and Powerful*. It's a Disney flick starring Rachel Weisz and..."

More finger snaps.

"Mila Kunis."

"Right. Mila Kunis. That's the music the clients requested." The scowl deepened. "Hell, no, I don't! Hold on."

He whipped his head around and barked at Gina. "You the new AC?"

"Yes."

"I'm Samuel DeGrange."

"Nice to…"

He brushed aside the pleasantries with an impatient hand. "Go upstairs and tell the DJ to pull his head out of his ass. The clients don't want Dorothy and Toto, for God's sake! Then make sure the bar supervisor knows how to mix the fizzy green juice concoction that's supposed to make the kids think they're dancing down a new, improved Yellow Brick Road."

Eight and a half hours later Gina was zipped into the Glinda the Good Witch costume that had been rented for her predecessor and making frantic last-minute changes to seating charts. Kallie the receptionist—now garbed as a munchkin—wielded a calligraphy pen to scribble out place cards for the twenty additional guests the honoree's mother had somehow forgotten she'd invited until she was in the limo and on her way from Temple with the newly bat mitzvahed Rachel.

Another six hours later, Gina collapsed into a green-draped chair and gazed at the rubble. Iridescent streamers in green and gold littered the dance floor. Scattered among them was a forgotten emerald tiara here, an empty party-favors box there. The booths where the seventy-five kids invited to celebrate Rachel's coming of age had fired green lasers and demolished video villains were being dismantled. Only a few crumbs remained of the fourteen-layer cake with its glittering towers and turrets. The kids invited to the party had devoured it with almost as much gusto as the more than two hundred parents, grandparents, aunts, uncles, cousins and family friends had drained the open bar upstairs.

Gina stretched out her feet in their glittery silver slippers and aimed a grin at the toothpick-thin Tin Man who flopped into the chair beside her.

"This party business is fun."

"You think?" Samuel shoved back his tin hat and gave her a jaundiced smile. "Talk to me again after you've had an inebriated best man puke all over you. Or spent two hours sifting through piles of garbage to find a guest's diamond-and-sapphire earrings. Which, incidentally, she calls to tell you she found in her purse."

"At least she let you know she found it," Gina replied, laughing.

"She's one of the few. Seems like our insurance rates take another jump after every event." He slanted her a sideways glance. "You did good tonight, St. Sebastian. Better than I expected when I read your résumé."

"Thanks. I think."

"You need to keep a closer finger on the pulse of the party, though. The natives got a little restless before the cake was brought out."

Gina bit her lip. No need to remind her new boss that he'd sent her out to the terrace to shepherd some underage smokers back inside right when the cake was supposed to have been presented.

"I'll watch the timing," she promised.

"So go home now. I'll do the final bar count and leave this mess to the cleaning crew."

She wasn't about to argue. "I'll see you tomorrow."

"Nine sharp," he warned. "We've got a preliminary wedding consult. I'll talk, you listen and learn."

She popped a salute. "Yes, sir."

"Christ! You got enough energy left for that?" He didn't wait for an answer, just shooed her away. "Get out of here."

The *Oz the Great and Powerful* bat mitzvah set the stage for the dozens of events that followed during the busy, busy month of May. Almost before she knew it Gina was caught up in a whirl of wedding and engagement and anniversary and graduation and coming-of-age parties. She gained both experience and confidence with each event.

So much so that Samuel soon delegated full responsibility for computing and placing orders with the subs for everything from decorations to bar stock. He also tapped her for fresh ideas for themes and settings. In rapid succession she helped plan a white-on-white wedding, a red-and-black "Puttin' on the Ritz" debutante ball and a barefoot-on-the-beach engagement party at a private Hamptons estate. And then there was her grand coup—snaring Justin Bieber for a brief appearance at the national Girl Scout banquet to be held in the fall. He was in town for another event and Gina played shamelessly on his agent's heartstrings until every teen's favorite heartthrob agreed.

Not all events went smoothly. Frantically working her cell phone and walkie-talkie, Gina learned to cope with minor crises like a forgotten kosher meal for the rabbi, a groom caught frolicking in the fourth-floor bridal suite shower with the maid of honor and a drunken guest held hostage by an irate limo driver demanding payment for damage done to the vehicle's leather seats.

In the midst of all the craziness she unpacked the boxes Dev's assistant had shipped back from L.A. and welcomed her sister and her new brother-in-law home from their honeymoon. Gina and Sarah and the duchess were all teary-eyed when the newlyweds departed again, this time to look at homes for sale close to Dev's corporate headquarters in California.

Miracle of miracles, Gina also managed to snag an appointment with the top OB doc on the short list of three Jack had emailed. She suspected he'd used his influence or family clout to make sure she got in to see one of them. She didn't object to outside help in this instance. The health of her baby took precedence over pride.

As promised, she called Jack's office to let him know about the appointment. A secretary routed her to his chief of staff.

"This is Dale Vickers, Ms. St. Sebastian. The ambassador is in conference. May I help you?"

"Jack asked me to let him know the date and time of my prenatal appointment. It's Thursday of next week, at three-fifteen, with Dr. Sondra Martinson."

"I'm looking at his calendar now. The ambassador is unavailable next Thursday. Please reschedule the appointment and call me back."

The reply was as curt as it was officious. Gina held out the phone and looked at it in surprise for a moment before putting it to her ear again.

"Tell you what," she said, oozing sweetness and light, "just tell Jack to call me. We'll take it from there."

The man must have realized his mistake. Softening his tone, he tried to regain lost ground.

"I'm sorry if I sounded abrupt, Ms. St. Sebastian. It's just that the ambassador is participating all next week in a conference with senior State Department officials. They're assessing U.S. embassy security in light of recent terrorist attacks. I can't overstate the importance of this conference to the safety and security of our consular personnel abroad."

Properly put in her place, Gina was about to concede the point when he made a suggestion.

"Why don't I call Dr. Martinson's office and arrange an appointment that fits with the ambassador's schedule?"

"That won't work. We need to work around my schedule, too."

"I'm sure you can squeeze something in between parties for twelve-year-olds."

The barely disguised put-down dropped Gina's jaw. What was with this character? Sheer obstinacy had her oozing even more saccharine.

"I'm sure I can. After all, the tab for our last twelve-year-old's party only ran to sixty-five thousand dollars and change. Just have Jack call me. We'll work something out."

"Really, Ms. St. Sebastian, we don't have to trouble the ambassador with such a trivial matter."

Heat shot to every one of Gina's extremities. Given her normally sunny and fun-loving disposition, she'd never believed that old cliché about seeing red. She did now.

"Listen, asshole, you may consider the ambassador's baby a trivial matter. I'm pretty sure he won't agree. The appointment is for three-fifteen next Thursday. End of discussion."

As instructed, she arrived at Dr. Martinson's office a half hour prior to her scheduled appointment. The time was required for a final review and signature on the forms she'd downloaded from the office website. She hadn't heard from Jack or from his stick-up-the-butt chief of staff. So when she walked into the reception area and didn't spot a familiar face, she wasn't surprised.

What did surprise her was how deep the disappointment went. She'd been so busy she hadn't had time to dwell on the confused feelings Jack Mason stirred in her. Except at night, when she dropped into bed exhausted and exhilarated and wishing she had someone to share the moments of her day with. Or when her body reminded her that she wasn't its sole inhabitant anymore. Or when she happened to spot a tall, tanned male across the room or on the street or in the subway.

"Don't be stupid," she muttered as she signed form after form. "He's making the world safer for our embassy people. That has to take precedence."

She was concentrating so fiercely on the clipboard in her hand that she didn't hear the door to the reception area open.

"Good, I'm not late."

The relieved exclamation brought her head up with a jerk. "Jack! I thought... Vickers said..."

Of all the idiotic times to get teary-eyed! How could she handle every crisis at work with a cheerful smile and turn into such a weepy wimp around this man? She had to jump off this emotional roller coaster.

"Vickers told me what he said." Grinning, he dropped into the chair beside hers. "He also told me what you said."

"Yes, well, you shouldn't piss off a preggo. The results aren't pretty."

"I'll remember that."

Guilt wormed through the simple, hedonistic pleasure of looking at his handsome face. She let the clipboard drop to her lap and made a wry face.

"You shouldn't have come. Vickers said you had a top-level conference going on all week."

"We wrapped up the last of the key issues this morning. All that's left is to approve the report once it gets drafted. I can do that by secure email. Which means," he said as he took the clipboard and flipped through the forms, "I don't have to fly back to D.C. right away. Here, you forgot to sign this one."

She scribbled her signature and tried not to read too much into his casual comment about extending his trip up from D.C. Didn't work. When he tacked on an equally casual invitation, her heart gave a little bump.

"If you don't have plans, I thought I might take you and the duchess to dinner tonight."

"Oh, I can't. I'm working a fiftieth anniversary party. I had to sneak out for this appointment."

"How about tomorrow?"

The bump was bigger this time. "Are you staying over that long?"

"Actually, I told Dale to clear the entire weekend."

"Ha! Bet he loved that."

"He's not so bad, Gina. You two just got off on the wrong foot."

"Wrong foot, wrong knee, wrong hip and elbow. How long has he worked for you, anyway?"

"Five years."

"And no one's ever told you he's officious or condescending?"

"No."

"It has to be me, then." Grimacing, she rolled out the reason she suspected might be behind his aide's less-than-enthusiastic response to her call. "Or the fact that the paparazzi will have a field day when they hear you knocked me up."

"They probably will," he replied, not quite suppressing a wince. "But when they do, you might want to use a different phrase to describe the circumstances."

"Really? What phrase do you suggest I use, Mr. Ambassador?"

He must have seen the chasm yawning at his feet. "Sorry. I didn't mean to come across as such a pompous jerk."

The apology soothed Gina's ruffled feathers enough for her to acknowledge his point. "I'm sorry, too. I know the pregnancy will cause you some embarrassment. I'll try not to add to it."

"The only embarrassing aspect to this whole situation is that I can't convince the beautiful and very stubborn mother of my child to marry me."

She wanted to believe him, but she wasn't that naive. She chewed on her lower lip for a moment before voicing the worry that had nagged her since Switzerland.

"Tell me the truth, Jack. Is this going to impact your career?"

"No."

"Maybe not at the State Department, but what about afterward? I read somewhere that certain powerful PACs think you have a good shot at the presidency in the not-too-distant future."

"Gina, listen to me." He curled a knuckle under her chin and tipped her face to make sure he had her complete attention. "We met, we were attracted to each other, we spent some time together. Since neither of us were then, or are now, otherwise committed, the only ones impacted by the result of that meeting are you, me and our baby."

"Wow," she breathed. "That was some speech, Mr. Ambassador. Those PACs may be right. You should make a bid for the Oval Office. You'd get my vote."

He feathered the side of her jaw with his thumb. "I'd rather get your signature on a marriage license."

Maybe…maybe she was being blind and pigheaded and all wrong about this marriage thing. So he didn't love her? He wanted her, and God knew she wanted him. Couldn't their child be the bridge to something more?

The thought made her cringe inside. What kind of mother would pile her hopes and dreams on a baby's tiny shoulders?

"We've had this discussion." Shrugging, she pulled away from his touch. "Let's not get into it again."

Surprise darkened his brown eyes, followed by a touch of what could have been either disappointment or irritation. Before Gina could decide which, a nurse in pink-and-blue scrubs decorated with storks delivering bundles of joy popped into the waiting room.

"Ms. St. Sebastian?"

"Right here."

"If you'll come with me, I'll get your height and weight and show you to an exam room."

Gina pushed out her chair. Jack rose with her. The nurse stopped him with a friendly smile. "Please wait here, Mr. St. Sebastian. I'll come get you in a few minutes."

The look on his face was more than enough to disperse Gina's glum thoughts. Choking back a laugh, she floated after the nurse. When Jack joined her in the exam room five minutes later, she was wearing a blue paper gown tied loosely in the front and a fat grin.

"I set her straight on the names."

"Uh-huh."

"Come on," she teased. "You have to admit it was funny."

The only thing in Jack's mind at the moment was not something he could admit. How could he have forgotten how full and lush and ripe her breasts were? Or had her pregnancy enhanced the creamy slopes he glimpsed through the front opening of her gown?

Whatever! That one glimpse was more than enough to put him in a sweat. Thoroughly disgusted, he was calling himself all kinds of a pig when the doctor walked in.

"Hello, Ms. St. Sebastian. I'm Dr. Martinson."

Petite and gray-haired, she shook hands with her patient before turning to Jack. "And you're Ambassador Mason, the baby's father?"

"That's right."

"I read through your medical and family histories. I'm so pleased neither of you smoke, use drugs, or drink to excess. That makes my job so much easier."

She included Jack in her approving smile before addressing Gina.

"I'm going to order lab tests to confirm your blood type and Rh status. We'll also check for anemia, syphilis, hepatitis B and the HIV virus, as well as your immunity to rubella and chicken pox. I want you to give a urine sample, as well."

Her down-to-earth manner put her patient instantly at ease...right up until the moment she extracted a pair of rubber gloves from a dispenser mounted on the wall.

"Let's get the pelvic exam out of the way, then we'll talk about what to expect in the next few weeks and months."

She must have caught the consternation that flooded into Gina's china blue eyes. Without missing a beat, the doc snapped on the gloves and issued a casual order.

"Why don't you wait outside, Ambassador Mason? This will only take a few moments."

Five

When Jack accompanied Gina out of the medical plaza complex and into the early throes of the Thursday evening rush hour, he was feeling a little shell-shocked.

The news that he would be a father had surprised the hell out of him initially. Once he'd recovered, he'd progressed in quick order from consternation to excitement to focusing his formidable energy on hustling the mother of his child to the altar. Now, with a copy of *A Father's Guide to Pregnancy* tucked in the pocket of his suit coat and the first prenatal behind him, he was beginning to appreciate both the reality and the enormity of the road ahead.

Gina, amazingly, seemed to be taking her pregnancy in stride. Like a gloriously painted butterfly, she'd gone through an almost complete metamorphosis. Not that she'd had much choice. With motherhood staring her in the face, she appeared to have shed her fun-loving, party-girl persona. The hysterical female who'd called Jack from Switzerland had also disappeared. Or maybe those personas had combined to produce this new Gina. Still bubbling with life, still gorgeous beyond words, but surprisingly responsible.

She'd listened attentively to everything the doctor said, asked obviously well-thought-out questions and made careful notes of the answers. She also worked the calendar on her iPhone with flying fingers to fit a visit to the lab for the required blood tests and future appointments with Dr. Martinson into her schedule.

In between, she fielded a series of what had sounded like frantic calls from work with assurances that yes, she'd confirmed delivery of the ice sculpture; no, their clients hadn't requested special permission from the New York City Department of Corrections for their grandson currently serving time at Rikers to attend their fiftieth wedding anniversary celebration; and yes, she'd just left the doctor's office and was about to jump in a cab.

Jack waited on the sidewalk beside her while she finished that last call. The sky was gray and overcast but the lack of sunshine didn't dim the luster of her hair. The tumble of shining curls and the buttercup-yellow tunic she wore over patterned yellow-and-turquoise tights made her a beacon of bright cheer in the dismal day.

Jack stood beside her, feeling a kick to the gut as he remembered exploring the lush curves under that bright tunic. Remembering, too, the kiss they'd shared the last time he put her in a cab. He'd spent more time trying to analyze his reaction to that kiss than he wanted to admit. It was hot and heavy on his mind when Gina finished her call.

"I have to run," she told him. "If you still want to take Grandmama and me to dinner, I could do tomorrow evening."

"That works."

"I'll check with her to make sure tomorrow's okay and give you a call."

He stepped to the curb and flagged a cab. She started to duck inside and hesitated.

Was she remembering the last time he'd put her in a cab, too? Jack's stomach went tight with the anticipation of taking her in his arms again. He'd actually taken a step forward when she issued a tentative invitation.

"Would you like to see where I work?"

The intensity of his disappointment surprised him, but he disguised it behind an easy smile. "Yeah, I would."

"It'll have to be a brief tour," she warned when they got in the cab. "We're in the final throes of an anniversary celebration with two hundred invited guests."

"Not including the grandson at Rikers."

She made a face. "Keep your fingers crossed he doesn't break out! I have visions of NYPD crashing through the doors just when we parade the cake."

"You parade cakes?"

"Sometimes. And in this instance, we'll do it very carefully! We're talking fifteen layers replicating the Cape Hatteras lighthouse that stands on the spot where our honorees got engaged."

She thumbed her iPhone and showed Jack an image of the iconic black-and-white striped lighthouse still guarding the shores of North Carolina's Outer Banks.

"We're doing an actual working model. The caterer and I had several sticky sessions before we figured out how to bury the battery pack in the cake base and power up the strobe light at the top without melting all his pretty sugar frosting into a black-and-white blob."

"I'm impressed."

And not just with the ingenuity and creativity she obviously brought to her new job. Enthusiasm sparkled in her blue eyes, and the vibrancy that had first snared his interest bubbled to the surface again.

"Hopefully, our clients will be impressed, too. We're decorating the entire venue in an Outer Banks theme. All sand, seashells and old boats, with enough fishnet and colorful buoys to supply the Atlantic fleet."

Unbidden and unwanted, a comparison surfaced between the woman beside him and the woman he'd loved with every atom of his being. The vivid images of Catherine were starting to fade, though, despite Jack's every effort to hang on to them. He had to dig deep to remember the sound of her laughter. Strain to hear an echo of her chuckle. She'd been so socially and politically involved. So serious about the issues that mattered to her. She had fun, certainly, but she hadn't regarded life as a frothy adventure the way Gina seemed to. Nor would she have rebounded so quickly from the emotional wringer of Switzerland.

As his companion continued her lighthearted description of tonight's event, Jack's memories of his wife retreated to the shadows once again. Even the shadows got blasted away when he and Gina exited the elevators onto the third floor of the Tremayne Group's midtown venue.

They could be on the Outer Banks, right at the edge of the Atlantic. Bemused, Jack took in the rolling sand dunes, the upended rowboat, the electronic waves splashing across a wall studded with LED lights.

"Wow. Is this all your doing?" he asked Gina.

"Not hardly. Mostly my boss, Samuel, and...uh-oh! There's Samuel now. He's with our big boss. 'Scuse me a minute. I'd better find out what's up."

Jack recognized the diminutive woman with the salt-and-pepper corkscrew curls at first look. Nicole Tremayne hadn't changed much in the past eight years. One of the underlings in her Boston operation had handled most of the planning for Jack's wedding to Catherine, but Nicole had approved the final plans herself and flown up from New York to personally oversee the lavish affair.

He saw the moment she recognized him, too. The casual glance she threw his way suddenly sharpened into a narrow-eyed stare. Frowning, she exchanged a few words with Gina, then crossed the floor.

"John Harris Mason." She thrust out a hand. "I should have made the connection when Gina demanded to know if Jack Mason had contacted me."

"I hope you told her no. She almost bit off my head when I offered to call and put in a word for her."

"She did? Interesting."

Chin cocked, Tremayne studied him through bird-bright eyes. She wasn't so crass as to come out and ask if he were the father of Gina's baby but Jack could see the speculation rife in her face.

"I was sorry to hear about your wife," she said after a moment.

"Thank you."

God, what a useless response. But Jack had uttered it so many times now that the words didn't taste quite as bitter in his mouth.

"Are you still in Boston?" she asked.

"No, I'm with the State Department now. Right now I'm assigned to D.C."

"Hmm." She tapped a bloodred nail against her chin. "Good to know."

With that enigmatic comment she excused herself and returned to her underlings. Gina rushed over a few moments later.

"I'm so sorry, Jack. We'll have to postpone the tour. I've got to take care of an ice-sculpture crisis."

"No problem. Just let me know if tomorrow evening's a go for the duchess."

"I will."

The following evening was not only a go, but the duchess's acceptance also came with an invitation for drinks at the Dakota prior to dinner.

Jack spent all that day at the NYPD Counterterrorism Bureau established after 9/11. While coordination between federal, state and local agencies had increased exponentially since that horrific day, there was always room for improvement. The NYPD agents were particularly interested in Jack's recent up-close-and-personal encounter with a rabidly anti-U.S. terrorist cell in Mali. They soaked up every detail of the terrorists' weaponry and tactics and poured over the backgrounds of two Americans recently ID'd as part of the group. Since the parents of one of the expatriates lived in Brooklyn, NYPD was justifiably worried that the son might try to slip back into the country.

Jack in turn received in-depth briefings on the Counterterrorism Bureau's Lower Manhattan Security Initiative. Designed to protect the nation's financial capital, the LMSI combined increased police presence and the latest surveillance technology with a public-private partnership. Individuals from both government and the business world manned LMSI's operations center to detect and neutralize potential threats. Jack left grimly hopeful that this unique publicprivate cooperative effort would prove a model for other high-risk targets.

He rushed back to his hotel and had his driver wait while he hurried upstairs to change his shirt and eliminate his fiveo'clock shadow. A half hour later he identified himself to a uniformed doorman at the castlelike Dakota. The security at the famed apartment complex had stepped up considerably after one of its most famous tenants, John Lennon, was gunned down just steps away from the entrance years ago. Jack had no problem providing identification, being closely scrutinized and waiting patiently while the doorman called upstairs.

"The duchess is expecting you, sir. You know the apartment number?"

"I do."

"Very good." He keyed a remote to unlock the inner door. "The elevators are to your left."

A dark-haired, generously endowed woman Jack remembered from the wedding reception answered the doorbell. She wore a polite expression but he sensed disapproval lurking just below the surface.

"*Hola.* I am Maria, housekeeper to *la duquesa* and auntie to Sarah and Gina."

Auntie, huh? That explained the disapproval. She obviously considered him solely responsible for the failure of the box of condoms he and Gina had gone through during their sexual extravaganza.

"Good evening, Maria. I saw you at Sarah's wedding but didn't get a chance to introduce myself. I'm Jack Mason."

"*Sí,* I know. Please come with me. *La duquesa* waits for you in the salon."

He followed her down a hall tiled in pale pink Carrara marble. The delicate scent of orange blossoms wafted from a Waterford crystal bowl set on a rococo side table. The elegant accessories gave no hint of how close the duchess had come to financial disaster. Jack picked up faint traces of it, however, when Maria showed him into the high-ceilinged salon.

The room's inlaid parquet floor was a work of art but cried for a hand-knotted Turkish carpet to soften its hard surface. Likewise, the watered silk wallpaper showed several barely discernible lighter rectangles where paintings must have once hung. The furniture was a skillful blend of fine antiques and modern comfort, though, and the floor-to-ceiling windows curtained in pale blue velvet gave glorious views of Central Park. Those swift impressions faded into insignificance when Jack spotted the woman sitting ramrod-straight in a leather-backed armchair, her cane within easy reach. Thin and frail though she was, Charlotte St. Sebastian nevertheless dominated the salon with her regal air.

"Good evening, Jack."

She held out a veined hand. He shook it gently and remembered her suggestion at the wedding that he use her name instead of her title.

"Good evening, Charlotte."

"Gina called a few moments ago. She's been detained at work but should be here shortly."

She waved him to the chair beside hers and smiled a request at Maria. "Would you bring in the appetizer tray before you leave?"

When the housekeeper bustled out, the duchess gestured

to a side table holding a dew-streaked bucket and an impressive array of crystal decanters.

"May I offer you an aperitif?"

"You may."

"I'm afraid I must ask you to serve yourself. The wine is a particularly fine French white, although some people find the Aligoté grape a bit too light for their tastes. Or..."

She lifted the tiny liqueur glass sitting on the table next to her and swirled its amber liquid.

"You may want to try *žuta osa*. It's produced in the mountains that at one time were part of the Duchy of Karlenburgh."

The bland comment didn't fool Jack for a second. He'd responded to too many toasts by foreign dignitaries and downed too many potent local brews to trust this one. He poured a glass of wine instead.

Maria returned with a silver tray containing a selection of cheeses, olives and prosciutto ham slices wrapped around pale green melon slices. She placed the tray on a massive marble-topped coffee table within easy reach of the duchess and her guest.

"Thank you." Charlotte gave her a smile composed of equal parts gratitude and affection. "You'd better leave now. You don't want to miss your bus."

"I'll take a later one."

Her quick glance in Jack's direction said she wasn't about to leave her friend and employer in his clutches. The duchess didn't miss the suspicion in her dark eyes.

"We're fine," she assured the woman. "Go ahead and catch your bus."

Maria looked as though she wanted to dig in her heels but yielded to her employer's wishes. The kitchen door swished shut behind her. Several moments later, her heavy footsteps sounded in the hall.

"Actually," Jack said when he resumed his seat beside the duchess, "I'm glad we have some time alone."

"Indeed?"

"As you know, Gina and I didn't spend all that much time together before our lives became so inextricably linked."

"I am aware of that fact."

Deciding he'd be wise to ignore the pained expression on Charlotte's face, Jack pressed ahead. "I'm just beginning to appreciate the woman behind your granddaughter's dazzlingly beautiful exterior. I'm hoping you'll help me add to that portrait by telling me a little more about her."

One aristocratic brow lifted. "Surely you don't expect me to provide ammunition for your campaign to convince Gina to marry you?"

"As a matter of fact, that's exactly what I'm hoping you'll provide."

"Well!" The brow shot up another notch. "For a career diplomat, you're very frank."

"I've found being frank works better than tiptoeing around tough issues."

"And that's how you categorize my granddaughter?" the duchess said haughtily. "A tough issue?"

"Ha!" Jack didn't bother to disguise his feelings. "Tough doesn't even begin to describe her. To put it bluntly, your granddaughter is the toughest, stubbornest, most irritating issue I've ever dealt with."

Oh, hell. The frozen look on his hostess's face said clearer than words that he'd overshot his mark. He was just about to apologize profusely when the facade cracked and the duchess broke into somewhat less than regal snorts of laughter.

"You do know," she responded some moments later, "that Gina says exactly the same thing about you?"

"Yes, ma'am, I do."

Still chuckling, she lifted her glass and tossed back the remainder of the amber liquid.

"Shall I pour you another?" Jack asked.

"Thank you, no. My doctor insists I limit myself to one a day. He's a fussy old woman, but he's kept me alive this long so I suppose I can't complain. Now, what do you want to know about Gina?"

Feeling as though he'd managed to negotiate a particularly dangerous minefield, Jack relaxed. "Whatever you feel comfortable sharing. Maybe you could start when she was a child. What kind of mischief did she get into?"

"Good heavens! What kind didn't she get into?" A fond smile lit the duchess's clouded blue eyes. "I remember one incident in particular. She couldn't have been more than seven or eight at the time. Maria had taken her and Sarah to the park. Gina wandered off and threw us all into a state of complete panic. The police were searching for her when she showed up several hours later with a lice-infested bag-lady in tow. She'd found the woman asleep under a bush and simply couldn't leave her on the cold, hard ground. I believe the woman stayed with us for almost a week before Gina was satisfied with the arrangements we worked out for her."

Charlotte's wry tale added another piece to the mosaic that was Gina St. Sebastian. Jack was trying to assemble the varied and very different sections into a coherent whole when the front door slammed.

"It's me, Grandmama. Is Jack here yet?"

The question was accompanied by the thud of something heavy hitting the table in the hall. Wincing, the duchess called out an answer.

"He is. We're in the salon."

With a kick in his pulse, Jack rose to greet her. His welcoming smile faltered and came close to falling off his face when she waltzed into the salon.

"Sorry I'm late."

"Eugenia!" the duchess gasped. "Your hair!"

"Pretty, isn't it?" Gina patted her ruler-straight, bright purple locks and shot her grandmother a mischievous grin. "We're doing a manga-themed birthday party tomorrow afternoon. I'm Yuu Nomiya."

"I don't have the faintest idea who manga or Yuu are, but I sincerely hope that color isn't permanent."

"It'll come out after a few washings." With that blithe assurance, she gave Jack an apologetic smile. "I'm sorry I kept you waiting. We haven't missed our dinner reservation, have we?"

"We've plenty of time." He struggled to keep his eyes on her face and off the neon purple framing it. "Would you like something to drink? I'm doing the honors."

"God, yes!"

She dropped onto the sofa in an untidy sprawl and caught the suddenly disapproving expressions on the two faces turned in her direction.

"What? Oh! I don't want anything alcoholic. Just tonic, with lots of ice."

Jack delivered the tonic and listened while Gina tried to explain the concept of Japanese manga comics to her grandmother. In the process, she devoured most of the contents of the appetizer tray.

To her credit, the duchess appeared genuinely curious about the phenomenon now taking the world by storm. Or perhaps she just displayed an interest for her granddaughter's sake. Whatever the reason, she asked a series of very intelligent questions. Gina answered them with enthusiasm…at first. Gradually, her answers grew shorter and more muddled. At the same time she slipped lower against the sofa cushions. When her lids drooped and she lost her train of thought in midsentence, the duchess sighed.

"Eugenia, my darling. You're exhausted. Go to bed."

The order fell on deaf ears. Her granddaughter was out like a light.

"I warned her," Charlotte said with affectionate exasperation. "The first few months especially sap a woman's strength."

"Dr. Martinson said the same thing."

"We'll have to forego dinner, Jack. She needs to rest."

"Of course."

When the duchess grasped her cane and aimed the tip at her sleeping granddaughter, he pushed out of his chair.

"Don't wake her."

Bending, he eased her into his arms. She muttered something unintelligible and snuggled against his chest. The scent and the feel of her tantalized Jack's senses. His throat tightening, he growled out a request for directions.

"Which way is her bedroom?"

Six

Gina was having the best dream. She was cradled in strong arms, held against a warm, hard chest. She felt so safe, so secure. So treasured. Like something precious and fragile, which even in her dream she knew she wasn't. Savoring the sensation of being sheltered and protected, she ignored a pesky pressure low in her belly and nuzzled her nose into something soft and squeezy.

The soft and squeezy, her hazy mind determined a moment later, was her pillow. And that irritating pressure was her bladder demanding relief. She pried up an eyelid and made out the dim outlines of her bedroom. The faint glow of the night-light always left on showed she was tucked under the satin throw she normally kept folded at the foot of the bed. She was also fully dressed.

Grunting, she got an elbow under her and sat up. Her slept-in clothes felt scratchy and twisted and tight. Long strands of purple hair fell across her eyes. She brushed them back and tossed aside the throw. Still groggy, she made her way to the bathroom. Once back in the bedroom she shed her clothes and slid into bed, between the sheets this time.

Sleep tugged at her. She drifted toward it on the vague

remnants of her dream. Those strong arms… That steady pulse of a heartbeat under her cheek…

"Jack?"

She sat up again, suddenly and fully awake, and flipped onto her other hip. The covers on the other side of the bed lay smooth and flat. Intense and totally absurd disappointment made her scrunch her face in disgust.

"Idiot! Like the man's going to crawl into bed with you? Right here, in the apartment? And Grandmama only a snore away?"

She flopped back down and yanked the sheet up to her chin. In almost the next breath, her disappointment took a sharp right turn into thigh-clenching need. The hunger shot straight from her breasts to her belly. From there it surged to every extremity, until even her fingernails itched with it.

She stared at the ceiling, her breath coming hot and fast. Images fast-forwarded in her mind. Jack leaning over her, his muscles slick and taunt. Jack laughing as she rolled him onto his back and straddled him. Jack's hands splayed on her naked hips and his jaw tight while he rose up to meet her downward thrust.

Oh, man! She should have expected this. One of the pamphlets Dr. Martinson had provided specifically addressed the issue of heightened sex drive during pregnancy. The rampaging hormones, the supersensitive breasts, the increased blood supply to the vulva— Taken together they could brew up a perfect storm of insatiable physical hunger.

Gina was there. Smack in the eye of the storm. She ached for Jack. She wanted him on her and in her and…

"Oh, for Pete's sake!"

Throwing off the sheet, she stalked to the antique dressing table with its tri-fold mirror, marble top and dozens of tiny drawers. She couldn't begin to count the number of hours she'd spent at this table. First as a youngster playing dress-up in Grandmama's pearls and Sarah's lacy peignoir. Then as a preteen, giggling with her girlfriends while they pirouetted in panties and training bras to show off their budding figures. After that came the high school years of mascara and eye shadow and love notes and trinkets from a steady stream of boys drooling over her nicely filled-out curves.

The notes and trinkets were long gone but her trusty vibrator was tucked in its usual drawer. She didn't have to resort to it often, but this...this gnawing hunger constituted a medical emergency.

So much of an emergency that the relief was almost instantaneous. And too damned short-lived! Gina tried to go from limp and languid into sleep. Jack kept getting in the way. Had he been bummed about dinner? Did he and Grandmama go without her? Would he try to see her again before he flew back to Washington?

She was forced to wait for the answers to those questions. With the manga birthday party set to kick off at 11:00 a.m., she had to leave for work before the duchess emerged from her bedroom. Maria came in at midmorning on Saturdays so Gina got no help from that quarter, either.

She toyed with the idea of calling Jack during the short subway ride to midtown, but all-too-vivid memories of last night's searing hunger kept her cell phone in her purse. The memories raised heat in her cheeks. She suspected that hearing his voice, all deep and rich, would produce even more graphic effects. She wasn't showing up for work with her nipples threatening to poke through bra and blouse.

That didn't stop said nipples from sitting up and taking notice, however, when Jack contacted her just after nine-thirty.

"How are you doing, sleepyhead?"

"Better this morning than last night." Jamming the phone between her chin and shoulder, she initialed the final seating plan and handed it to Kallie to add table numbers to name tags. "Sorry I zonked out on you."

"No problem. The duchess didn't want to leave you, so we ordered in."

"Corned beef on rye from Osterman's, right?"

"How did you know?"

"That's what we usually order in."

"We had a nice, long talk while we ate, by the way."

"Uh-oh! Did she leave any stones from my misspent youth unturned?"

"One or two. She said you'll have to turn over the rest yourself. She also said she was meeting with her opera club this evening. So that leaves just us. We can do a make-up dinner. Unless you have to work..."

He'd left her an easy out. It said much for Gina's state of mind that she didn't even consider taking it.

"I'm doing the party kickoff but Samuel's taking cleanup. I should be done here by three."

"I'll pick you up then."

"Kind of early for dinner," she commented.

"We'll find something to do."

His breezy confidence took a hit when she slid into the cab he drove up in. Groaning, she let her purpled head drop onto the seat back.

"Next time I tell you I'm helping with a birthday party for a slew of eight- and nine-year-olds, be kind. Just shoot me right between the eyes."

"That bad, huh?"

"Worse."

"Guess that means you're not up for a stroll down Fifth Avenue."

"Do I look like I'm up for a stroll?"

"Well..."

She angled her head and studied him through a thick screen of purple-tipped lashes. "You, bastard that you are, appear relaxed and refreshed and disgustingly up for anything."

Jack laughed and decided not to bore her with the details of his day, which had kicked off at 4:32 a.m. with a call from the State Department's twenty-four-hour crisis monitoring desk. They reported that an angry crowd had gathered at the U.S. Embassy in Islamabad, and a debate was raging within the department over whether to reinforce the marine guard by flying in a fleet antiterrorist security team. Thankfully, the crowd dispersed with no shots fired and no FAST team required, but Jack had spent the rest of the morning and early afternoon reading the message traffic and analyzing the flash points that had precipitated the seemingly spontaneous mob.

Although the crisis had been averted, Jack knew he should have jumped a shuttle and flown back to D.C. His decision to remain in New York another night had surprised him almost as it had his chief of staff, Dale Vickers.

Jack had first met Dale at Harvard, when they both were enrolled in the Kennedy School of Government. Like Jack, Dale had also gone into the Foreign Service and had spent almost a decade in the field as a Foreign Service Officer until increasingly severe bouts of asthma chained him to a desk at State Department headquarters. *Chained* being the operative word. Unmarried and fiercely dedicated, Vickers spent fourteen to sixteen hours a day, every day, at his desk.

Jack appreciated his second-in-command's devotion. He didn't appreciate the disdain that crept into Vickers's voice after learning his boss intended to stay another night in New York.

"We've kept your relationship with Ms. St. Sebastian out of the press so far, Ambassador. I'm not sure how much longer we can continue to do so."

"Don't worry about it. I don't."

"Easy for you to say," Dale sniffed, displaying the prissy side he didn't even suspect he possessed. "Media relations is my job."

"I repeat, don't worry about it. If and when the story breaks, Ms. St. Sebastian and I will handle it."

That was met with a short, charged silence. Jack had worked with Vickers long enough now to know there was more to come. It came slowly, with seeming reluctance.

"You might want to discuss the slant we should give Ms. Sebastian's pregnancy with your father, Ambassador. He expressed some rather strong views on the matter when he called here and I told him you were in New York."

"First," Jack said coldly, "I don't want you discussing my personal affairs with anyone, including my father. Second, there is no slant. Gina St. Sebastian is pregnant with my child. What happens next is our business. Not the media's. Not the State Department's. Not my father's. Not yours. Got that?"

"Yes, sir."

"Good. I'll let you know when I book the return shuttle to D.C."

Fragments of that conversation played in Jack's mind now as he studied the purple-tipped lashes framing Gina's eyes. When his gaze drifted from those purple tips to her hair, he found himself repressing an inner qualm at the prospect of bumping into some member of the paparazzi. Jack could only imagine his father's reaction to seeing Gina splashed across the tabloids in her manga persona.

John Harris II still mourned Catherine's death but in recent years he'd turned his energy to finding a suitable replacement. Preferably someone with his daughter-in-law's family wealth and political connections. He would accept an outsider if pushed to the edge. But Gina...?

"What are you thinking?" she asked, yanking Jack back to the present.

Everything fell away except the woman next to him. He relaxed into a lazy sprawl, his thighs and hips matched with hers. "I'm thinking I skipped lunch. How about you? Did you scarf down whatever you ordered up for that slew of eight-and nine-year-olds?"

"Puh-leez." Her shoulders quivered in an exaggerated shudder. "My system can only take so much sugar."

Her system, and her baby.

Only now did Gina appreciate the 180-degree turn her diet had taken. She'd cut out all forms of alcohol the moment she'd suspected she was pregnant. After her initial appointment with Dr. Martinson, she'd also cut out caffeine and started tossing down neonatal vitamins brimming with iron and folic acid. She hadn't experienced any middle-of-the-night cravings yet but suddenly, inexplicably, she had to have a foot-long smothered in sauerkraut.

"How does a picnic sound?" she asked. "One of my favorite street vendors works a corner close to Bryant Park. We could grab a couple of fat, juicy hot dogs and do some serious people watching."

"I'm game."

Bryant Park encapsulated everything Gina loved about New York. Located between 5th and 6th Avenues and bounded on the eastern side by the New York Public Library, it formed an island of leafy green amid an ocean of skyscrapers. On weekdays office workers crowded the park's benches or stretched out on the lawn during their lunch hours. If they had the time and the ambition, they could also sign up for a Ping-Pong game or backgammon or a chess match. Out-of-towners, too, were drawn to the park's gaily painted carousel, the free concerts, the movies under the stars and, glory of glory, the superclean public restrooms. Chattering in a dozen different languages, tourists wandered the glassed-in kiosks or collapsed at tables in the outdoor restaurant to take a breather from determined sightseeing.

This late in the afternoon Gina and Jack could have snagged a table at the Bryant Park Grill or the more informal café. She was a woman on a mission, however. Leaning forward, she instructed the cab driver to cruise a little way past the park and kept her eyes peeled for an aluminum-sided cart topped by a bright yellow umbrella.

"There he is. Pull over."

Mere moments later she and Jack carried their soft drinks and foil-wrapped treasures into the park. Gina had ordered hers doused with a double helping of sauerkraut. Jack had gone the more conservative mustard-and-relish route. The scent had her salivating until they snagged an empty bench.

"Oh, God," Gina moaned after the first bite. "This is almost better than sex."

Jack cocked a brow and paused with his dog halfway to his mouth.

"I said 'almost.'"

If she'd had a grain of common sense, she would have left it there. But, no. Like an idiot, she had to let her mouth run away with her.

"Not that I've had anything to compare it to in the past couple of months," she mumbled around another bite.

"We can fix that."

Jack tossed the words out so easily, so casually, that it took a second or two for his meaning to register. When it did, Gina choked on the bite she'd just taken.

"I've been doing my assigned reading," he said as he gave her a helpful thump on the back. "*A Father's Guide to Pregnancy* says it's not uncommon for a woman's libido to shoot into the stratosphere, particularly during the first trimester. It also warned me not to feel inadequate if I don't satisfy what could turn into an insatiable appetite."

He didn't look all that concerned about the possibility. Just the opposite. The wicked glint in his brown eyes positively challenged Gina to give him a shot.

She wanted to. God, she wanted to! Just looking at his beautiful mouth with a tiny smear of mustard at the corner made her ache to lean in and lick it off. She had to gulp down a long slug of Sprite Zero to keep from giving in to the impulse.

"I appreciate the offer," she said with what she hoped was a cheeky smile. "I'll keep it in mind if I run out of batteries."

"Ouch."

He put on a good show of being wounded, but when the laughter faded from his eyes she saw the utter seriousness in their depths.

"I know you want a relationship based on more than just sex, Gina. I'm hoping we can build that partnership."

"I know you are."

"We're not there yet," he admitted with brutal honesty, "but we're getting closer."

Ha! He could speak for himself. She was standing right on the edge, and every moment she spent with this man cut more ground from under her feet. All it would take was one gentle push. She'd fall for him so fast he wouldn't know what hit him.

Unfortunately, everything else would fall with her. Her fledgling career. Her self-respect. Her pride. She was just starting to feel good about herself. Just beginning to believe she could be the responsible parent she wanted so desperately to become.

Oh, hell! Who was she kidding? She would dump it all in a heartbeat if Jack loved her.

But he didn't. Yet.

So she wouldn't. Yet.

Consoled by the possibilities embedded in that little three-letter word, she tried to keep it light. "Too bad this isn't horseshoes. We would score points for close. Let's just…let's just press on the way we have been and hope for a ringer."

Stupid metaphor but the best she could come up with at the moment. Jack looked as if he wanted to say more but let it go. They sat knee-to-knee in the sunshine and devoured their hot dogs. Or more correctly, Gina devoured hers. Jack had set his on the unwrapped foil to pop the top of his soft drink. He took a long swig and rested the can on his knee while he watched two twentysomethings duking it out at the Ping-Pong table. The crack of their paddles smacking the ball formed a sharp counterpoint to the carousel's merry tune and the traffic humming along 6th Avenue.

"This is nice," Jack commented. "I don't get to just sit and bask in the sun much anymore."

"Uh-huh."

He stretched an arm along the back of the bench. "Did you come here often when you were growing up?"

"Yep."

Her abbreviated responses brought his gaze swinging back to her just in time to catch the covetous looks she was giving his not-yet-consumed weenie. She didn't bother to plead innocence.

"Are you going to eat that?"

"It's all yours. Or shall I go get you another one doused with sauerkraut?"

She gave the question serious consideration before shaking her head. "This will do me."

The remains disappeared in two bites. Semi-satisfied, Gina leaned against the bench and stretched out her legs. His arm formed a comfortable backrest as she replied to his earlier query.

"I couldn't even hazard a guess how many times I've been to Bryant Park. Maria used to bring Sarah and me to ride the merry-go-round or ice-skate on Citi Pond. Grandmama would come, too, after shopping on Fifth Avenue or to wait while we girls hit the library."

"Your grandmother's a remarkable woman."

"Yes, she is."

"Are she and Sarah the only family you have left?"

"There are some distant cousins in Slovenia. Or maybe it's Hungary. Or Austria. To tell the truth, I'm not real sure which countries got which parts of Karlenburgh after the duchy was broken up."

"Has Charlotte ever gone back?"

"No, never. She doesn't say so, but I know it would be too painful for her."

"What about you?" He toyed with the ends of her hair, still straight, still purple. "Have you ever visited your ancestral lands?"

"Not yet. I'd like to, though. One of these days…"

She could sit here for hours, she thought lazily. Listening to the crack of the Ping-Pong paddles, watching the tourists nose through the kiosks, nestling her head on the solid heat of Jack's arm. She didn't realize her eyelids had fluttered shut until his amused voice drifted down to her.

"You going to sleep on me again?"

"Maybe."

"Before you zone out completely, let's set a date for you to make a visit to D.C. My folks are anxious to meet you."

That woke her up. The little she knew about Jack's family suggested they probably wouldn't welcome her with open arms. Not his father, anyway. But she'd promised. Digging into her purse, she checked the calendar on her iPhone.

"I can't do next weekend. Does the second weekend in June work for you?"

"I'll make it work. Go back to sleep now."

Seven

Gina ended up making the jaunt down to Washington a week earlier than expected. Her change of plans kicked off the following Thursday morning with a summons to Samuel's office, where her boss relayed a request from the head office.

"Nicole just called. She needs you to fly down to D.C. You've got a reservation on the two-twenty shuttle."

"Today?"

"Yes, today. TTG's coordinating a black-tie reception and private, prerelease movie showing for two hundred tomorrow evening."

"And Elaine needs help?"

Elaine Patterson managed the TTG's Washington venue. Gina had met the trim, elegant brunette once when she'd flown to New York for a meeting with Samuel.

"Elaine's father had a heart attack. She's in Oregon and her assistant just checked into the ICU with a bad case of pancreatitis, whatever the hell that is. The rest of the staff is too junior to handle a function this large. Nicole wants you to take charge."

Samuel shoved a folder across his desk. "Here are faxed copies of the timetable, menu, floor plans, proposed setup, list of suppliers and contact phone numbers. I had them also email copies so you'll be able pull 'em on your iPad in case you need to make changes on the fly. You can stay in the venue's bridal suite. It's fully equipped and stocked."

"But…"

"I'll cover the consult you have scheduled for this afternoon."

"What about the Hanrahan retirement party on Saturday? I'm lead on that."

"I scanned the file. From the looks of the checklist, you've got everything in good shape. I'll take care of the last few prep tasks and get Kallie to pull floor duty with me."

Gina thought fast. She'd have to call Maria to see whether she could come in Sunday and check on Grandmama. If she could, Gina might extend her stay in D.C. for another day, possibly two.

The prospect of spending those days with Jack made her heart do its own version of a happy dance. She could feel it skittering and skipping as she let drop a casual comment.

"My calendar's pretty light on Monday. I don't have anything scheduled that can't be moved. I may take some comp time and stay over in Washington."

"Fine by me." He flapped a hand. "Just get your butt in gear."

She got her butt in gear!

A call made while the cab whisked her uptown confirmed Maria would be happy to check on *la duquesa* Sunday afternoon. When Gina dashed in and explained the arrangement, Grandmama issued an indignant protest.

"I'm neither crippled nor incapacitated, Eugenia. There's no need for Maria to come all the way in to check on me."

"She's not doing it for you, she's doing it for me."

"Really," the duchess huffed. "It's not necessary."

"I know. Just humor me, okay? The thing is, I may stay

over in D.C. a day or two. Jack wants me to meet his parents. If they're available, I'll try to cram in a visit."

"Indeed?"

That bit of news stifled any further objections from her grandmother. Her faded blue eyes lingered thoughtfully on Gina's face for a moment before she commented dryly, "How fortunate the purple washed out of your hair."

Extremely fortunate, Gina thought as she rushed into the bedroom. She hurried out again after stuffing toiletries, a sequined tuxedo jacket she appropriated from Sarah's closet, black satin palazzo pants and some casual clothes into a weekender.

"I'll call you," she promised, dropping a kiss on her grandmother's cheek.

She hit the lobby and had Jerome flag her a cab to La-Guardia. Collapsing in the backseat, she fished out her phone and called Jack. His cell phone went to voice mail, so she left a quick message. For added insurance, she called his office and got shuffled to his chief of staff. Her nose wrinkling, she asked Vickers to advise his boss that she was flying down to Washington.

"Certainly, Ms. St. Sebastian."

He sounded a little more polite but about a mile and half from friendly. Gina wanted to ask him what his problem was but she suspected she already knew the answer.

She made her flight with all of five minutes to spare. When the adrenaline rush subsided and the plane lifted off, she rested her head against the seat back. The next thing she knew, the flight attendant was announcing their imminent arrival at Ronald Reagan National Airport. Gina blinked the sleep out of her eyes and enjoyed her view through the window of the capital's marble monuments.

The short nap left her energized and eager to plunge into the task ahead. She wheeled her weekender through the airport with a spring in her step and exited into a beautiful June day only slightly tainted by the exhaust pluming out of the cars and taxis and shuttles lined up outside the terminal.

Gina didn't have to dig deep to know why she was so jazzed. The idea that Nicole trusted her enough to step in at the last minute and take charge of a major event had given her self-confidence a shot in the arm.

Then there was the chance she might cram in some time with Jack. That possibility prodded her to whip out her cell phone and take it off airplane mode. The flashing icon indicating a text from Jack put a smile on her lips.

Just heard you're en route to D.C. Call when you arrive.

She crossed the street to the parking garage and aimed for the rental car area while she tried his private number. He answered on the second ring.

"You're here?"

The sound of his voice moved the smile from her lips to her heart. "I'm here. Just got in."

"This is a surprise. What brought you to D.C.?"

For once she managed to catch herself before blurting out the truth. He didn't need to know the possibility of spending some time with him was one of the reasons—the main reason—she'd jumped at this job.

"I'm a last-minute stand-in to coordinate an event tomorrow night."

"Which event?"

"A fancy-schmancy cocktail party and prerelease showing of the new action flick starring Dirk West."

Gina wasn't a real fan of the shoot-'em-up, blow-'em-up type movies West had been making for several decades but she knew every new release pulled in millions.

"The event's being hosted by Global Protective Services," she told Jack. "According to their company propaganda, they're—"

"One of the largest private security contractors in the

world," he interrupted. "They have more boots on the ground in Afghanistan right now than the U.S. military. Rumor is they put up most of the money for the movie. Probably because the script makes a very unsubtle case for decreasing the size of our standing armies and increasing the use of private mercenaries."

Holding the phone to her ear, Gina skimmed the Hertz reservation board to find the parking slot for the car Kallie said would be waiting for her.

"Sounds like this shindig would be right up your alley," she commented as she started down the long row of parked vehicles, "but I didn't see your name on the attendee list."

"That's because I declined the invitation. I might have to rethink that, though, if you're going to be working the event."

"Oh, sure," she said with a laugh. "Screw up the head count, why don't you?"

"I won't eat much," he promised solemnly.

"Well…" She found her car and tossed her briefcase onto the passenger seat. "I guess I can add you to the list."

"That takes care of tomorrow, then. What's on your agenda tonight?"

"I've got what's left of the TTG crew standing by." She slid into the driver's seat but waited to key the ignition. "We're going to go over the final task list and walk through the venue."

"How long will that take?"

"I have no idea."

She hesitated a moment before laying the possibility of an extended stay on him. Would she really be up to meeting his parents after working this event? Yes, dammit, she would.

"I told Samuel I might take a couple extra days in D.C. If it fits with your schedule and theirs, maybe we could work in a visit with your folks."

"We'll make it fit. I'll give them a call and arrange a time. Where are you staying?"

"At TTG's L'Enfant Plaza venue. We have a full bridal suite on the top floor."

"A bridal suite, huh?" His voice dropped to a slow, warm caress. "Want some company?"

God, yes! She gripped the phone, almost groaning at the idea of rolling around with Jack on the Tremayne Group's signature chocolate-brown sheets. Instant, erotic images of their bodies all sweaty and naked buzzed in her head like a swarm of pesky flies.

"Thanks for the offer," she said, making a valiant attempt to bat away the flies, "but I'd better pass."

Somewhat to her disappointment Jack didn't press the issue.

"You sure you can't sneak away for an hour or two and have dinner with me?" he asked instead.

Desire waged a fierce, no-holds-barred, free-for-all with duty. The old, fun-loving Gina would have yielded without a second thought. The new, still fun-loving but not quite as irresponsible Gina sighed.

"Sorry, Jack. I really need to spend this afternoon and evening prepping for the event."

He conceded with his usual easy charm. "I understand. I'll see you tomorrow."

Jack disconnected, swung his desk chair around and settled his gaze on the slice of Washington visible from his third-floor office. Since he held ambassadorial rank, he rated a full suite at the State Department's main headquarters on C Street.

The thirties-era building was originally designed to house the War Department, but the war planners outgrew it before it was completed. When they moved into the Pentagon in 1941, State inherited this massive structure constructed of buff-colored sandstone. It and its more modern annexes were located in the area of D.C. known as Foggy Bottom, so named because this section of the city was once a dismal, gray-misted swamp. Many of the talking heads who filled today's airwaves with their dubious wisdom liked to suggest the decisions coming out State were still pretty foggy and swampy.

The windows in Jack's office gave a narrow view down 21st Street to the National Mall, with the Lincoln Memorial at one end and the Washington Monument at the other. On good days he could almost catch the glitter of sunlight bouncing off the reflecting pool. The view didn't hold a particle of interest at the moment.

All his thoughts centered on Gina. The news that she was coming to Washington had proved the only bright spark in an otherwise grim morning spent reviewing casualty reports and incident analyses from twenty years of attacks on U.S. diplomatic outposts. Just the sound of her voice and merry laugh lightened his mood.

Thoughtfully, Jack tipped back his chair. Simply knowing that Gina was here, on his home turf, sparked a need that dug into him with sharp, fierce claws. Her image was etched in his mind. Those bright blue eyes. That luscious mouth. The tumble of white-blond curls.

The image shifted, and he pictured her manga'ed mane. God, what if she was still sporting that look? He could only imagine his father's reaction. The thought produced a wry grin as he swung his chair around and dialed his parents' number.

Jack brought his tux in to the office with him the next morning and changed before leaving work that evening. Anxious to see Gina, he arrived at L'Enfant Plaza early.

The plaza was named for Pierre Charles L'Enfant, the French-born architect recruited by General LaFayette to serve as an engineer with George Washington's Continental army. A long rectangle, the plaza was bordered on three sides by an amalgamation of office buildings, government agencies, retail shops and hotels. One of I. M. Pei's iconic glass pyramids dominated the center. A sister to the pyramid in front of the Louvre, it rose from a lower level with gleaming majesty.

The spot was a good choice for evening events. Foot and vehicle traffic died out when the surrounding offices emptied, leaving plenty of underground parking for guests. Or they could hop off the Metro and let the escalators whisk them up to the plaza. Jack had opted for plan B and emerged from the Metro's subterranean levels into a balmy June evening. Tiny white lights illuminated the trees lining two sides of the plaza. Centered between those sparkling rows, the lighted pyramid formed a dramatic backdrop for lavishly filled buffet tables and strategically placed carving stations.

Two dozen or so other early arrivals grazed the tables or clumped together in small groups with drinks in hand. Jack took advantage of the sparse crowd and lack of lines to hit one of the S-shaped bars set up close to the pyramid. He kept an eye out for Gina as he crossed the plaza but didn't spot either her blond curls or a waterfall of purple. Nor did he find a bartender behind the ebony-and-glass counter. He angled around to check the other bars and saw an attendant at only one. Flipping and tipping bottles, the harried attendant splashed booze and mixers into an array of glasses and shoved them at the tuxedoed waitstaff standing in line at his station.

The fact that three of the four bars weren't ready for action surprised Jack until he spotted Gina, a male in a white shirt and black vest and a plump female with a radio clipped to her waist hurrying out onto the plaza. The man peeled off in the direction of one unattended bar, the woman aimed for another. Gina herself edged behind the ebony S where Jack stood.

"Shorthanded?" he asked as she whipped bottles of champagne out of a refrigerated case and lined them up on the bar.

She rolled her eyes. "Just a tad."

When she started to attack the foil caps, he moved behind the bar to help. She flashed him a grateful look and set him to popping corks while she extracted champagne flutes from a rack beneath the counter.

"I should be in the media center making a last check of the seating," she told him, "but I've been on the phone with the bar subcontractor for twenty friggin' minutes. He's supposed to be sending replacements for their no-shows. You can bet this is the last time the jerk will do business with TTG."

The fire in her eyes told Jack that was a safe bet.

"Keep your fingers crossed the replacements get here before the real hordes descend," she muttered as she began pouring champagne into the tall crystal flutes.

He nodded toward the crowd emerging from the bank of elevators. "I think they're descending."

"Crap." She slapped the filled flutes onto a tray and hooked a finger at one of the waitstaff. "You're over twenty-one, right?"

"Right."

"Take this and start circulating."

"I'm a food server," he protested.

"Not for the next half hour, you're not. Take it! I've cleared it with your boss."

Champagne sloshing, she thrust the tray at him and reached under the counter for more flutes.

"Good thing the subcontractors aren't union," she said fervently. "My ass would be grass if I got TTG crosswise of the culinary workers and bartenders local."

Jack eyed the racks of glasses, bottles and nozzles behind the counter. Everything appeared to be clearly labeled.

"I've fixed a few martinis and Manhattans in my time. I'll pull bar duty until your replacements arrive. You go do your thing in the media center."

"No way! I can't let you sling booze. You're a guest."

"I won't tell if you don't. Go. I've got this."

Jack had no trouble interpreting the emotions that flashed across her expressive face. He could tell the instant the idea of John Harris Mason III dishing up drinks at Global Protective Service's big bash struck her as too irresistible to pass up.

"All right," she conceded, laughter sparkling in her eyes. "But let's hope Nicole doesn't hear about this. My ass won't just be grass. It'll be mowed and mulched."

"And it's such a nice ass." He couldn't help it. He had to reach behind her and caress the body part under discussion. "Trust me, sweetheart, I won't let anyone mow or mulch it."

She backed away and tried to look stern, but the light still danced in her eyes. "I can't believe you just did that."

Jack couldn't believe it, either. He'd do it again, though, in a heartbeat. Or better yet, drag her upstairs to that bridal suite she'd mentioned and caress a whole lot more than her ass. Sanity intruded in the form of the gray-haired senior senator from Virginia.

Thomas Dillon broke away from the group he was with and strolled over to the bar. "Jack?"

The senator looked from him to Gina and back again. Clearly he didn't understand what an ambassador-at-large was doing behind the drinks counter, but he contained his confusion behind a broad smile.

"I thought I recognized you, son. How's your father?"

"He's still kicking butt and taking names, Senator. What can I get you to drink?"

"Pardon me?"

"I'm pulling special duty tonight. What would you like?"

Despite the near-disastrous start, the remainder of the event went off without a hitch. Most of the invitees were jaded Washingtonians who had attended too many black-tie functions to do more than guzzle down the free booze and food, but Jack heard more than one guest comment on the quality of both.

His replacement arrived before he'd had to mix up more than a dozen drinks. He surrendered his post with some reluctance and mingled with the other guests. Jaded they might be, but the arrival of the movie's star started a low buzz. Gina had returned to the plaza and stood next to Jack while Dirk West graciously made the rounds.

"Wow," she murmured, eyeing his shaved head and six-feet-plus of tuxedo-covered muscle. "He looks tougher in real life than he does on the screen."

Tough, and extremely savvy. West worked the crowd like a pro and seemed to sense instinctively the real power brokers and potential backers. He might have been aided in that by the CEO of Global Protective Services, who stuck to the star's side like a barnacle and made a point of steering him over to Jack.

"This is Ambassador John Harris Mason," he said by way of introduction. "He's the man who faced down a cell of armed insurgents in Mali a few years ago."

"I read about that." West crunched Jack's hand in his. "Sounded like a pretty hairy situation. I might have to send a script writer to ferret out the details that didn't get into print."

Jack could have told him not to bother since most of the details were still classified but West had already turned his attention to Gina.

"And who's this?"

The bronze-edged name tag pinned to her lapel should have given him a clue. He ignored it, concentrating all his star power on her face.

"Gina St. Sebastian." She held out her hand and had it enfolded. "I'm with the Tremayne Group. We're coordinating this event."

West's appreciative gaze made a quick trip south, edged back up. "You ever considered taking a shot at acting, Ms. St. Sebastian?"

"I've toyed with the idea once or twice."

"If you decide to do more than toy, you give me a call."

Global's CEO was more interested in Jack's connections

at the State Department than the acting aspirations of the hired hands.

"I hear you've got a meeting with the Senate Intelligence Committee next week regarding embassy security, Ambassador. I've got some ideas in that regard."

"I'm sure you do."

"I'd like to discuss them with you. I'll have my people call and set up an appointment."

His mission accomplished, he steered West to the next group. Jack waited until they were out of earshot to fill Gina in on his conversation with his parents.

"I got ahold of my folks. They're anxious to meet you, but mother's chairing a charity auction tomorrow evening so I told them we'd drive down for Sunday brunch."

"Sunday brunch works for me."

"Good. That leaves tomorrow for just you and me."

She started to comment, but spotted the plump brunette with the radio clipped to her waist signaling from across the plaza.

"Gotta go. It's almost showtime."

She turned, spun back and flashed one of her megawatt smiles.

"Thanks for helping out earlier. Remind me to pay you for services rendered."

"I will," he murmured to her retreating back. "I most certainly will."

Jack carried fantasies of the various forms that payment might take with him into the plush media hall. They teased his thoughts all through Dirk West's explosive attempts to single-handedly save the world from evil. But not even his wildest imaginings could compete with reality when a tired but triumphant Gina invited him up to the bridal suite several hours later.

Eight

Gina had tried to convince Jack he didn't need to hang around while she signed off on the final tally sheets and supervised the breakdown. She'd honestly tried. Yet she couldn't suppress a little thrill of pleasure when he insisted on waiting for her to finish up.

So she'd extended the invitation to join her upstairs. When they entered the lushly appointed suite, though, all she wanted to do was plop down on the sofa, kick off her shoes and plunk her feet on the coffee table. Which was exactly what she did. And all she would have done if Jack hadn't plopped down beside her!

"That's some view," he commented lazily, his eyes on the dramatic vista of the floodlit capital dome framed by the suite's windows.

"Mmm."

She only half heard him. Her mind was still decompressing after the pressure-packed night. He responded by tugging loose his bow tie and popping the top button of his dress shirt before patting his lap.

"Here."

She blinked, suddenly very much in the present. She didn't trust either his simple gesture or her body's instant response to it. He read the sudden wariness in her face and patted his thighs again.

"I've been told I give a pretty good foot massage. Swing your feet up and see if you agree."

Oooooh, yeah! Gina most definitely agreed. Ten seconds after he went to work on her toes and arch, she was approaching nirvana. Groaning with pleasure, she wedged deeper into the corner of the sofa.

"If you ever decide to give up ambassadoring, you could make a bundle plying the foot trade."

"I'll keep that in mind."

Curious, she eyed him through the screen of her lashes. "What *are* you going to do when you give up ambassadoring?"

"Good question."

His clever, clever fingers worked magic on the balls of her right foot before moving to the left.

"What about those PACs I read about?" she asked. "The ones that think you've got the makings of a future president?"

"*Future* being the operative word. There are a few steps I'd have to take in between."

"Such as?"

"Running for public office, to start with. I've been just a career bureaucrat up to this point."

"Su-u-ure you have. I wonder how many career bureaucrats go toe-to-toe with armed terrorists."

"Too many, unfortunately. Still, elected office is almost a required stepping stone to anything higher. Except for the war heroes like Washington and Eisenhower, almost all of our presidents served as either governors or members of Congress."

"So run for governor. Or Congress. You'd make a great senator or representative. More to the point, someone's got to get in there and straighten out that mess."

"Am I hearing right?" Ginning, he pulled on her toes.

"This enthusiastic endorsement can't be coming from the same woman who's called me obnoxious and uptight and a few other adjectives I won't repeat."

"You are obnoxious and uptight at times. Other times..." She circled a hand in the air, trying to pluck out one or two of his less irritating traits. "Other times you surprise me, Mr. Ambassador. Like tonight, for instance, when you got behind the bar. You went above and beyond the call of duty there."

"I'm a man of many talents," he said smugly. "And that reminds me. I was promised payment for services rendered."

"So you were. Have you given any thought to what form that payment should take?"

"Oh, sweetheart, I haven't thought of anything else all evening."

Red flags went up instantly. Gina knew she was playing with fire. Knew the last thing she should do was slide her feet off his lap and curl them under her, rising to her knees in the process.

All she had to do was look at him. The tanned skin, the white squint lines at the corners of his eyes, the square chin and the strong, sure column of his throat. Like a vampire hit with a ravenous hunger, her weariness disappeared in a red flash. She had to taste him. Had to lean forward and press her mouth to the warm skin in the V of his shirt. Had to nip the tendons in his neck, the prickly underside of his chin, the corner of his mouth.

And of course, he had to turn his head and capture her lips with his. There was nothing gentle about the kiss. Nothing tentative. It went from zero to white-hot in less than a heartbeat. Mouths, teeth, tongues all engaged. Hips shifted. Hands fumbled. Muscles went tight.

Jack moved then, tipping her back onto the cushions. He came down with her, one leg between hers, one hand brushing her hair off her face. Careful not to put all his weight on her middle but taut and coiled and hungry.

She could feel him get hard against her hip. The sensation shot a hot, fierce rush through her veins. Shoving his jacket lapels aside, she tugged his starched shirt free of the satin cummerbund and tore at the buttons. When she got to the shoulder muscle underneath, she ran her palm over the smooth curve, then felt it bunch under her fingers as Jack's hand went to her waist. The two buttons on her borrowed sequin jacket proved a flimsy barrier. Jack peeled back the lapels and came to a dead stop. Every muscle and tendon in his body seemed to freeze.

"God."

It was half prayer, half groan. His brown eyes hot with desire, he brushed a finger along the lace trimming her demi-bra.

"Good thing I didn't know this was all you had on under those sequins. It was hard enough making it through the movie."

Gina tucked her chin and surveyed her chest with something less than enthusiasm. The underwired half cup of black silk and lace mounded her breasts almost obscenely.

"I've gone up another whole size," she muttered in disgust. "I had to buy all new bras."

Jack picked up on her tone and wisely didn't comment. Good thing, because she probably wouldn't have heard him. All it took was one brush of his thumb over her sensitized nipple and she was arching her back. And when he tugged down the lace and caught the aching tip between his teeth, every part of her screamed with instant, erotic delight.

She arched again, and he took what she offered. His hands and mouth and tongue drove her higher and higher. The knee he wedged between her thighs and pressed against her center almost sent her over the edge.

"Wait!" Gasping, she wiggled away from the tormenting knee. "Wait, Jack!"

He raised his head, a shudder rippling across his face. Disgust followed a moment later.

"Sorry. That was a little more than you probably expected to pay for my bartending services."

When he started to sit up, Gina grabbed his lapels and kept him in place. "Hold on, Ambassador. That little tussle doesn't even constitute minimum wage. I just...I just thought we should shed a few more layers."

Jack stared down at her, eyes narrowed. He knew as well as she did they wouldn't stop at a few layers. He was damned if he'd give her a chance to change her mind, though. Getting the stubborn Gina St. Sebastian into bed ranked almost as high up there as getting her to the altar.

"Shedding is good," he said with a crooked grin that masked his sudden iron determination. "I'll start."

His tux jacket hit the floor. The cummerbund and shirt followed a moment later. He held out a hand and helped her to her feet, taking intense satisfaction from the play of her greedy hands over his bare chest.

Once he'd disposed of the sequined jacket, he helped her shimmy out of her black satin pants. His self-control took a severe hit when he got a look at the hipsters that matched her black lace bra. They dipped to a low V on her still-flat belly and barely covered her bottom cheeks.

He cupped his hand over those sweet, tantalizing curves and brought her against him. He saw her eyes flare when she felt him against her hip, rock-hard and rampant. Her head tipped. Red singed her cheeks.

"Okay," she exhaled in a low, choked voice. "I really, really need to make payment in full. But the two of us going to bed together doesn't change anything."

The hell it didn't.

Jack kept that thought to himself as he scooped her into his arms and strode toward the bedroom.

The Tremayne Group had done their guest suite up right. A king-size bed sat on a raised dais, its chocolate-brown comforter draping almost to the floor. Mounds of brown, aqua and silver-trimmed pillows piled high against the padded headboard. Floor lamps gave the corners of the room a subdued glow, while a crystal dish filled with creamy wax pebbles emitted a faint scent of vanilla.

Jack absorbed the details with the situational awareness that was as much instinct as training. That alertness had kept him alive in Mali and served him well in so many other tense situations. But it shut down completely when he stretched Gina out on the soft, fluffy ocean of brown. Her hair spilled across the comforter in a river of pale gold. Her eyes were hot blue and heavy. Her long, lush body drove every thought from his mind but one.

Aching for her, he yanked down the zipper of his pleated black slacks. He discarded them along with his socks and jockey shorts, joined her on the bed and ran his hand over the flat planes of her belly.

"You are so incredibly gorgeous."

Her stomach hollowed under his palm even as she gave a breathless, delighted chuckle.

"Flattery will get you everywhere, Ambassador."

He slid his hand under the lace panties and found the wet heat at her center. Her head went back. Her lips parted. As Jack leaned down to cover her mouth with his, he realized he didn't want to be anywhere but here, with this woman, tasting her, touching her, loving her.

He was rougher than he'd intended when he stripped off her underwear. More urgent than he ever remembered being when he pried her knees apart and positioned himself between her thighs. And when she hooked her calves around his and canted her hips to fit his, he lost it.

Driven by a need that would shock the hell out of him when he analyzed it later, he thrust into her. It was a primal urge. An atavistic instinct to claim his mate. To brand her as his. Leave his scent on her. Plant his seed in her belly.

Except he'd already done that.

The thought fought its way through the red haze of Jack's

mind. He went stiff, his member buried in the hot satin that was Gina. Hell! What kind of an animal was he? He levered up on his elbows, blinking away the sexual mists that clouded his vision. When they cleared, he saw Gina glaring up at him.

"What?" she demanded.

"I didn't mean to be so rough. The baby…"

"Is fine! I, however, am not."

To emphasize her point, she hooked her calves higher on his and clenched her vaginal muscles. Jack got the message. Hard not to, since it damned near blew off the top of his head. He slammed his hips into hers again. And again. And again.

They could only spend so many hours in bed. Theoretically, anyway. Jack would have kept Gina there all day Saturday but even he had to come up for air. Since they wouldn't drive down to his parents' house in Richmond until the following day, he offered to show her his favorite spots in D.C. She approved the proposed agenda, with two quick amendments.

"I'd like to see where you live. And where you work."

Jack had no problem with either. Gina had packed clothes for the weekend but he had to get rid of his tux before he could appear in public again. That naturally lent itself to a first stop at his town house.

It was classic Georgetown. Three narrow stories, all brick. Black shutters. Solid brass door knocker in the shape of a horse's head. Gina's nose wrinkled when Jack mentioned that the detached garage at the back had once been slave quarters, but she was gracious enough to acknowledge he'd taken occupancy of the ivy-covered premises long after those tragic days.

The framed photo of Catherine still occupying a place of honor on the entryway table gave her pause, though. Almost as much as it gave Jack. He stood next to Gina as she gazed at the black-and-white photo.

It was one of his favorite shots. He'd taken it after losing yet another tennis match to his hypercompetitive wife. She laughed at the camera, her racquet resting on her shoulder. Her dark hair was caught back in a ponytail. A sweatband circled her forehead. All her energy, all her pulsing life, shone in her eyes.

"I bet she kept you jumping," Gina murmured.

"She did."

Almost too much.

The thought darted into Jack's mind before he could block it. That energy, that formidable legal mind, the all-consuming passion for politics. He'd had to march double time to keep up with her. More than once he'd wished she'd just relax and drift for a while.

The thought generated a sharp jab of guilt. Jack had to work to shrug it off as he left Gina to explore the town house's main floor and went upstairs to change. He came back down a half hour later, showered and shaved and feeling comfortable in jeans and his favorite University of Virginia crewneck.

"You sure you want to swing by my office? There's not a whole lot to see but we can make a quick visit if you want."

Gina forced a smile. The pictures of his wife scattered around the town house had gotten to her more than she would admit. She'd spotted several shots of Catherine alone. Several more of Catherine with Jack. The perfect marriage of smarts and ambition.

And here Gina was, trying desperately to anchor herself after years of flitting from job to job, man to man. Her life to this point seemed so frivolous, so self-centered. How could Jack have any respect for her?

She buried her crushing doubts behind a bright smile. "I've never been to the State Department. I'd like to see it."

"Okay, but don't say I didn't warn you."

Gina took Jack's disclaimer with a grain of salt. It should have been a teaspoon, she decided when he escorted her through State's echoing marble halls and into his impressive suite of offices.

The first thing she noticed was the view from the windows of the outer office. It cut straight down 21st Street to the Lincoln Memorial Reflecting Pool and presented a narrow, if spectacular, slice of Washington.

The second item that caught her attention was the individual in jeans, a button-down yellow shirt and round eyeglasses hunched over a computer. She shouldn't have been surprised that Jack's people were dedicated enough to come in on weekends. And when he introduced her to his chief of staff, she tried hard to bury her antipathy behind a friendly smile.

"I'm glad to finally meet you, Dale."

That was true enough. She'd been curious about this man. More than curious. She wasn't usually into stereotypes, but her first glimpse of Dale Vickers pegged him immediately as a very short, very insecure male suffering from a rampaging Napoleon complex. He kept his desk between him and his boss. Also between him and Gina. She had to reach across it to shake his hand. He acknowledged her greeting with a condescending nod and turned to his boss.

"I didn't know you were coming in this morning."

What a prick! Gina couldn't see why Jack put up with him until she spotted the framed 4x6 snapshot on the man's workstation. Catherine *and* Jack *and* Dale Vickers with their arms looped over each other's shoulders. All smiling. All wearing crimson sweatshirts emblazoned with the Harvard logo.

Images of Catherine Mason hovered at the back of Gina's mind for the rest of the day. She managed to suppress them while Jack gave her a private tour of the State Department's hallowed halls. Ditto when they took advantage of the glorious June afternoon to stroll the banks of the Potomac and cheer the scullers pushing against the vicious current.

After browsing the upscale shops in Georgetown Mall,

Jack took Gina to his favorite Thai restaurant later that evening. The owner greeted him with a delighted hand pump.

"Mr. Ambassador! Long time since we see you."

"Too long, Mr. Preecha."

The slender Asian whipped around, checked his tables and beamed. "You want by the window, yes? You and...?"

He made a heroic effort to conceal his curiosity when Jack introduced Gina. She felt it, though, and as soon as they were seated and their drink order taken, the question tumbled out.

"Did you and Catherine come here often?"

"Not often. We'd only lived in D.C. four or five months before she died. Do you like shumai? They serve them here with steamed rice and a peanut ginger sauce that'll make you swear you were in Bangkok."

The change of subject was too deliberate to ignore. Gina followed the lead.

"Since I have no idea what shumai are and have never been to Bangkok, I'll take your word on both."

Shumai turned out to be an assortment of steamed dumplings filled with diced pork, chicken or shrimp. She followed Jack's lead and dipped each morsel in ginger or soy sauce before gobbling it down. Between the dumplings, steamed rice, golden fried tofu triangles, some kind of root vegetable Gina couldn't begin to pronounce and endless cups of tea, she rolled out of the restaurant feeling like a python just fed its monthly meal. Too stuffed for any more wandering through Georgetown. Almost too stuffed for sex. When she tried to convince Jack of that sad state of affairs, though, he just laughed and promised to do all the work.

He followed through on his promise. The chocolate-brown sheets were a tangled mess and Gina was boneless with pleasure when he finally collapsed beside her.

For the second night in a row she fell asleep in his arms. And for the second morning in a row, she greeted the day cradled in the same warm cocoon.

She came awake slowly, breathing in Jack's scent, twitching her nose when his springy chest hair tickled her nose. It felt right to cuddle against his side. Safe and warm and right.

Slowly, without Gina willing them, the images she'd glimpsed of Jack's wife yesterday took form and shape in her mind. For an uneasy moment, she almost sensed Catherine's presence. Not hostile, not heartbroken at seeing her husband in bed with another woman, but not real happy, either.

"We'd better get up and get moving."

Jack's voice rumbled up from the chest wall her ear was pressed against. "Sunday brunch is a long-standing family tradition," he warned, stroking her hair with a lazy touch. "Hopefully, it'll just be us and my parents today but you should be prepared for the worst."

"Great! Now he tells me."

She could do this, Gina told herself as she showered and blow-dried her hair and did her makeup. She could run the gauntlet of Jack's family, all of whom had known and no doubt adored his wife. She wasn't looking forward to it, though.

And damned if she couldn't almost hear Catherine snickering in the steamy air of the bathroom.

Nine

Light Sunday–morning traffic was one of the few joys of driving in Washington. Jack's Range Rover whizzed through near deserted streets and crossed the 14th Street Bridge. The Jefferson Memorial rose in graceful symmetry on the D.C. side of the bridge. The gray granite bulk of the Pentagon dominated the Virginia side. From there they shot south on 395.

Once south of the Beltway, though, Jack exited the interstate and opted instead to drive a stretch of the old U.S. Highway 1. Gina understood why when he pulled into the parking lot of the Gas Pump Café just outside Woodbridge.

"We won't sit down for brunch until one or two. And this place," he said with a sweeping gesture toward the tin-roofed cafe, "serves the best biscuits and gravy this side of the Mason-Dixon line."

Gina hid her doubts as she eyed the ramshackle structure. It boasted a rusting, thirties-era gas pump out front. Equally rusty signs covered every square inch of the front of the building. The colorful barrage advertised everything from Nehi grape soda to Red Coon chewing tobacco to Gargoyle motor oil. The scents of sizzling bacon and smoked sausage that emanated from the café, though, banished any doubts the place would live up to Jack's hype.

It didn't occur to Gina that he'd made the stop for her sake until they were seated at one of the wooden picnic tables. He obviously didn't consider the slice of toast and half glass of orange juice she'd downed while getting dressed adequate sustenance for mother and child. She agreed but limited her intake to one biscuit smothered in gravy, two eggs, a slab of sugar-cured ham and another glass of juice. Since it was just a little past nine when they rolled out of the café, Gina felt confident she would be able to do justice to brunch at one or two o'clock.

She also felt a lot more confident about meeting Jack's family. Strapped into the Range Rover's bucket seat, she patted her tummy. "Hope you enjoyed that, baby. I sure did."

Jack followed the gesture and smiled. "Have you started thinking about names?"

She didn't hesitate. "Charlotte, if it's a girl."

"What if it's a boy?"

She slanted him a sideways glance. He'd left his window cracked to allow in the warm June morning. The breeze lifted the ends of his dark gold hair and rippled the collar of his pale blue Oxford shirt. He'd rolled the cuffs up on his forearms and they, too, glinted with a sprinkling of gold.

She guessed what was behind his too-casual question. If Jack won his on-going marriage campaign, he no doubt envisioned hanging a numeral after his son's name. John Harris Mason IV. Not for the first time, Gina wondered if she was being a total bitch for putting her needs before Jack's. Why did she have to prove that she could stand on her own two feet, anyway? This handsome, sophisticated, wealthy man wanted to take care of her and the baby. Why not let him?

She sighed, acknowledging the answers almost before she'd formulated the questions. She would hate herself for giving up now. That had been her modus operandi her entire adult life. Whenever she got bored or developed a taste for something new, she would indulge the whim.

But she couldn't quit being a mother. Nor did she want to give up a job she'd discovered she was good at. Really good. Then again, who said she had to quit? The Tremayne Group's Washington venue had plenty of business.

All of which was just a smoke screen. The sticking point—the real, honest-to-goodness sticking point—was that Jack didn't love her. He'd been completely honest about that. Although...the past two nights had made Gina begin to wonder if what they did feel for each other might be enough. Uneasy with that thought, she dodged the issue of boys' names.

"I haven't gotten that far," she said lightly. "Tell me about your parents. Where they met, how long they've been married, what they like to do."

Jack filled the rest of the trip with a light-handed sketch of a family steeped in tradition and dedicated to serving others. His mother had been as active in volunteerism over the years as his father had in his work for a series of presidents.

Gina might have been just the tiniest bit intimidated if she hadn't grown up on stories of the literary and social giants Grandmama had hobnobbed with in her heyday. Then, of course, there was her title. Lady Eugenia Amalia Therése St. Sebastian, granddaughter to the last Duchess of Karlenburgh. That and five bucks might get her a cup of coffee at Starbucks but it still seemed to impress some people. Hopefully, she wouldn't have to resort to such obvious measures to impress Jack's folks.

She didn't. Fifteen minutes after meeting John II, Gina knew no title would dent the man's rigid sense of propriety. He did not approve of her refusal to marry his only son and give his grandson the Mason name.

"Now, John," his wife admonished gently. She was a soft-spoken Southern belle with a core of tempered steel beneath her Donna Karan slacks and jewel-toned Versace tunic. "That's a matter for Gina and Jack to decide."

"I disagree."

"So noted," Ellen Mason said dryly. "Would you care for more iced tea, Gina?"

There were only the four of them, thank goodness. They were sitting in a glass-enclosed solarium with fans turning overhead. A glorious sweep of green lawn shaded by the monster oaks that gave the place its name filled the windows. The Masons' white-pillared, three-story home had once been the heart of a thriving tobacco plantation. The outlying acres had been sold off over the decades, but the current owner of Five Oaks had his lord-of-the-manner air down pat.

"I'd better not," Gina replied in response to Ellen's question. "I'm trying to cut out caffeine. Water with lemon would be great."

Jack's mother tipped ice water from a frosted carafe and used silver tongs to spear a lemon wedge. "We didn't worry about caffeine all those years ago when I was pregnant. That might explain some of my son's inexhaustible energy."

Her guest kept a straight face, but it took some doing. Ellen's son was inexhaustible, all right. Gina had the whisker burns on her thighs to prove it.

"I know you must have questions about this side of your baby's family tree," the older woman was saying with a smile in her warm brown eyes. "We have a portrait gallery in the upper hall. Shall I give you a tour while Jack and his father catch up on the latest political gossip?"

"I'd love that."

The duchess had taken Gina and Sarah to all the great museums, both at home and abroad. The Louvre. The Uffizi. The Hermitage. The National Gallery of Art in Washington. As a result Sarah had developed both an interest in and an appreciation for all forms of art. Gina's knowledge wasn't anywhere near as refined but she recognized the touch of a master when she saw it. None of the portraits hanging in the oak-paneled upstairs hall had that feel. Still, the collection offered a truly fascinating glimpse of costumes and hairstyles from the 17th century right down to the present.

Gina paused before the oil of Jack's grandfather. He wore the full dress uniform of an army colonel, complete with gold shoulder epaulets and saber. "My grandmother knew him," she told Ellen. "She said he and your mother-in-law attended a reception she once gave for some sultan or another."

"I've read about your grandmother," her hostess commented as they moved to the next portrait, this one of Ellen and her husband in elegant formal dress. "She sounds like an extraordinary woman."

"She is." Lips pursed, Gina surveyed the empty space at the end of the row. "No portrait of Jack and Catherine?"

"No, unfortunately. We could never get them to sit still long enough for a formal portrait. And…" She stopped, drew in a breath. "And of course, we all thought there was plenty of time."

She turned and held out both hands. Gina placed hers in the soft, firm fold.

"That's why I wanted this moment alone with you, dear. Life is so short, and so full of uncertainties. I admire you for doing what your heart tells you is right. Don't let Jack or his father or anyone else bully you into doing otherwise."

The brief interlude with Ellen made her husband a little easier to bear. John II didn't alter his attitude of stiff disapproval toward Gina but there was no disguising his deep affection for his son. He not only loved Jack. He was also inordinately proud of his son's accomplishments to date.

"Did he tell you he's the youngest man ever appointed as an ambassador-at-large?" he asked during a leisurely brunch that included twice-baked cheese grits, green beans almondine and the most delicious crab cakes Gina had ever sampled.

"No, he didn't," she replied, silently wishing she could

sop up the béchamel sauce from the crab cakes with the crust of her flaky croissant.

"Then he probably also didn't tell you some very powerful PACs have been suggesting he run for the U.S. Senate as a first step toward the White House."

"Dad…"

"Actually," Gina interrupted, "I read about that. I know those PACs love Jack. And he and I talked about his running for office the other night."

John II paused with his knife and fork poised above his food. "You did?"

"Yep. I told him he should go for it."

"Dad…"

Once again the father ignored the son's low warning. His lip curled, and a heavy sarcasm colored his voice. "I'm sure our conservative base will turn out by the thousands to support a candidate with an illegitimate child."

"That's enough!"

Jack shoved away from the table and tossed down his napkin. Anger radiated from him in waves. "We agreed not to discuss this, Dad. If you can't stick to the agreement, Gina and I will leave now."

"I'm sorry." The apology was stiff but it was an apology. "Sit down, son. Please, sit down."

Ellen interceded, as Gina suspected she had countless times in the past. "Jack, why don't you take our guest for a stroll in the rose garden while I clear the table and bring in dessert?"

Gina jumped up, eager for something to do. "Please, let me help."

"Thank you, dear."

A decadent praline cheesecake smoothed things over. Everyone got back to being polite and civilized, and Ellen deftly steered the conversation in less sensitive channels.

Gina thought they might make it through the rest of the

visit with no further fireworks. She nursed that futile hope right up until moments before she and Jack left to drive back to Washington. At his mother's request, he accompanied her into her study to pick up a flyer about an organization offering aid to abused children overseas she wanted him to look at.

That left Gina and John II standing side by side in the foyer for a few moments. An uncomfortable silence stretched between them, broken when he made an abrupt announcement.

"I had you investigated."

"What?"

"I hired a private investigator."

Gina's brows snapped together, and her chin tipped in a way that anyone familiar with the duchess would have recognized immediately as a warning signal.

"Did you?"

"I wanted him to chase down rumors about the other men you might have been involved with."

Her hand fluttered to her stomach in a protective gesture as old as time. "The other men I might have screwed, you mean."

He blinked at the blunt reply, but made no apology. "Yes."

The thought of a private investigator talking to her friends, asking questions, dropping insinuations, fired twin bolts of anger and mortification. Gina's chin came up another inch. Her eyes flashed dangerously.

"Why go to the expense of a private investigator? A simple DNA test would have been much cheaper."

"You were in that clinic in Switzerland. Jack flew over right after you called him. I told him to insist on a paternity test, but..." He broke off, grimacing. "Well, no need to go into all that now. What I want to say is I accept that you're carrying my grandchild."

"How very magnanimous of you."

The icy response took him aback. He looked as though

he wanted to say more, but the sound of footsteps stilled him. Both Jack and his mother sensed the tension instantly. Ellen sighed and shook her head. Her son demanded an explanation.

"What's wrong?"

"Nothing," Gina said before his father could respond. "Nothing at all. Thank you for a lovely lunch, Ellen."

She kissed the older woman's cheek before offering a cool glance and a lukewarm handshake to Jack's father.

"Perhaps I'll see you again."

He stiffened, correctly interpreting the threat buried in that polite "perhaps."

"I certainly hope so."

"All right," Jack said as the Range Rover cut through the tunnel of oaks shading the drive. "What was that all about?"

Gina wanted to be cool about it, wanted to take the high road and shrug off the investigation as inconsequential, but her roiling emotions got the better of her. She slewed around as much as the seat belt would allow. Anger, hurt and suspicion put a razor's edge in her words.

"Did you know your father hired a P.I. to investigate me?"

"Yes, I…"

"With or without your approval?"

"Christ, Gina." His glance sliced into her. "What do you think?"

She was still angry, still hurt, but somewhat mollified by his indignation. Slumping against the seat back, she crossed her arms. "Your father's a piece of work, Ambassador."

Which was true, but probably not the smartest comment to make. Jack could criticize his father. He wouldn't appreciate an outsider doing so, however, any more than Gina would tolerate someone making a snide comment about the duchess. The tight line to Jack's jaw underscored that point.

"I'm sorry," she muttered. "I shouldn't have said that."

He accepted the apology with a curt nod and offered one

of his own. "I'm sorry, too. I should have told you about the investigation. The truth is I didn't know about it until after we got back from Switzerland and then it just didn't matter."

Her anger dissipated, leaving only an urgent question. "Why not, Jack? Didn't you...? Don't you have any doubts?"

"No. Not one." The rigid set to his shoulders eased. His reply was quiet and carried the ring of absolute truth. "We may disagree on a number of important issues, marriage included, but we've always been honest with each other."

Her eyes start to burn. She refused to cry, she flatly refused, but she suddenly felt miserable and weary beyond words. "Look," she said tiredly, "this has been a busy few days. I may have overdone it a bit. I think...I think I'd better fly back to New York this evening."

He knifed her a quick look. "Is it the baby?"

"No! The baby's fine."

"Then it's my father." Another sharp glance. "Or is it us?"

"Mostly us." She forced a smile. "You have to admit we didn't get much sleep the past two nights. I need to go home and rack out."

"Is that what you really want?"

"It's what I really want."

The drive back to D.C. took considerably less time than the drive down to Richmond. No cutting off to ramble along Route 1. No stops at picturesque cafés. Jack stuck to the interstate, and Gina used the time to check airline schedules. She confirmed a seat on a 7:20 p.m. flight to New York. It was a tight fit, but she could make it if she threw her things in her weekender and went straight to the airport.

"You don't have to wait," she told Jack as he pulled into the parking garage at L'Enfant Plaza. "I can grab a cab."

"I'll drive you."

She was in and out of TTG's guest suite in less than twenty minutes. A quick call ensured the cleaning crew would come in the following day. The key cards she sealed in an envelope and slid under the door to the main office. Elaine Patterson, manager of the Washington venue, was due back tomorrow. Gina would coordinate the after-event report with her and tie up any other loose ends by email.

Her emotions were flip-flopping all over the place again when Jack pulled up at the airport terminal. Part of her insisted she was doing the right thing. That she needed to pull back, assess the damage to her heart done by the nights she'd spent in his arms. The rest of her ached for another night. Or two. Or three.

If Jack were experiencing the same disquiet, it didn't show. He left the Range Rover in idle and came around to lift out her weekender. His expression was calm, his hand steady as he buried it in her hair and tilted her face to his.

"Call me when you get home."

"I will."

"And get some rest."

"Yes, sir."

"I'll see you at our next doctor's appointment, if not before."

Before would be good, she thought as she closed her eyes for his kiss. Before would be very good.

When she climbed out of a cab outside the Dakota almost seven hours later, her ass was well and truly dragging. Her flight had been delayed due to mechanical problems before being canceled completely. The passengers had sat for well over an hour on the plane before being shuffled off and onto another. She'd called Jack once she was aboard the alternate aircraft so he wouldn't worry, and again when she landed at LaGuardia.

Since they'd touched down at almost midnight, she didn't call her grandmother. The duchess would have gone to bed hours ago and Gina didn't want to wake her. Feeling dopey with exhaustion, she took a cab into the city. Jerome wasn't on duty and she didn't know the new night doorman except to nod and say hello. Wheeling her suitcase to the elevator, she slumped against the mirrored wall as it whisked her upward.

The delicate scent of orange blossoms telegraphed a welcome to her weary mind. She dropped her purse and key next to the Waterford crystal bowl filled with potpourri. Her weekender's hard rubber wheels made barely a squeak as she rolled it over the marble tiles.

She'd crossed the sitting room and was almost to the hall leading to the bedrooms when she caught the sound of a muffled clink in the kitchen. She left the suitcase in the hall and retraced her steps. Light feathered around edges of the swinging door between the dining room and kitchen. Another clink sounded just beyond it.

"Grandmama?"

Gina put out a hand to push on the door and snatched it back as the oak panel swung toward her. The next second she was staring at broad expanse of black T-shirt. Her shocked glance flew up and registered a chin shadowed with bristles, a mouth set in a straight line and dark, dangerous eyes topped by slashing black brows.

Ten

Everything Gina had ever learned or heard or read about self-defense coalesced into a single, instinctive act. Whipping her purse off her shoulder, she swung it with everything she had in her.

"*Hé!*" The intruder flung up his arm and blocked the savage blow. "*Várj!*"

"*Várj* yourself, you bastard!"

Gina swung again. This time his arm whipped out and caught the purse strap. One swift tug yanked it out of her hands.

"If you've hurt my grandmother…"

She lunged past him into the kitchen. Her fingers wrapped around the hilt of the largest knife in the upright butcher-block stand.

"*Jézus, Mária és József!*" The stranger chopped his hand down on her wrist, pinning it to the counter. "Stop, Eugenia. Stop."

The terse command pierced her red haze of fear but her heart still slammed against her chest as the questions tumbled out. "How do you know my name? What are you doing here? Where's my grandmother?"

"The duchess is in her bedroom, asleep, I presume. I am

here because she invited my sister and me to stay. And I know your name because we're cousins, you and I."

"Cousins?"

"Of a sort."

When she tugged her wrist, he released his brutal grip. A smile softened the stark angles of his face. "I'm Dominic. Dominic St. Sebastian. I live in Budapest, but my parents came from Prádzec. Your grandmother's home," he added when she looked at him blankly.

It took her a moment to recognize the name of the town on the border between Austria and Hungary, in the heart of what was once the Duchy of Karlenburgh.

"I don't understand. When did you get here?"

"This afternoon." He gestured behind him to the coffee-maker just starting to bubble and brew on the counter. "It's midnight in New York, but morning in Hungary. My body has yet to adjust to the time change and craves its usual dose of caffeine. Will you join me for coffee and I'll explain how Anastazia and I come to be here, in your home."

"No coffee," Gina murmured, her hand fluttering to her stomach as she tried to absorb the presence of this dangerous-looking man in her grandmother's kitchen.

He was as sleek and as dark as a panther. Black hair, black shirt, black jeans slung low on his hips. The T-shirt stretched taut across a whipcord-lean torso. The hair was thick and razored to a ragged edge, as though he didn't have time or couldn't be bothered with having it styled.

"Tea, then?" he asked.

"Tea would be good." Slowly getting her wind back, Gina nodded to the cabinet behind his head. "The tea caddy is in there."

"Yes, I know." His smile reached his eyes. "The duchess told me to make myself to home. I took her at her word and explored the cupboards."

Whoa! This man's face cast in hard angles and tight lines was one thing. The same face relaxing into a lazy grin was something else again. Gina had a feeling Dominic St. Sebastian could have his pick of any woman in Budapest. Or pretty much anywhere else in the world.

The fact that he knew his way around a tea caddy only added to the enigma. While the fresh-made coffee dripped into the carafe, he brewed a pot of soothing chamomile. Moments later he and Gina were sitting across from each other with steaming mugs in hand.

"So," he said, slanting her a curious look. "The duchess never spoke to you of me or my family?"

His speech held only a trace of an accent. A slight emphasis on different syllables that made it sound intriguing and sexy as all hell. Wondering where he'd learned to speak such excellent English, Gina shrugged.

"Grandmama told my sister and me that we had some cousins, four or five times removed."

"At least that many times. So we could marry if we wished to, yes?"

The tea sloshed in her mug. "Excuse me?"

"We're well outside the degree of kinship forbidden by either the church or the law. So we could marry, you and I."

A sudden suspicion darted into Gina's consciousness. Despite the duchess's seeming acceptance of her granddaughter's single-and-pregnant status, was she resorting to some Machiavellian scheming?

"Just when did my grandmother invite you and your sister to New York?"

"She didn't. I had to come on business and since Anastazia had never been to the States, she decided to accompany me. When we phoned the duchess to arrange a visit, she invited us for tea. She was so charmed by my sister that she insisted we stay here."

Charmed by his sister? Gina didn't think so.

"How long will you be in New York?"

"That depends on how swiftly I conclude my business. But not, I hope, before I get a chance to know you and the duchess. I've heard many tales of her desperate flight after the duke's execution."

"She doesn't speak of those days. I think the memories still haunt her."

"Is that why she's never returned to Austria, or traveled to any part of what is now Hungary?"

"I think so."

"That's certainly understandable, but perhaps some day she will visit and allow Anastazia and me to return her gracious hospitality. She would find everything much changed."

"I'm sure she would."

"You must come, too. I would enjoy showing you my country, Eugenia."

"Gina, please. Grandmama's the only one who calls me Eugenia, and then it's generally because I've screwed up."

"And does that happen often?"

She made a face. "Far more often than either of us would like."

The tea and the European rhythm of Dominic's speech had combined to bring Gina the rest of the way down from the adrenaline spike of her scare. When she reached bottom, weariness hit like a baseball bat.

Her jaw cracked on a monster yawn. She barely got a hand up in time to cover it and gave Dominic a laughing apology.

"Sorry 'bout that. It's been a long day."

"For me, also." His mesmerizing onyx eyes held hers. "Shall we go to bed?"

Okay, she had to stop attaching sexual innuendo to every word that came out of the man's mouth.

They took their mugs to the sink. Dominic rinsed them while Gina emptied the coffeemaker. He flicked off the kitchen light as they passed through the swinging door, plunging them both into temporary blindness.

Gina had grown up in this apartment and was intimately familiar with every piece of furniture a mischievous girl could crawl under or hide behind. She also knew which sharp edges to avoid, blind or not. Instinctively, she angled to the left to skirt the corner of a marble-topped table.

The move brought her into contact with Dominic's thigh, and his hand shot out to save her from what he must have assumed was a near fall.

"Careful."

For the second time that night he'd captured her arm. Gina wasn't quite as quick to shake off his hold this time.

"Thanks. I assume Grandmama put Anastazia in my sister's room and you in the study?"

"Is the study the baronial hall with the oak paneling and crown molding?" he asked dryly.

"It is." They stopped outside the double sliding doors. "Here you go. I guess I'll see you in the morning. Correction. Make that later in the morning."

His fingers slid from her forearm to her elbow to her wrist. Raising her hand, he bowed and dropped a kiss on it with old-world charm right out of the movies.

"*Aludj jól,* Gina."

"And that means?"

"Sleep well."

"*Aludj jól,* Dominic."

She left him standing by the sliding doors and reclaimed her suitcase. No light shone from under the door to her grandmother's room, so Gina slipped quietly into her own. She was asleep almost before her head hit the pillow.

She woke mere hours later. Grunting at what felt like a bowling ball resting atop her bladder, she rolled out of bed and headed for the bathroom.

When she snuggled between the sheets again, sleep didn't descend as swiftly. And when it did, it brought confusing dreams of a shadowy figure whose hair morphed from black to gold to black again.

Since Samuel wasn't expecting her back from Washington for another day, possibly two, Gina didn't feel compelled to go in to the office the next morning. Good thing, because she didn't wake up a second time until almost nine.

She took her time in the shower, wondering if she'd dreamed that kitchen encounter last night. It was so surreal, and so unlike her grandmother to invite complete strangers to stay in their home. Maybe she was more tied to the land of her birth than she let on.

Gina followed the scent of coffee and cinnamon toast to the kitchen, where Maria was turning fresh toast onto a plate.

"There you are. Dominic told us, *la duquesa* and me, that you came in late last night."

"I just about jumped out of my skin when I came in last night and bumped into him." Dying for a cup of coffee, Gina poured a glass of apple juice instead. "I'm surprised Grandmama invited him and his sister to stay here."

"Me, as well. But they are very nice and have made your grandmother smile. You will see," Maria said, flipping the last of the toast onto the platter.

"Here, I'll take that."

The scene in the sunny, green-and-white breakfast room certainly seemed to give credence to Maria's comment. The duchess was holding court, her snowy hair in a crown of braids, her chin feathered by the high lace collar of her favorite lavender silk blouse. Her smile was far from regal, though. Wide and lively, it transformed her face as she carried on an animated conversation with her guests in their native language.

But it was those guests who stopped Gina in her tracks. In the bright light of day, Dominic appeared every bit as dangerous as he had last night. Must be that European, unshaved whisker thing. Or his preference for black shirts. This one was starched cotton and open-collared, showing just a hint of a silver chain at his throat.

The woman seated across from him was almost as riveting. Her hair fell well past her shoulders, as lustrous and raven-black as her brother's. Her cheekbones were high and sharp, her mouth a glistening red. Thick lashes framed dark eyes with just the hint of a slant. If the rest of her was as striking as that sculpted face, the woman could walk into any modeling agency in New York and sign a high six-figure contract within minutes.

All of a sudden Gina felt fat and dumpy and just a tad jealous of the way these two outsiders seemed to have glommed on to her grandmother. That lasted only until the duchess spotted her. Her lined face lit up with love.

"You're awake at last. Come and join us, dearest."

Dominic pushed back his chair and took the platter of toast so Gina could bend to give her grandmother a kiss. The look he gave her banished any lingering nasty thoughts. Fat and dumpy wouldn't have put such an admiring gleam in his eyes.

"Good morning, cousin. Did you sleep well?"

"Very."

"You must let me introduce my sister. Anastazia, this is..."

"Eugenia Amalia Therése," the brunette said in an accent noticeably heavier than her brother's.

She, too, pushed back her chair and came around the table. Holding out both hands, she kissed Gina's cheeks. "I have been so eager to meet you, cousin. I, too, was named for the Archduchess Maria Amalia of Parma." She wrinkled her perfect nose. "I am Anastazia Amalia Julianna. Such long names we have, yes?"

Despite her cover-model looks, she was open and friendly and engaging. Gina couldn't help but smile back.

"We do indeed."

"You must call me Zia. And I will call you Gina."

That thorny matter settled, they joined the others at the table. Gina helped herself to two slices of cinnamon toast while her grandmother gave them all a rare glimpse into the family archives.

"Poor Archduchess Maria Amalia," she said with a wry

smile. "Married against her will to a mere duke while two of her sisters became queens. Marie Antoinette of France and Marie Caroline of Naples and Sicily."

Charlotte took a sip of her tea and shared another historical tidbit.

"The three sisters were reportedly very close. They often exchanged letters and portraits and gifts. One of the last letters Marie Antoinette smuggled out of her prison was to Amalia."

"I'm told there's a miniature of their mother, the Empress Marie Therese of Austria, in your Metropolitan Museum of Art," Zia said eagerly. "It is one of the places I hope to visit while I am here."

"You must get Eugenia to take you. She spent many hours at the Met as a child."

"Oh, but I must not impose." The brunette turned her brilliant smile on Gina. "From what your grandmother has told us, you're very busy with your work."

"Actually, I'm off today. We can go this afternoon, if you like."

"I would! And you, Dom. You must come, too, to see this long-dead ancestor of ours."

His gaze met and held Gina's. His mouth curled in a slow smile. "I'll have to see if I can reschedule my afternoon appointment."

Gina didn't get a chance to corner her grandmother until midmorning. Zia had gone out onto the terrace to check her phone for voice messages and emails. Dominic retreated to the study to make some calls. As soon as he was out of the room, Gina pounced.

"Okay, Grandmama, 'fess up. What's behind this sudden spurt of hospitality to distant relatives you've never met."

"Really, Eugenia! I should hope I'm not so lacking in generosity as to let two young and very charming relations stay in a hotel when we have plenty of room here."

"But you don't know anything about them."

"That's what Dominic said when I extended the invitation. He tried to refuse, but I insisted."

"Did either of them tell you what they do for a living?"

"Dominic does some kind of security work. Anastazia just got her MD degree from Semmelweis University in Budapest."

Gorgeous and smart and a doc. Another nasty little worm of jealousy poked its head up. Gina might have started feeling dumpy and fat again if Dominic hadn't come back into the room.

"I'm yours for the afternoon, if you're sure you wish to..."

He broke off and pivoted on the balls of his feet in the direction of the hall. Startled, Gina strained to hear in the sudden silence and picked up a faint buzz.

"Oh, that's my phone. I left it in my purse on the hall table last night. Excuse me."

The call had already gone to voice mail when she fished the phone out of her jam-packed bag. She saw the name on caller ID and stabbed the talk button just in time.

"Hello, Jack."

"Hi, Gina. I just wanted to check and see how you're feeling after your long odyssey last night."

The sound of his voice stirred the usual welter of confused emotions. Despite her abrupt departure yesterday, she couldn't believe how much she missed him. How much she ached for him.

"I'm good," she said, "although I decided not to go in to work since I had the day off, anyway."

"So you're going to put your feet up and rest, right?"

"Pretty much. Although I did agree to take my cousins to the Met this afternoon."

"Cousins?"

"Two of them. Dominic and his sister, Anastazia. Their parents came from Prádzec, which was once part of the Duchy of Karlenburgh."

"And is now in Hungary."

Trust an ambassador-at-large to know that. The phone to her ear, Gina wandered toward the end of the hall. Dom sat next to her grandmother's chair and appeared to be amusing her with some anecdote.

"Did the duchess know they were coming?" Jack asked.

"They surprised her. Me, too! I thought Dom was a burglar when I came chest-to-chest with him last night."

"They were there, in the apartment when you got home?"

"They're staying here."

That was met with a short silence.

"What did you say their names were again?"

"Dominic and Anastazia St. Sebastian. She's just finished med school and he does something in security. Grandmama didn't get the specifics."

She caught a flash of sunlight as the terrace doors opened and Zia rejoined the group.

"Oh, there's Anastazia. I'd better go, Jack."

"Gina…"

"Yes?"

"About this weekend—"

"It was just me," she interrupted quickly. She hadn't had time to sort through everything that had happened during their days together. And the nights! Dear God, the nights.

"Chalk it up to hormones run amok. I'll talk to you soon, okay?"

"Okay."

She blew out a breath and hit the end button, but some of the emotions Jack had stirred must have shown in her face when she walked into the sitting room. She couldn't hide them from the duchess. Her faded blue eyes locked onto to Gina's.

"Who was that, dearest?"

"Jack."

"Hmm."

The odd inflection in that murmur snared the interest of

both guests. They were too polite to ask, however, and the duchess left it to Gina to elaborate.

"Jack Mason. He's an ambassador-at-large with the U.S. State Department in Washington."

Dominic's expression of casual interest didn't change but just for a second she thought she saw something flicker in his dark eyes. Like the duchess, he must have sensed there was more to the call than she wanted to reveal.

Oh, hell. Might as well let it all hang out.

"He's the father of my baby."

After Gina disconnected, Jack spent several long moments staring at the slice of the Mall viewable through his office windows. Their brief conversation ricocheted around in his mind.

Two of them. From Hungary. They surprised her. Chest-to-chest.

He wanted to believe it was his recent showdown with the Russian Mafia thugs who'd spilled across the borders of Eastern and Central Europe that prompted him to reach for the phone. Yet he couldn't get that chest business out of his head.

His chief of staff answered the intercom. "What's up, boss?"

"I need you to run a check on a pair from Hungary. They say they're siblings and are going by the names Dominic and Anastazia St. Sebastian."

Eleven

The next few days flew by. Gina got caught up at work. During her spare hours she showed Zia and Dominic the best of New York. She also delighted in the slow unfurling of her grandmother's memories. Prompted by her guests' presence and their gentle probing, the duchess shared some of her past.

She'd kept it locked inside her for so long that each anecdote was a revelation. Even now she would only share those memories that gave glimpses of a girl born into a wealthy, aristocratic family, one who'd grown up with all Europe as her playground. A fascinated Gina learned for the first time that her grandmother might have qualified as an Olympic equestrian at the age of fifteen had her family allowed her to compete. She'd retaliated for their adamant refusal by insisting she be allowed to study Greek and Roman history at Charles University in Prague.

"Prague is such a romantic city," the duchess mused to her audience of three over a dinner of Hungarian dishes prepared by Zia and Dominic as a small thank-you to their hostess.

Candles flickered in tall silver holders. The remains of the meal had been cleared away but no one was in a hurry to leave the table. A Bohemian crystal decanter of *pálinka* sat within easy reach. Double-distilled and explosively potent, the apricot-flavored brandy had been a gift from Zia and Dom. The duchess and her guests sipped sparingly from balloon-shaped snifters. Gina was more than content with a goblet of diet cranberry juice and the dreamy expression on her grandmother's face.

"That's where I first met the duke," the duchess related with smile. "In Prague. There'd been talk off and on about a possible liaison between our families but nothing had come of it at that point."

"So what was he doing in Prague?" Gina asked.

"He'd evidently decided it was time to take a wife, and came to find out if I was scandalously modern as the rumors said."

She took a sip of brandy and a faraway look came into her eyes.

"When he walked into the café where my friends and I were having dinner, I didn't know who he was at first. All I saw was this tall, impossibly handsome man with jet-black hair and the swarthy skin of his Magyar ancestors. Even then, he had such a presence. Every head in the café turned when he walked over to my table," she murmured. "Then he bowed, introduced himself, and I was lost."

The duchess paused, drifting on her memories, and Gina's gaze drifted to Dominic. His olive-toned skin and dark eyes indicted Magyar blood ran in his veins, too.

A nomadic, cattle-herding tribe that swept into Europe from the Steppes, the Magyars were often depicted in art and literature as the early Hungarian equivalent of America's Wild West cowboys. Gina was back in the 8th or 9th century, picturing Dominic riding fast and low in the saddle, when the intercom sounded.

She returned to the present with a start. The buzz brought the duchess out of her reverie, as well. A small frown of annoyance creased her forehead.

"I'll get it," Gina said.

She crossed to the intercom's wall unit and saw the flashing light signaling a call from the lobby. "Yes?"

"It's Jerome, Lady Eugenia. There's a gentleman to see you. Mr. John Mason."

Jack! Surprise and pure, undiluted delight flooded her veins.

"Send him up! Excuse me," she said to the three interested parties at the table. "I need to get the door."

She rushed to the entryway and out into the hall, wishing she'd spiffed up a little more for this evening at home. Oh, well, at least she still fit into her skinny jeans. And her crab-apple-green stretchy T-shirt did accent her almost-nursing-mother boobs.

When Jack stepped out of the elevator, Gina forgot all about her appearance and devoured his. Ohmanohman-ohman! Hungarian cowboys had nothing on tall, tanned Virginians.

The sight of him erased last weekend's awkward moments. Her hurt and indignation over learning that his father had hired a P.I. evaporated. Ditto the poisonous little barbs planted by his obnoxious chief of staff. Double ditto the ache in her heart when she'd spotted the pictures of Catherine at his home. Like the duchess had so many years ago, all Gina needed to do was look at this man and know she was lost.

"What are you doing here?"

"Two reasons. One, I didn't like the way our weekend ended. I'm still kicking myself for letting you leave with little more than a peck on the cheek."

"Oh. Well. I suppose we can correct that."

"You suppose right."

When he hooked her waist, she went into his arms eagerly, joyfully. He buried a hand in her hair and more than made up for any deficiencies in their parting.

Gina could have stayed there forever. The feel and the taste and the scent of him wrapped around her like warm silk. She felt his heart beating under her spread palms, breathed in the heady mix of aftershave and male.

When he raised his head, her heart was in her smile. "You said there were two reasons. What's the second?"

The pause was brief, hardly more than half a breath, but still noticeable.

"I missed you."

"Was it that hard to say?" she teased.

"You try it."

"I missed you." It came so easily she added a little embellishment. "Bunches."

The murmur of voices inside the apartment snagged Jack's attention. "Did I catch you at a bad time?"

"No, we finished dinner a while ago and are just sitting around the table talking. Come meet my cousins."

She led him to the dining room and had time to note widely varied reactions before she made the introductions. Zia's first glimpse of the newcomer brought her elbows off the table and a look of instant interest to her face. As her eyes raked Jack over, a slow, feline smile curved her lips.

Gina couldn't help herself. She was bristling like a barnyard cat when she noticed Dominic's expression. It was as shuttered as his sister's was open. The duchess's, on the other hand, was warm and welcoming.

"Good evening, Ambassador. It's good to see you again."

The title sent Zia's brows soaring. Her gaze whipped from Jack to Gina and back again, while Dominic slowly pushed his chair back from the table and stood.

"It's good to see you, too, Duchess." Jack crossed the dining room to take her hand. "I'm sorry to barge in like this."

"No need to apologize. Allow me to introduce my guests. They're visiting from Hungary."

"So Gina told me."

"Anastazia, may I present Ambassador Jack Mason."

He was at his most urbane with the sultry brunette. A smile, a lift of her hand, a light kiss on the fingers.

"You must call me Zia," she purred. "And I will call you Jack, yes?"

"Igen."

"How wonderful! You speak our language."

"Only enough to order a drink in a bar."

"In Hungary," she laughed, "that is more than enough. This is my brother, Dominic."

Jack rounded the table and extended his hand. It was a simple courtesy, a universal gesture recognized the world over. Yet there was something about the look accompanying it that made Gina pause. The message was subtle. Almost *too* subtle. She caught a hint of it, though, or thought she did.

So did Dominic. His smile took on a sardonic edge, his eyes a sudden glint as he shook Jack's hand.

"We've met before, Ambassador, although I doubt you'll remember."

"I remember. I also remember you were using another name at the time."

The two men ignored the surprise that produced among the women. Their gazes locked, they seemed to be engaged in a private and very personal duel.

"I was, indeed," Dominic drawled. "And you, as I recall, had not yet acquired your so very impressive diplomatic credentials."

The duchess's notions of propriety didn't include what was fast assuming the air of an Old West showdown in her dining room. With a touch of irritation, she thumped her hand on the table to get the combatant's attention.

"Do sit down, both of you. Jack, would you care to try this very excellent cognac? Or there's coffee if you prefer."

"Cognac, please."

"Gina, if you'll get another snifter perhaps Jack or Dominic will condescend to tell us where or when they met before."

The acidic comment found its mark. While Gina retrieved a cut crystal snifter from the graceful Louis XV china cabinet that took up almost an entire wall, the tension between the two men eased by imperceptible degrees. She brought the snifter to the table and splashed in the aromatic brandy as Dom yielded the floor to Jack with upturned palms.

"It's more your story than mine, Ambassador."

Jack accepted the snifter with a murmured thanks and addressed himself to the duchess. "Dominic and I met a number of years ago in Malta. I was on a UN fact-finding mission investigating the transshipment of young women kidnapped from Eastern Europe and sold to wealthy purchasers in the Arab world."

"Dear Lord!" The duchess shot her guest a sharp, questioning look, but he merely gestured for Jack to continue.

"While the UN team was in Malta, we heard rumors of a shipment coming in from Albania. We worked with Interpol and the Maltese authorities to intercept the trawler transporting the merchandise. There were six girls aboard, all between the ages of fifteen and twenty, all drugged to the gills."

Jack lifted the balloon goblet and swirled its contents. His gaze shifted from the duchess to the man sitting across of him.

"The captain of the trawler was killed in the cross fire. That's the word that was put out, anyway."

"What do you mean?" Gina demanded. "Was the captain killed or wasn't he?"

She didn't like where this was going. Had she and her grandmother been too trusting? Had they accepted too readily that Dom and Zia were who they said they were? With a sinking sensation, she remembered how dangerous Dom had seemed that first night, when she'd come home and surprised him in the kitchen.

"The captain went down," Jack confirmed, "but not in a cross fire. Evidently he spotted the intercept boats on his radar and started dragging the girls to the rail. He was going to throw them overboard and get rid of the incriminating evidence before we closed in. That's when he took a shot point-blank to the forehead."

Dom lifted a shoulder. "The bastard had one of those kids shoved against the rail. There was no time to negotiate."

"I don't understand." Gina frowned at her cousin. "Were you on one of the intercept boats?"

"I was on the trawler."

"What?"

He leaned forward, acknowledging her shock. "I was undercover, Gina. I'd been working to take down the head of that particular white slavery ring for months, but I couldn't allow the captain to murder those girls."

"Or blow your cover," Jack murmured in the stunned silence that followed.

Dom's glance slewed back to him. "Or blow my cover."

"Funny thing about that." Jack swirled his cognac again, his eyes never leaving Dom's face. "Interpol put out the word that the second crewman on the trawler escaped after being taken into custody. Yet there was never any record made of the arrest. And the officer who supposedly took the man into custody disappeared two days later."

Dom's smile didn't quite make it to his eyes. "The Albanians play rough."

Gina couldn't believe they were sitting in this elegant dining room, sipping brandy and cranberry juice from Baccarat crystal while calmly discussing kidnapped fifteen-year-olds and death on the high seas. She glanced at her grandmother and found the same incredulity on the duchess's face. Even Zia looked stunned. Evidently her brother's undercover persona was news to her, too.

"I'm curious," Jack said. "Where did you go from Malta, St. Sebastian?"

"I had several assignments. As did you, Mason."

"You're no longer with Interpol."

It was a statement, not a question, but Dominic responded

with a quick, slashing grin. "Not anymore. I'm now what you might term an independent entrepreneur."

And just like that, the ominous spell was broken. He was Gina's cousin again. Handsome, charming, exotic and more intriguing than she'd ever imagined.

She made the fatal mistake of saying so when she walked Jack to the door an hour later.

"I had no idea my cousin was an undercover agent."

"Isn't that the whole point of 'undercover'?"

The acerbic comment raised Gina's brows.

"I suppose," she replied. "But still, you have to admit it's all pretty James Bondish."

"If you say so. Are you tired?"

The abrupt change of subject made her blink. It also made her realize she wasn't the least tired. Probably because the hour was still relatively early. Either that, or the extraordinary conversation at the dinner table had stimulated her. Or just standing here, so close to Jack, set every one of her nerves to dancing.

"Not really. Why?"

"I'm staying at the Excelsior. It's only a few blocks from here. Do you feel like getting out for a little while? We still need to talk about last weekend."

Cold, hard logic dictated a negative. She still hadn't completely sorted through the confused feelings left over from their weekend together. Luckily, Gina had never been particularly concerned with logic. At that moment, looking up into Jack's brown eyes, all she knew was that she craved an hour or two or six alone with him.

She'd never been the kind to play games, much less hide her feelings. Coyness didn't factor anywhere into her makeup. A smile of eager anticipation slid into her eyes as she tipped her head toward the dining room.

"Hang loose. I'll tell Grandmama and the others not to wait up for me."

* * *

They opted to walk to the Excelsior. The June night was too balmy and the city lights too enticing to take a cab for a few short blocks. When they reached the lobby of the Dakota, she steered him away from the main entrance on West 72nd toward the inner courtyard.

"This way. It's shorter."

They exited on 73rd and cut back to Central Park West. Somehow Gina's hand found her way into Jack's as they strolled past the imposing bulk of the Museum of Natural History. And somehow, when they were in the elevator shooting up to his suite, his lips found hers.

She couldn't blame the heat that raced through her on hormones. It was Jack. All Jack. Only Jack. He stoked her senses. Fired her blood. She made herself wait until he keyed the door to his room before she pounced. Then there were no holds barred.

"I hope this is what you had in mind when you asked if I wanted to get out for a while," she muttered as she tore feverishly at his shirt buttons.

"Pretty much."

His voice was low and rough. So were his hands. Dragging up the hem of Gina's T-shirt, he cupped her aching breasts. All it took was one flick of his thumbs over her supersensitive nipples to have her moaning. On fire for him, she locked her mouth and her body with his. They were both half-naked when she threw a glance around the luxurious sitting room.

"There's a bed here somewhere, right?"

"Oh, yeah."

The bedroom was as palatial as the rest of the suite. All crown molding and watered silk wallpaper. Not that either of them noticed. The bed was the center of their focus. Four ornately carved posts. Champagne-colored gauze dripping from each corner. A silk duvet in the same color just begging to be yanked back.

Jack did the honors before tumbling Gina onto the cool sateen sheets. Standing beside the bed, he stripped off the rest of his clothes. Her greedy eyes feasted on his muscled chest. His washboard ribs and flat stomach. His rampant sex.

Gina had to cup him. Had to taste him. Rolling onto her knees, she scooted to the edge of the mattress and wrapped her hand around him. He was hot to her touch. Hot and ridged and already oozing. The milky bead at the tip of his erection stirred a deep, feminine thrill. The idea that she could bring her man to this point with just a kiss, just a stroke, set a torch to her own wild desire. Dipping her head, Gina took him in her mouth.

Jack stood it as long as he could. Then the atavistic need that had been building in him since the moment he'd walked into the duchess's apartment swept everything else aside. He wanted to claim this woman. Mark her as his.

Driven by that primal instinct, he pushed her onto the pillows and followed her down. She spread her legs for him willingly, eagerly, and Jack sank into her. Her hips rose, rammed into his. Once. Twice. Again. Then she opened her eyes and the red mist that had obscured Jack's mind cleared.

This was Gina of the bright, contagious smile.

Gina, who enticed and excited him.

Gina, who'd erased everything and everyone else from his mind.

Jack came out of a deep sleep with his customary, instant awareness. The hotel room was still dark, the silence deep, although a faint gray light was just beginning to show at the edge of the drapes blanketing the window.

Gina lay sprawled at his side. Soft puffs of air escaped her lips with each breath. Not quite snores but close enough to make him smile. With slow, careful moves he nudged down the knee digging into his hip and eased out of bed.

His slacks and shorts lay where he'd dropped them. He

pulled them on but left his belt unbuckled and shirt lying where it was as he crossed to the window. Lifting the drape a crack, he saw the city hadn't yet roared to life. Like Jack, it was enjoying the final quiet moments before the rush of the day.

He stared at the shadowy bulk of the Museum of Natural History across the street and tried to remember the last time he'd felt so relaxed. More important, the last time his world had felt so right. Not since Catherine, certainly.

Or even before.

The traitorous thought slipped in before he could block it. Only here, in the dim stillness, with Gina just a few feet away, could he admit the painful truth.

Catherine had been all brilliant energy. Athletic, competitive, totally committed to the causes she believed in. Loving and living with her had demanded the same high level output from Jack.

Would he have burned out? Would they?

Or would they have found what he'd somehow found so swiftly and so unexpectedly with Gina? Jack struggled to find the right word for it. It wasn't peace. Or contentment. Or certainty. God knew, there was nothing certain or predictable about Eugenia Amalia Therése St. Sebastian!

Nor was what he felt for her wrapped up in the baby. The fact she was carrying his child played, of course. No way it couldn't. But what had Jack by the throat right now was Gina. Just Gina.

Christ! Why didn't he just admit it? He was in love with her. Everything about her. Okay, she pissed him off royally at times. And yes, she was one of the most stubbornly hardheaded females he'd ever encountered. Yet everything inside him warmed at the thought of waking up next to her for the next…the next…

His jaw locked. Whirling, he strode back to the bed and sat on the edge.

"Gina. Wake up."

She grunted and tried to burrow into her pillow.

"Wake up."

"Wha...?" She raised a face half-obscured by a tangle of hair and blinked owlishly. "What?"

"Sit up a moment."

Grumbling, she rolled onto a hip and wiggled up against the headboard. The sheet came with her in a waterfall of Egyptian cotton.

"This better be good," she muttered.

She shoved her hair out of her face and tucked the sheet around her breasts, scowling at him through still sleepy eyes. He figured that was as good as he would get.

"Okay, here's the deal. I love you. I want to wake up beside you every morning for as long as we have together. The problem is, neither of us knows how long that might be."

He gripped her upper arms. His fingers dug into soft flesh as he pressed his point.

"I learned the hard way there are no guarantees. You... we have to grab whatever chance at happiness we have now, today. I understand you're still trying to sort through all the changes going on in your life right, but..."

"Wait! Just hold on!"

She pulled away from him, and Jack smothered a curse. He'd overplayed it. Pushed her too hard. He was falling back to regroup when she scrambled off the bed, sheet and all, and pointed a finger at him.

"You stay right where you are. I have to pee. And wash my face. And brush my teeth. Afterward, I'm going to come back to bed and you're going to repeat part of your speech."

"Which part?"

She looked over her shoulder on her way to the bathroom. The smile she sent him lit up the entire room.

"The I-love-you part."

Jack sat there, grinning like an idiot.

* * *

He was still grinning when he heard a faint click coming from the sitting room. A second later, the outer door thudded back against the wall and three men rushed in.

Jack reacted instantly. His one thought, his only thought, was to direct them away from Gina. Springing to the far side of the bed, he grabbed the only available weapon. He had his arm back to hurl the nightstand lamp when the bald giant leading the pack leveled a silenced semiautomatic. The beam of his laser sight painted a red eye dead-center in Jack's naked chest.

"Don't be foolish, Ambassador."

He recognized the voice even before Dominic St. Sebastian stepped from behind baldy's hulking frame.

Twelve

"Now," Gina said gleefully as she yanked open the bathroom door, "let's pick up where we…"

She stopped dead. Clutching the towel she'd wrapped around her like a sarong, she gaped in stunned disbelief at the frozen tableau that greeted her. Jack, gripping a table lamp like a baseball bat. A monster with a shaved head aiming a gun at his chest. Another stranger eying her half-naked body with a leer. And Dom, his dark eyes flashing an urgent message she couldn't even begin to interpret.

"Wh…?" She backed up an involuntary step, two, hit the bathroom door frame. "What…?"

"Very nice, Ambassador." The leering stranger's accent was so thick Gina's shocked mind could barely understand him. "Your woman would bring a good price, yes?"

"Jack! Dom!" Her frantic gaze whipped from one to the other. "What's going on?"

Dom stepped toward her, still telegraphing a signal that refused to penetrate her frantic brain.

"Listen to me, Gina. These men and I have some unfinished business to take care of, business that involves Jack. When you wake, you will understand."

"When I…when I wake?"

A small, apologetic smile altered his grim expression for a moment. Just long enough to distract Gina from the blow that clipped her chin and snapped her head back. She felt Dom catch her as she crumpled. Heard Jack snarl out a curse. Sensed some sort of violent movement on the other side of the room, followed by a low pop.

Then everything faded to black.

She came to slowly, dazed and disoriented. As the gray mist cleared, she discovered she was stretched on the unmade bed. Alone. With the towel draped over her naked body.

She also discovered that her jaw hurt like nobody's business. The ache cut through her lingering haze. A montage of images leaped into her head, sharp and cold and terrifying. The men. Dom. The gun with its ugly silencer.

"Jack!"

Terror engulfing her, Gina shoved off the bed. The violent lunge brought a dark, dizzying wave. She had to reach out a hand to steady herself for a moment, as the towel puddled around her ankles. As soon as the wave receded enough to reclaim her scant body covering, she rushed into the sitting room.

Nothing. No one. Not a table out of place. No overturned chairs. No Jack, or any strangers.

Or Dom.

She hadn't fully processed those moments right before her cousin clipped her, hadn't really understood the vivid images that had popped into her head. She strung them together now, and the pattern they formed made her want to retch.

Dom! Dear God, Dom! What was he involved in? Why had he led those men to Jack? What did they want?

Five exhausting hours later, Gina still didn't have an answer to any of those questions. Neither did the small army of city, state and federal officials who'd descended on the Excelsior in response to her 911 call.

Two uniformed NYPD officers arrived hard on the heels of hotel security. They were followed in a bewildering succession by two plainclothes detectives; a CSI team to scour the suite for fingerprints and other evidence; a grim-faced individual who identified himself as being with the city's counterterrorism unit; two agents from the regional FBI office; a liaison from the governor's office in Albany; a Department of Homeland Security rep and a tall, angular woman from the State Department's New York Office of Foreign Missions, who'd been sent at the urgent request of her boss to find out what the hell happened to Ambassador-At-Large Mason.

Senior FBI Agent Pamela Driskell assumed charge of the hastily assembled task force. It was done with tact and a smooth finesse that told Gina the agent had considerable prior experience dealing with prickly jurisdictional issues.

"Section 1114 of Title 18 U.S. Code assigns the FBI the responsibility for protecting officers and employees of the United States," she explained in a peaches-and-cream Southern drawl at odds with her short, no-nonsense hair and stocky frame. "Now tell me everything you know about this cousin of yours."

Gina started with the surprise visit by Dom and his sister and ended with last night's startling revelations.

"I didn't get all the details. Just that he and Jack—Ambassador Mason—crossed paths some years ago during a UN mission investigating white slavery."

Driskell shot a look at the State Department rep. "You know anything about that?"

"No, but I'll check it out."

Whipping out her BlackBerry, the woman turned away. Driskell swung back to Gina.

"What else?"

"Dom—my cousin—was an undercover agent at the time. Working for Interpol."

"That right? Well, we'll check that out, too. Now I think it's time we talk to your cousin's sister."

She flapped a hand to get the attention of everyone else in the suite.

"Y'all have any further questions for Ms. St. Sebastian? No? Okay, I'm taking her home. Kowalski and I will interview Anastazia St. Sebastian."

When Gina and her escort arrived, Jerome was at his station. Concern etched deep grooves in his seamed face, and his shocked gaze went to the bruise that had blossomed on her chin.

"It's not as bad as it looks," she assured the doorman.

Actually, it was worse but Jerome didn't need to know that.

"Two police officers arrived earlier," he reported.

Gina nodded. Driskell had requested NYPD dispatch the officers. Just in case Dom made an appearance.

"One officer's waiting in the lobby," Jerome said with a worried frown. "The other went up to the duchess's apartment. Can you tell me what's going on, Lady Eugenia?"

Special Agent Driskell started to intervene but Gina held up a palm. "It's okay. I've known this man all my life. I feel safer with him on the door than any five FBI agents."

Driskell hiked a brow but didn't argue the point. "We're investigating the suspected kidnapping of Ambassador Jack Mason," she said instead. "We have reason to believe Dominic St. Sebastian may be involved."

"No!" Jerome reeled back a step. "I don't believe it!"

"Why not?"

He had to stop and think about his instinctive denial. "I've seen Mr. St. Sebastian and his sister with the duchess," he said after a moment. "They're so good with her. So caring and solicitous."

Driskell's curled lip said what she thought of caring and solicitous. "What time did you come on duty this morning?"

"Nine o'clock."

Too late for the events that happened at the Excelsior hours earlier, but Driskell tried, anyway.

"Have you seen two men loitering anywhere in the vicinity? One big and bald? The other smaller, with a heavy accent?"

Jerome drew himself up, all wounded dignity under his summer uniform. "If I'd seen anyone loitering in the vicinity of the Dakota, you may rest assured I would have seen they were attended to."

"I'll take that as a no," Driskell said in her deceptively soft, magnolia-petal drawl.

The uniformed cop in the lobby reported no sighting of Dominic St. Sebastian, his suspected accomplices, or Ambassador Mason. The cop who'd been assigned to wait in the duchess's apartment gave the same report.

Gina only half heard him. Her attention went straight to her grandmother. The duchess sat as straight-spined as ever in her high-backed chair. Maria huddled with shoulders hunched in the chair beside hers. Both women showed worried, strained faces. And both jerked their heads up when Gina walked in.

"Eugenia!"

Relief flooded the duchess's face. Then she seemed to fold into herself, like someone who'd been granted a reprieve from her worst fears.

Gina rushed across the room and dropped to her knees beside the woman who'd always been her anchor. The terror she'd been holding at bay rose up again but she choked it back. She wasn't about to aggravate her grandmother's heart condition by indulging in a fit of hysterics like she really, really wanted to.

"I'm okay, Grandmama."

"What happened to your face?"

She hesitated but couldn't find any way around the truth. "Dom knocked me unconscious."

"No!"

The single syllable arced through the air like summer lightning. Sudden. Tense. Electrifying. Gina jerked her head around and saw Zia leap off the sofa. Her face was ablaze, her eyes feral.

"My brother would not strike a woman!"

"Guess again," Gina snapped.

"I don't believe you!"

The savage denial pulled her up short. Jerome and Anastazia. That made two people in less than five minutes who refused to accept Dom's role in the morning's events.

Her grandmother made a third.

"I can't believe it, either," the duchess said in a more shaky voice than Gina had ever heard coming from her. "Please, Eugenia. Introduce me to these people. Then for heaven's sake sit down and tell us what happened. Zia and Maria and I have been imagining every sort of horrible disaster."

The introductions didn't take much time. The telling took only a little longer. What could Gina add to the stark facts? She'd emerged from the bathroom. Found Dom and two strange men in Jack's suite. Dom stepped forward, knocked her out. She woke alone.

"I cannot understand any of this," Zia said fiercely. "But whatever happened, Dom had some reason for his actions."

Agent Driskell chose to exert her authority at that point. "We'd like to talk to you about your brother, Ms. St. Sebastian."

"It's Dr. St. Sebastian," Zia interrupted acidly.

"Right." The agent turned to the duchess. "Is there some place my partner and I can speak privately with Dr. St. Sebastian?"

"Yes, of course. Maria, will you show them to the breakfast room?"

The kitchen door swished behind them, leaving Gina and her grandmother alone for a few precious moments.

"Eugenia, for God's sake, be honest with me." The duchess held out a trembling hand. "Did you fall? Hurt yourself or the baby?"

"No." She took her grandmother's hand and sank into the chair Maria had just vacated. "Dom caught me before I hit the floor."

"He knocked you unconscious but didn't let you fall? This...none of this makes any sense."

"I know."

She was no closer to understanding when Agent Driskell and her partner departed some time later. Before leaving, Driskell gave Gina a business card imprinted with her office and cell phone numbers.

"There's a chance your cousin or whoever's he's working with may try to reach you. If they do, call me at once."

"I will," Gina promised, slipping the card into the pocket of her jeans. "And you'll call me immediately if they contact someone in Jack's office?"

Driskell nodded. "In the meantime, we'll pull the police officer here in the apartment but keep one in the lobby just in case."

With the agents' departure, an uneasy silence gripped the four women. Maria broke it by pushing heavily to her feet.

"You must eat, *Duquesa*. All of us must. I will make a frittata."

She swished through the swinging door to the kitchen, leaving Gina and the duchess to face a clearly worried Zia.

"I knew my brother had worked with Interpol," the Hungarian said with a deep crease between her brows, "but I was not aware he was...he was..." She waved a hand, as though trying to pull down the right word.

"An undercover agent?" Gina supplied.

"*Igen!* An undercover agent." Her accent reflected her agitation. The Eastern European rhythm grew more marked with each word. "Dominic never spoke of such things to me. Nor to our parents."

Gina wanted to believe her. Her aching chin dictated otherwise.

"He said last night he's no longer with Interpol," she reminded Zia coolly. "As I recall, he mentioned that he's now an independent entrepreneur. What, exactly, does that mean?"

Her cousin's eyes flashed. "I don't know. He has business all over. Many parts of the world. Something to do with security. But…I don't know."

She raked a hand through her silky black hair. She was dressed casually today in navy leggings and a belted, cream-colored tunic with a scoop neckline that dipped off one shoulder. Tall and slender and impossibly elegant, she stirred Gina's frumpy, dumpy feelings again.

Of course, it didn't help that she'd been in such a hurry to jump back into bed with Jack this morning that all she'd done in the bathroom was pee, splash her face with cold water and brush her teeth. Nor was her appearance uppermost in her mind when she'd come to. After her panicked 911 call, she'd scrambled into the same jeans and crab-apple stretchy T-shirt she'd worn last night. If she'd dragged a comb through her hair, she couldn't remember it. Makeup had never entered her mind. Aside from the ice pack Agent Driskell's partner had thrown together with a towel and minicubes from the wet bar to keep her jaw from swelling, Gina had given zero thought to how she looked.

She was feeling that omission now. She wanted a shower, a hairbrush, a change of clothes and another ice pack in the worst way. She hated to take the time for even a quick scrub, though. What if Agent Driskell called? Or Dom? Or Jack?

She was still debating the issue when Zia addressed the duchess. "This is very awkward for you," she said stiffly. "And for me. I think perhaps I should pack my things and… and Dom's…and go to a hotel."

The duchess frowned but before she could reply the cordless phone on the table beside her chair rang. Gina dived for it, praying fervently. Jack! Please, God, let it please be Jack!

"Hello?" Stabbing the talk button, she fumbled the receiver to her ear. "Hello?"

"Gina! Thank God!"

She had to strain to hear her sister's voice over the roar of some kind of engine.

"Grandmama called us early hours and hours ago," Sarah shouted above the noise. "She said you'd been in some kind of an incident. Are you okay?"

"I'm fine."

"The baby?"

Gina laid a hand over her still-flat stomach. Dom had caught her just as her knees crumpled. She hadn't hit the floor. Hadn't bruised anything but her chin. Which, she realized belatedly, must have been his intent.

"Also fine," she assured Sarah. "What's that noise? Where are you?"

"Just about to touch down at the 34th Street Heliport."

"You're here? In New York?"

"Dev ordered his private jet two minutes after Grandmama called. We'll be at the Dakota shortly. Gina, you're not hurt? You swear you're not hurt?"

"I swear."

"Okay, see you in a bit."

Gina cut the connection, battling the almost overwhelming urge to burst into tears. Dammit! These kamikaze hormones were killing her! But just knowing that the sister who always was and always would be her closest friend had rushed to New York on the basis of a single phone call made her want to bawl.

She fought back the tears and sent the duchess a tremulous smile. "That was Sarah."

"So I gathered. They're in New York?"

"They're about to touch down at the 34th Street Heliport."

Her grandmother's paper-thin eyelids fluttered down, as though in prayer. "Thank heavens."

When her lids lifted again, relief was stamped all across her face. "If anyone can get to the bottom of all this, Dev can."

Gina wasn't sure what her brother-in-law could do that two dozen assorted city, state and federal law officials couldn't. She'd put her money on Dev, though. He didn't have to play by the same rules those officials did.

"Now I must leave," Zia said, returning to the topic she'd introduced before the phone call. "Your other granddaughter comes, yes? You will need the bedroom for her."

"Why don't we wait until Sarah and Dev arrive before we decide that?" the duchess suggested.

Zia wasn't fooled. Neither was Gina. They both knew the duchess intended to keep their only connection to Dom on a short leash until Dev had a chance to talk to her.

Her cousin acknowledged as much with a curt nod. "Very well."

Then the stiffness went out of her spine. Like an elegant doll that suddenly lost its stuffing, Zia collapsed onto the sofa and put her head in her hands.

"Dominic is the best of all brothers," she said on a small moan. "I don't understand this. I don't understand any of this."

Her distress was so genuine, so obviously unfeigned. If Zia loved her brother even half as much as Gina loved Sarah, this crazy situation had to be tearing her apart.

The realization gave Gina more of a sense of kinship with her cousin than she'd felt at any point before. It brought her out of her chair and halfway across the sitting room before the buzz of the intercom sent her spinning toward the wall unit. The flashing number on the panel signaled a call from the lobby.

"It's Gina, Jerome."

"There's a gentleman to see you, Lady Eugenia. Mr. John Mason says…"

"Send him up!"

Thank God, thank God, thank God! Jack had returned from wherever he'd disappeared to.

She raced to the front door and flung it open. She was dancing from foot to foot in wild impatience when the elevator doors pinged open. Like a stork hit by lightning, she froze with one foot lifted in the air.

Jack's father stalked out of the elevator, his face red with suppressed fury. "What the hell have you involved my son in?"

Thirteen

She fell back a step, stunned by the vicious accusation. Before she could respond, before she could even think of a response, Zia came running down the hall.

"Come quickly! Special Agent Driskell's on the phone. She thinks they have a link to the kidnappers."

Gina spun on one heel and raced for the sitting room. Footsteps pounded behind her but she had no thought for Jack's father at the moment. Her heart pounding, she snatched up the phone the duchess held out and jammed it to her ear.

"This is Gina St. Sebastian. What's happening?"

"We just got a tip from Interpol," Pam Driskell said with barely suppressed excitement. "Antonio Cordi disappeared from their radar three days ago and may have entered the U.S. under a fake passport."

Like that told Gina anything!

"Who's Antonio Cordi?"

"He's the suspected capo of a vicious crime family operating out of southern Italy. Unfortunately, no one's been able to penetrate the family or get close enough to pin anything on him."

"You're kidding!" She gripped the phone with a white-knuckled fist. "What connection does Jack—Ambassador Mason—have to a Mafia don?"

A grim, white-faced John Harris Mason II surged into her field of view. "I can answer that."

Gina had the phone plastered against her ear, trying to assimilate John II's startling announcement, when she heard a commotion in the foyer. Her heart jumped into her throat.

Jack! Dom! Please God, let it be one of them!

She was hit with alternating waves of crushing disappointment and heartfelt joy when Sarah and Dev appeared. Waving a frantic hello, she relayed the latest development to Special Agent Driskell.

"Ambassador Mason's father is here at our apartment. He says he's got information about this Antonio Cordi."

"Keep him there! My partner and I are only a few blocks away. We'll return immediately."

Her thoughts whirling, Gina inserted the phone into its base. "Agent Driskell wants you to hang loose. She's on her way back here."

The thump of a cane against the parquet floor commanded her attention. "I believe introductions are in order, Eugenia."

"Oh. Right. Grandmama, Sarah, Dev, Zia…this is Jack's father, John Mason. John, this is my grandmother, sister, brother-in-law and…and cousin."

She hadn't intended the stumble over that last part. In her heart of hearts, Gina refused to believe Dom had gone over to the dark side. She still hadn't been able to come up with an explanation for his role in this morning's extraordinary events, though. Neither had his sister. Their unanswered questions hung over the room like a black cloud.

Zia acknowledged as much with a terse nod in the general direction of the newcomers. Which left Gina to pray the duchess hadn't heard the accusation flung at her by Jack's father in the hall a few moments ago. If Charlotte had, blood might yet be spilled.

Mason skated on that one, thank God. The duchess rose

from her chair with the aid of her ebony cane and held out a blue-veined hand.

"I'm sorry we have to meet under such unhappy circumstances, John. I may call you John, mightn't I?"

He gave a curt nod, his thoughts obviously spinning more on his son than on social niceties.

"Good, and you may call me Charlotte. Now, please, sit down and tell us what connection your son has to a Mafia don."

Mason a dismissive gesture with one hand. "I'll wait for the FBI."

Gina chalked the rudeness up to the worry that had to be gnawing at him but cringed at the expression his brush-off put on her grandmother's face.

"Gina says this FBI agent is on the way to take my statement. I'll wait and..."

"No, sir, you will not."

The duchess's cane whipped up and took aim at his chest.

"Look at that bruise on my granddaughter's chin," she commanded with icy hauteur. "If you have an explanation for why her cousin felt compelled to strike her and disappear into thin air with your son, I want to hear it. Now."

Gina guessed John II rarely, if ever, tucked his tail between his legs and backed off. He didn't exactly do either at that point, but he offered a stiff reply.

"I can't tell you why this...this cousin of Gina's struck her or how *he's* involved in this situation. I have my suspicions," he said, his jaw tight, "but nothing solid to base them on. All I can tell you is that I once headed a delegation chartered to examine international banking practices that shielded money laundering, both in the U.S. and abroad. We spent months in South America, more months in Europe digging into accounts reputedly owned by an Italian crime organization called the 'Ndrangheta."

"Go on," the duchess instructed as she resumed her seat. "And for heaven's sake, do sit down."

The demand for at least a semblance of normality drained the last of John II's hostility. He sank into a chair, looking suddenly haggard and far older than his years.

Gina and Sarah and Zia huddled together on the sofa. Dev took the straight-backed chair at the duchess's gilt-edged escritoire. Every pair of eyes was locked on Jack's father as he reduced what had to be a dramatic tale of international crime and intrigue to a few, stark sentences.

"We were in Rome. With the help of the Italian authorities, we'd actually begun to decipher the labyrinthine flow of third- and fourth-tier transactions. One of those tiers led to a member of the 'Ndrangheta named Francesco Cordi."

"I thought his name was Antonio," Gina said, frowning.

"Francesco is—was—Antonio's brother.

"Was?"

"Francesco's dead."

John scrubbed a hand over his face. It was evident to everyone in the room he still carried vivid memories of those days in Rome.

"He didn't like us nosing around in his business and decided to let us know about it. Two of my associates were incinerated when their vehicle was firebombed. We found out later I was next on the hit list. Fortunately—or unfortunately as it now turns out—Jack flew over to Rome at the first sign of trouble. He was with me when Francesco made his move." A fleeting smile creased the retired diplomat's face. "There wasn't a whole lot left of him to send home to his brother Antonio."

"Who's now here, in the States," Gina explained for Sarah and Dev. "The FBI says they got a tip that…"

The buzz of the intercom had her springing her off the sofa.

"That must be Agent Driskell and her partner now."

It wasn't. Her stomach sank like a stone when Jerome announced another visitor.

"I'm sorry to bother you, Lady Eugenia, but there's a Mr. Dale Vickers in the lobby."

Jack's obnoxious chief of staff. That's all she needed! Squeezing her eyes shut, Gina pressed her forehead against the wall.

"He wishes to speak with you. Shall I send him up?"

Hell, no! She knew darn well the officious little turd possessed no vital information relating to his boss's kidnapping. If he had, he would have taken it straight to the FBI. She would also bet he'd already used the weight of his office to extract every detail he could from them. Now he wanted to hear it straight from the horse's mouth.

She guessed she couldn't blame him. Vickers and Jack went back a long way. He had to be as shaken as everyone in the room. Sighing, Gina raised her head.

"Send him up."

Mere moments after the short, tightly wired Vickers said hello to Jack's father and was introduced to others, he confirmed Gina's cynical guess. The man had spoken to just about every local, state and federal official involved into the case.

"They can't tell me a damned thing beyond the basics. All they could confirm was that you and the ambassador were screwing around when he got snatched and…"

"Stop right there, young man!"

Incensed, the duchess tilted her chin to a dangerous angle.

"You will address Lady Eugenia with courtesy and respect or you will leave this apartment immediately."

"I…"

"Do we understand each other?"

"I just…"

"A simple 'yes, ma'am' will do."

"Yes, ma'am."

Despite the tension engulfing the room, Gina and Sarah exchanged a small smile. The sisters had seen their grandmother reduce bigger and stronger men than Dale Vickers to quivering blobs of sorry.

Vickers's next comment erased any inclination to smile, however. Too wired to accept the duchess's icily polite invitation to have a seat, he paced the sitting room.

"I know it was clutching at straws, but I even thought this might have something to do with the face-to-face between the ambassador and the CEO of Global Protective Services at that little soiree TTG put on last weekend."

Little soiree? Gina swallowed an indignant huff. She had to work hard to refrain from suggesting Vickers take a short leap off a tall building.

Unaware he'd ignited her fuse, the staffer proceeded to send her straight into orbit. "If Global's power structure thought the ambassador was going to undercut them on the fat embassy security contract they're trying to land, they might want him out of the picture. When I called Nikki, though, she assured me…"

"Whoa! Back up a minute. Did you just say you called Nikki?" Gina asked incredulously. "Nicole Tremayne? My boss?"

"Of course I called her. She appreciates the business we've sent TTG's way since you and the ambassador…uh…" He caught the duchess's warning glance. "Since you and the ambassador started seeing each other. But I knew she didn't understand the awkward position you put him in by enticing him to attend an event sponsored by Global."

Gina barely heard the last, insulting remark. She was still dealing with the shock of learning that Jack and his staff had funneled business to TTG.

Her pride crumbled. Like an old, rotted rowboat, it just fell apart right before her eyes. What a fool she was! All these weeks she'd thought, she'd actually believed, she was making her own mark at TTG.

She struggled to her feet. She refused to burst into tears in front of Vickers, but her throat was thick when she reminded the assembled group that Special Agent Driskell and her partner were expected at any moment.

"Sarah, would you show them in when they get here? I need to... I need to..."

She didn't trust herself to finish. With a vague gesture toward the arched hallway leading to the rear of the apartment, she turned on her heel. Her eyes were burning by the time she made it the bath linking her bedroom with Sarah's old room. She dropped the lid to the stool and sank down sideways, crossing both arms on the counter beside it.

Strangely, the tears didn't gush. Gina stared at the wall, her pride in shreds, and waited for the usual flood to burst through the dam. It took a moment for her to understand why the tsunami didn't happen.

None of it mattered. Not her job or TTG or Vickers's snide comments. The *only* thing that mattered right now was Jack's safety. She would eat crow or humble pie or black, slimy worms if that would bring him back to her.

She was still staring blankly at the wall when Sarah tapped on the bathroom door.

"Gina? Are you okay?"

"Mostly."

"May I come in?"

She mumbled an assent and almost lost it when her sister eased down onto her knees beside the stool. Gina had counted on Sarah to bail her out of so many of life's little catastrophes. Turned to her, too, to soothe the ruffled feathers of the men she'd fallen for, then dropped with such careless abandon.

"It'll be okay," Sarah murmured, stroking her hair. "It'll be okay. Judging by everything I've heard in the past few minutes, Jack's been in tight spots before. He'll find a way out of this one, too."

Halfway across town Jack was was hungry, hurting and totally pissed.

He'd been sitting on his ass for hours now in a wobbly

chair with one leg shorter than the other. His arms were twisted behind his back. Plastic restraints cut into his wrists. The wound from the bullet that had grazed his upper arm had scabbed over, but the trail of dried blood it left itched like the devil under the shirt and suit coat he'd been told to pull on before they'd departed his hotel suite.

Jack had complied with the order. Hell, with Dominic St. Sebastian cradling an unconscious Gina in his arms, Jack would have jumped out the eighth-story window if so ordered to prevent the bastard from hurting her any worse.

He'd had time these past hours to think about that, though. How fast St. Sebastian had put himself between Gina and his two pals with guns. How quickly he'd clipped her, then caught her before she hit the floor. As though he wanted to neutralize her and get her out of the picture immediately, before the other goons turned their weapons in her direction.

If so, he hadn't bothered to communicate his strategy to Jack. Or anything else, for that matter. St. Sebastian and the shorter of his two pals had disappeared right after they'd dumped Jack in this abandoned warehouse.

They'd left the shaved-head Goliath to stand guard. The giant had heaved his bulk up twice in the past six hours, both times to take a leak. He'd sprayed the grimy brick wall like a fire hose, adding his contribution to the stench of vomit, urine and rat feces littering what was obviously a hangout for homeless druggies. He'd also grunted into a cell phone a few times in a heavy dialect Jack couldn't understand but otherwise refused to say a word.

Shifting in his chair to ease the ache in his shoulder joints, Jack decided to take another shot at him. "Hey! Num nuts! I know you won't respond to English."

He tried Spanish again, then French, then his limited Russian. All he got was a sneer and a shake of the thug's massive head.

Okay. All right. Jack couldn't wait any longer. If the nine or ten layers of local, state and federal officials he knew had to be looking for him hadn't closed in on the warehouse by now, odds were pretty damned good they wouldn't. If Jack were going to get out of this mess, he had to do it on his own.

For the fifth or sixth time he did a visual sweep of the warehouse. Rat droppings weren't the only objects littering its dim, cavernous interior. A stained mattress, some moldy fast-food sacks and a scatter of rusted tin cans gave ample evidence of prior occupation. So did the syringes dropped on the concrete floor.

His glance lingered on the syringes. He'd considered those earlier but the damned things were plastic, not glass. Even if he could toe one within reach, somehow get it into his hands and break the barrel before the gorilla noticed, the plastic shard wouldn't cut through the restraints.

He'd have to go with a rusted can. The closest was about four feet away. Its lid was jagged and bent back, as though someone had used an old-fashioned can opener to get at the contents, then tossed it aside.

He couldn't wiggle the rickety chair that far without getting Goliath all excited. He had to take a dive. Probably more than one. He just hoped to hell he didn't knock himself unconscious when he hit the cement floor.

"Hey! You!"

Goliath slewed a disinterested glance Jack's way.

"I need to take a leak, too."

Hard to pantomime without the use of your arms. He tipped his chin toward his fly. When that didn't produce results, he nodded toward the urine-splashed wall, arced his arms behind him to clear the chair and started to push to his feet.

His guard grunted a warning. Jack ignored it. He was almost upright when the giant lunged out of his own chair and swung the beefy fist gripping his silenced semiautomatic.

The blow knocked Jack sideways. He crashed to the cement. The rickety chair went with him. Goliath said something that was obviously a warning and hooked a paw under

Jack's arm. Of course, he had to grab the one grazed by the bullet.

When Jack grimaced in pain, amusement lit Goliath's broad, flat face. He muttered a few words that no doubt translated to "serves you right, asshole" and righted the over-turned chair. He shoved Jack into it and headed back to his own.

"I have to piss."

His jaw set, Jack started to rise again. And again, Goliath let fly with a backhanded blow. And this time, he couldn't be bothered to right the chair or haul his hostage up into it.

Jack's lips curled in a snarl. His eyes never left the gorilla's. Muttering profanities that only seemed to increase the big man's amusement, he got a grip on the rusted can he'd landed almost on top of. He maneuvered it with his fingertips until he turned the jagged lid inward. As he sur-reptitiously sawed at the plastic restraints, he wondered fleetingly how long it had been since his last tetanus shot. No matter. Lockjaw was the least of his worries right now. His gut told him Dominic St. Sebastian's pals played for keeps.

He got confirmation of that just moments after the gi-ant's cell phone buzzed. Goliath picked up the instrument, glanced at the number displayed on the screen and hit Talk. Two grunts later, he set the phone down. A few moments after that, a door at the far end of the warehouse opened.

Still lying on his side, Jack curved his body so his front faced the door and his wrists were hidden behind his back. The damned can lid was slippery with blood from slicing into his skin, but the grim realization that it was now or never kept him razoring at the restraints.

He also kept his eyes on the three men who came through the door. One he recognized from the hotel. The second was a stranger. The third was Dominic St. Sebastian. His fea-tures seemed to freeze when he spotted the body sprawled on the concrete. Then his eyes caught Jack's. He flashed a swift, silent message, but before Jack could interpret that damned thing, the stranger took a wide-legged stance a few yards away. He was dressed in a sleek gray suit and white wing tips. A distant corner of Jack's mind was wondering who the hell wore wing tips anymore when a vicious smile cut across the man's swarthy face.

"I have waited a long time for this, Ambassador."

"That right?"

"I thought to take you in Washington, but security there is too tight. How convenient that you have a woman here in New York."

The jagged lid took another slice out of Jack's thumb. He couldn't work the lid too hard with the stranger's eyes on him, but he didn't give up.

"Convenient for you, maybe," he drawled. "Not so much for me. Who the hell are you, anyway?"

"I am Antonio Cordi, the brother of Francesco Cordi. Perhaps you remember him?"

"Yeah, I remember him. Hard to forget the man who tried to gun down my father."

"And failed, unfortunately. We don't often miss our targets."

"'We' being you and the other scumbags who comprise 'Ndrangheta."

Jack was all too familiar with the confederation of Italian families that rose to power after the Cosa Nostra's decline in the 1990s. By forming alliances with Central and South American drug cartels, 'Ndrangheta had gone global and was now one of the world's most powerful criminal organizations. Its members were up to their hairy armpits in drug trafficking, prostitution, extortion, weapons smuggling and kidnappings for ransom. One U.S. State Department white paper estimated that their illegal activities accounted for more than $43 billion in 2007 alone—or approximately three percent of Italy's total gross domestic product.

Jack had gotten up close and personal with only one member of the clan, when his dad had been tapped to lead a delegation exploring the extent to which the 'Ndrangheta's money laundering had infiltrated the international banking system. The delegation followed one of the links to Francesco Cordi. When they dug a little too deep, Cordi retaliated by going after the high-ranking members of the delegation. Two died when their car was firebombed. Jack flew to Rome as soon as he heard about it and was with his father when Cordi came after him.

He had no regrets about taking Cordi down. Not then, not now. Even though he'd been advised by several concerned Italian officials that every member of the 'Ndrangheta swore a blood oath to always, *always* avenge the death of one of their own.

So he wasn't surprised when Cordi's brother slid a hand inside the jacket of his pearl-gray suit. Or that the hand emerged holding a blue steel Beretta.

Fourteen

Gina had never been inside a military command post but she suspected they couldn't be any more crowded or more tense than the apartment once Special Agent Driskell and her partner arrived.

With the duchess's permission, the FBI agents commandeered the study to interview Jack's father in private. That left Gina, her grandmother, Sarah, Dev, Zia and the obnoxious Dale Vickers to pick at the buffet lunch Maria had miraculously managed to augment with the arrival of each new wave of visitors.

Gina re-ee-eally wanted to tell Vickers to find somewhere else to squat, but the man was so worried about his friend and boss she didn't have the heart to kick him out of their unofficial command center. Besides, he and Dev seemed to have formed an unlikely partnership.

She tried to set aside her animosity for Vickers and study the two men objectively as they sat across from her, with the remains of the buffet lunch still littering the table. Jack's chief of staff was in an expensive-looking suit with his tie loosened and the top button of his shirt popped. Dev wore jeans and a faded, light blue denim shirt with the sleeves rolled up. With his broad shoulders, close-cropped black hair and tanned skin, he looked as if he spent more time on his parents' New Mexico ranch than in boardrooms all around the globe. Yet anyone looking at the two men could easily pick out the power broker. Dev Hunter exuded the utter confidence that came with having built a multinational aerospace corporation from the ground up.

"Are you sure Jack had his cell phone on him when he left Washington?" he asked Vickers.

"I'm sure."

Frowning, Dev worked the buttons of his handheld device. "It's not emitting a signal."

"I could have told you that," Gina said. "Someone..."

She scrunched her forehead and ran through a mental litany of officials who'd responded to her 911 call. The NYPD detectives? The guy from the counterterrorism office? Pam Driskell? Aside from the short, stocky FBI agent, they were all pretty much a nameless, faceless blur now.

"I can't remember who, but someone ran a trace on Jack's cell phone within moments of showing up at the Excelsior. Maybe several someones. They said any recently manufactured cell phone has a built-in tracking device that allows eavesdroppers to pinpoint its location to within just a few feet."

"Unless the battery is removed," Dev muttered, playing with his gizmo. "Which must be the case here, or the ultra high frequency cargo container signal receptor we're developing for MilSatCom would pick it up."

"The what for the who?"

"I can't speak to the 'what,'" Sarah said as Dev continued to scowl at the instrument in his hand, "but the 'who' is the Military Satellite Communications System."

When both the duchess and Gina turned to stare at her, she smiled at their look of astonishment. "Don't be so surprised. I've been receiving a crash course on all things military since we got back from our honeymoon."

"You're serious?"

"As serious as the self-contained, bolt-on/bolt-off special operations surveillance system mounted in the belly of a C-130," she said solemnly.

Gina tried, she really tried, to picture her oh-so-elegant sister in one of the retro designer classic outfits she loved clambering around the belly of a C-130. Not that Gina knew what a C-130 was, exactly.

"What about your brother?" Dev asked Zia, cutting into Gina's wild imaginings. "Do you know Dom's cell phone number?"

"Of course," she said wearily. "But the police ran a trace on that, too, with no results."

"With all due respect to our various law enforcement agencies, they don't yet have access to the kind of technology I'm talking about here. It's still in the developmental stage and... Well, damn! That's it!"

Dev's exclamation shot up the tension level among the others in the room. The women all sat up in their chairs. Vickers hunched closer as Dev whipped out his own cell phone.

"That's what?" Vickers asked.

Shaking his head in obvious self-disgust, Dev tapped a number on his speed dial. "Why the hell didn't I think of it before?"

"Think of what?"

"Hold on." He put the phone to his ear. "Pat, I need the MilSat access code for the gamma version of CSR-II. I've been trying to get on using the beta version but... Yeah, I know. I know. Just get me the damned code."

"Ooooh," Sarah murmured, her green eyes dancing, "that's going to cost him."

"Pat Donovan is Dev's right-hand man," Gina explained to a bewildered Zia. "He's a wizard. Really, I think the man has magical powers. He can move mountains with a single phone call."

"If not mountains, at least the occupants of an entire Parisian hotel," Sarah recalled. "I don't know what kind of a bonus Dev paid him for that particular trick but I have a feeling it ran to big bucks."

"Say again," Dev barked into the phone, his brows knit. "Right. Right. Okay, got it. What? Yeah, we'll talk about that later."

He disconnected and switched to his handheld device. The thing looked so innocuous. Just a small, wafer-thin box with a greenish-colored digital screen and a set of icons that appeared with the tap of a finger. It fit in the palm of Dev's hand and could easily be mistaken for a smart phone, except this little gadget could evidently bounce signals off the moon or something.

He was entering a long involved code when the sliding doors to the study slammed back. Every head turned in surprise as Driskell's partner raced out and made a beeline for the foyer. Driskell herself was right on his heels, with Jack's dad staggering white-faced behind them.

The FBI agent paused only long enough to throw out a terse explanation. "We've got a report of shots fired. Initial indications are the situation may involve the ambassador."

"Involve *how?*" Gina jumped up. The violent movement sent her chair crashing to the floor. "Agent Driskell, wait! Is Jack hurt?"

"Or my brother?" Zia demanded as she, too, surged to her feet.

"I don't know," the FBI agent replied on the run. "I'll contact y'all as soon as I do."

"I'm coming with you!"

Gina shouted to an empty space. Driskell was already out the front door, leaving a frozen tableau of tension and fear in her wake. Dev shattered the silence with an abrupt command.

"Gina, do you have Driskell's cell phone number?"

She could hardly speak past the terror lodged like a spiked ball in her throat. "Yes."

Wedging a hand into the pocket of her jeans, she extracted

the business card Driskell had given her earlier. Dev snatched it from her fingers and entered the number on his device. Mere seconds later, his blue eyes lit with fierce satisfaction.

"Okay, I've got her." He swung toward the foyer. "Let's go."

Gina, Zia, Jack's dad and Dale Vickers all wheeled in a swift formation that would have done a platoon of marines proud. Their syncopated turn didn't impress Dev.

"Whoa! We can't all—"

"Do not say it!" Zia interrupted. Her dark eyes blazed and her accent went thick with passion. "I am a doctor. If Dom... If anyone is hurt, I can help."

"I'm going, too," Jack's dad growled.

Dale Vickers didn't say a thing but his pugnacious expression dared anyone, Dev included, to try and stop him.

Sarah was the only who exhibited any restraint. "I'll stay with Grandmama." Her gaze drilled into her husband. "But please, please, be careful."

"I will." Dev strode for the foyer. "We'll have to take two cabs."

"Sarah!" Gina called over her shoulder. "Buzz down and tell Jerome to get on his whistle. We need two taxis, like pronto!"

The doorman had them lined up and waiting at the curb when they all poured out of the elevators. Dev aimed for the lead vehicle and issued orders in a voice that said he wasn't allowing vetoes this time.

"Gina, you and Zia with me. Vickers, you follow with Mr. Mason."

They scrambled into their assigned cabs. Gina and Zia took the backseat of the first, Dev folded his tall frame into the front.

"Hey, mon," the cabbie said in a lilting Caribbean accent that matched his shoulder-length dreadlocks and colorful orange, green, yellow and black knit cap. "Where ya goin'?"

"Straight down Central Park West until I tell you to turn."

The cabbie shrugged and activated his meter. As the leafy green of the park zipped by, Dev kept his narrowed gaze on the street grid filling his screen.

Gina edged forward on her seat and looked over his shoulder. All she could see was a tiny red dot racing along the grid.

"Is that Driskell?"

"It is."

"What happens if she gets or makes a call? You won't lose the track, will you?"

"Heads in my R-and-D division will roll if I do."

Not quite reassured by that grim prediction, Gina groped for her cousin's hand. Zia threw her a glance filled with equal parts hope and determination.

"They will be okay, your man and my brother. But to make sure..." She squeezed Gina's fingers. "I shall say a special prayer to Saint Stephen. He is the patron saint of your grandmother's homeland, you know."

No, Gina didn't know. At this point, though, she would pray to any celestial being who might intercede on Jack and Dom's behalf.

As if sensing how close her cousin was to a total meltdown, Zia tried to distract her with details about the saint. "He is Istvan in our language. He was born in 965 or '67 or '75. No one knows for sure. His father was Grand Prince Géza of Hungary. His mother, the daughter of Gylua of Transylvania."

The mention of Transylvania diverted Gina long enough for all-too-vivid images of werewolves springing out of coffins to flash into her mind. Or was it vampires who rose from the dead? For God's sake! Who cared?

Zia refused to let her cousin's wildly careening thoughts and emotions overwhelm her. Speaking calmly, slowly, soothingly, she related how the eventual Saint Istvan married Giselle of Bavaria and ascended to the throne of the Magyars on the death of his father. How he discouraged pagan customs and strengthened Christianity by a series of strict laws. How he was devastated by the death of his oldest son, Emeric, in a hunting accident, after which his cousin, Duke Vazul, took part in an assassination conspiracy.

"The attempt failed," Zia related as Dev issued a sharp order to the cabbie to cut across town. "Vazul had his eyes gouged out and molten lead poured in his ears."

"Umm," Gina murmured.

Her eyes were on that blinking red dot, her thoughts anywhere but with some long dead saint.

"Without a living heir, King St. Istvan asked the Blessed Virgin Mary to take the Hungarian people as her subjects and become their queen. He died on the same feast day that commemorates the assumption into heaven of the Blessed Virgin Mary, yes?"

"What? Oh. Right."

Gina had no idea what her cousin had been talking about. Her focus was on the bridge ahead. As a native New Yorker, she understood why the cabbie balked.

"I don't do runs to that part of Brooklyn," he said with a head shake that set his dreadlocks swinging.

"There's an extra five hundred in it for you," Dev countered.

"Say no more, mon."

As they cruised onto the bridge, Gina twisted around. The second cab was still following. She dropped back in her seat, wondering how much Jack's dad had offered his driver.

Once across the bridge they entered a twilight zone of abandoned warehouses and crumbling industrial facilities. The area had formerly been home to the Brooklyn Navy Yard and had died a painful death in the '60s or '70s. Gina knew a comeback was planned, but it was still a ways off.

Artists and commercial activities rented space in the cavernous building that hadn't collapsed under the weight of time and disuse. She saw a bright pink neon sign indicating a movie studio. Another, slightly less attention-grabbing billboard advertised Brooklyn Grange Farm. The farm supposedly utilized 45,000 square feet on the roof of Building 3, wherever that was. Sadly, all too many of the structures showed an endless vista of graffiti-covered walls, trash-strewn yards fenced off with razor wire, and row after row of broken windows.

With every deserted block the cab skimmed past, Gina's hopes dipped lower and lower. They hit rock-bottom when the taxi turned a corner and she spotted what looked like twenty or more emergency vehicles dead ahead.

The cabbie screeched to a halt a half block away. "Hey, mon, I can't cruise close to no cop cars. They might have dogs with 'em."

"Christ," Dev muttered, "what are you hauling in... Oh, hell, never mind."

He shoved a wad of bills at the driver and shouldered open the door. Gina and Zia scrambled out at the same time.

"Stay here until I scope out the situation," Dev ordered brusquely.

"No way," Gina said, her frantic gaze locked on the two ambulances parked side by side amid the other vehicles.

She took off after Zia, who'd already broken into a dead run. All Dev could do at that point was curse and charge after her. If shots were fired from any of the broken windows staring sightlessly down at them, he'd damned well better get in front of Gina and shield her body with his. Sarah would never forgive him if her sister got hurt. Zia would just have to take her chances.

The cabbie barely waited for them to clear his vehicle before screeching into a three-point turn. He almost swiped the second cab's fender when he peeled off. Dev heard the shriek of brakes, the thud of doors slamming, the slam of footsteps on pavement as Vickers and Jack's father raced down the street.

Luckily, they all reached the protective screen of emergency vehicles without shots erupting from the warehouse. The uniformed officer on the perimeter looked as if he might draw his weapon, though, when the two women leading the charge ignored his command to stop. Parting like the proverbial Red Sea, they started to go around him.

"Hey! Hold it right there."

He made a grab for the closest, which happened to be Zia, and got a face full of raging female.

"*Vagyok orvos!* Ach! I am doctor! Doctor!"

Her unleashed emotions made her accent so heavy that the English was almost indistinguishable from the Hungarian. Neither made an impression on the uniformed officer.

"Look, lady, you…all of you…better not take another friggin' step until I see some ID, log you in and get clearance to…"

"*Ide,* Anastazia!"

The shout came from an unmarked vehicle parked inside the cordon. Zia whirled and gave a glad cry. The rest of the group spun around, as well. Gina registered a half-dozen wildly careening thoughts as she watched Dominic stride toward them.

Blood seeped from a slash high on one cheek. One eye was swollen shut. He wasn't in handcuffs. And he was alone.

Dear God! He was alone.

With a sob of sheer terror, she dodged the uniformed officer and broke into another run. He gave a shout, but interpreted a short air-chop from Dominic as a signal that his duty lay in keeping the rest of the crowd corralled.

Ten steps later, Gina flung herself at Dominic. Her fists hammered a frantic drumbeat on his chest. "Where's Jack? What did you do with him? If you or those thugs you were with hurt him, I'll carve out your heart and shove it down your throat."

Dom's eyes widened, and Gina shocked even herself with the viciousness of the threat. A distant corner of her mind registered a flicker of surprise that she hadn't burst into her by-now-usual flood of tears. Her otherwise volatile hormones seemed to have narrowed to a single, deadly and completely primal urge.

If this man—if any man—had harmed her mate, she'd make that Italian crime organization Jack's dad mentioned seem like a bunch of playful kindergarteners.

"Tell me, dammit. Where's Jack?"

Dom caught her pounding fists before they did serious damage to his chest wall. "He's there, Gina." Keeping a careful grip on her wrists, he angled her around. "Talking with some agents from the FBI."

She spotted him the same moment he followed Agent Driskell's nod and glanced over his shoulder. In the ten seconds it took for Gina to wrestle out of Dom's hold and Jack to sprint the fifty or so yards separating them, she saw that he was as bruised as her cousin.

But it was his eyes that lit her heart up like the Fourth of July. His fierce, unguarded expression. The raw, male pheromones shooting off him like live sparks when he caught her in his arms. Her blood singing with joy, she returned his kiss with every ounce of relief, of desire, of love that was in her.

Swift, frightening sanity came in the form of a sticky residue that transferred from the sleeve of his dark charcoal suit coat to Gina's palm. In her mad rush to his arms, she hadn't noticed the stain.

She couldn't miss it now. It left her palm a rusty red and a lump of dismay the size of a basketball bouncing around in her stomach. Gently, gingerly, she tried to ease away from the injured arm.

"You're hurt."

"So are you."

He curled a knuckle under her chin and angled her chin to survey the ugly bruise.

"I thought slamming my fist into your cousin's eye made up for this," he said, murder in his voice. "Looks like he still has some payment coming."

"You gave Dom his black eye?" Gina couldn't make sense of any of this. "If he was part of the plot to kidnap you, why isn't he under arrest?"

"Long story. Why don't we…?" He broke off, his gaze going to the men who now approached. "Hello, Dad. Dale."

Jack didn't seem the least surprised to see his father or chief of staff. Gina backed away to give them access to the man they all loved. She could share him with his family. With his obnoxious assistant. With his memories of Catherine.

And with the child they would welcome to the world in just a few short months. Lost in a love undiminished by the past or constrained by the present, Gina acknowledged there was more than enough of Jack Mason to go around.

Fifteen

Once again the duchess's spacious apartment served as command central. Most of the key players in the day's drama sat elbow-to-elbow at the dining table, relieving their tension with their choice of coffee, iced tea, fruit juice, *žuta osa* or the last of the double-distilled *pálinka*.

The duchess and Jack's father had opted for the brandy. Jack, Dev, Zia and Dom braved the throat-searing kick of the liqueur. Dale Vickers went with coffee, while Gina and Sarah chose juice. The duchess insisted Maria fill her own glass rather than trying to keep everyone's topped off and just sit down.

Pam Driskell put in a brief appearance, as did Jerome. The doorman had delegated his post to a subordinate to accompany the FBI agent upstairs. He'd abandoned his dignity long enough to wrap Gina in a fierce hug. He then shook Jack's hand, told him how happy he was to see him safe and went back to work.

The only major players who failed to put in an appearance were Antonio Cordi and his two thugs. Cordi because he was dead, shot through the heart during the violence that erupted inside the warehouse just moments before the police arrived. One of his hired hands was also deceased, the big one Jack bitingly referred to as Goliath. He'd had his jugular sliced by the lid of a rusty tin can and had bled out before the EMTs arrived. The second thug was now a guest of the U.S. government and likely to remain so for a long, long time.

Even now, huddled at the table that could seat twenty comfortably with the leaves in, Gina felt sick at the thought of how close both Jack and Dom had been to being on the receiving end of a bullet.

"Cordi must have wondered if my well-publicized departure from Interpol was a blind," Dom related after tossing back another restorative shot of *pálinka*. "He allowed me into the outer fringe of 'Ndrangheta but never let me get close enough to gather the evidence we needed to nail him."

"So to get close to the capo," Jack drawled, "you suggested using your kinship to Gina as a means to get to me."

"Cordi had sworn a blood oath to avenge his brother," Dom said with an unrepentant shrug. "He would have gotten to you eventually. I merely proved my loyalty by offering to set up the hit."

Gina still couldn't believe the tangled web of lies and deceit Dom had lived for almost a year. Danger had stalked him with every breath, every step.

Zia was even more appalled. She'd had no idea her brother had infiltrated one of Europe's most vicious crime organizations. Or that he'd arranged this "business" trip to New York City for a specific, and very deadly, purpose.

"No wonder you balked at my decision to accompany you," she said, scowling.

"You would not have accompanied me, had I not been sure I could keep you safe from danger."

"Not to mention," Dev guessed shrewdly, "the fact that she added to your credibility with the duchess."

"Yes, there was that consideration." A wry smile curved Dom's lips. "You don't know my sister very well, however, if you think my objections carried any weight with her. If I hadn't been certain I could keep her safe, I would have been forced to chain her to a wall in the dungeon of the crumbling castle the Duchess Charlotte once called home."

Jack's voice cut across the table like a serrated knife blade. "Too bad you couldn't offer the same guarantees for Gina."

"Ah, yes."

Dom's glance went to the bruise on Gina's chin. His one eye was still swollen shut, but the other showed real chagrin. "I very much regret having to hurt you, cousin. My associates had become impatient, you see, and I had to act or risk blowing my cover."

His glance slewed to Jack, then back to Gina. A rakish glint replaced the regret in his good eye. "If you would but let me," he murmured, "I would kiss away the hurt."

Jack answered that. This time his tone was slow and lazy but even more lethal. "You really do like living on the edge, don't you, St. Sebastian?"

"That's enough!"

The sharp reprimand turned every head to the duchess. Her chin had tilted to a degree that both Gina and Sarah recognized instantly, and her faded blue eyes shot daggers at the two combatants.

"May I remind you that you're guests in my home? Dominic, you will cease making such deliberately provocative comments. Jack, you will stop responding like a Neanderthal ready to club all rivals. Gina…"

When her gimlet gaze zinged to her youngest granddaughter, Gina jerked upright in her chair. She'd been on the receiving end of that stare too many times to take it lightly.

"What did I do?"

"It's what you haven't done," the duchess informed her. "For pity's sake, tell Jack you love him as much as he so obviously loves you and get on with planning your wedding."

A few moments of stark silence greeted the acerbic pronouncement. Jack broke it with a cool reply. "With all due respect, Duchess, that's something Gina and I should discuss in private."

His father joined the fray with a sudden and explosive exclamation. "Bull hockey!"

"Dad..."

John II ignored his son's warning glance. The face he turned to Gina wore a mix of regret and resolution. "I know I acted like an ass when you came to visit us at Five Oaks."

"Pretty much," she agreed politely.

"I need to apologize for that. And for the ugly name I called you earlier this morning," he added with a wince.

"Christ, Dad, what the hell did you...?"

"Be quiet, Jack. This is between Gina and me."

John Harris Mason II hadn't lost his bite. His son matched him glower for glower but yielded the floor. Once again, the older man addressed Gina.

"That was unforgivable. I hope you'll chalk it up to a father sick to death with worry over his son."

"Consider it chalked," she said with a shaky smile.

Oh, boy! Her emotions were starting one of their wild swings. Now that the danger to Jack had passed and she was surrounded by everyone she loved most in the world, she wasn't sure how long she could hold out before dissolving into wet, sloppy tears.

Jack's father didn't help matters. He leaned forward, his gaze holding hers. "I've never seen anyone turn Jack on his head the way you have, Gina."

"Is that...?" She gulped. "Is that good?"

"Oh, yes. More than I can say. You've shaken him out of the mold I tried... We all tried," he said with a glance at Dale Vickers, "to force him into."

He paused. His throat worked, sending his Adam's apple up and down a few times. When he could speak again, his voice was raw with emotion.

"Jack's mother would be proud to call you daughter. So would I."

That did it. Gina could feel her face getting all blotchy with the effort of holding back tears. "I...I..."

Shoving back her chair, she resorted to her most trustworthy excuse for beating an instant retreat.

"I have to pee."

Sarah had followed her when she'd retreated to the bathroom earlier in the afternoon. This time it was Jack. Except he didn't knock, as her sister had. Nor did he ask for permission to enter. He just barged in and kicked the door shut behind him.

Luckily, Gina hadn't really needed to go. Her panties weren't around her ankles. The skinny jeans she'd been wearing for what now felt like two lifetimes were still zipped up. She was on the pot, though, and the tears she'd tried so hard to stem streamed down her cheeks. Like Sarah, Jack sank to his knees beside the stool. Unlike Sarah, he didn't hesitate to drag Gina off the throne and into his arms.

"Don't cry, sweetheart. Please, don't cry."

He held her, rocking back and forth, while the residual stress and tension and fear poured out via her tear ducts.

"It's…it's the hormones," she said through hiccuping sobs. "I never cry. Never! Ask Sarah. Ask…ask Grandmama. They'll tell you."

"It's okay."

"Noooo," she wailed, "it's not."

She grabbed the front of his shirt. His bloodied shirt. He hadn't had time to change, either.

"I didn't get a chance to tell you this morning, Jack. I…I didn't think I'd ever get a chance to tell you. I love you."

"I know, darling."

"No, you don't!"

The tears evaporated, replaced by an urgency that reached deep into her core.

"I think…" She shook her head. "Scratch that! I know I fell a little bit in love with you our first weekend together. I'm not sure when I tumbled all the rest of the way, but I'm all the way there."

"Me, too, my darling."

His smile was all Jack. Charming, roguish and so damned sexy Gina could feel her tears drying and another part of her starting to get wet.

"So what do you think?" he said, dropping a kiss on her nose. "Want get off the floor, go back into the dining room and tell your grandmother to start planning a wedding?"

"No."

His confidence took a hit, but he recovered fast. Shaking his head, he acknowledged his gaffe. "I'm such a jackass. How could I forget you're the world's greatest event coordinator?"

"Yeah, right."

Those damned hormones! Gina could for the sneer curled her lip and the sulky response she couldn't hold back.

"I can't be that great if you had to send Washington business TTG's way."

"What are you talking about?"

"Dale told me you steered business to TTG." She made a heroic effort to keep the hurt out of her voice. "I appreciate it, Jack. I really do. It's just that I wanted to… I was trying to… Oh, crap!"

The hand that took her chin and tilted it up was anything but gentle.

"Listen to me, Eugenia Amalia Thérése St. Sebastian. I'm going to say this once, and once only. If Dale Vickers or anyone else in my office steered business to TTG, they did it without my knowledge or consent. You got that?"

The fire in his blue eyes convinced her as much as the uncomfortable grip on her still sore chin.

"I've got it."

"You'd better," he said, the anger still hot. "Now, do you want to work the wedding arrangements yourself or not?"

"Not."

"Dammit all to hell! I'm past being civilized and modern and reasonable about this. If I have to lock you in those chains your cousin talked about and drag you to the altar, I will. One way or another, you're going to marry me."

"Oooooh."

Gina batted her eyes and thought about leading him on a little longer. She decided against it, primarily because she wasn't quite sure he wouldn't follow through with that bit about the chains.

"As much as I might enjoy the kinky aspects of your proposal," she breathed, "I think we should go for something a little more traditional."

"Then for God's sake," he bellowed, "tell me what the hell you want."

Whoa! What happened to the smooth, polished diplomat who'd seduced her with his charm and sophisticated wit? This glimpse of the angry male under Jack's urbane shell thrilled and made her just a tad nervous. Yielding to the age-old feminine instinct to soothe and soften and placate her mate, Gina stroked his cheek.

"What I want," she said, "is for us to get off the bathroom floor. Then we'll make a call to your mom and get her up here on the next flight. After which, we'll haul ass to a lab and have our blood drawn so we can stand up before the nearest justice of the peace."

Jack agreed with the last portion of her agenda, if not the first. Instead of pushing to his feet and pulling her up with him, he kept her anchored to the fluffy bath mat. The fire went out of his eyes, the irritation out of his voice.

"Are you sure that's what you want?" he asked in a much subdued tone.

"That's what I want."

"No big fancy wedding? No exotic theme?"

"No big fancy wedding." With silent apologies to Nikki and Samuel and Kallie, she lied her heart out. "No exotic theme. Just you and me and our immediate families in front of a JP."

* * *

Gina should have known that plan wouldn't hold up against the combined assault of her sister, her grandmother and Jack's mom, Ellen. All right, maybe she didn't really want it to. She'd given too much of herself and her energy to the party-planning business. In her heart of hearts, she secretly wished for at least a little splash.

Still, she had to work to overcome her irritation when her boss called less than an hour after Gina and Jack had emerged from the bathroom and announced their intentions to the assembled entourage. Vickers, Gina thought immediately. The little toad probably had TTG on his speed dial.

"Gina," Nikki gushed in her rapid-fire way, "I just heard! You've finally come to your senses."

"I…"

"I'm so, so glad you've agreed to marry your sexy ambassador."

"I have, but…"

"Listen, kiddo, I know Jack is hot to get you to the altar before you change your mind. I also know you want to keep the wedding small and intimate, but the midtown venue's available Thursday evening."

"Nikki…"

"My office, ten tomorrow morning. We'll hammer out the details. Oh, and bring your grandmother. I've been wanting to meet her since the day my father announced he was leaving my mother for her. God, I wish he had! Might have saved me thousands of dollars in shrink fees. *Ciao,* my darling. And don't worry. TTG will send you off in grand style."

Send you off in grand style.

The blithe promise had been intended to reassure. It acted instead like a bucket of frigid water. Every spark of Gina's newfound joy got a thorough dousing.

Grandmama, she thought on a wave of dismay. How could she move to D.C. and live with Jack? Not that he'd remain in

D.C. much longer. Vickers had hinted he was being considered for a major diplomatic posting. London was a definite possibility. So was Athens.

Heartsick, she caught Sarah's eye and telegraphed a silent signal. Her sister's hidden antenna were obviously in full receive mode. She nodded and moments later pushed through the swinging door to the kitchen. As soon as she saw Gina's face, concern clouded her green eyes.

"What's the matter?"

"Nothing out of the ordinary," Gina said bitterly. "I'm just being my usual, selfish self."

"Selfish how?"

"I didn't even think about Grandmama when I agreed to marry Jack. She's so looking forward to the baby. She's already talking about converting the study to a nursery. How can I just flit off and leave her alone?"

"She wants you to be happy. She wants both of us to be happy. You know she does."

Gina might have believed her if not for the guilt clouding Sarah's forest-green eyes. She'd experienced the same wrenching pangs before her wedding to Dev. They hadn't eased until Gina posed the possibility of moving back into the Dakota.

"Dev said he could set up a temporary headquarters here in New York," Sarah reminded her sister. "We could still do that. Or…"

The swish of the swinging door cut off whatever alternate Sarah had intended to propose. She and Gina both turned to face Zia.

"I'm sorry to intrude," she said. "But I wished to speak to you both, and this may be my only chance before Dom and I move to a hotel."

The heavy, stress-induced accent had disappeared. Zia was once again their gorgeous, self-assured cousin.

Or a third sister. One demanding to be included in this

girls-only enclave. The thought struck Gina all of two seconds before Zia gave it flesh and blood.

"As Gina knows," she said to Sarah, "I've just finished my last year of medical school at Semmelweis University in Budapest. It's a very prestigious institution and...well..."

She shrugged, as if to downplay what both sisters knew had to be a major accomplishment. "I've been offered a number of residencies in pediatric medicine," she continued after a moment. "One of them is at Kravis Children's Hospital. That's why I insisted on accompanying Dom on this visit. I...I have an interview with the head of the residency program tomorrow," she finished on a note of uncharacteristic hesitation.

"That's wonderful," Sarah said with unfeigned delight. "You and Grandmama will be able to visit and get to know each other better."

"Yes, well..." Zia's glance shifted from one sister to the other. "The duchess has invited me to live with her, should I do my three-year residency here in New York City. I'm overwhelmed by her generosity but I don't wish to impose on her. If the idea concerns you...either of you...or in any way makes you think I'm taking advantage of her, please tell me."

Gina wished she were a better person. She really did! Here she was, wracked with guilt one moment at the prospect of leaving her grandmother alone. In the next, she was battling a toxic niggle of jealousy at the idea of this ultra-smart, ultra-achieving woman taking her place in the duchess's heart.

And of course, because Zia *was* so damned smart, she read every emotion that flitted across Gina's face.

"I will not live here if you don't wish it," she said quietly. "Or you, Sarah. I know how much you love the duchess. How much she loves you. If it will cause you or her heartache, I'll turn down the offer from Kravis. None of you will ever hear from me again."

Gina knew the speech came straight from the heart. But it was the mist that sheened her cousin's dark eyes that obliterated any and every doubt. Somehow, someway, the knowledge that brilliant, self-assured Anastazia St. Sebastian was susceptible to human emotion made everything all right.

The jealousy fell away, leaving only a profound thankfulness. Smiling, she reached out and squeezed Zia's hand.

"I think it would be wonderful for Grandmama to have your company."

Sixteen

Nicole Tremayne came through as promised. TTG sent Gina and Jack off in grand style.

The balmy June evening was perfect for an outdoor ceremony. Thousands of tiny white lights gleamed in the topiary trees outlining the terrace of TTG's midtown venue. More lights sheathed in filmy white netting were hung in graceful loops to form an archway from the reception room to the dais. The platform itself was framed by antique wrought-iron. The intricate iron work was painted pearl-white and intertwined with netting, lights, ivy and fragrant yellow honeysuckle.

Gina and Jack had kept the guest list small. Relatively small, that is, compared to the hundreds who usually attended TTG's functions. Still, the attendees filled eight rows of white chairs arranged in a semicircle on the terrace overlooking the East River.

Gina's coworkers at TTG came as guests for a change instead of employees. Jerome and his wife had been invited, of course, and Maria beamed from her seat in the front row. Dominic sat beside her, his black eye still noticeable but considerably reduced in size and discoloration.

Jack's guests filled the seats on the other side of the aisle.

Following her son's wishes, Ellen had been ruthless. She'd axed every one of the political cronies her husband had tried to add to the list. Only Jack's family, close personal friends and associates survived the hatchet. In his case, though, "close" included the Secretary of State, the current U.S. Ambassador to the U.N. and Virginia's lieutenant governor.

"You ready, Gina?"

Kallie was the only of her fellow employees not seated out front. She'd volunteered to get the major players in place and cue the music. The wings in her red hair were yellow tonight in keeping with the yellow roses that wreathed the hair of the bride and her attendants.

The event coordinator in Gina had her taking a quick peek through the gauze curtains to make sure everyone was where they were supposed to be. Sure enough, Jack waited under the wrought-iron arch with his groomsmen. Dev stood tall and handsome beside him. Dale Vickers was arranged next to Dev. Gina grimaced inwardly but reminded herself of her resolution to *try* to build a better relationship with the little toad.

She let the curtain drop and sent a smile to the other three women clustered with her in the small anteroom. Her grandmother, regal in royal blue silk and lace, looked like the grand duchess she was. Gina had asked Zia to be one of her attendants. And Sarah, of course. They were each wearing the dress of her choice. Zia had hit the shops on 5th Avenue and found a body-hugging gold silk sheath that dipped to her waist in the back. With her black hair piled loosely on top of her head, the rear view was sure to drop most of the male jaws in the house when she glided down the aisle.

Sarah's dress was one of the retro classics she still favored despite Dev's repeated attempts to get her to buy out Rodeo Drive. This one was a Balenciaga that fell in soft, shimmering folds in the same vivid green hue as the Russian emerald Dev had slipped on her finger when they'd become engaged.

Gina's choice of rings was more traditional, if you could

call a three-carat marquise traditional. Particularly since Jack had upped the weight from her original choice and had the stone set in a band studded with another three carats of baguettes.

The diamonds' glitter didn't compare to the sparkle in Gina's smile as she gave Kallie the go-ahead. "I am so ready."

She wasn't sure, but she thought Sarah and the duchess let out a collective sigh of relief. Even Zia perked up as the music swelled and she led the way down the aisle. Sarah gave her sister a quick kiss and went next. Then Gina slipped her arm through her grandmother's.

As they made their slow progress under the arch of netting and tiny white lights, Gina couldn't believe how her world had changed so drastically in such a short time. Was it only two months since Grandmama had made this same, slow walk with Sarah? Two and a half months since Gina had peed on a little purple stick and felt her world tilt off its axis? Those frantic days might have happened in another life, to another person. Everything in Gina's world now was right and bright and perfect.

The duchess seemed to agree. When she and her youngest granddaughter reached the dais, her faded blue eyes shone with love. "My dearest Eugenia. I'm so very proud of you."

Gina wouldn't cry! She wouldn't! She wanted to, though. Big, fat, wet, sloppy tears that would streak her entire face with mascara.

Uh-oh! Jack must have sensed how close she was to a meltdown. He took a hasty step forward, smiling as he relieved the duchess of escort duty.

"I'll take it from here."

Bending, he dropped a kiss on his soon-to-be-grandmother-in-law's cheek. She murmured something for his ears only. Probably the same death threat she'd issued to Dev, Gina guessed, threatening him with unspeakable agony if he hurt so much as a single hair on her head.

Jack acknowledged the warning with a solemn nod. Then

his eyes were on Gina. Only on Gina. Her glorious smile, her tumble of silvery blond curls, her laughing blue eyes. He tucked her arm in his, amazed and humbled by the fact he'd been given the precious gift of love twice in one lifetime.

In all the excitement of the past week, he and Gina had almost missed their second appointment with their OB doc. They'd gone in yesterday and had the first ultrasound done. Jack carried a copy of the scan in his tux pocket now, right next to his heart. As far as his parents knew, he and Gina would welcome the Mason family's first set of twins.

First things first, though! Jack's number one priority at the moment was getting a wedding band on Gina St. Sebastian's finger. He practically dragged her into position on the dais and issued a swift instruction to the senior judge of the U.S. Court of Appeals for the Second Circuit, who also happened to be his former college roommate.

"Let's do this!"

Epilogue

What an exciting, frightening, wonderful week this has been! Eugenia, my darling Eugenia, finally admitted what I've known since the day she returned from Switzerland. She's in love, so very much in love, with the father of her babies. Babies! I can't wait to cradle them in my arms, as I once held Gina.

Then there's Sarah, my lovely Sarah. It makes my heart sing to see her so happy, too. I suspect it won't be long before she and Dev start their family, as well.

I thought my life's work would be complete when I escorted those two precious girls down the aisle. How odd, and how wonderful, that another young and vibrant twosome has helped fill the void of losing them. Dominic goes back to Hungary in a few days and is pressing me to return to my homeland for a visit. I shall have to think about that. In the meantime, I'll share Anastazia's trials and tribulations as she begins what I know will be a grueling residency.

Who would have imagined my plate would be so full at this late stage in my life?

From the diary of Charlotte,
Grand Duchess of Karlenburgh

* * * * *

THE GIRL HE'D OVERLOOKED

CATHY WILLIAMS

PROLOGUE

JENNIFER looked at her reflection in the mirror. She had died and gone to heaven! Fantastic restaurant, fantastic food, even the ladies' room was fantastic. Beige marble everywhere and delicate little hand towels, a basket of them, to be picked, used and discarded. Could things get any better? Her cheeks were pink, her eyes were glowing.

She leaned forward and for the first time her physical shortcomings did not rush towards her in a wave of disappointment. She was no longer the too tall, too big-boned girl with the hair that was slightly too unruly and a mouth that was too wide. She was a sexy woman on the brink of the rest of her life and, best of all, James was out there, waiting for her. James, *her date*.

Jennifer Edwards had known James Rocchi all her life. From the small window of her bedroom in the cottage that she had shared with her father, she could daily look out to the distant splendour of his family home—The Big House, as she and her father had always called the Rocchi mansion, with its sweeping drive and imposing acres of stunning Victorian architecture.

As a kid, she had worshipped him and had trotted behind him and his friends as they had enjoyed themselves in the acres and acres of grounds surrounding the house. As a teenager, she had developed a healthy crush on him, blushing and awkward whenever he returned from boarding school, although, several years older than her, he couldn't have been more oblivious. But she was no longer a teenager. She was now twenty-one years old, with a degree in French firmly behind her and a secondment to the Parisian office of the law firm in which she had spent every summer vacation working only days away.

She was a woman and life couldn't have felt any better than it did right now, right here.

With a little sigh of pleasure, she applied a top up of her lip gloss, patted her hair, which she had spent ages trying to straighten and mostly succeeded, and headed back out to the restaurant.

He was gazing out of the window and she took a few seconds to drink him in.

James Rocchi was a stunning example of the sort of aggressively good-looking alpha male that could turn heads from streets away. Like his father, who had been an Italian diplomat, James was black-haired and bronze-skinned, only inheriting his English mother's navy-blue eyes. Everything about him oozed lethal sex appeal, from the arrogant tilt of his head to the muscled perfection of his body. Jennifer had seen the way other women, usually small blonde things he had brought back with him from university, had followed him with their eyes as if they couldn't get enough of him.

She was still finding it hard to believe that she was actually here with him and she took a deep breath and reminded herself that *he had asked her on a date*. It gave her just the surge of confidence she needed to walk towards him and she blushed furiously as he turned to look at her with a slow smile on his face.

'So…I've arranged a little surprise for you…'

Jennifer could barely contain her breathless excitement. 'You haven't! What is it?'

'You'll have to wait and see,' he told her with a grin. He leaned back, angling his body so that he could stretch his legs out. 'I still can't believe that you've finished university and are heading off to foreign shores...'

'I know, but the offer of a job in Paris was just too good to pass up. You know what it's like here.'

'I know,' he agreed, understanding what she meant without her having to explain. Wasn't this one of the great things about her? he thought. They had known each other for so long that there was hardly any need to explain references or, frankly, sometimes, to finish sentences. Of course, Paris for a year was going to be brilliant for her. Aside from her stint at university, which, in Canterbury, had hardly been a million miles away, he couldn't think of a time that she had ever left here and, however beautiful and peaceful this slice of Kent was, she should be champing at the bit to spread her wings and fly farther afield. But he didn't mind admitting to himself that he was going to miss her easy companionship.

Jennifer helped herself to another glass of wine and giggled. 'Three shops, a bank, two offices, a post office and no jobs! Well, I guess I could have thought about travelling into Canterbury...seeing what I could land there but...'

'But that would have been a waste of your French degree. I guess John will miss having you around.'

Jennifer wanted to ask if *he* would miss having her around. He worked in London, had taken over the running of his father's company when, in the wake of his father's death six years previously, the vultures had been circling, waiting to snap it up at a knock-down price. At the time he had barely been out of university but he had skipped the gap year he had planned and returned to take the reins of the company and haul it into the twenty-first century. London was his base but he travelled out to the country regularly. Would he miss having her around on those weekends? Bank holidays?

'I won't be gone for the rest of my life.' Jennifer smiled, thinking of her father. 'I think he'll manage. He has his little landscaping business and, of course, overseeing your grounds. I've been working to get him computer literate so that we can Skype each other.' She cupped her face in her hands and looked at him. He was only just twenty-seven but he looked older. Was that because he had been thrown into a life of responsibility at the highest possible level from a very young age? He had had little to do with his father's company before his father had died. Silvio Rocchi had barely had anything to do with it himself. While he had carried out his diplomatic duties, he had delegated the running of the company to his right-hand men which, as it turned out, had not been the best idea in the world. When he died, James had been the young up-start whose job it had been to sack the dead wood. Had that forged a vein of steel inside him that had turned the boy quickly into the man?

She could have spent a few minutes chewing over the conundrum but he was saying something, talking about her father.

'And it's just a thought but he might even enjoy having the place to himself, who knows?'

'Well, he'll get *used to it*.' But enjoy? No, she couldn't really see that happening. Her earliest memories were of her and her dad as a unit. They had weathered the storm of her mother's death together and had been everything to each other ever since.

'I think,' James murmured, glancing over her shoulder

and leaning towards her to cover her hand with his, 'your little surprise is on its way...'

Jennifer spun around to see two of the waiters walking towards her and felt a stab of sudden disappointment. They were holding a cake with a sparkler and huge bowl of ice cream liberally covered with chocolate sauce and coloured sweets. It was the sort of thing a child would have been thrilled by, not a grown woman. She glanced over her shoulder to James, and saw that he was lounging back, hands clasped behind his head, smiling with an expression of satisfaction so she smiled too and held the smile as she blew out the sparkler to an audience of clapping diners.

'Really, James, you shouldn't have.' She stared down at more dessert than anyone could hope to consume in a single sitting, even someone of her proportions. The awkward girl she had left behind threatened to return as she gazed down at his special gesture.

'You deserve it, Jen.' He rested his elbows on the table and carefully removed the sparkler from the cake. 'You did brilliantly at university and you've done brilliantly to accept the Paris job.'

'There's nothing *brilliant* about accepting a job.'

'But Paris...when my mother told me that you'd been offered it, I wasn't sure whether you had it in you to take it.'

'What do you mean?' It seemed rude to leave the melting ice cream and the slab of cake untouched, so she had a mouthful and looked away from him.

'You know what I mean. You haven't strayed far from the family home...university just around the corner so that you could pop in and check on John several times a week, even though you were living out...'

'Yes, well—'

'Not that that's a bad thing. It's not. The world would be a better place if there were more people like you in it. We

certainly would be reading far fewer stories in the news-
papers of care homes where ageing relatives get shoved
and forgotten about.'

'You make me sound like a saint,' Jennifer said, stabbing some cake and dipping it into the bowl of ice cream.

'You always do that.'

'What?'

'Somehow manage to turn cake and ice cream into
slush. And you always manage to do...*that*...'

'What?' She could feel her irritation levels rising.

'Get ice cream round your mouth.' He reached over
to brush some ice cream off and the fleeting touch of his
finger by her mouth almost made her gasp. He licked the
ice cream from his finger and raised his eyebrows with
appreciation.

'Very nice. Bring that bowl closer and let's share.'

Jennifer relaxed. This was more like it. Three glasses
of wine had relaxed her but she hadn't been able to banish
all her inhibitions. His treating her like a kid was probably
going to bring them all back but clinking spoons as they
dipped into the same bowl, exchanging mouthfuls of ice
cream and laughing...

Once again she felt intoxicated with anticipation.

She made sure to lean forward so that he could see her
cleavage, which was daringly on display. Normally, she
wore much plainer clothes, big jumpers in winter and loose
dresses in summer. But, for this date, she had splashed out
on a calf-length skirt and although the silky top was still
fairly baggy, its neckline was more risqué.

It was strange but, although she had no qualms about
wearing tight jeans and tight tops at university, the standard uniform for students, the thought of wearing anything
tight in front of James had always brought on a mild panic
attack. The feel of those lazy blue eyes resting on her had

always resulted in an acute bout of self-consciousness. His girlfriends were always so petite and so slim. In her head, she had always been able to hear his comparisons whenever he looked at her. Loose clothes had been one way of deflecting those comparisons.

'So,' he murmured, 'will you be leaving any broken hearts behind?'

It was the first time he had ever asked her such a directly personal question and she shivered pleasurably as she shook her head, not wanting, *under any circumstances*, to let him get the impression that she wasn't available.

'Absolutely no one.'

'You surprise me. What's wrong with those lads at university? They should have been forming a queue to ask you out.'

Jennifer blushed. 'I went on a couple of dates, but the boys all seemed so young, getting drunk at clubs and spending entire days in front of their computer games. None of them seemed to take life seriously.'

'At eighteen and nineteen, life is something not to be taken seriously.'

'*You* did when you were barely older than that.'

'As you may recall, I had no choice.' Jennifer was the only woman who could get away with bringing his private life into the conversation. She was, in actual fact, the only woman who knew anything at all about his private life and, even with her, there was still a great deal of which she was unaware.

'I know that and I know it must have been tough, but I honestly can't think of anyone who would have risen to the occasion the way you did. I mean, you had no real experience and yet you went in there and turned it all around.'

'I'll make sure that you're the first on the guest list when I get knighted.'

Jennifer laughed and pushed the plate of melting ice cream away from her, choosing instead to have a bit more wine and ignoring James's raised eyebrows.

'I'm being serious,' she insisted. 'I can't think of a single guy I knew at university who would have been capable of doing what you did.'

'You're young. Life shouldn't be about looking for a guy who can take the world on his shoulders. In fact, it should be about the guy who hasn't grown up yet. Believe me there's plenty of time to buckle down and realise that life's no picnic…'

'I'm not young!' Jennifer said lightly. 'I'm twenty-one. Not that much younger than you, in actual fact.'

James laughed and signalled to the waiter for the bill. 'You haven't done justice to those desserts.' He changed the topic when she would have had him pursue this tantalising personal conversation. 'I've always admired your sweet tooth. So refreshing after some of the girls I've dated in the past, who think that swallowing a mouthful of dessert constitutes an offence punishable by death.'

'That's why they're so skinny and I'm not,' she said, fishing hopefully for a compliment, but his attention was on the approaching waiter and on the bill being placed in front of him.

Now that the evening was drawing to a close, she could feel her nerves begin to get the better of her, although the copious amounts of wine had helped. When she stood up, she swayed ever so slightly and James reached for her with a concerned expression.

'Tell me you haven't had too much to drink,' he murmured. 'Hang onto me. I'll make sure you don't topple over.'

'Of course I'm not going to topple over! I'm a big girl. I need more than a few glasses of wine to topple over!' She loved the feel of his arm around her waist as they strolled out of the restaurant. It was August and still balmy outside. The fading light cast everything into shadow but the street lights had not yet come on and the atmosphere was wonderfully mellow and intimate. She surreptitiously nestled a little closer to him and tentatively put her arm around his waist. Her heart skipped a beat.

She was five ten and in heels, easily six foot, but at six foot three he still made her feel gloriously small and feminine.

She could have stayed like this in silence but he began asking her about Paris, quizzing her about the details of her job, asking her what her apartment would be like and reassuring her that, if it wasn't up to scratch, she was to remember that his company had several apartments in Paris and that he would be more than happy to arrange for her to stay in one of them.

Jennifer didn't want that. She didn't want him doing the big brother thing and imagining that she wanted him to take care of her from a distance so she skirted around his offer and reminded him that she wasn't in need of looking after.

'Where has this sudden streak of independence come from?' he asked teasingly, and his warm breath rustled her hair. He was smiling. She heard it in his voice.

They had reached his car, and she felt the loss of his arm around her as he held open the passenger door for her to step inside.

'I remember,' he said, still smiling and turning to look at her as he started the engine, 'when you were fifteen and you told me that you couldn't possibly get through your maths exam unless I sat and helped you.'

Never thinking that he had better things to do, just

pleased to be able to bask in his attention for a couple of hours as he had patiently helped her.

'I must have been a complete pain,' she said truthfully.

'Or a pleasant distraction.'

'What do you mean?'

'I was buried under work trying to fish my father's company out of its woeful state of affairs. Helping you and listening to all your school gossip often gave me a much-needed break from the headache of running a company.'

'But what about your girlfriends?'

'I know,' James said ruefully. 'You would have thought that they would have provided a distraction, but at that juncture in my life I didn't need their demands.'

'Well, that was such a long time ago. I can't even remember any of that school gossip.'

'And if I recall, you went on to get an A in your maths…'

Jennifer didn't say anything. The restaurant was only a matter of thirty minutes away from the house. In the blink of an eye, they would be back at the cottage and she would be able to show him that she really and truly was no longer the kid who had asked for help with her homework or filled him in on the silly happenings in her life whenever he happened to be down for the weekend. Maybe he wouldn't be entirely surprised…? After all, he *had* asked her out on a date!

She replayed that lovely feeling of having his arm around her and resisted the temptation to reach out and cover his hand with hers.

They drew up to the cottage in comfortable silence. Set in the grounds of the manor house, it was originally designed to house the head butler, but it had been annexed years before the Rocchis had moved in by a wily investor who had seen it as an efficient way of making some additional money. It was a happy coincidence that her father had bought the tiny two-bedroom place at around the same time as the Rocchis had moved into the manor house. Her own mother had died when she, Jennifer, had been just a toddler and Daisy Rocchi, unable to have any more children after James, had become a surrogate mother, bypassing all rules and conventions that predicated against two families of such differing incomes becoming close.

'Dad's not in.' Jennifer turned to look at James and cleared her throat. 'Why don't you…um…come in for something to drink? You barely had any of that wine tonight.'

'If I had thought ahead, I would have booked a taxi for us instead of driving myself.'

'Well, I know there's some wine in the fridge and I think dad's got a bottle of whisky in the cupboard. His once-a-month vice, he tells me.' She wasn't sure what she would do if he turned down her offer but he didn't and she breathed a sigh of relief as he said no to the alcohol but opted for a cup of coffee instead.

Inside the cottage, she switched on the lamp in the sitting room instead of the harsher overheard light and urged him in while she prepared them coffee with shaking hands. She was trying very hard to recapture the excitement and confidence she had felt earlier on in the restaurant as she had gazed at her reflection in the mirror and told herself that this *date* had arrived at just the perfect time, when she was still riding the crest of a wave, with her finals behind her and an exciting new job ahead of her.

She was so lost in her thoughts that she almost sent both mugs of coffee crashing to the ground as she turned to find James lounging in the doorway to the kitchen. Very carefully, she rested the mugs on the pine kitchen table and took two steps to close the distance between them.

Now or never, Jennifer thought with feverish determination. She had nurtured this crush for way too long. All through her time at university, she had tried to make herself like the boys who had asked her out, but her thoughts had always returned to James. His heart-stopping sex appeal and their shared history were a potent, heady combination and she had never quite managed to break free of its spell.

'I…I liked what you did earlier…' The palms of her hands were sweaty with nerves.

'You mean the cake and ice cream?' He laughed and looked down at her. 'Like I said, I know what a sucker you are for sweet things.'

'Actually I was talking about after that.'

'Sorry. I'm not following you.'

'When you put your arms around me on the way to the car. I liked that.' She slid her hand over his chest and nearly fainted at the hard body underneath her fingers. 'James…' She looked up at him and before she could chicken out she closed her eyes and tiptoed up to reach him. The first taste of his cool mouth sent a charge of adrenaline racing through her body and with a soft moan she kissed him harder, reached up to wind her arms around his neck as her body curved against his.

Her breasts were aching, her heart was beating like a drum. Every nerve in her body was alive with sensations she had never felt with anyone in her life before. Every kiss she had ever shared with other boys was drowned out by the scorching heat of this kiss. She felt his response as he kissed her back and that response was enough for her to take his hand and guide it underneath the loose shirt, up to the lacy bra that she had worn especially.

She was so lost in the moment that it was a few seconds before she realised that he was gently but firmly detaching himself from her and it was a few more seconds before it sank in that this was not a gesture preparatory to taking her upstairs. This much-longed-for evening was not going to end in her bedroom, making love while candles flickered in the background. She had agonised over her choice of linen, ditching her usual flowery bedcovers for something plain instead. He wasn't going to see any of it.

'Jennifer...'

Unable to bear the gentleness in his voice, she spun around with her arms tightly clasped around her body.

'I'm sorry. Please go.'

'We need to talk about what...what happened just then.'

'No. We don't.' She refused to look up as he circled round to face her. She kept her eyes pinned to his shoes while her body went hot and cold with mortification. She was no longer a sexy woman on a date with the guy for whom she had spent years nursing an inexhaustible infatuation. She bitterly wallowed in the reality that she was an awkward and not particularly attractive woman in a stupid, newly purchased outfit who had just made a complete fool of herself.

'Look at me, Jen. Please.'

'I got the wrong end of the stick, James, and I apologise. I thought...I don't know what I thought...'

'You're embarrassed and I understand that but—'

'Don't say any more!'

'I have to. We're friends. If we leave this to fester, things will never be the same between us again. I enjoy your company. I wouldn't want to lose what we have. For God's sake, Jennifer, at least *look at me*!'

She looked up at him and for the first time the sight of him didn't thrill her.

'Don't beat yourself up, Jen. I kissed you back and for that I apologise. I shouldn't have.'

But he had and she knew why. What man wouldn't suc-

cumb to a woman who flung herself at him? It was telling that he had come to his senses in a matter of seconds. Even with everything on offer, she hadn't been able to tempt him.

'You're young. You're about to embark on the biggest adventure of your life—'

'Oh, spare me the pity talk,' Jennifer muttered.

'I'm not *pitying you.*' He stuck his hands in the pockets of his trousers and shook his head in frustration.

'Yes, you are! I've been a complete idiot and I've put us both in an awkward position and none of it is your fault! Okay, so when you asked me out to dinner tonight, I thought it was more than just two friends having a meal. I fooled myself into believing that you might have begun to see me as a woman instead of the girl next door! Instead of the clumsy, ungainly, unappealing, borderline unattractive girl next door.'

'Don't put yourself down. I don't like it.'

'I'm not putting myself down.' She managed to meet his eyes without flinching although it cost her every ounce of will power. 'I'm being honest. I've had a crush on you—'

'And there's nothing wrong with that…'

'You knew.'

'It was endearing.'

'Well, a pleasant distraction from when your pocket-sized blonde bombshells were being too demanding, at any rate.'

'You had a schoolgirl crush and there's nothing sinful about that,' James told her with such sincerity that she itched to slap him. 'But you're young. I know you said that you're only a few years younger than me, but in terms of experience we're light years apart. Trust me when I tell you that in a year's time you'll have forgotten all about this. You'll have met some nice lad…'

'Yes,' Jennifer parroted dutifully, wanting this entire

conversation to be over so that she could go upstairs and bury herself under the freshly laundered covers.

He sighed and shook his head. This was a Jennifer he didn't recognise. Gone was the smiling, malleable girl. Had he known that she had a crush on him? Yes, of course he had, although he had never openly addressed the issue. Now, for the first time, he could sense her locking him out. He understood but it was a strange sensation and he didn't like it.

'Your feelings for me are misplaced,' he told her roughly. 'I wasn't lying when I told you that you want to enjoy your youth with boys who are uncomplicated and fun-loving.'

'You make it sound as though I was looking for... looking for something more than just...'

'A romp in the sack?'

Mortified, Jennifer shrugged.

'You deserve a lot more than I could give you.'

By which, she thought, *you mean that there's nothing you're interested in giving me aside from a peck on the cheek every now and again and lots of good advice about how to live my life.*

He was being patronising and the worst of it was that he wasn't even aware of it.

'Don't worry about me, James,' she said with a forced smile, relieving him of the obligation to keep thinking about her feelings because he was a decent human being. 'I'll be fine. These things happen.' Two steps back, putting distance between them. 'I probably won't see you before I leave.'

'No.'

'Of course I'll keep in touch and I'm sure we'll bump into one another now and again.' One more step back.

'You'll be all right, will you?'

Jennifer chose to interpret this at face value and she looked at him with a polite, unfocused expression. 'Of course I will. As I told you, the job I'll be doing over there isn't going to be substantially different than what I've done over the summer vacations. Naturally, I'll be following through on a lot more and there'll be a great deal of translating but I'm sure I'll be able to handle it.'

'Right. Good.'

'So.'

James hesitated and raked his fingers through his hair.

'Thanks for dinner, James…and I'll see you…'

She remained frozen to the spot as he brushed past her, pausing fleetingly, as though hesitant to leave.

What did he think she was going to do? Jennifer wondered. Fling herself out of her bedroom window because he had rejected her? Was she so pathetic in his eyes that he doubted her ability to get over the slight?

The soft click of the front door closing signalled his departure and it was only once she was certain that he had left the cottage that Jennifer slumped.

She closed her eyes and thought of the excited girl who had bought a new outfit especially for her big date. She remembered her anticipation at having him all to herself over dinner. She had dreamt of seduction and of finally having this crazy crush of hers fulfilled. It suddenly felt like a million years ago and, although a year wasn't long, it was long enough to say goodbye to that person.

CHAPTER ONE

EXCEPT one year became two, which became three, which became four. And in all those four years, Jennifer had not once set eyes on James. Each Christmas, she had contrived to bring her father over to Paris for the holidays, which he had loved. What had begun as a one-year placement, during which she could consolidate her French, had seen her rise through the company, and as she had risen so too had her pay cheque. She found that she could afford to holiday with her father abroad, and on those occasions when she *had* returned to England she had been careful with her visits, always making sure that they were brief and that James was nowhere in the vicinity.

He had walked out of the cottage four years previously and she had fled to Paris, her wounds still raw. She couldn't imagine ever facing him again, and not facing him had developed into a habit. He had emailed her, and she had been happy enough to email back, but on the occasions when he had been in Paris she had excused herself from meeting him on grounds of being too busy, prior engagements, not well, *anything* because the memory of him gently letting her down remained, that open wound quietly hurting somewhere in the background of her shiny new life.

Except now...

She had nodded off on the train and woke with a start as it pulled into the station.

When she looked through the window it was to see that the flurries of snow that she had left behind in London were a steady fall here in Kent. The weather was always so much harsher out here. She had forgotten.

At six-thirty in the evening the train was packed with commuters and fetching her bags was chaotic, with people jostling her on all sides, but eventually she was out of the train and braving the freezing temperatures and snow on the platform.

She wasn't planning on staying long. Just long enough to sort out the problems in the cottage, problems she had learnt about via an email from James who had been checking his house in his mother's absence and had happened to walk down to the cottage to take a look only to find water seeping out from under the front door. Her father was away on his annual post-Christmas three-week holiday to visit his brother in Scotland. The email had read:

You can pass this on to your father, but I gather you're in the country so you might want to check it out yourself instead of ruining your father's fishing trip. This, of course, presupposes that you can interrupt your busy schedule.

The tone of the email was the final nail in the coffin of their enduring friendship. She had run away and, never looked back, and over time, the chasm between them had become so vast that it was now unbreachable terrain. His emails, which had been warm and concerned at the beginning of her stint in Paris, had gradually become cooler and more formal, in direct proportion to her avoidance tactics. It occurred to her that she actually hadn't heard from him at all for at least six months.

In Paris, she could tell herself that she didn't mind, that this was just the way things had turned out in the end, that their friendship had always been destined to run its course because it had been an unrealistic union of the inaccessible boy in the manor house and the childishly doting girl next door.

But now here, back in Kent, his email was a vaguely sexy reminder of how things used to be.

She wheeled her suitcase out to where a bank of taxis was only just managing to keep the snow on their cars from settling by virtue of having their engines running. Everywhere, the snow was forming a layer of white.

The water had been cleared, James had informed her, but there was a lot of collateral damage, which she would have to assess for the insurance company. He had managed to get the heating started. So at least when she arrived at the cottage, she wouldn't freeze to death. She hoped he might have left her some fresh provisions before he cleared off, on his way to Singapore for a series of meetings, he had politely informed her in his email, but she wasn't banking on it.

That was how far their friendship had devolved. When Jennifer thought about it for too long, she could feel a lump of sadness in her throat and she had to remind herself of that terrible night when she had made such a fool of herself. Someone better and stronger might have been able to survive that and laughingly put it behind them so that a friendship could be maintained, but she couldn't.

For her, it had been a devastating learning curve and she *had* learnt from it.

She gazed out of the window of the taxi but could barely see anything because of the snow. Deep in the heart of the Kent countryside, the trip, in conditions like this, would take over an hour. She settled in for the long haul and let her thoughts drift without restraint.

It had been a while since she had returned to the cottage for any length of time. She and her father had spent summer in Majorca, two weeks of sun and sea, and every six weeks she brought him over for a weekend. She loved the fact that she could afford to do that now. She knew that there was a part of her that was reluctant to return to the place that held so many memories of James, but that was fine because her father was more than happy to travel out to see her and she always, always made sure that she met Daisy, James's mother, for lunch in London when she was over on business. She had politely asked about James and given evasive non-answers whenever Daisy showed any curiosity as to why they no longer seemed to meet. Eventually his name had been quietly dropped from conversations.

To think of him moving around in the cottage made something in her shiver. Sometimes, a memory of the scent of him, clean and masculine and woody, would surface from nowhere, leaving her shaken. She hoped that scent wouldn't be lingering in the cottage when she got there. She was tired and it was too cold to run around opening windows to let out an elusive smell.

By the time they reached the cottage, driving was becoming impossible.

'And they predict at least a week of this,' the driver said bitterly. 'Business is bad enough as it is without Mother Nature getting involved.'

'Oh, this won't last,' Jennifer said airily. 'I've got to be back in London by day after tomorrow.'

'Lots of clothes for an overnight stay.' The driver struggled up to the door with the case, unable to wheel it in the snow.

'I'll be leaving one or two things behind. Clearing out old stuff.'

She paid him, thinking of the task that lay ahead. Aside from sorting out the cottage, she would be bagging up all those frumpy clothes that had once been the mainstay of her wardrobe. None of them would fit any more. In the space of four years, she had been seduced by Parisian chic. She had lost weight, or maybe, thanks to her daily run, the weight had just been reassigned. At any rate, the body she had once avoided looking at in the mirror now attracted wolf whistles and stares from strangers and she was not ashamed to wear clothes that accentuated it. Nothing revealing, that would never be her style, but fashionable and figure hugging. Her untamed hair had been tamed over the years, thanks to the expert scissors of her hairdresser. It was still long, longer even than it used to be, but it was cleverly layered so that the frizz had been replaced with curls.

The cottage was in complete darkness although the door was surprisingly unlocked. She lugged the suitcase through and slammed the door shut behind her, luxuriating for a few seconds in the blissful warmth, eyes closed, lights still off because she just wanted to enjoy the cottage before she could see all the damage that had been caused by the flood.

And then she opened her eyes and there he was. Lounging against the door that led into the kitchen.

The cottage hadn't been in complete darkness, as she had first thought. No, one of the kitchen lights had been switched on, but the kitchen was at the back of the house and the door leading to it had been shut when she had entered.

She literally froze on the spot.

God, he hadn't changed. He was still as beautiful as

he always had been, still the man who towered over other men. His hair was shorter than it had been four years ago and she could tell from the shadow on his jawline that he hadn't shaved. In the space of a few seconds, during which time Jennifer felt her breath catch in her throat, she took in everything. The lean, long body in a pair of jeans and an old striped rugby jumper, the sleeves of which were shoved up to the elbows, those amazing deep blue eyes, now focused on her in a way that made her head swim.

Disastrously, she felt herself catapulted back to the young, naive girl she had once been.

'James. What on earth are you doing here?' She knew that her hand was trembling when she hit the light switch. 'You told me that you would be leaving the country!'

'I should be in the air right now but the weather got in the way of those plans. It's been a long time, Jennifer...'

The silence stretched and stretched and stretched and she had to fight to maintain her self-control. Four years of independence, of cutting herself free from those infantile ties that had bound her to this man, and she could feel them melting and slipping away. She could have wept. Instead, she let the little ball of remembered bitterness and anger form into a knot inside her stomach and she began to get rid of her coat, which was heavy and damp from the snow.

'Yes. Yes, it has. How are you?' She forced a stiff smile but her heart was thumping like a sledgehammer.

'I thought I'd stay in the cottage until you got here, make sure you arrived safely. I wasn't sure whether you were going to drive or take the train.'

'I...I took the train.' Her car was parked outside her friend's house in London where she stayed every time she came back to the city. 'But there was no need for you to hang around here. You know I can take care of myself.'

'You've certainly been doing a very good job of that

while you've been in Paris. My mother frequently regales me with news of yet more promotions.'

She still hadn't taken a single step towards him because her feet appeared to be nailed to that one spot in the hallway.

He was the first to break the spell, turning away and heading into the kitchen, leaving her to follow him.

He hadn't said a word about how much she had changed. How could he have failed to notice? But then, why was it so surprising when he had never really noticed her? The ease she had once felt in his company was nowhere to be found and it was a struggle thinking of polite conversation to make.

'It's been a very successful posting for me,' Jennifer said politely. 'I never thought that I'd end up staying over there for four years but as I accepted more and more responsibility, the work became more and more challenging and I found myself accepting their offers to stay on.'

'You look like a visitor, standing there. Sit down. You might as well forget about getting anything done tonight. We can work on detailing what will need to be done to the cottage tomorrow.'

'We? Like I said, there's absolutely no need for you to help me with this. I plan on having it all finished by tomorrow afternoon and I'll be leaving first thing the following morning.' This was not how two old friends, meeting after years of separation, would act. Jennifer knew that. She could hear the sharp edge to her voice and, while she was dismayed by it, she was also keenly aware that it was necessary as a protective tool, because just looking at him rooting around in the fridge with his back to her threatened to take her down memory lane and that was a journey she wasn't willing to make.

'Good luck arguing with the weather on that score.'

'What are you doing in the fridge?'

'Cheese, eggs. There's some bread over there, bought yesterday. When the snow started, I realised I might find myself stuck here and if I was stuck here, then you would be as well, so I managed to make it down to the shops and got a few things together.'

'Well, that was very kind of you, James. Thank you.'

'Well, isn't this fun?' He fetched a bottle of wine from the fridge, something he had bought along with the food, she was sure, and poured them both a glass. 'Four years and we're struggling to pass the time of day. Tell me what you've been up to in France.'

'I thought I just had. My job is very invigorating. The apartment is wonderful.'

'So everything lived up to expectation.' He sat back in the kitchen chair and took a deep mouthful of wine, looking at her over the rim of the glass. God, she'd changed. Did she realise just how much? He couldn't believe that the last time he'd seen her had been four years ago, but then she had made sure to be unavailable whenever he'd happened to be in Paris, and somehow, whenever she'd happened to be in the UK, he'd happened to be out of it.

She had cut all ties with him and he knew that it had all happened on that one fateful night. Of course, he didn't regret the outcome of that evening. He had had no choice but to turn her down. She had been young and vulnerable and too sexy for her own good. She had come to him looking for something and he had known, instinctively, that whatever that something was he would have been incapable of providing it. She had been trusting and naive, not like the hard-edged beauties he was accustomed to who would have been happy to take whatever was on offer for limited duration.

But he had never suspected that she would have walked out of his life permanently.

And changed. And had not looked back.

'Yes.' Jennifer played with the stem of her wine glass but there was no way that she was going to drink any of it. 'Everything lived up to expectation and beyond. Life has never been so good or so rewarding. And what about you, James? What have you been up to? I've seen your mother over the years but I really haven't heard much about you.'

'Shrinking world but fortunately new markets in the Far East. If you like, I can go into the details but doubt you would find it that fascinating. Aside from the challenging job, what is Paris like for you? Completely different from this neck of the woods, I imagine.'

'Yes. Yes, it is.'

'Are you going to expand on that or shall we drink our respective glasses of wine in silence while we try and formulate new topics of conversation?'

'I'm sorry, James. It's been a long trip with the train and the taxi and I'm exhausted. I think it's probably best if you went up to your house and we can always play the catch-up game another time.'

'You haven't forgotten, have you?'

'Forgotten what?'

'Forgotten the last time we met.'

'I have no idea what you're talking about.'

'Yes. Yes, I think you do, Jen.'

'I don't think there's anything to be gained by dragging up the past, James.' She stood up abruptly and positioned herself by the kitchen door with her arms folded. Not only were they strangers, but now they were combatants, squaring up to each other in the boxing ring. Jennifer didn't dare allow regret to enter the equation because just looking at him like this was making her realise that on some deep, instinctive level she still responded to him. She didn't know whether that was the pull of familiarity or the pull of an attraction that refused to remain buried and she was not willing to find out.

'Why don't you go and change and I'll fix you something to eat, and if you tell me that you're too exhausted to eat, then I'm going to suspect that you're finding excuses to avoid my company. Which wouldn't be the case, would it, Jen?'

'Of course not.' But she could feel a delicate flush creep into her cheeks.

'Nothing fancy. You know my culinary talents are limited.'

The grin he delivered was an aching reminder of the good times they had shared and the companionable ease they had lost.

'And don't,' he continued, holding up one hand as though to halt an interruption, 'tell me that there's no need. I know there's no need. Like I said, I'm fully aware of how independent you've become over the past four years.'

Jennifer shrugged, but her thoughts were all over the place as she rummaged in the suitcase for a change of clothes. A hurried shower and she was back downstairs within half an hour, this time in a pair of loose grey yoga pants and a tight, long-sleeved grey top, her hair pulled back into a ponytail.

It had always been a standing joke that James never cooked. He would tease her father, who adored cooking, that the kitchen was a woman's domain, that cooking wasn't a man's job. He would then lay down the gauntlet—an arm-wrestling match to prove that cooking depleted a man of strength. Jennifer used to love these little interludes; she used to love the way he would wink at her, pulling her into his game.

However, he was just finishing a remarkably proficient omelette when she walked into the kitchen. A salad was in a bowl. Hot bread was on a wooden board.

'I guess I'm not the only one who's changed,' Jennifer said from the doorway, and he glanced across to her, his eyes lazily appraising.

'Would you believe me if I told you that I took a cookery course?'

Jennifer shrugged. 'Did you?' She sat at the table and looked around her. 'There's less damage than I thought there would be. I had a look around before I went to have a shower. Thankfully, upstairs is intact and I can just see that there are some water stains on the sofa in the sitting room and I guess the rugs will have to be replaced.'

'Have we finished playing our catch-up game already?' He handed her a plate, encouraged her to help herself to bread and salad, before taking up position opposite her at the kitchen table.

Jennifer thought that this was the reason she had avoided him for four years. There was just *too much* of him. He overwhelmed her and she was no longer on the market for being overwhelmed.

'There's nothing more to catch up on, James. I can't think of anything else I could tell you about my job in Paris. If you like I could give you a description of what my apartment looks like, but I shouldn't think you'd find that very interesting.'

'You've changed.'

'What is that supposed to mean?'

'I barely recognise you as the girl who left here four years ago. Somewhere in my memory banks, I have an image of someone who actually used to laugh and enjoy conversing with me.'

Jennifer felt the slow burn of anger because *he* hadn't

changed. He was still the same arrogantly self-assured James, supremely confident of their roles in life. She laughed and blushed and he basked in her open admiration.

'How can you expect me to laugh when you haven't said anything funny as yet, James?'

'That's *exactly* what I'm talking about!' He threw his hands up in a gesture of frustration and pushed himself back from the table. 'You've either had a personality change or else your job in Paris is so stressful that it's wiped out your sense of fun. Which is it, Jen? You can be honest with me. You've always been open and honest with me, so tell me: have you bitten off more than you can chew with that job?'

'I know that's what you'd like me to say, James. That I'm hopelessly lost and can't handle the work in Paris.'

'That's a ridiculous statement.'

'Is it? If I told you that I was having a hard time and just couldn't cope, then you could be the caring, concerned guy. You could put your arm round my shoulder and whip out a handkerchief for me to sob into! But my job is absolutely brilliant and if I wasn't any good at it, then I would never have been promoted. I would never have risen up the ranks.'

'Is that what you think? That I'm the sort of narrow-minded, mean-spirited guy who would be happy if you failed?'

Jennifer sighed and pushed her plate away.

'I know you're not mean-spirited, James, and I don't want to argue with you.' She stood up, began clearing the dishes, tried to think of something harmless to say that would defuse the high-voltage atmosphere that had sprung up.

'Leave those things!' James growled.

'I don't want to. Tomorrow's going to be a long day and

the less I have to do in the kitchen, tidying up stuff that could be done now, the better. And by the way, thank you very much for cooking for me. It was very nice.'

James muttered something under his breath but began helping her, drying dishes as she began washing. Jennifer felt his presence as acutely as a live charge. If she stepped too close, she would be electrocuted. Being in his presence had stripped her of her immunity to him and it frightened her, but she wasn't going to give in to that queasy feeling in the pit of her stomach. She launched into a neutral conversation about their parents. She told him how much her father enjoyed Paris.

'Because, as you know, he stopped going abroad after Mum died. He once told me that it had been their dream to travel the world and when she died, the dream died with her.'

'Yes, the last time I came here for the weekend, he was waiting for the taxi and reading a guide book on the Louvre. He said it was top on the agenda. He's been ticking off the sights.'

'Really?' Jennifer laughed and for an instant James went still. He realised that the memory of that laugh lingered at the back of his brain like the refrain from a song that never quite went away. Suddenly he wanted to know a lot more than just whether she enjoyed her job or what her apartment was like. She had always, he was ashamed to admit to himself, been a known quantity, but now he felt curiosity rip through him, leaving him bemused.

'You've opened up a door for John,' he drawled, drying the last dish and then leaning against the counter with the tea towel slung over his shoulder. 'I think he's realised what he's been missing all these years. He was in a rut and your moving to Paris forced him out of it. I have a feeling that he's going to get bored with weekends to Paris pretty soon.'

'We don't just stay in Paris,' Jennifer protested. 'We've been doing quite a bit of Europe.' But she was thrilled with what James had told her. It was a brief window during which, with her defences down, they were back to that place they had left behind, that place of easy familiarity, two people with years and years of shared history.

She glanced surreptitiously at him and edged away before that easy familiarity could get a little too easy, before her hard-won independence began draining away and she found herself back to the girl in the past who used to hang onto his every word.

'In fact, I've already planned the next couple of weekends. When the weather improves, we're going to go to Prague. It's a beautiful city. I think he'd love it.'

'You've been before, have you?'

'Once.'

'And this from the girl who grew up in one place and never went abroad, aside from that school trip when you were fifteen. Skiing, wasn't it?'

Yes, it certainly was. Jennifer remembered it distinctly. James's father had just died and he had been busy trying to grapple with the demands of the company he had inherited. He hadn't been around much and when, after the skiing trip, she had seen him for the first time after several weeks, she had regaled him with a thousand stories of all the little things the class had done. The cliques that had subdivided the groups. The quiet girl, usually in the background, who had come out of her shell because she was one of only a handful who had been any good at skiing.

'Yes, that's right.'

'And who did you go to Prague with?' James enquired casually. 'I've actually been twice. Romantic city.' He

turned to fill the kettle and found that he was keenly await-
ing her response.

Jennifer frowned. She was relieved that he had his back
to her. Her first instinct was to tell him that her private
life was none of his business. She quickly decided that it
was one thing being scrupulously polite, but if she began
to actively push him away he would start asking himself
why and they would be back to the subject she was most
desperate to avoid: her mistimed, unfortunate pass at him.
He would really be in his element then, she concluded bitterly, holding her hand and trying to assure her that she
shouldn't let the memory of it interfere with her life, that
their friendship was so much more important than a silly
non-escapade. She would be mortified.

'Yes. It's a very romantic city. I love everything about
it. I love the architecture and that terrific feeling of a place
almost suspended in time. Don't you agree?'

'So who did you go with? Or is it a deep, dark secret?'
He chuckled and turned round to face her, moving to hand
her a mug of coffee and then sitting down and pulling one
of the chairs in front of him so that he could fully relax,
using the spare chair as a footrest.

'Oh, just a guy I met over there.'

'A guy!'

'Patric. Patric Alexander. Just someone I met at a party
a while back...'

'Well.' He didn't know why he was so shocked at this.
She had always been sexy, although it was fair to say that
she had never realised it. She was still sexy and the only
difference was that Paris had made her realise just how
much.

'French guy, is he?' James heard the inanity of his question and his lips thinned although he was still smiling.

'Half French. His mother's English.' She gulped down

her coffee and stood up with a brisk smile. 'Now, I really think it's time for you to head back to your house, James. I have unpacking to do and I want to be up fairly early to make a list of what needs doing. Hopefully not that much. I noticed that the rug in the sitting room's already been rolled. Thank you for that.'

'Thank God there's no carpet downstairs. The joys of flagstones when there's a flood! Why didn't this Patric guy come to help you?'

'Because he's in Paris.' She moved to the door and frowned when he remained comfortably seated at the table.

'The name doesn't ring a bell. I'm sure your father would have mentioned him to me in passing—'

'Why would he?' Jennifer snapped.

'Because I'm his friend…? How long have you been going out with this Patric guy?'

'I really don't want to be having this conversation with you.'

'Because you feel uncomfortable?'

'Because I'm tired and I want to go to sleep!'

'Fair enough.' James took his time getting to his feet. 'I wouldn't want to be accused of prying and I certainly wouldn't want to make you feel uncomfortable in any way…' He walked towards her and, the closer he got, the tenser she could feel herself becoming.

'I'm perfectly comfortable.'

'I just wonder,' he mused, pausing to invade her personal space by standing only inches in front of her, a towering six-feet-three inches of pure alpha male clearly hell-bent on satisfying his curiosity, 'whether you avoided me over the years because you were reluctant to let me meet this man of yours…'

'I was not *avoiding you* over the years,' Jennifer muttered uncomfortably. 'I thought we corresponded very frequently by email…'

'And yet every time I happened to be in Paris, you were otherwise occupied, and every time you happened to be in this country, I was out of it…'

'The timings were always wrong.' Jennifer shrugged, although she could feel hot colour rising to her face and she stared down at the ground with a little frown. 'Patric and I are no longer involved,' she finally admitted, when the silence became unbearable. 'We're still very good friends. In fact, I would say that he's my closest confidant…'

This time she did look at him and James knew instantly, from the genuine warmth of her smile, that she was being completely truthful.

The girl who had always turned to him, the girl who had matured into a woman he hadn't seen for nearly four years, now had someone else to turn to.

'And what about you?' she asked, because if he could ask intrusive questions then why shouldn't she? 'Is there anyone significant in your life at the moment, James?'

James was still trying to get over a weird feeling of disorientation. He tilted his head to one side, considering her question.

'No. No one at the moment. Until recently, I was involved with an actress…'

'Blonde?' Jennifer couldn't resist asking and he frowned at her and nodded.

'Petite? Fond of very high heels and very tight dresses?'

'Did my mother mention her to you? I got the impression she wasn't bowled over by Amy…'

'No, your mother didn't mention anyone to me. In fact,' she added with a hint of smugness, 'your mother and I haven't really discussed you at all. I'm just guessing because those are the sort of girls you've always been interested in. Blonde, big hair, small, very high heels and very tight dresses.' Jennifer couldn't help herself, even though dipping into this subject would be to open a door to all the insecurities she had felt as a young woman, pining for him and comparing herself incessantly to the girls he would occasionally bring back to the house. Amy clones. She took a deep breath and fought her way through that brief reminder of a time she would rather have forgotten.

James flushed darkly.

'Nothing changes,' she said scornfully.

'Really? I wouldn't say that's true at all.'

'You still go out with the blonde airheads. Daisy still despairs. You still only have relationships that last five seconds.'

'But you don't still have a crush on me…'

That softly spoken remark, a lazy, tantalising question wrapped up in a statement, was like a bucket of freezing water thrown over her and she stepped back as though she had been slapped.

What had she been thinking? Had she been so shocked to find him in the cottage that she had forgotten how efficiently he could get under her skin? She had managed to keep her distance so how was it that they had somehow drifted into a conversation that was so personal?

'That was all a long time ago, James, and, like I said, there's nothing to be gained from rehashing the past.'

'Well…' He finally began strolling to where his coat was hanging over the banister. She wondered how she had managed to miss that when she had walked in but, of course, she hadn't been expecting him. 'I'll be heading off but I'll be back tomorrow and please don't tell me that there's no need. I'll roll the other carpets. Get them into one of the outbuildings and keep them dry so that they can be assessed for damage when this snow decides to stop and someone from the insurance company can come out.'

'I'm sure that can wait,' Jennifer said helplessly. 'I won't be here long. I plan on leaving…well…if not tomorrow evening, then first thing the following morning…'

James didn't say anything. He took his time wrapping his scarf round his neck, then he pulled open the front door so that she was treated to the spectacular sight of snow swirling madly outside, so thick that she could barely make out the fields stretching away into the distance.

'Good luck with that.' He turned to her. 'I think you'll find that we might both end up being stuck here…'

With each other. Jennifer tried not to be completely overwhelmed at the prospect of that. He wasn't going to stay cooped up in his house when he thought that she needed help in the cottage. He would be *around* and she had no idea how long for. Certainly, the snow looked as though it was here for the long haul and the house and cottage were not positioned for easy access to handy, cleared roads. They were in the middle of nowhere and it would not be the first time that heavy snow would leave them stranded.

But maybe it was for the best. She couldn't hide away from him for ever. Sooner rather than later she would be returning to the UK to live. Her father wasn't getting any younger and she had enough on her CV to guarantee a job, or at least a good prospect of one. When that happened, she would be seeing him once again on weekends.

She decided that this was fate.

'You could be right,' she said with more bravado than she felt. 'In which case, thank heavens you're here! I mean, I adore Patric, but I have to be honest and tell you that an artist probably wouldn't be a huge amount of practical help at a time like this…'

CHAPTER TWO

AN ARTIST? Jennifer had gone out with *an artist*? James could scarcely credit it. She had never shown any particular interest in art, per se, so how was it that she had been enticed into an affair with an artist? And who else had there been on the scene? He was disconcerted to find that she had somehow managed to escape the box into which he had slotted her and yet why should he be? People changed.

Except, there had been something smug about her tone of voice when she had implied that *he* had changed very little over the years. Still going out with the same blonde bimbos.

He was up at the crack of dawn the following morning and one glance out of the window told him that neither of them would be going anywhere, any time soon. If anything, the snow appeared to be falling with even greater intensity. Drifts of it were already banking up against the sides of the outbuildings and his car was barely visible. It was so silent out here that if he opened a window he would have been able to hear the snow falling.

Fortunately, the electricity had not been brought down and the Internet was still working.

He caught up with outstanding emails, including informing his secretary that she would have to cancel all meetings for at least the next couple of days, then, on the spur of the moment, he looked up Patric Alexander on an Internet search engine, hardly expecting to find anything because artists were a dime a dozen and few of them would ever make it to the hall of fame.

But there he was. James carried his laptop into the sprawling kitchen, which was big enough to fit an eight-seater table at one end and was warmed by the constant burn of a four-door bottle-green Aga. Mug of coffee in one hand, he sipped and scrolled through pages of nauseating adulation of the new up-and-coming talent in the art world. Patric was already garnering a loyal following and a clientele base that ensured future success. The picture was small, but James zoomed into it and found a handsome, fair-haired man surrounded by a bevy of beautiful women, standing in front of a backdrop of one of his paintings.

He slammed shut the lid of the computer, drained his coffee and was in a foul mood when, minutes later, he stood in front of the cottage and banged on the knocker.

It was barely eight-thirty and so dark still that he had practically needed a torch to find his way over. Even with several layers of clothing, a waterproof and the wellies he had had since his late teens, he could feel the snow trying to prise its way to his bare skin. His mood had slipped a couple of notches lower by the time Jennifer eventually made it to the door and peered out at him.

'What are you doing here so early?'

'It's too cold for us to make conversation in a doorway. Open up and let me in.'

'When you said you were going to come over, you never told me that you would be arriving on my doorstep *with the larks*.'

'There's a lot to do. What's the point in sleeping in?' He looked at her as he removed his coat and scarf and gloves and sufficient layers to accommodate the warmth of the cottage. She was in a pair of faded jeans and, yes, she really *had* changed. Lost weight. She looked tall and athletic. She had pulled back her hair and it hung down her back in a centre braid. 'I hope I didn't wake you? I've been up since five-thirty.'

'Oh, bully for you, James.' The day suddenly had the potential to be unbearably long. He followed her to the kitchen, sat down and seemed pleasantly surprised when she began cracking eggs into a bowl. He hadn't had any breakfast. Great if she could make some for him as well. Did she need a hand?

'I thought you said that you had made sure to buy some food?'

'Oh, the fridge at home is stocked to capacity but I didn't think to make anything for myself.'

'Even though you were up *at five-thirty*? It never crossed your mind that you could pour yourself a bowl of cereal? Grab a slice of toast?'

'When I start working, nothing distracts me. And small point of interest…I don't eat cereal. Can't stand the stuff. Just bits of cardboard pretending to be edible and good for you.'

Jennifer had spent a restless night. This was the last thing she needed and she turned to him coolly.

'This isn't going to work, James.'

'What?'

'*This!* You strolling over here and making yourself at home!'

'It's impossible to stroll in this weather.'

'You *know* what I mean! If you think that you need to help, to get the rugs to the outbuildings, then that's fine, but you can't just waltz in here for the day. I have things to do!'

'What?'

'I have to clear some cupboards and I have lots of work to catch up on if it turns out that I can't leave tomorrow as planned!' She felt his eyes on her as she turned round to pour some eggs into a frying pan.

'It makes sense for us to share the same space, Jen. What's the point having the heating going full blast in my house when I'm the only person in it?'

'The point is *you won't be under my feet*!'

'I'm going to be doing some heavy lifting on your behalf today, Jennifer. It's hardly what I would call *being under your feet*.'

'I'm sorry,' she muttered with a mutinous set to her mouth. 'I'm very grateful for the practical help you intend to give me but—'

'Okay. You win, Jennifer. I don't know why you want to draw battle lines, but if that's what you're intent on doing, then I'll leave you to get on with it.'

He stood up and Jennifer spun round to look at him. Was this what she really wanted? To make an enemy out of the person who had always been her friend? Because she found it difficult being in the same room as him?

'I don't want to draw battle lines,' she said on a heavy sigh. 'I just don't want you to...to think that nothing's changed between us.' She flicked off the stove and moved to sit at the table. The past was still unfinished business. That clumsy pass had never been discussed and she had carried it with her for four years. The memory of it was still so bitter that it had shaped all her relationships over the past four years, not that there had been many. Two. The first, to a young French lawyer she had met through work, had barely survived three months and, although he had laboured to win her over, she had been hesitant and eventually incapable of giving him the commitment he had wanted.

Patric had been her soul mate from the start and they had had three years of being friends before they decided to take that step further. It was a relationship that should have worked and yet, try as they had, she had not been able to capture the sizzle, the breathless excitement, the aching anticipation she had felt for James.

She knew that all of that was just a figment of her imagination. She knew that she had to somehow find it in her to prise herself out of a time warp that had her trapped in her youth, but eventually she and Patric had admitted defeat and had returned, fortunately, to being the close friends they had once been.

He had laughingly told her that there was no such thing as a friend with benefits. She had told herself that she needed to find a way of blocking James out of her head. She wasn't an impressionable young girl any more.

James looked at her in silence.

'I know I…I made that awful pass at you all those years ago. We never talked about it…'

'How could we? You left the country and never looked back.'

'I left the country and then life just became so hectic…' Jennifer insisted. 'I suppose to start with,' she said, conceding an inch but determined to make sure that an inch was the limit of her concessions, 'I *did* think that it might be awkward if we met up. I *may* have avoided you at first but then, honestly, life just became so busy…I barely had time to think! I guess I could have come back to England more frequently than I did, but Dad's never travelled and it was fun being able to bring him over, take him places. It was the first time I've ever been able to actually afford to take him on holiday…' The egg she had been scrambling had gone cold. She relit the stove and busied herself resuscitating it, keeping her back to him so that she could guard her expression from those clever, perceptive deep blue eyes, which had always been able to delve into the depths of her. She couldn't avoid this conversation, she argued to herself, but she wasn't going to let him know how much he still affected her.

She was smilingly bland when she placed a plate of toast and eggs in front of him.

'I think what I'm trying to say, James, is that I've grown up. I'm not that innocent young girl who used to hang onto your every word.'

'And I'm not expecting you to be!' But that, he realised, was exactly what he had been expecting. After four years of absence, he had still imagined her to be the girl next door who listened with eagerness to everything he had to say. The smiling stranger he had been faced with had come as a shock, and even more surprising was the fact that his usual cool when dealing with any unexpected situation had apparently deserted him.

'Which brings me to this: I don't want for there to be any bad feeling between us, but I also don't want you thinking that because we happen to be temporarily stranded here, that you have a right to come and go as you please. You've seen to the little flooding problem in the cottage and I'm very grateful for that but it doesn't mean that you now have a passport to my home.'

'Point taken.'

'And now I expect you're angry with me.' She hadn't wanted to say that but it just slipped out and she could have kicked herself because, as the new woman she claimed to be, would she still care what he thought of her? Why couldn't she be indifferent? She hadn't seen him for *four years*! It seemed so unfair that after all this time her heart still skipped a beat when he was around and it was even more unfair that she inwardly quailed at the thought of antagonising him.

'I'm glad you said what was on your mind. Honesty being the best policy and all that.' He dug into his breakfast with relish. 'Did your father tell you that he's thinking of doing a cookery course? This, incidentally, is my way of trying to normalise the situation between us. Because you've changed doesn't mean that we've lost the ability to communicate.'

Jennifer hesitated, apprehensive of familiarity, but then decided that, whether she liked it or not, there were too many strands of their lives that were interwoven for her to pretend otherwise.

'He told me,' she said, relaxing, with a smile. 'In fact, the last time he came over, just before Christmas, he brought all his prospectuses so that I could give him some advice. Not that I would be any good at all when it comes to that sort of thing.'

'You mean being in Paris, surrounded by all that French cuisine, wasn't enough to stimulate an interest in cooking?'

'The opposite,' Jennifer admitted ruefully. 'When there's so much brilliant food everywhere you go, what's the point trying to compete at home?'

'You must have picked something up.' James saluted her with a mouthful of egg on his fork. 'This scrambled egg tastes pretty perfect.'

'That's the extent of it, I'm afraid. I can throw a few things together to make something passable for an evening meal but no one I've ever entertained has really expected me to produce anything cordon bleu. In fact, on a couple of occasions, friends in Paris actually showed up with some store-bought delicacies. They always said that they wanted to make life easier for me but, personally, I suspected that they weren't too sure what they might be getting.' She laughed and their eyes met for a few seconds before she hurriedly looked away.

There was no way that she was going to return to her comfort zone but this felt good, chatting to him, relaxing, dropping her guard for a while.

'And what about you?' she asked. 'Do you still avoid that whole domestic thing?'

'Define *avoid that whole domestic thing*.'

'You once told me that you always made sure that the women you dated never went near a kitchen just in case they started thinking that they could domesticate you.'

'I don't remember saying that.'

'You did. I was nineteen at the time.'

'Remind me never to have conversations of a personal nature with any woman who has perfect recall.' He had forgotten just how much he had told her over the years, superficial stuff and yet stuff he probably would never have told any other woman. 'Your father has been trying to lure me into cooking. Every time I've popped over, he's shown me one of his new recipe books. A few months ago I came for a few days to oversee some work my mother was having done in the house, and your father asked us both to dinner here. We were treated to an array of exotic meals and I was personally given a lecture on the importance of a man having interests outside work. Have you any idea how difficult it is for a man to defend himself from a dual-pronged attack? Your father preached to me about learning to enjoy my leisure time and my mother made significant noises about the correlation between hard work and high blood pressure.'

Jennifer laughed again, that rich, full-bodied laugh that reminded James of how much he had missed her uncomplicated company over the years. Except now…nothing was as uncomplicated as it once was. They could skim the surface with small talk and reach a place in which they both felt comfortable, but he realised that he wanted to dig deeper. He didn't want to just harp back to the good old days. He didn't want to just keep it light.

'I thought I'd see if that Patric guy of yours had a presence on the Internet.' He changed the subject, standing up and waving her to sit back down when she would have helped him clear the table.

Jennifer went still. Why, she wanted to ask, would he do that?

'Oh?'

'He's well reviewed.'

'Why would you want to check up on him?' she asked abruptly. 'Did you think that I was lying? Made him up?'

'Of course I didn't!' He shook his head in frustration as they teetered back to square one after their fragile truce.

'Then what? Why the curiosity?'

He looked at her closed, uninviting expression and scowled. She might have loosened up for a few minutes, but the bottom line was she wanted their relationship to remain on the safe, one-dimensional plane it had always occupied.

He thought back to that crossroads moment, when, four years ago, she had offered herself to him. Hell, he could still taste her mouth on his before he had gently pushed her away. In fact, thinking about it, he wondered whether he had ever really put it behind him.

'Call it human nature,' he gritted. 'Is it a taboo subject? Am I getting too close to showing a perfectly normal interest in the person you are *now*?'

Jennifer couldn't argue with that. *She* was the one at fault. It was only natural that he would want to exchange more than just polite pleasantries about their past or idle chit-chat about their parents. It wasn't his fault that she felt threatened whenever she thought about him getting too close and the reason she felt threatened was because she still had feelings for him. She didn't know what exactly those feelings were, but they were defining the way she responded. It was crazy.

It was going to be very tiring if they continually veered between harmless small talk and bitter arguments. Worse, he would wonder why.

'Patric isn't a taboo subject. I just think that I already told you everything there is to know about him, and what I didn't you probably gleaned from the Internet. He's a big name in Europe. Or at least, he soon will be. His last exhibition was a huge success. Everything sold and he has a number of galleries vying to show his work.'

James had read all of that in the glowing article on the computer. They had not stinted in their praise.

'You were never into art.'

'I…I…never really thought that it would be something practical to do so I dropped it at school and really, around here…well, museums and art galleries aren't a dime a dozen. I think I started realising how much I loved art when I went to university…so it was easy to fall in love with it in Paris where it's all around you…'

'And the French guy was all part and parcel of the falling-in-love process?'

Jennifer shrugged. 'We were close friends first. Maybe I got caught up in his passion and enthusiasm over the years. I don't know.'

'And it didn't work out in the end.'

'No. It didn't. Now, why don't you start getting the rugs together and I'll give you a hand? There's a great wad of tarpaulin in the coal shed at the back of the cottage. If I get that, then we can cover the rugs and hopefully they won't get too wet when we lug them over.'

What little personal conversation she had submitted to was over. James was receiving that message loud and clear. He had never been one to encourage touching confidences from women. Events in his past had conspired to put a cynical spin on every relationship he had, although that was something he kept to himself. It was weird that he was now increasingly curious to find out more about Jennifer. It was almost as though he had suddenly discovered that his faithful pet could spout poetry and speak four languages.

He wondered whether his sudden interest was a result of being marooned with her by the snow, compounded by the fact that he hadn't seen her in years. Had he met her at his mother's house, would they have skirted over the same ground, played their usual roles and then parted company to meet again in three weeks' time and repeat the process?

Hauling rugs into an outbuilding seemed an inadequate substitute to having his curiosity sated, but he dropped the subject and, for the next couple of hours, they worked alongside each other in amicable companionship, exchanging opinions on what would and wouldn't need to be done to the cottage. It was an old place and prone to all the symptoms of old age. Things needed replacing on a frequent basis and an updating process was long overdue.

'Right,' Jennifer said, once they were back in the cottage. 'You're going to have to go now, James.'

The past couple of hours were a warning to her that she had to be careful around him. She had always found his charm, his wit, his intelligence, irresistible and time, it appeared, had not diminished his appeal in that area. He could still make her laugh, and wading through the fast-falling snow was a great deal safer than sitting in a cosy kitchen where they had eye-to-eye contact.

What alarmed her were those casual touches, the brush of his gloved fingers against her arm, the feel of his thigh next to hers as they had manoeuvred the rug into the out-building, laughing and looking at the collection of junk they had had to shift to make room.

Her body had felt alive; her skin had tingled. She had been that twenty-one-year-old girl again, yearning to be touched. At least, it had felt like that. What if this whole unforeseen situation, trapped in the snow, made her do something regrettable? It was barely a thought that she allowed to cross her mind, but she knew that it was there, like an ugly monster shifting lazily underneath the defences she had laboured to pile on top of it. What if, on the spur of the moment, she let her hand linger just a little bit too long on his arm? What if she held his look for too long?

He was no longer the cardboard cut-out hero of her youth. She had moved on from blind infatuation and now, here, she was beginning to see the complex man who told her how tough it was moving from being a carefree student to a man who needed to run a company. He shared thoughts about his mother, getting older and living in a house that was too big for her, and she could see the worry etched on his face.

She didn't like it or perhaps, scarily, she liked it too much. He was easy and relaxed with her because he still considered her a friend. She was wary with him and she had to be because, beyond any friendship, there were still feelings buried there and they frightened her.

So spending the afternoon in the cottage together, be-cause *it made sense*, just wasn't going to do.

'I have some clothes I need to box up and also some work to do because, you're right, it doesn't look likely that

I'm going to make it back to London tomorrow. In fact, I'll be lucky if I get out of here by the weekend. So...'

Neither of them had had a chance to change and her hair was damp from the falling snow. Dark tendrils curled around her face. Her cheeks were pink from the cold and the woollen hat she had put on was pulled down low, almost down to her eyes, huge and brown and staring purposefully at him. Unlike the babes he dated, she had a dramatic, intelligent face, a face he found he liked looking at.

'I can't think of the last time I was chucked out of a woman's house,' he said, raising his eyebrows. 'Come to think of it, I can't think of the last time I did anything manual with a woman.'

'I doubt any of your girlfriends would be any good in conditions like these. Deep snow and kitten heels don't go well together. And I'm not a woman, I'm a friend.'

'Thanks for reminding me,' James murmured. 'I was in danger of forgetting...'

Jennifer drew in a shaky breath. What did that mean? No. She refused to waste time speculating on the things he said and reading meanings into throwaway remarks. She knew from experience that that was a road that led nowhere and, anyway, she *didn't care about him*. She had spent *four years* putting him behind her!

'Perhaps later this evening we can share a quick meal. Or I could come up to the house. It *does* seem silly for us to eat on our own when we could join rations.'

'And I could cook for you.' His voice was warm and amused. 'Adding yet something else to the steadily growing list of things I don't do with women but I do for you.'

Was he flirting with her? 'You can if you want to,' she countered sharply, 'but if not you're more than welcome to come here and have something with me or we could just reconvene in the morning and take it from there. You have my mobile number, don't you?'

'I think it's one of the things you omitted to give me when you left...' Once upon a time his charm would have swept her off her feet. Now, it slid off her, leaving her unaffected. In fact, leaving her irritated.

'Then let's exchange mobile numbers now just in case there's a change of plan. If I find that I'm behind with all the stuff I want to do, then I'll contact you.'

'And are you going to get in touch with John and let him know what's happened?'

'No.' Tell her father? That she was holed up in the cottage in the middle of a snowstorm with James? His imagination would be on overdrive if she did that! He had been all too aware of her childish crush! She had been so young and disingenuous...incapable of hiding her emotions, wearing her heart on her sleeve like any impressionable teenager. He had never known about that disastrous final dinner she had had with James. At least, he had never known the details but he was as sharp as a tack. He had known that it hadn't lived up to expectations because the following day she had been quiet, avoiding his questions. And then she had left for Paris and never seen James again. 'No. You were right to get in touch with me and leave Dad out of this. He doesn't get to see Anthony often and he looks forward to his three-week holiday up there. Anyway, the transport links are terrible at the moment. He would have a hard time returning and there's nothing he can do here that I can't manage.'

'How does it feel?' James asked softly and she stared at him with a perplexed frown.

'What are you talking about?'

'To be in charge.'

'I'm not in charge of anything,' Jennifer mumbled,

dipping her head. She wondered whether it was a compliment to be seen as a woman *in charge*. Maybe from someone else it would have been, but from James…? 'Well, maybe I *am* in charge,' she amended, refusing to be drawn into thinking that there was something wrong with not being a helpless feeble woman incapable of doing anything useful in case a nail got chipped. 'Dad's not getting any younger. He's going to be sixty-eight on his next birthday and he's been complaining about tiring more easily. He jokes about it, but I can tell from when we've been walking around Paris that he's not as spritely as he used to be.'

'And where does that leave you, I wonder?'

'I'm not saying that Dad has suddenly become old and feeble!'

'I'm curious as to how long you intend to work in Paris…'

'That's a big subject for us to suddenly start discussing,' Jennifer said, fighting the irresistible temptation to confide. Patric might be a wonderful friend and a sympathetic confidant, but he wasn't James. James who had known her for most of her life and who knew her father better than anyone else.

'Is it?' He shrugged and shot her a crooked smile. 'Am I stepping too close to something personal?'

'Of course not,' Jennifer said uncomfortably, hating the way he found it so easy to return to their familiarity while she continued to fight against it tooth and nail because in her head it represented a retrograde step. 'I…yes, I've been thinking about that, wondering whether it might not be time to return to England…'

'But you're worried that you've settled into a lifestyle that agrees with you and you might just get back here and have difficulty slotting back in. This isn't Paris.'

'I've made a lot of friends,' Jennifer said defensively.

'I know the work and I'm very well paid... I don't even know whether I'd be able to find a similar job over here! I keep abreast of the news. There are no jobs!'

'Plus you hate change and the biggest thing you've ever done is go to Paris and reinvent yourself...'

'Stop trying to shove me back in time. I'm not that person any more.' But yes, she had never liked change even though she had never had a problem adapting to different circumstances. Secondary school had been a challenge, but she had done it and it had been fine. University, likewise. However, she had had no choice in either of those. Paris, as he had said, had been her big step. Returning to England would be another.

'No, you're not,' James said quietly, while she continued to glare at him. 'I would have no problem giving you a job, Jennifer. There are a lot of opportunities in my company for someone fluent in French with the level of experience you've had. In fact, I have access to a number of company apartments. It would be an easy matter for me to sort one of them out for you...'

'No, thank you!' Jennifer could think of nothing worse than breaking out of her comfort zone only to be reduced to handouts from James Rocchi. In Paris, she had been her own person. She shuddered to think how it would be if she were to be working in his company and renting one of his apartments. Would he be dropping in every two minutes with one of his blonde Barbies on his arm to check up on her and make sure that she was okay? Nosing into her private life and expressing surprise if she happened to be dating someone? Maybe looking up this, as yet, fictitious someone on the Internet so that he could check for himself that she wasn't dating someone unsuitable? Or maybe just checking out of curiosity, the way he had with Patric?

'I mean,' she amended hurriedly, 'that's a generous

offer but I haven't made any decisions as to whether or not I'll be returning just yet, anyway. And when I *do* decide to return…well, I would want to find my own way. I'm sure my boss in Paris will supply me with excellent references…'

James tried not to scowl as she smiled brightly at him, a big, glassy smile that set his teeth on edge. He was so used to her malleability! Now, in receipt of this polite dismissal, he felt strangely impotent and piqued.

'I'm sure he would.'

'And I've managed to save quite a bit while I've been over there. I stayed in a company flat and they kindly let me carry on there at a very subsidised rate after my one-year secondment was at an end. In fact, I would probably be able to put down a deposit on a small place of my own after a while. Not in London, of course. I would have to travel in. But definitely in Kent somewhere. I could work in London, because that's where the jobs are, and commute like most people have to do. So…thanks for the offer of one of your company flats, but there's no need to feel duty-bound to be charitable.'

'And on that note, I think I'll leave.'

She let him. She saw him to the door, where they made polite noises about the continuing bad weather. He suggested that he come over to the cottage to eat because it would be easier for him to tackle the short distance in blizzard conditions; he was sure he had a pair of skis lurking in a cupboard somewhere from his heady teenage years. She smiled blandly.

Inside it felt so wrong to be closing the door on him with this undercurrent of ill feeling between them.

Her head was telling her to let go of the past and find new ground with him, as he obviously wanted to do with her. New, inoffensive ground. Her heart, however, was beating to a different tune.

She spent the remainder of the day clearing out cupboards and bagging old clothes. She couldn't believe the rubbish she pulled out of her wardrobe. The cottage was small and yet the cupboard in her bedroom was like the wardrobe in Narnia—never ending. She had binned the outfit she had worn all those years ago on their disastrous dinner date in a fit of humiliation and hurt, but the shoes were still there, stuffed at the back, and she pulled them out and relived that night all over again.

Then she worked on her computer. She didn't know how long the connection would last. Paris seemed like a million light years away and when she managed to talk to Patric, she found it hard to imagine that she had once thought that he might be the one for her.

She tried not to look at the clock and told herself that she honestly didn't care whether James came over to the cottage for dinner or not. Yes, sure, some adult company would be nice. Eating pasta for one while the snow bucketed down outside was a pretty lonely prospect. She told herself that she likewise didn't care if he had taken offence at her rejection of his offer of a job and a place to rent. She could have handled it differently, but the message would have amounted to the same thing whatever. On both counts, she knew that she was kidding herself. She was keyed up to see him later. Like an addict drawn to the source of her addiction, she craved the way he made her feel.

By six, she was glancing at the clock on the mantelpiece, and when her mobile vibrated next to her on the sofa, she had to fight back the disappointment at the thought that he would be at the other end of the line informing her that he had decided to give their arrangement a miss.

CHAPTER THREE

'IF YOU'RE calling to tell me that you won't be coming over tonight for dinner, then don't worry about it. Not a problem. I still have so much work to do, anyway! You wouldn't believe it! Plus I'm going to take the opportunity to catch up with some of my frie...'

'Jennifer, shut up.'

'How dare you?'

'You need to do exactly what I say. Get dressed in some warm clothes, come out of your cottage and head for the copse behind it. You know the one I mean.'

'James, what's going on? You're scaring me.'

'I've had a bit of an accident.'

'You...*what*?' Jennifer stood up, felt giddy and immediately sat back down. Every nerve in her body had gone into sudden, panicked overdrive. 'What do you mean?'

'There were some high winds here a couple of days ago. Just before you came. Some fallen branches in the copse behind the cottage and a tree that's about to go and is dangerously close to one of the overhead cables.'

'You tripped over a branch on your way here?'

'Don't be ridiculous! How feeble do you think I am? After I left you earlier, I got back to the house, did some work and then thought that I might as well see if I could bring the tree down, get it clear of the overhead power lines.'

In a flashback springing from nowhere, she had a vivid memory of him as a young boy not yet sixteen, strapped halfway up one of the towering trees that bordered the house, chainsaw in one hand, reaching for a branch that had broken, while underneath his parents yelled for him to get down *immediately*. He had grown up in sprawling acres of deepest countryside and had always loved getting involved in the hard work of running the estate. He had had a reckless disregard for personal safety, had loved challenging himself. She had adored that about him.

'I can't believe you could have been so stupid!' she yelled down the phone. 'You're not sixteen any more, James! Give me five minutes and *don't move.*'

She spotted him between the swirling snow, just a dark shape lying prone, and the worst-case scenarios she had tussled with as she had flung on her jumper and scarf and coat and everything else smashed into her with the force of a ten-ton block of granite. What if he had suffered concussion? He would be able to sound coherent, make sense, only to die without warning. That had happened to someone, somewhere. She had read it in the news years ago. What if he had broken something? His spine? Fractured his leg or his arm? There was no way that a doctor would be able to get out here. Even a helicopter would have trouble in these weather conditions.

'Don't move!' She had brought two tablecloths with her. 'You can use these to cover yourself with and I'm going to get that table thing Dad uses for wallpapering. It can be rigged up like a stretcher.'

'Don't be so melodramatic, Jen. I just need you to help me up. The snow's so soft that it's impossible. I seem to have pulled a muscle in my back.'

'What if it's more serious than that, James?' she cried, kneeling and peering at him at close range. She shone her torch directly at his face and he winced away from the light.

'Would you mind directing the beam somewhere else?'

She ignored him. 'What I'm saying is that you shouldn't move if you think you might have done something to your spine. It's one of the first things you learn on a first-aid course.'

'You've done a first-aid course?'

'No, but I'm making an educated guess. Your colour looks good. That's a brilliant sign. How many fingers am I holding up?'

'What?'

'My fingers. How many of them am I holding up? I need to make sure that you aren't suffering from concussion…'

'Three fingers and move the bloody torch, Jennifer. Let me sling my arm around your neck and we're going to have to hobble to the cottage. I don't think I can make it all the way back to the house.'

'I'm not sure…'

'Okay, here's the deal. While you debate the shoulds and shouldn'ts, I'm going to pass out with hypothermia. I've pulled a muscle! I don't need the blankets and a makeshift stretcher, although I'm very grateful for the suggestion. I just need a helping hand.'

'Your voice sounds strong. Another good sign.'

'Jennifer!'

'Okay, but *I'm still not sure…*'

'I can live with that.'

He slung his arm around her neck and she felt the heavy, muscled weight of him as he levered himself up, with her help. The snow was thick and their feet sank into its depth, making it very difficult to balance and walk. It was little wonder that he hadn't been able to prise himself up. Even with her help, she could tell that he was in pain, unable to stand erect, his hand pressed to the base of his back.

They struggled back to the cottage. She had draped the tablecloths around him, even though he had done his best to resist and the torch cast a wavering light directly ahead, illuminating the snow and turning the spectral scenery into a winter wonderland.

'I could try and get hold of an ambulance service...' she suggested, out of breath because even though he was obviously doing his best to spare her his full weight, he was still six feet three inches of packed muscle.

'I never knew you were such a worrier.'

'What do you expect?' she demanded hotly. 'You were supposed to stroll over for dinner...'

'Didn't I tell you that it's impossible to stroll in snow this deep?'

'Stop trying to be funny! You were supposed to come to the cottage for dinner and the next time I hear from you, you're calling to tell me that you decided to chop down a tree and you're lying on the ground with a possible broken back!'

'I'm sorry if I worried you...'

'Yes,' Jennifer muttered, still angry with him for having sent her into a panic, still deathly worried that he was putting on a brave face because that was just the sort of man he was, 'well, you *should* be.'

'Have you cooked something delicious?'

'You shouldn't talk. You should conserve your energy.'

'Is that something else you picked up on the first-aid course you never went to?'

She felt her lips twitch and suppressed a desire to laugh. She got the feeling that he was doing his utmost to distract her from her worry, even though he would have been in a lot of discomfort and surely worried about himself. That simple generosity of spirit brought a lump of emotion to her throat and she stopped talking, for fear of bursting into tears.

Ahead of them the well-lit cottage beckoned like a port in a storm.

'Here at last.' She nudged open the door and deposited him on the sofa in the sitting room, where he collapsed with a groan.

He didn't have a broken spine. Nor was anything fractured. That much she had figured out on the walk back. He had pulled a muscle. Painful but not terminal.

She stood back, arms folded, and looked at him with jaundiced eyes.

'Now, admit it, James. It was very silly of you to think you could sort out that tree, wasn't it?'

'I managed to do what needed doing,' he countered. 'I fought the tree and the tree lost. The pulled muscle in my back is just collateral damage.'

Jennifer snorted in response. 'You'll have to get out of those clothes. They're soaking wet. I'm going to bring down some of Dad's. They won't be a terrific fit, but you'll have to work with it. Tomorrow I'll fetch some from your house.' She was resigned to the fact that they would now be stranded together, under the same roof.

James, eyes closed, grunted.

'But first, I'll go get you some painkillers. Dad keeps them in bulk supply for a rainy day. Or an emergency like this.'

'I don't do painkillers.'

'Too bad.'

Her father was shorter than James and thinner. She had no idea how his clothes would stretch to accommodate James's more muscular frame, but she chose the biggest of the tee shirts, a jumper and a pair of jogging bottoms with an elasticated waist, which were a five-year-old legacy from her father's days when he had decided to join the local gym, which he had tried once only to declare that gyms were for idiots who should be out and about.

'Clothes,' she announced, back in the sitting room, where the open fire kept the room beautifully warm. 'And first, painkillers.' She handed him two tablets with a glass of water and watched as he reluctantly swallowed them.

'You make a very good matron.' He handed her the glass of water and sighed as he began to defrost.

He grinned but she didn't find it very amusing. He had been a complete fool. He had, as was his nature, been so supremely confident of his strength that it would never have occurred to him that sorting out a tree in driving snow might have been an impossible mission. He had worried her sick. And beyond both those things, she was stupidly annoyed to be compared to a *matron*. She privately and illogically rebelled against being the friend upon whom he could rely in a situation like this, the girl who wouldn't baulk in a crisis and was used to the harsh easterly conditions, the tall, well-built girl who could tackle any physical situation with the best of them. She wanted to be seen as delicate and fragile and in need of manly protection, and then she was annoyed with herself for being pathetic. Old feelings that she thought she had left behind seemed to be waiting round every corner, eager to ambush the person she had become.

'I'll leave you to get into some fresh clothes,' she said shortly. 'And I'll go and prepare us something to eat.'

She turned to walk away and he reached out to catch her hand and tug her to face him.

'In case you think I'm not grateful for your help, I am,' he said softly.

Jennifer didn't say anything because he was absentmindedly rubbing his thumb on the underside of her wrist, and for the first time since she had been flung into his company she had no resources with which to fight the stirrings of desire she had been trying so hard to subdue. She could barely breathe.

'I don't know what I would have done if you hadn't been here.'

'That's all right,' Jennifer croaked, then cleared her throat, while she wondered whether to snatch her hand out of his gently, delicately, caressing grasp.

'I know you weren't expecting to find me here when you arrived but I'm glad I was. I've missed you.'

She wanted to shout at him that he shouldn't use words like that, which made her fevered irrational brain start thinking all sorts of inappropriate things.

'Have you missed *me* or was I replaced by your hectic life and new-found independence?'

'I...I don't know what you expect me to say to that, James...' But she wondered whether this was his way of reasserting the balance between them, putting it back to that place where he could be certain that he knew where she stood, a place where the power balance was restored.

'Of course—' she pulled her hand away from him and took a step back '—I thought about you now and again and hoped that you were doing well. I meant to email you lots more than I actually did and I'm sorry about that...'

He looked at her in unreadable silence, which she was the first to break.

'I'll leave you to change.'

'I think it would probably be a good idea if I were to dry off a bit. It won't take long, but it'll be easier to get these clothes off if they aren't damp.'

'Makes sense.' Her nerves were still all over the place

and those fabulous midnight-blue eyes roving over her flushed face felt as intimate as his thumb had on her wrist.

'You've just come from outside. Sit for a while and get dry before you think of cooking.'

'Well...maybe just for a few minutes...' She sat on the chair closest to the fire and nervously looked at him. She had thought he hadn't changed at all in the past four years but he had. There was a tough maturity about him that hadn't yet crystallised when she had last seen him. His rise in the world of business had been meteoric. She knew that because, just once, she had given in to temptation and devoured everything she could about him on the Internet. She had discovered that he no longer limited himself to the company he had inherited, he had used that as a springboard for taking over failing companies and had gained a reputation for turning them around in record time. And yet, he had continued to resist the lure of marriage. Why? Was he so consumed by work that women were just satellites hovering on the periphery? Or did he just still enjoy playing the field which, as an eligible, staggeringly rich, good-looking bachelor, would have been a really huge field?

She felt the urge to burst through her self-imposed barrier and ask him and stifled it. She remembered the last time she had misread a situation.

'You've grown up,' he said so softly that she had to strain forward to hear him. 'You've lost that open, transparent way you used to have.'

'People *do* grow up,' she said abruptly.

'Were you hurt by that guy? That's the question I've been asking myself.'

For a few seconds, Jennifer didn't follow where he was going and then she realised that he was talking about Patric.

'He's my best friend!'

'Not sure that says anything.' James slanted her a look that made her go red. 'Were you in love with him? Did he break your heart? Because you seem a lot more cynical than you did four years ago. Sure, people change and grow up, but you're much more guarded now than you were then.'

Jennifer was lost for words. His take on her was revealing. He might have known, years ago, that she had a crush on him, but he obviously had never suspected the depth of her feelings. *She* had not really suspected the depth of her own feelings! It was only as she began dating that she realised how affected she had been by James's rejection, how deep her feelings for him ran. And returning here… all those feelings were making themselves felt once again.

The last thing she needed was him trying to get into her head!

'I love Patric,' she told him tightly. 'And I don't want to be psychoanalysed by you. I know you're probably bored, lying there unable to do anything, but I can bring you your computer and you can work.' The devil worked on idle hands and right now James was very idle.

'My computer's back at my house,' he said irritably, 'and I won't have you braving the snow to get it. I've done enough work for the day, anyway. I can afford to take a little time off.'

'Your mother would be pleased to hear that. She thinks you work too hard.'

'I thought you never talked about me with my mother.'

Jennifer shook her head when he grinned at her and stood up. 'I'm going to go and fix us something to eat. Get changed when you feel your clothes are dry enough.'

'What's on the menu?'

'Whatever appears on the plate in front of you.' She left

to the sound of his rich chuckle and she sternly stifled the temptation to laugh as well.

Her head was full of him as she went about the business of turning a bottle of crushed tomatoes, some cream and some mushrooms into something halfway decent to have with some of the tagliatelle her father kept in abundant supply in the larder. James annoyed her and alarmed her the way no one else had ever been able to, but he also made her laugh when she didn't want to and held her spellbound when she knew she shouldn't be. So what did that say about the state of her defences? She had thought that by seeing him again, she would have finally discovered that his impact had been diminished. She had foolishly imagined that she would put her demons to rest. The very opposite had happened, and, although she hated the thought of that, she was practically humming under her breath as she prepared their meal.

When she thought about him lying on the sofa in the sitting room, a wonderful, excited and *thoroughly forbidden* heat began spreading through her and she couldn't stop herself from liking it.

She took him his food on a tray and he waved her help aside as he struggled into a sitting position.

'The painkillers are kicking in.' He took a mouthful of food and then wondered where the wine was. Oh, and while she was about it, perhaps she could bring him some water as well.

Halfway through the meal, about which he was elaborately complimentary, he announced that he was now completely dry. He magnanimously informed her that there would be no need to wash his clothes, even though she hadn't offered.

'I have more than enough at home to get me through an enforced stay,' he decided, and Jennifer frowned at him.

'How long are you planning on staying?' she asked, not bothering to hide the sarcasm, and then she looked at him narrowly when he shrugged and smiled.

'How long is a piece of string?'

'That's no kind of answer, James.'

'Well, weather wise, even if the snow stops in the next five minutes, which is highly unlikely, we won't be leaving here for another couple of days. We both know that this is the last port of call for the snow ploughs. It's too deep for either of us to drive through and, in my condition, I can't do much about clearing it. That said, I don't think it's going to abate for at least another twenty-four hours, anyway. Longer if the weather forecast is to be believed.'

'Well, you're certainly the voice of doom,' Jennifer said, removing his tray from him, putting it on top of hers and sitting back down because she was, frankly, exhausted, despite having had a very lazy day, all things considered.

'I prefer to call it the voice of reality. Which brings me to point two. I can't go back to my house. I'm going to need help getting back on my feet. I'm putting on a brave front, but I can barely move.' She hadn't exactly been the most welcoming of friends when she had discovered him in the cottage, but, hell, however hard she fought it, there was still something there between them. Friendship, attraction…he didn't know. He just knew that the frisson between them did something for him. As did looking at her. As did hearing her laugh and seeing her smile and catching her slipping him sidelong looks when she didn't think his attention was on her. He relished this enforced stay and, while his back was certainly not in a particularly good way, he silently thanked it for giving him the opportunity to get to the bottom of her.

Jennifer was torn as to whether to believe him or not. On the one hand, he had always claimed to have the constitution of an ox. He was known to boast that he never fell prey to viruses and that his only contact with a doctor had been on the day of his birth. He surely wouldn't lie when it came to admitting pain.

On the other hand, he didn't look in the slightest regretful about his circumstances. In fact, for someone in the grip of back pain, he seemed remarkably breezy.

Breezy or not, she couldn't send him hobbling back to his house although the thought of him in the cottage with her made her stomach tighten into knots of apprehension. Four years of hiding had been rewarded with such a concentrated dose of him that she was struggling to maintain the fiction that the effect he had on her was history. It wasn't. Anything but.

'So...as it stands, I'm going to have to fetch clothes for you for an enforced stay of indefinite duration, plus your laptop...plus I'm going to have to feed and water you...'

'There's no need to sound so thrilled at the prospect...'

'This just isn't what I banked on when I began this journey to the cottage.'

'No,' James said drily, 'because you didn't even expect to find me here.'

'But I'm glad I did,' she told him with grudging truthfulness. 'Four years is a long time. I was in danger of forgetting what you looked like.'

'And have I lived up to expectation?'

'You look older than you are,' Jennifer said snidely, because his ego was already big enough as it was.

'That's very kind of you.' But he grinned. That boyish, sexy grin that had always been able to set her pulses racing. 'Now you're going to have to do me yet another favour, I'm afraid.'

'You want coffee. Or tea. Or something else to drink. And you'd like something sweet to finish off the meal.

Maybe a home-made dessert of some kind. Am I along the right lines?'

'Could I trust you to make me a home-made dessert?' he asked lazily. 'Don't forget that my knowledge of your love of cooking goes back a long way...' He held her eyes and Jennifer, skewered by the intensity of his gaze, half opened her mouth to say something and discovered that she had forgotten what she had been about to say. Colour slowly crawled into her face and, to break the suffocating tension, she stood up to get the two plates and carry them into the kitchen.

'So tea or coffee, then,' she said briskly. 'Which is it to be? Dad has a million varieties of tea you could choose from. The larder seems to have had a massive overhaul ever since he decided to take up cooking. Apparently one brand of tea is no longer good enough.'

'I need you to help me undress.'

'I beg your pardon?'

'I can't manoeuvre to get the trousers off, even though the painkillers are beginning to kick in.'

Jennifer froze. For a few seconds all her vital functions seemed to shut down. When they re-engaged, she knew that, in the name of this friendship that they were tentatively rebuilding, she should think nothing of providing the help he needed. He had no qualms asking for it. He wasn't going into meltdown at the thought of her touching him. She had loftily told him that he should see her as a friend rather than a woman, so what was he going to think if, *as a friend*, she told him that she couldn't possibly...?

'Have you tried?'

'I don't need to try. Every time I make the smallest movement, my back protests.'

Jennifer took a deep breath and walked towards him. What choice did she have?

James slung his arm over her shoulders, felt the softness of her skin underneath the jumper she was wearing, breathed in her clean fresh scent, the smell of the cold outdoors still lingering on her skin.

'Well, thank goodness I'm not one of these five-foot-nothing girls you go out with,' she managed to joke, although her vocal cords felt unnaturally dry and strained. 'You would still be lying in the snow outside or else dragging yourself back to the house the best you could.'

'Why do you make fun of yourself?'

'I don't.' She helped him into a sitting position. His skin was clammy. Underneath the breezy façade, he was obviously in a great deal of discomfort, yet he had not taken it out on her. While she had been reluctantly catering to his demands and not bothering to hide the fact that she wasn't overjoyed at having him under her roof, he had been suffering in silence. Shame and guilt washed over her.

'You do. You've always done it.' He had unbuttoned his shirt and he grimaced as she eased him out of it, down to the white tee shirt underneath. 'I remember when you were sixteen laughing at yourself, telling me about the outfits your friends were wearing to go out, making fun of your height and—'

'I can't concentrate when you're talking!' She was red-faced and flustered because those were memories she didn't want thrown at her.

'You're a sexy woman,' he said roughly.

'I'll help you to your feet so that we can get the trousers off.' He thought *she was a sexy woman*. Why did he have to say that? Why did he have to open a door in her head through which all sorts of unwanted thoughts could find their way in? He hadn't thought she was *a sexy woman* four years ago, she reminded herself fiercely. Oh, no! Four years ago he had shoved her away!

She didn't have to look at him as she began easing the trousers off. On their downward path, she was aware of black tight-fitting underwear, the length and strength of his legs, his muscled calves. She was in danger of passing out, and even more so when she heard his voice in her head telling her that she was a sexy woman.

Patric had never made her feel this way when he had told her that she was sexy. Hearing Patric tell her that she was sexy had made her want to giggle uncontrollably.

'This is crazy,' she said in a muffled voice, her face bright red as she sprang back to her feet and snatched the jogging bottoms she had earlier brought down.

'Why is it crazy?'

'Because you…you need a professional to help you. A qualified nurse! What if I do something wrong and you… you damage yourself?' She was mesmerised by the sight of his legs, the dark hair on them, the rock hardness of his calves. She didn't dare allow her eyes to travel farther up. Instead, she focused furiously on the jogging bottoms and his feet as he stepped into them, supporting himself by his hand on her shoulder.

'I thought you already gave me all the vital checks?'

'Not funny, James! There. Done!'

'Tee shirt. Might as well get rid of that as well.' He slowly sank back down on the sofa.

Jennifer wondered whether this would ever end. He thought she was *sexy*. What did he feel as her fingers made contact with his skin? Did it do anything for him, considering he thought that she was *a sexy woman*? She fought back the tide of inappropriate questions ricocheting in her head and pulled his tee shirt off, where it joined the rest of his now barely damp clothes on the ground, and helped him with the tee shirt she had grabbed from her father's chest of drawers.

None of the clothes fitted him properly. The jogging bottoms were too short and the tee shirt was too tight. He should have looked ridiculous but he didn't. He just carried on looking sinfully, unfairly, disturbingly sexy.

'Okay. I'm going to stick these in the wash and have a shower and then I'll make you some coffee. I'm sure Dad has some sleeping tablets somewhere in his bedroom from when he did his back in a few years ago. Shall I get them for you?'

'Painkillers are about as far as I'm prepared to go when it comes to taking tablets.'

Jennifer shrugged and backed towards the door, clutching the clothes in one hand like a talisman.

Anyone would imagine, he thought with sudden irritation, that she had been asked to walk on a bed of hot coals. She made lots of noises about friendship but her body language was telling a different story. This wasn't the girl upon whom he had always thought he could rely. This wasn't the girl fascinated by his stories and willing to go the extra mile for him. This was a woman inconvenienced by his presence, a woman determined to keep him at a distance. He had hurt her once and she had moved on, leaving him behind in her wake. The knowledge was frustrating. He wondered how well he had ever known her. She had skimmed over her relationship with the Frenchman and had mentioned no other guys, although he was sure that there would have been some. The woman was a knockout. But whereas once she would have happily confided in him, leaving no detail out, this was no longer the case. He could remember a time when she had laughed and told him little stories about the people she went to school with and, later, to university. No more.

Fair's fair, he thought. Did she know *him*? He was uneasily aware that a relationship flowed two ways. It was something he was poorly equipped for. His relationships with women were disposable and had always involved more effort on their part than on his.

James was not given to this level of pointless introspection and he pushed it aside.

'Well, it's up to you,' she was saying now with a dismissive shrug. 'I think, as well, that you should sleep down here. The sofa is big enough and comfortable enough and it'll save you the trip up the stairs. There's a downstairs toilet, as you know…I know the bath is upstairs but I'm sure you'll be able to manage things better…tomorrow…after you've had a good night's sleep…' She hoped so because she drew the line at helping him into a bath or under the shower. Just thinking about it made her feel a little wobbly.

Having delivered that speech in a surprisingly calm, controlled, neutral voice, she fled up the stairs, had a very quick shower, which was blissful, and then returned to the sitting room with an armful of bed linen. She had expected to find him still lying on the sofa but he wasn't. He had moved to one of the chairs and switched the television on. Wall-to-wall coverage of the weather.

Quickly and efficiently, she began making up the sofa with two sheets, the duvet which she had pilfered from her father's bed, likewise the pillows.

'You probably shouldn't be taxing your back too much,' she said, hovering by the sofa because she didn't intend to stay down and watch television with him. There was danger in this pretend domesticity and she had no intention of falling prey to it.

'The more I tax it, the faster I'll be back on my feet,' James said curtly, realising, from her dithering, that she had no intention of being in his company any more than was strictly necessary. Her body language was telling him that, whatever common ground they had managed to carve out for themselves, she still hadn't signed up to be stuck with him in the cottage for an indefinite period of time. That was beyond the call of duty.

'Aren't you going to relax and watch some television with me?' he asked, perversely drawn to hearing her confirm what was going through his head, and his mouth twisted cynically as she shook her head and stammered out some excuse about still having to clear the kitchen, being really tired after the day's events, needing to finish some emails she had started earlier in the afternoon…

'In that case,' he said coolly, 'I wouldn't dream of keeping you. If you make sure that the painkillers are at hand, then I'll see you in the morning.' He stood up, waved aside her offer of assistance and made his way back to the sofa, where he lay down carefully as she left the sitting room, closing the door quietly behind her.

CHAPTER FOUR

IT DIDN'T take long for Jennifer to work out that James made a very demanding patient.

She awoke the following morning at seven-thirty and tiptoed downstairs to discover that the light in the sitting room was on, as was the television, which was booming out the news. James was on the sofa and she stood for a moment in the doorway to the sitting room with her dressing gown wrapped tightly around her, drinking him in. She had hoped to simply grab a cup of coffee and retreat back to her bedroom for a another hour's worth of sleep, but he noticed her and glanced across broodingly at her silhouette.

'There's no end to this snow,' were his opening words. The curtains had been pulled open as if to reinforce his darkest suspicion that they were, indeed, still stranded in a sea of white. 'The last time it snowed like this, life didn't return to normal for two weeks. I have work to do.'

'That goes for the both of us,' Jennifer muttered, ungluing herself from the doorway and stepping into the sitting room to toss a few logs into the now-dead fire.

She had exhausted herself wondering how she was going to deal with James under her roof. She had feverishly analysed the heady, unhealthy mix of emotions his presence generated, had shakenly viewed her loss of calm as a dangerous and possibly slippery slope to a place she couldn't even begin to imagine, a place where she once again became captive to feelings she had spent years stuffing away out of sight. Now she realised that, while she had been consumed with her own emotional turmoil, he likewise was counting down to when they could part company.

She sourly wondered if *making the best of things* was becoming a strain. Add to that the fact that he was now out of action and she could understand why he was contemplating the still-falling snow with an expression of loathing.

'I've had to let Paris know that I can't say when I'll be back. I'm missing Patric's next exhibition, which I had been looking forward to. You're not the only one desperate to get out of here!'

James wondered whether she could make things any clearer. If she had had skis, he would not have been surprised to find her strapping them to her feet so that she could use them.

And who cared whether she happened to be missing her ex-boyfriend's exhibition? He thought back to the fair-haired man with the earring and the fedora and scowled. They had gone out and broken up. Who, in God's name, remained good friends with their ex-partner? It was unhealthy. His mood, which had been grim the night before when she had made it clear that the last thing she wanted was his company, became grimmer in receipt of this unwanted piece of information.

'I've been up since five,' James told her, levering himself into a sitting position.

'Wasn't the sofa comfortable?'

'It's big but so am I. I wouldn't say it's been the most amazing night's sleep. My back was in agony.'

'I left some painkillers…'

By way of response, James held up the plastic tub and tipped it upside down. 'Not enough and I didn't have the energy to hobble into the kitchen to see if I could find more. Your father has an eccentric way of storing things.'

Jennifer, ashamed because she had spared little thought for his back in between her own inner confusion, instantly told him to wait right there, that she would get him some painkillers immediately, something stronger than paracetamol.

'Where am I supposed to go?' James asked sarcastically. 'I am literally at your mercy.'

Jennifer almost grinned. He was always so masterful, so much in control, the guy who was never fazed by anything and yet here he was now as sullen and as sulky as a child deprived of his Christmas treat because the body on which he depended had let him down.

'I like the sound of that,' she told him and he quirked an eyebrow and then reluctantly smiled.

'Really? So what do you intend to do with me?'

Jennifer didn't know whether there was any kind of double meaning to that soft drawl, but she felt the hairs on the back of her neck stand on end.

'Well...' be brisk and keep it all on an impersonal level two friends thrown together against their will, two friends who had absolutely no history '...first of all I shall go and get you some painkillers. A full tub of them, although don't have to tell you that under no circumstances are you to go over the allotted dosage—'

'There's a career in nursing crying out for you—'

'And then—' she ignored his interruption '—I shall light that fire because this room is pretty cold—'

'Fire went out some time around two in the morning.'

'You were up at two in the morning?'

'Between the sudden drop in temperature and the agony in my back, sleep was difficult.'

Jennifer, distracted from her list of things to do, wasn't sure whether to believe him or not. The advantage to their familiarity with one another was that there was no need to continually try and be entertaining or even talkative. The disadvantage was that he would see no need whatsoever to be on his best behaviour.

'And then I shall go up to your house and fetch whatever it is you want me to fetch.'

She didn't give him time to ask any questions. Instead, she went to the kitchen, located a box of strong painkillers and took them in with a glass of water.

'You'll have to help me into a sitting position.'

'Honestly, James, stop milking it.' But she helped him up and she knew, although she could barely admit it to herself, that she liked the feel of his body. She could tell herself that she had to be careful until the cows came home, but it was heady and treacherously thrilling to touch him, even if the touching, like this, was completely innocent.

Flustered, she turned her attention to the dead fire, and she began going through the routine of relighting it. It was something she had done a million times. More logs would have to be brought in from the shed outside. She hoped that they would have been cut. Her father was reliable when it came to making sure that they were well stocked over the winter months. Snow, at some point, was inevitable and it never paid to take something as simple as electricity for granted. Too many times it had failed, leaving them without heating.

James edged himself up a bit more and watched, fascinated, as she dealt expertly with the fire. He had turned down the volume on the television when she had entered the sitting room and the flickering light from the TV picked out the shine in her long, wavy hair, which fell across her face as she knelt in front of the fireplace.

She wasn't one of those useless, helpless women who thought that their role in life was to be dependent. Her slender hands efficiently did what had to be done. Her robe had fallen open and he could see her tee shirt underneath and the shorts that she slept in. Sensible sleeping wear and never, he thought, had he ever seen anything so damned sexy.

James was taken aback by the sudden ferocity of his arousal and he realised that it had been there from the start, practically from the moment he had laid eyes on her again. He whipped the duvet over him because she wouldn't have been able to miss the definition of his erection underneath the jogging bottoms that she had brought down for him the evening before and that he was still wearing.

His breath caught in his throat when, eventually, she stood up, all five foot leggy ten, and brushed her hands together to shake off some of the woody dust and ash. She had forgotten that she was supposed to clutch the dressing gown around her and now he had an eyeful of long, shapely legs and the brevity of a tee shirt that delineated full, firm breasts. He thought back to four years previously when she had offered herself to him, thought back to how close he had come to taking what had been on offer, only pulling back because he had known, instinctively, that a vulnerable girl with little experience didn't need a man like him. Desire for her now slammed into him and he half closed his eyes.

'No wonder you have to pull that duvet over you.' Jennifer walked towards him and James looked at her. She was resting her hands on her waist and wore a reproving expression. 'It's cold in here even with the heating on. You should have yelled for me to come down and light the fire. I would have understood that you couldn't do it yourself.'

James shifted and dragged his eyes away from those abundant orbs barely contained underneath the skimpy tee shirt. In resting her hands on her waist, she had pushed aside the dressing gown and was it his imagination or could he see, in the grey, indistinct light, the outline of her nipples?

'I was hardly about to do that when you made it clear that taking care of me for five minutes was a chore,' he said gruffly, dragging his eyes away from the alluring sight.

Jennifer flushed guiltily in the face of this blunt accusation. He couldn't even look her in the face and she could understand why. She had been a miserable friend, taking out her insecurities on him when he had done nothing but try and fix the gaping hole four years of absence had left in their friendship. In return, she had sniped, chastised and been grudging in her charity. God, he was probably close to truly disliking her.

When she thought about that, about him really not wanting to spend time in her company, she was filled with a sour, sickening anguish.

Although she had been at pains to avoid him for four long years, she had never, actually, thought about the simple truth, which was that she had engineered the destruction of a long-standing friendship. She had thought that the choice was a simple one. All or nothing. And in Paris she had managed to kid herself that nothing was achievable. It wasn't. Her heart picked up speed and she longed for him to look at her again instead of averting his eyes from her the way he would have averted them from a stranger who couldn't be bothered to help out in a crisis.

'I'm sorry if that was the impression I gave you, James. I didn't mean to. It's not a chore. Of course, it isn't.'

'You've made it perfectly clear that this is the last place on the face of the earth you want to be, especially when there's the exciting pull of Paris, parties and important exhibitions to view.'

'I never said anything about parties,' Jennifer mumbled. Disconcertingly, the exhibition that she had been looking forward to when she had left Paris now held little appeal. Technicolor reality was happening right here and everything else had been reduced to an out-of-focus, inconsequential background blur.

'And Patric will be fine hosting his exhibition without me. In fact, sometimes those things can be a little bit tiring.'

James, who couldn't think of the blond man without feeling distinctly uptight, pricked up his ears. He looked as she perched on the side of the sofa and picked absently at the tassel on one of the cushions, which she had rescued from the ground where it had landed at some point during the night.

'Really?' he asked in an encouraging voice and she shot him a guilty look from under her lashes.

James kept his eyes firmly fixed on her face because anywhere else would have been disastrous for the array of responses his body was having in her presence. Those were definitely her nipples outlined against the soft cotton tee shirt. He could see the tips of them. It was just one reason to make sure he looked directly at her face, although even that made him feel a little giddy.

'I love art and I just love going to exhibitions and, of course, I would do anything in the world to help Patric out, but sometimes it gets a little boring at those dos. Lots of glamorous people trying to outdo one another. The women are always dripping with jewellery and most of the men barely look at the paintings because they are into investment art. You see, Patric's parents are rather well connected so the guest list is usually...well...full of the Great and the Good...'

'Sounds tedious,' James murmured. 'Can't stand that kind of thing myself...'

'It *can* be a little dull,' Jennifer confided. 'But the financial climate is tough out there and art is a luxury buy at the end of the day. Patric has no option but to put up with stuff like that.'

'Maybe he enjoys it...' James was keen to insinuate that the wonderful best-buddy-confidante thing might have been something of an illusion. People who go abroad could be very susceptible to the kindness of strangers. 'He certainly looked on top of the world in those pictures I saw of him. Big grin, lots of hot babes around him...'

'He always has a lot of hot babes around him.' Jennifer laughed. 'He's that kind of person. Women are attracted to him. He doesn't try to hide his feminine side.'

'You're telling me that the man's gay?'

'I'm telling you no such thing!' But she found herself laughing, right back in that place where they had always been so good together. 'He's just in tune with women, likes talking about the things they like talking about, and he's also a massive flirt.'

James wanted to ask her if that was why they had broken up. Had she, perhaps, caught him in bed with one of those hot babes to whom he had been pouring out his heart, showing his sensitive side, while simultaneously chatting about clothes and shoes and feelings?

But regrettably she was standing up and telling him that she would go and get changed and get the day started.

'I'll bring you some breakfast,' she said, 'just as soon as I've had a shower. Er...' Should she ask him whether he wanted a shower? A bath, maybe, if he was up to that?

She decided not to because just the thought of helping him get undressed made her feel light-headed and horribly, horribly turned on.

'Er...I won't be long...' She thought about helping him get naked, wondered what he would look like and felt faint at the thought of it. 'You can make a list of what you want me to bring back from the house for you and I'll need your key. I know Dad has one but I have a feeling he keeps it on his key ring, which he took with him to Scotland.'

For the first time since she had arrived at the cottage and run slap bang into James, Jennifer was feeling on top of the world as she quickly showered and changed into a pair of faded jeans, a vest, a tee shirt, a jumper and some very thick knee-high socks. She knew why. Keeping him at a continual distance was hard work. Of course, she wasn't about to start being overly chummy, giggling and forgetting that he was the guy who had broken her young heart, but it was just a hell of a lot easier to let him in just a little.

At any rate she had no choice, did she? He was laid up, unable to move. She *had* to physically help him! If she could open up and be friends with him once more, it would just prove that she had got over him! More or less! Those niggly, confused, tumultuous, excited feelings she was having would therefore be nothing to worry about!

The list was ready when she returned. On it he had written, 'laptop, charger, clothes'.

'But before you disappear,' he said, making it sound as though she were Scott of the Antarctic, 'I'm feeling a little peckish...'

She was still feeling strangely upbeat when, forty-five minutes later, she headed off to his house. The estate was so vast that no other dwelling could be glimpsed from any window in the house. In summer, the trees shielded the view of the house but those trees now were bare and heavy with snow and it was a battle against the wind and the snow to make it to the front door. She had been to the house before but never to his bedroom, which she managed to locate by a process of elimination. The top of the house was comprised of a suite of rooms, and was virtually closed off, used only for guests. Of the other bedrooms, only one, apart from Daisy's, resembled a room that was occupied.

Deep burgundy floor-length drapes were pulled open so that she could see, outside, the steady swirl of the never-ending snow. Most of the pale carpet was covered by a sprawling Persian rug and a massive four-poster bed dominated much of the room. It was neatly made up but, when she leaned against the doorframe and closed her eyes, she could picture James lying on it, wickedly, sensationally sexy, with dark satin sheets lightly covering his bronzed muscular body. Then she pictured him on that sofa, with the duvet over him as she perched on the edge and chatted to him, so close that their bodies had been practically touching. She blinked guiltily and the image was gone.

Locating a handful of clothes took no time at all but it felt uncomfortable gathering them up, jumpers, trousers, tee shirts and underwear. Designer items neatly laundered and tossed into the drawer indiscriminately. She had grabbed two plastic bags before leaving the cottage and she stuffed all the items inside and then hunted down his laptop computer and charger, both of which were in the kitchen where he had left them before his heroic mission to fell the tree.

She had left him lying on the sofa and he was still there when she finally returned, although he had decided that he couldn't remain prone for ever.

'I can manage to move a bit when the painkillers kick in,' he announced, liking the way the wet made the waves in her long hair turn into curls. Her dark hair was dramatic against the paleness of her skin and he didn't think he had ever noticed before how long her lashes were or how satiny smooth her complexion.

'But I don't think it's going to do any good if I try and work sitting up on the sofa,' he pushed himself up, flexed his muscles and grimaced when his back made itself felt. 'I should be upright. You'd probably know that if you'd done that first-aid course you never got around to doing.'

'So what are you suggesting?' Jennifer asked drily.

'Well...I can use that chair over there but you might have to bring me some sort of desk. We can position it by the bay window.'

'What sort of desk did you have in mind, sir?'

'Would it be asking too much for you to get the one I use at the house? It's roughly eight by four.' He grinned and felt a kick when she grinned back at him and shook her head with an elaborate sigh.

'I suppose I could bring down my dressing table. It's small and light and it'll have to do.' She glanced down at the clothes she had brought over in the plastic bag. 'Can you manage to change yourself?'

'Only after I've had a shower, but I figure I can just about make it up the stairs myself. If you could lend me a towel...'

She did and while he showered—she could hear the water and could picture him standing under it—she cleared the little dressing table and manoeuvred it down the stairs where she set up a miniature work station for him. An office away from his office with a view of the snowy landscape.

The cottage was small and, having avoided him the night before, leaving him to watch television on his own, she resigned herself to the fact that she wasn't similarly going to be able to avoid him during daylight hours. She could work in the kitchen and she would, but even stretching her legs would entail walking into the sitting room.

Far from feeling discomforted by the prospect of that, as she had the evening before, she felt as if something had changed between them. Despite her best efforts, she had stopped fighting herself and relaxed.

He had forgone the hassle of shaving and he emerged half an hour later with wet hair and just enough of a stubble so that he looked even darker and sexier. Reluctantly she was forced to admit that neither Patric nor Gerard, the erstwhile lawyer with whom she had tried to forge a relationship, were a patch on James when it came to sheer animal sex appeal.

He took himself off to the sitting room with a pot of coffee and Jennifer tried to concentrate on catching up with her emails in the kitchen. It was almost impossible. Eventually, she began reading some of her father's recipe books, amused when she noticed a number of pages creased, dishes he had either tried or else had put on a list to try at some stage.

In the midst of trying to decide whether she should just abandon all hope of concentrating on work and start cooking something a little more ambitious for their dinner, she was interrupted by the sound of a book hitting the ground with force and she yelped and jumped to her feet.

James was standing by the window with his hand pressed against the base of his back and scowling. He turned as she entered and greeted her with, 'Why do people resist doing something when they must know that it's for their own good!'

Jennifer looked down at the heavy book that had hit the floor. It was her father's gardening tome.

'Apologies. I had to throw something.'

'Do you throw something every time you get frustrated?' she asked, moving to collect the book and replace it on the little coffee table.

'My favoured way of releasing stress is to go to the gym and punch-bag it out of my system. Unfortunately that's impossible at the moment.' He felt a lot less stressed now that she was in the room. 'What are you doing in the kitchen? Are you working?'

'I'm reading a recipe book and wondering whether I should chance cooking something a little more ambitious a bit later. Shall I get you something to eat? Drink?'

'No, but you can sit and talk to me.' He gave up the chair in favour of the sofa and lay down with a sigh of intense relief.

'Your secretary must have a nightmarish time working for you,' Jennifer commented, moving to the comfy chair by the fire and tucking her legs under her.

She marvelled at how easy it was to slide back into this easy companionship and how much she was appreciating it, having feared it to be lost and gone for good. She tried not to think that it was no good for her and then decided that she was just, finally, dealing with things in an adult fashion. Not hiding, not fighting, just accepting and moving on. What could be dangerous or unhealthy about that? Besides, she enjoyed looking at him, even though she hated admitting that weakness to herself. She liked seeing him rake his fingers through his hair as he was doing now. It was a gesture that had followed him all through his teenage years.

'My secretary loves working for me,' he denied. 'She can't wait to start work in the mornings.'

Jennifer imagined someone young, pretty and adoring, following him with her eyes and working overtime just to remain in his company, and suddenly was sick with jealousy. 'She's in her sixties, a grandmother, with a retired husband who gets under her feet. Working for me is like having a permanent holiday.'

The relief that flooded her set up a series of alarm bells in her head and she resolutely ignored them. So that crush she had had might not have been quite as dead and buried as she had hoped, but she could deal with that!

He was grinning at her and she smiled back and said something about his ego, but teasingly, blushing when he continued to look at her with those fabulous deep blue eyes.

'So tell me why you threw the book,' she said, still feeling a little hot and bothered by his lingering stare. She knew that it wasn't good to feed an addiction, however much you thought you were in control, but she found she just couldn't stand up and walk back to the kitchen and carry on reading recipe books.

'A couple of months ago, we finalised a deal with a publishing company. On the whole a lucrative buyout with a lot of potential to go somewhere, but one of the subsidiary companies is having a problem toeing the line.'

Jennifer leaned forward, intrigued. She remembered reading about that buyout on the Internet. 'What do you mean *toeing the line*?'

'They need to amalgamate. They have a niche market but it makes no money. The employees could be absorbed into the mainstream publishing company and get on board with ebooks but they're making all sorts of uncooperative noises and refusing to sign on the dotted line without a fight. Of course, they could be made to toe the line but I'd rather not take on board disgruntled employees.'

Jennifer had worked with a couple of small publishing houses in Paris, one of which specialised in maps, the other in rare limited edition books. She had been fascinated to

find how differently they were run from their mainstream
brothers and how different the employees were. They were
individually involved in their companies in a way ordinary
employees tended not to be. Both had successfully broken away from the umbrella of the mother company and
both were doing all right but hardly brilliantly. Without
any security blanket, it was tough going.

She peppered him with questions about the legal standing of the company he was involved with, quite forgetting
her boredom in the kitchen when she had been unable to
concentrate on work.

Digging into her experiences with similar companies,
she expanded on all the problems they had faced when
they had successfully completed management buyouts.

'You want to work with them,' she said earnestly. 'You
can exploit a different market. It doesn't all have to be
about ebooks and online reads. I personally think it's
worth having that niche market operating without interfer-
ence because it really lends integrity to the bigger picture.'

James, who had had no real idea of what Jennifer did
in Paris, had only known that whatever she did, she did
extremely well, was impressed by the depth of her knowledge and the incisiveness of her ideas. She also knew all
the legal ins and outs should this small arm of his publishing firm decide to break away. He found himself listening to her with interest and when, pink cheeked, she
finally rounded up her rousing argument for not trying
to force them to fit into a prescribed mould, he nodded
slowly and frowned.

'Very good,' he said slowly, and she flushed with pleasure. 'So you think I should stop trying to close this minor
arm of the business and let the employees do their own
thing?'

'Not *do their own thing*,' Jennifer said, 'but with some

one good in charge, you might be pleasantly surprised to find that there's room in this computerised world of ours to accommodate things that don't want to or can't be computerised. There are still people out there with a love of old things and we should encourage that.'

'And what would you say if I told you that I have just the person for that job in mind?'

'Have you? I guess I always thought that the people who work for you were bright young things who wouldn't want to get tied up with something they might see as old-fashioned.'

'Oh, some of the bright young things could be easily persuaded into tying themselves into something old-fashioned if the pay was right. Money is always the most effective arm twister.'

'Ye-es...' She dragged out that single syllable as she thought about what he said. 'But you also need someone who's really interested in what they're doing and not doing it just because the pay cheque at the end of the month is fat.'

'The person I have in mind is bright, passionate and would do a damn good job.'

'That's brilliant. Well...enough of me spouting my opinions. Do you feel a little less frustrated now or am I going to hear that gardening book hit the ground again? Not that I mind, but maybe you could give me a little advance warning so that I don't jump out of my skin when I happen to be holding a knife about to chop something up for our dinner!' She began standing up and he waved her back down.

'I like you spouting your opinions,' he said, which made her flush with pleasure again. 'The girl I knew just used to hang onto mine.'

And the guy I knew and with whom I was so infatuated never encouraged me to have my own...

The shift in their relationship now stared her in the face. Two adults finding ground that was equal, so different from what they once had, so different and *so much more rewarding.*

From nowhere floated those little words he had said when she had still been fighting him, still trying to prove to him how little he meant to her...

You're a sexy woman. Her heart skipped a beat and her skin began to tingle. He might respect her opinions, she thought, but that didn't mean that he had suddenly stopped seeing her as the girl next door. This time, when she tried to dredge up the hurt she felt she had suffered at his hands all those years ago, it eluded her. It was in the process of being replaced by something else. For the very first time, she thought back to that night and tried to see herself through his eyes. Young, naive, infatuated, gullible. What a poor proposition. She shook her head, clearing it of the muddle of thoughts now released to show themselves.

'I know. How boring for you.'

'Boring...never...'

'Who,' she said hurriedly, because that thoughtful look in his eyes was doing all sorts of weird things to her, 'do you have in mind for this job, then? And do you think he'll like being taken away from what he's doing to head up something that might not be a profitable concern?'

'It's a she...'

All at once Jennifer's overactive imagination, the very one she had tried to subdue, was back in play, throwing up images of a little blonde thing, cute and brainy, simpering and doing whatever was asked of her. One of his loyal employees, like his secretary only much younger and not married.

'The only fly in the ointment,' James said, watching her very carefully and marvelling at the fact that she still didn't seem to have a clue where this conversation was leading, 'is that she doesn't actually work for my company.'

'She doesn't?'

'Nope. In fact, she doesn't even work in the country.' He let those words pool in silence between them and smiled as it began to dawn on her that he was asking her to work for him.

'*I* can't work for you, James!'

'Why not? You said yourself that you were thinking of returning to England, that your father is getting older and will need you around more than he has done... Have you changed your mind about that?'

'No, but—'

'And this isn't a job offered to you out of charity. You talked yourself into it, as a matter of fact. Everything you said is spot on. It'll be the biggest challenge of your life and I guarantee you'll love every second of it.'

'Surely you have people within your company who are more qualified for the position.'

'None as passionate as you and certainly none with the required experience in dealing with a tiny, stubborn company that refuses to shift with the times.'

'I don't know what to say...'

'Then think about it.' He closed his eyes and listened to her soft breathing. 'Now what were you saying about that exciting meal you were going to prepare for me...?'

CHAPTER FIVE

'I never said that it was going to be *exciting...*'

'And you'll give some consideration to my offer while you cook...'

'Are you sure you're being serious about this, James? You've never worked with me. I don't want you to get back to London and realise that you did the wrong thing because you weren't in your normal surroundings. I can't afford to jack my job in to discover that you've made a mistake.'

'I never make mistakes.'

'And you're never laid up, yet here you are. Laid up.'

'Do you ever do anything without putting up an argument?' But his slow smile addled her. 'I mean it. You'd be perfect for the job. You can join that little team and you can all argue together about the ills of capitalism and big conglomerates wiping out small concerns.'

'Is that what they've been saying to you?' She grinned, liking the sound of that team already.

'Something like that. I've never met a more stubborn bunch of people. They've been allowed to be fully self-accounting, thanks to their very woolly-headed, charming, eighty-two-year-old boss and, now that they face the threat of being held to account, they refuse to surrender. I think one of them may have said something along the lines of they'll go down fighting. None of them have realised that they've already been taken over and they don't have much choice but to get with the programme.'

'But you're not hard-hearted enough to force them.'

'Like I said, a disgruntled employee is worse than no employee at all.'

Her heart flipped over. James Rocchi might be powerful and ruthless, but he was also fair-minded and sympathetic. He was all those things she had always seen under the surface.

'And what about their eighty-two-year-old boss? Did they feel betrayed that he'd sold them out?'

'It wasn't a hostile takeover,' James said. 'Far from it. Edward Cable was a friend of my father's even though he was considerably older. He came to me for a rescue bid. One of the big publishing houses wanted them. They were a failing company but he was reluctant to sell out to someone who would pick them apart and throw aside the bits they didn't want without thought to the employees. I have next to no experience with publishing companies and no desire to add one to my stable but...'

'But you felt you had to do the decent thing.'

'Perhaps it was my sensitive, feminine side coming out...'

Jennifer wished he would stop doing that, making her laugh, making her see him as the three-dimensional man she had never glimpsed as a young girl.

'Edward was extremely grateful to me and I could afford to buy him out. In actual fact, like I said, the company has a lot of promise. There's enough there for them to carry that little wayward arm of their company which is what I suspect he's been doing all these years.'

'Then why the need to sell?'

'Because they were making less and less money and he's never had a family. No children to inherit. A family business in a fast-moving world that doesn't have much time for family businesses unless they're incredibly well run with top-of-the-range IT departments that can take them into the twenty-first century.'

'I'll think about it.' She stood up, flexed her legs and headed out to the kitchen with a lot on her mind.

Should she take a job that would require her to work for James? If that had been suggested when she had been in Paris, hunkered down with him out of sight, she would have run a mile from the idea, but out here, forced to face him once again, she was discovering that he was not the *bad guy* of her imagination. And the job sounded as though it could be fun. In fact, it sounded like a job that would be right up her street. Should she turn it down because it involved James? Should she let pride get in the way of a good deal?

She prepared a meal on autopilot. They were now running out of fresh vegetables and, with the snow still falling and no idea when she would next be seeing a shop, she made do with tinned vegetables. Her father's larder was well stocked. It was the sort of larder that would keep a small family in food for weeks in the event of a nuclear fall-out.

She was busily opening a can when she heard James's deep velvety voice at the door and she started and spun round to see him lounging indolently against the door-frame. Immediately her body went into overdrive. How was it that he was capable of dominating the space around him so that it was impossible to remain detached?

'I've come to lend a hand.' He pushed himself away from the door and sauntered into the kitchen to peer over her shoulder. 'What feast are you preparing?'

'Nothing.'

He picked up the recipe book that she was following in a half-hearted way and scrutinised it, reciting the ingredients and then checking them off on what he could spy on the counter.

Up close and personal, his presence next to her was making it impossible to think straight and she snatched the recipe book from his hands.

'You're not supposed to be in here!' she informed him. 'You're supposed to be out there. Working. I put a lot of effort in dragging my dressing table downstairs for you because you couldn't possibly make do with the sofa and the coffee table.'

'Now you make me sound fussy.'

Her eyes slid over to where he was picking up one of the onions, which he began to peel.

'You *are* fussy,' Jennifer grumbled. 'Most people would have made do.'

'These things are fiddly.'

'Have you never peeled an onion before?'

'Look at me and tell me what you think.'

Jennifer glanced at him. His eyes were watering and he wiped one with the back of his hand.

'You're the only woman who can make me cry like this,' he murmured. She felt warm colour flood her cheeks while she mentally slapped herself on the wrist because he was just teasing her. He'd always enjoyed teasing her. He had once told her that he liked to see her blush. Now that she had stopped sniping at him, he was once again comfortable teasing her. Still, she looked away abruptly and told him not to be silly, to leave the wretched onion alone, that too many cooks spoiled the broth...

'Ah, but many hands make light work,' he quipped, carrying on with the task, 'and it's only fair that we both share the cooking duties. Besides, it gives me an opportunity to try and persuade you to work for me. I want to lock you up and throw away the key before you have time to consider other options.'

'It's tempting,' Jennifer admitted. 'But I don't want to have anyone think that I got a job because of my connections to you. It wouldn't feel right and it would compromise my working conditions. There's such a thing as office politics, although you probably don't know that because you're the head of the pile.'

'I'd be your boss on paper but in reality you'd report through a different chain of command. The company isn't even lodged in my head office. They're housed in an old Victorian building in West London, far from the madding crowd, and I shall let them continue to lease the premises. Makes more sense than dragging them into central London. So you'd be far away from me.'

He'd moved on to the peppers and was making short work of cutting them into strips. He was quick but untidy. He was a typical male with a cavalier approach to food preparation. Bits of discarded pepper were flicked into the sink or else accidentally brushed onto the ground. He might be helping but she would spend an hour afterwards cleaning up behind him. Instead of finding the prospect of that frustrating, she had to conceal a smile of indulgence. God, what was happening to her? Were her brains in the process of being scrambled like the eggs she had cooked for him the day before?

'I don't know how much notice I would have to give my boss in Paris.' She was determined to ignore the increasingly potent effect he was having on her. 'It's usually one month but they've been very good to me and I wouldn't want to leave them in the lurch.'

'Naturally.' He looked around for something else to chop and decided to avoid the mushrooms, which looked grubby. Giving up on his good deed, he washed his hands and moved on to the less onerous task of pouring them both something to drink. A glass of wine. Rules of normality were suspended out here, so why not? He leaned against the counter and watched as she started putting things together. She didn't try and impress him with her culinary skills. Twice she apologised in advance for something she was sure would taste pretty appalling. She ignored the scales and the measuring cup. She was a breath of fresh air.

He didn't like women who went out of their way to try and impress him. He had fallen victim once, many years ago, to a woman's wiles and he had vowed never to repeat the mistake. He never had. Nothing was as off-putting as the woman who wanted to display her culinary talent. Behind that, he could always read the unspoken text. *Let me show you what a good catch I am and then maybe we could start talking about the next stage.*

For James, there was never a next stage. At least not in the foreseeable future. He supposed that one day he would start thinking about settling down, but he would recognise that day when and if it came, and so far it was nowhere on his horizon.

'And then there's the question of leaving your friends behind.' He sipped his wine and resisted the temptation to brush that wayward tendril of hair from her cheek.

'I think we'll all make the effort to keep in touch,' Jennifer said drily. She looked at her concoction and hoped for better things when it had done its time in the oven. For the moment, there was nothing else to add and she began tidying the counters, nudging him out of the way and allowing him to press the glass of wine into her hand.

James wanted to ask her how much she would miss the French fedora man but he couldn't work out how to introduce him into the conversation. Nor could he quite understand why he was bothered by the thought of her ex-boyfriend, anyway. She suddenly turned to him and he flushed to have been caught staring at her.

'So I'm assuming you're on board…'

'Yes.' She made her mind up. She wasn't going to let a once-in-a-lifetime prospect slip away from her for the wrong reasons. She wasn't going to let the past dictate the present or the future. 'I'm on board. Of course, I'll have to hear the complete package.'

'I think you'll find that it will be a generous one. Shame we have no champagne. We could have cracked a bottle open to celebrate.'

Jennifer wasn't sure of the wisdom of that. Alcohol, James and her increasingly confusing emotions didn't make good bedfellows. With the cooking out of the way, she edged to one of the kitchen chairs, sat down and watched him there by the kitchen sink, sipping his wine and contemplating her over the rim of his glass.

'And I expect you'll turn this down, but there will always be a company flat for you to stay in, should you choose.'

'You're right. I've turned it down. Ellie…my friend in London…I've maintained the rent on a room in her house. I always knew that I'd be back in London and it's there, waiting for me.' She wondered what his place was like. Did he live in a house? An apartment? She wanted the background pieces to slot together so that the picture in her head could be more complete. What did that mean?

'Do you know—' she laughed lightly '—that I don't actually know where you live in London?'

'Kensington.' And you could have known, James thought, if you had kept in touch. He pictured her in his sprawling apartment, wrestling with a cookery book and trying to turn a recipe into something appetising. He pictured her with a glass of wine in her hand, laughing that rich, full-throated laughter. The image was so sudden, so unexpected, that he shook his head to clear it and frowned.

'How lovely.' That slight frown reminded her that perhaps she was being nosy.

'Well, it's big although I'm not sure you would find it lovely.' *What would she look like sitting across from him at his dinner table? With her elbows resting on the glass surface? Laughing?*

'Why?'

'It's very modern and I know you've never liked modern things.'

'I could have changed.'

'Have you?'

'Not that much,' she admitted, swirling the drink in her glass and then taking a sip. 'That's one reason why I've continued to rent the room in Ellie's house. I love where it's located and I love the fact that it's small and cosy and Victorian. There's a garden and in summer it's absolutely beautiful.'

James thought that she would have loathed the company flat, which was modelled along the lines of his own apartment, although half the size. Pale walls, pale wooden flooring, pale furniture, abstract paintings on the walls, high-tech kitchen with all mod cons known to mankind.

'I think you should email your office and give them advance warning of your plan to return to the UK. The sooner we can get this sorted, the better.' Now that she had agreed to the job, he couldn't wait to get her to sign on the dotted line.

'And you're sure you don't want to interview anyone else for the position?'

'Never been more sure of anything in my life.'

'And how is your back feeling, James? I'm sorry I haven't asked sooner. I've just been thinking about this whole job thing...'

'A near lethal diet of painkillers is doing its job.' He walked towards her. He couldn't get images out of his mind, images of her in his apartment, images of her looking at him the way he knew he wanted to look at her, images of her turning to him, raising her lips to his, closing her eyes...

He remembered the feel of her from all those years ago when he had gently turned her away and was rocked by the realisation that he had never cleared his head of the memory. He wondered whether it was because she was so much taller and so much more voluptuously endowed than the women he had dated before and since. She had offered herself to him as a naive girl and he hadn't hesitated in turning her away because to do otherwise would have been to have taken advantage of her gullibility. Now, the offer was no longer on the cards but he wanted her. He wanted her as the woman she had become. Independent, outspoken, challenging. In every respect, so different from the airheads of his past.

When he thought about the Frenchman, he had to subdue the sudden surge of jealousy. He wasn't a jealous man and yet, there it was, the green-eyed monster buried underneath his cool.

'But the pain is still there. Might have to see the doctor when I get back to London. Might...' he leaned against the kitchen table, directly in front of her so that she had to look up to meet his eyes '...have to go to a physiotherapist. Who knows? When something happens to your back, the consequences can last for years...'

'Really?'

'Really,' he confirmed seriously. 'Which is why I'm thinking that it might be a good idea if you could maybe massage my back for me.'

'Massage your back?'

'It's a big ask but I don't want to wake up at two in the morning again in agony. I also don't want to find that when this snow's disappeared, I'm still laid up and can't get back out to work.'

'And you think a massage is going to help you?'

'I don't think it can do any harm. I wouldn't have asked you two days ago. I realise you had some kind of problem with me...'

'I didn't have a problem with you,' Jennifer said awkwardly. 'I was just surprised to find you here.'

'But we seem, thankfully, to have put whatever differences you may have had with me to rest, which is why I feel comfortable about asking you to do this...unless, of course, you'd rather not help me out here...would fully understand...'

'Well, just while the chicken's in the oven. I guess.' *Massage?* If he knew how disobedient her thoughts about him had been, that would be the last suggestion to leave his mouth. He had rejected her once. He would run a mile if he thought that there might be any temptation on her part to repeat her folly.

Not that she would. But she still felt uncertain about touching him, even in a way that wasn't sexual. What excuse would she give to shoot his request down in flames? As he had said, their differences had been overcome, they were back on safe ground, friends but without the complications of her having a crush on him... He felt nothing for her. He would wonder why she couldn't help him out, especially if, as he had intimated, the pulled muscles in his back could have lasting repercussions.

'Five minutes,' he agreed. 'It might make all the difference...'

Back in the sitting room, which was wonderfully warm with the open fire burning, James stripped off his top. In truth, his back still protested vehemently at any extreme movement, although he acknowledged that he had exaggerated just a little. He lay face down on the sofa and waited as she pulled a couple of cushions over so that she could kneel on the ground next to him.

His skin was cool as she began kneading his firm, bronzed back. He had the perfect physique. Broad shoulders, tapering to a narrow waist and long, muscular legs. There was a mantra playing in her head, one she was forcing herself to repeat: *He's just a friend, how nice to be pals once again, pals always help each other out...*

She could feel his body relax under the pressure of her fingers. She, on the other hand, couldn't be further from relaxed. Her pulses were in free fall and her heart was racing so fast that she could scarcely breathe properly. It was just as well his back was to her. If not, she was certain that he would be able to see the telltale traces of a woman...

Turned on. She stopped massaging and informed him that she would have to check the chicken.

'Surely it won't be ready yet.' He turned over before she had time to stand up and suddenly she was no longer safely staring at his back but instead looking straight at him, lying there, sexily semi clad. 'Raw chicken...not recommended by any major chef...'

'Yes...well...' There was no way that she would allow her eyes to drift down to his bare chest and even meeting his eyes with some semblance of self-control was a trial.

'That felt good.'

Jennifer licked her lips nervously. There was a subtle change in the atmosphere. He was holding her glance for too long and she couldn't tear her eyes away from his. The mantra had fragmented into worthless pieces and she was only aware of the changes in her body as he continued to stare at her.

'Sit.' He shifted his big body a little and patted a space next to him on the sofa. Idiotically, Jennifer obeyed. She wasn't quite sure why.

Her fingers were resting lightly on her lap and she nearly passed out when he reached to entwine his fingers with hers, although he didn't take his eyes away from her face.

Jennifer found that she was nailed to the sofa as he began doing that thing with his thumb, rubbing it gently on her hand so that her breathing became jerky and uneven and her mouth went dry.

When the silence became too much to bear, she finally found her voice and said, shakily, 'What are you doing?' She didn't want to look at their enmeshed fingers because to do that would have been to acknowledge that she knew exactly what he was doing. Caressing her. Was it some kind of weird *thank-you-great-massage* caress? Was he aware of what it was doing to her? Was this a *friendly thing*?

'I'm touching you,' James murmured in a voice that implied that he was as surprised by the gesture as she was. 'Do you want me to stop?'

Jennifer was having trouble getting past the first part of his statement. This was what she had seemingly spent a lifetime fantasising about. The four years she had spent telling herself that daydreams played no part in reality, that he had never been attracted to her, that she had to *wake up and smell the coffee*, floated away like early morning mist on a summer day.

'Yes! No...this isn't...isn't appropriate...'

'Why isn't it?'

'You know why…' There was a very good reason but she couldn't quite remember what exactly it was and, while she was trying to figure it out, he drew her slowly down towards him.

A buzz of nervous excitement ripped through her. She was the kid opening her eyes on Christmas Day, wondering if the much-longed-for present would live up to expectation… She knew that no good would come of any physical contact with him, that she wanted, had always wanted so much more than he could ever offer, and yet his pull was magnetic and irresistible and her curiosity and raw longing far too powerful.

She closed her eyes on a soft sigh and their mouths touched, a sweetly exploring caress, then he reached both his hands into her hair, brushed his thumbs along her neck and didn't give her the opportunity to surface as the gentle exploration turned into something wonderfully, erotically hungry.

Jennifer lowered herself onto him and her breasts squashed against his chest. In between drowning in his kisses, she surfaced to tell him in a shaky voice that they really shouldn't be doing this…that he wasn't himself… that the chicken in the oven was going to burn…

He, for his part, laughed softly and informed her that this was exactly what they should be doing.

His hand had moved from the nape of her neck to slide underneath her top. He stroked her back, his hand moving upwards until he was brushing her bra strap. He carried on kissing her while he unclasped it.

'I'm not one of your Polly Pockets…' Along with a shudder of intense excitement, she felt the hangover of self-consciousness that had always afflicted her in his presence. He liked them little. She wasn't.

'Stop talking,' James commanded huskily. 'Let me see you.'

Jennifer arched up into an awkward sitting position and he shoved her top up. Bountiful breasts tumbled out, breasts that were much more than a handful, breasts a man could lose himself in. He groaned.

'I've died and gone to heaven,' he breathed unevenly. Her nipples peeped over the unclasped bra. With her head flung back and her long, curly hair tumbling down her back, she was the epitome of sexiness, a wanton goddess the likes of which he had never seen before.

Once she had offered herself to him. Only now could he receive that offering. He touched the tips of her nipples with his fingers, circling them and trying not to explode with desire as the tips firmed and stiffened in response. She was panting and moaning softly, little noises that inflamed him. He didn't know how long he would be able to indulge in foreplay because he was losing his self-control fast. When she edged upwards on the sofa so that her breasts now dangled provocatively close to his mouth, he circled her waist with his hands, determined to take things as slowly as he could.

It felt like an impossible task, requiring heroic efforts beyond his control, as he gently levered her down so that he could suckle on a proffered nipple. He drew the pulsing bud into his mouth and luxuriated in tasting her. He was a big man with big hands and her lush breasts suited them perfectly. How could he ever have been satisfied with those thin women with jutting hip bones and small breasts?

The sofa was big but they still had to wriggle to find comfortable positions. While they did, he continued sucking her nipples and massaging her breasts. He could have carried on for ever.

'This sofa isn't ideal,' he broke free to tell her.

'I can lay the duvet in front of the fire…'

'Do it without your clothes on. I want to see every naked inch of your perfect body.'

Jennifer stood up and slowly stripped off her clothes. She wasn't inexperienced but removing every item of clothing while her man looked on with rampantly appreciative eyes was new to her. She felt deliciously, thrillingly wanton. He had been vocal in his praise for her body, had lavished attention on breasts that were big by anyone's standards, had hoarsely told her that she was beautiful. Any lingering self-consciousness she might have had had disappeared under the onslaught of his compliments. In fact, she felt heady and sexy and bursting with self-confidence.

As she began pushing aside the coffee table that sat in the centre of the room, making space for the king-sized, thick, soft duvet, he told her to take her time. When it was time for her to fetch the duvet from the sofa, he stood up and began undressing, more slowly than he might have had his back not still been aching.

The breath caught in her throat as the images she had stored in her head were replaced by the reality. When he was completely naked, he held her eyes and then motioned for her to look at him as he touched himself. He was a big man and everything about him was impressively big, including the erection his hand circled.

In her wildest, fiercest day dreams, she had never imagined that it could feel so good to be standing here, naked, on the brink of making love to this man. She walked over to him and removed his hand so that she could replace it with her own. To feel him throb against the palm of her hand…

Was she doing the right thing? Never had anything felt

so right. She stretched up to kiss him and this time they kissed long and tenderly.

'You'll have to do the work,' he murmured, breaking free and leading her towards the duvet. 'Don't forget that I'm a man with a bad back…'

'I wouldn't want to do further damage,' Jennifer returned, guiding his hand to her breast. 'I remember what you said about bad backs never going away…'

'I'd be happy to swap the health of my back for an hour in bed with you.'

How easy it would be to allow words she'd never thought she would ever hear to get to her. How easy to lose herself in the excitement of the moment. A little core of practical common sense cautioned her against jumping into this wonderful situation feet first, without any thought for rocks that might lie beneath.

This was what she wanted. She had waited a long time and she knew now that she had spent the past four years waiting. How long would she have waited? She didn't know. But that didn't mean that this was the beginning of every dream she had ever had coming true. That wasn't how life worked.

They lay down on the duvet, which was mercifully soft.

She curved her body against his, drawing her leg over his thigh, and riffled his dark hair with her fingers.

When she looked at his impossibly handsome face, she saw the past entwined with the present, the boy as he had been and the man he had become. The feelings she had had for him, which had started with the sweet innocence of infatuation, had grown and matured and had never gone away. Being thrown together in the cottage had made her realise that. What she felt for him was no longer infatuation. Neither had it been four years ago. Infatuation didn't have much of a life span; it would have faded over time, replaced by other experiences.

She loved him and she knew, without quite understanding why, that any mention of love would have him running for cover. She took this on board and knew that she still wanted to be right here with him, even if her feelings left her exposed and vulnerable.

'You are beautiful,' he interrupted her chain of thoughts and she smiled sadly.

'I don't want to kill the moment, but that's not what you said four years ago.'

'Four years ago you were a child.'

'I was twenty-one!'

'A very young twenty-one,' James murmured, stroking her hair away from her face. 'Too young for someone as jaded as me. You've grown up in the past four years, Jennifer.'

Grown up but still as vulnerable as that twenty-one-year-old girl had been. She nodded and kissed him and pushed uncomfortable thoughts to the back of her mind. Her nipple tingled and throbbed as it rubbed against his chest. She straddled him and eased her body up so that when she lowered it he could take her nipple into his mouth and suckle on it until her body was alive with sensation. She groaned as he slipped his hand between her legs and began caressing her, rubbing fingers along the sensitised, slippery groove until she could hardly bear the exquisite, agonising need to be completely fulfilled.

'Not fair,' she murmured into his mouth, but she moved her hips sensuously against his exploring hand and he laughed with rich appreciation.

'I want to taste you,' he groaned, easing her into an upright position so that she was kneeling over him and he could fully take in the beauty of her spectacular body.

Her heavy breasts were amazing, her nipples dark and perfectly formed and the patch of dark hair nestled between her thighs was as sweet and aromatic as honey. He clasped her from behind and nudged her closer to his mouth.

Jennifer rested her hands flat against his shoulders and shuddered at the first touch of his tongue tasting her. He took his time, licking and exploring and then falling back when she thought she couldn't take any more. She was cresting a wave except, just when the wave threatened to break, it simply ebbed and began building again. It was the most incredible experience. She had wondered what it would be like to be with him. Nothing like this. This was way, way better than anything she had conjured up in her head.

'I can't take any more of this,' she gasped, when he had, once again, brought her almost to the point of no return.

She slid off him to lie on her side where she could try and let her breathing return to normal, but how could it when he was nudging his thigh between hers and sending her right back to the brink?

'I can't take much more myself,' James admitted shakily. 'I never lose control but I'm in danger of doing so very soon.'

'Shall I see how much stamina you have...?'

She wriggled around so that while he explored her with his mouth, she could likewise explore him with hers. He was rock hard and tasting him made her want to swoon, as did his continuing exploration of the delicate groove between her legs.

Their mutual need was frantic by the time her mouth joined his in a wet, musky, greedy kiss.

'I need you. Now.'

And I love you so much, was the reply that flew through
her head. 'I need you too,' she returned huskily.

'Are you protected?'

'I'm not at the moment but I can be…'

CHAPTER SIX

JENNIFER'S bag was lying on the ground next to the chair. She unzipped it and rustled in the side pocket where a memento of that non-event four years ago lay. The condom, optimistically bought and never used for a love-making session that had never happened, had been through a lot. It had jostled next to coins and make-up and packets of chewing gum. It had been transferred from bag to bag, a secret talisman and a permanent reminder of her youthful foolishness. It had even drowned and been resuscitated when, on a boat trip with her father in Majorca, she had accidentally dropped her bag in the sea.

Fetching it out of its compartment felt like fate.

'Not yet.' He caught her hand as she was about to tear open the little packet. 'My back feels up to a little bit more foreplay...'

In truth, he felt fighting fit and this time she was the one lying on the duvet as he explored every glorious inch of her succulent body. She tossed beneath him and he pinned her down, subjecting her to the onslaught of his mouth and tongue and hands. Their bodies were slick with perspiration when, unable to take any more, she cried out for him to enter her.

The condom that had been through the wars was finally serving its purpose and as he thrust into her she bucked and cried out in ecstasy. The feel of him inside her was beyond all expectations. He was big and powerful and he filled her in a way she would never have dreamed possible. It was as if their bodies were made for each other. They moved in perfect rhythm and her orgasm, when she finally came, was wave upon wave of such pleasure that her whole body quivered and shook from the strength of it.

The used condom joined the logs burning in the open fire and she curved her body against his with a gurgle of contentment.

'Amazing,' James murmured softly. 'It's done my back a world of good. I think we'll have to carry on with this method of physiotherapy if I'm to improve and suffer no lasting damage.'

Jennifer had never felt so blissfully happy and completely whole. For the first time in her life, her body was complete.

Then she wondered how long the physiotherapy was destined to continue. She glanced outside through the window and the snow reminded her that this was a snatched moment in time.

'Pretty incredible.' She brushed his cheek with her hand. He had shaved earlier but she could feel the stubble already trying to make a reappearance. She nuzzled his chin and settled on top of him so that she could feel every inch of his body underneath her.

'Everything you dreamed of?' There was laughter in his voice but the navy-blue eyes were solemn.

'I'm not going to feed your ego by telling you how great it was, James.' She unglued herself from him to allow his hands to wedge over her breasts where he could tease her nipples.

'Cruel woman.' He laughed out loud this time and continued to roll the pads of his thumbs over her nipples, which were already standing to attention even though it had only been minutes since they had been lavished with devotion. 'I'm tempted to punish you by not allowing you to get any sleep tonight. In fact, if I had my way I wouldn't let you leave my side...'

And he almost succeeded in doing just that. At least for the next forty-eight hours, during which the snow began to slacken in its fury and the unremitting leaden grey skies gradually showed glimpses of pale, milky blue.

Jennifer yielded to the bubble in which there were just the two of them, playing house like babes in the wood and making love wherever and whenever, which was everywhere and often. Her one condom had done its job but James had more at the house because he would never, she assumed, take risks of any kind with any woman.

He told her repeatedly that he couldn't get enough of her and, with every smile and every touch, she fell deeper and deeper into love. It consumed her and it was only when, lying on her bed, wrapped up with him, she looked outside and noticed that the snow had finally and completely stopped.

'It's not snowing any longer,' she said and James followed her gaze to see that she was right. He hadn't even noticed. In fact, over the past three days there was a great deal that he hadn't noticed. Starting with the state of the weather and ending with his work, which he had rudimentarily covered. Most of the time, his computer lay on the dressing table, which neither of them had bothered to relocate to the bedroom, untouched.

'If I know anything about the weather here, we'll wake up tomorrow morning to find bright sunshine and the snow melted.'

She couldn't prevent a certain wistfulness from creeping into her voice because with the end of the snow came the beginning of the questions that she had conveniently put to one side. What happened next? Where did they go from here? Was this a relationship or was it only a consequence of the fact that they had been cooped up for days on end?

She wasn't about to start asking questions, though.

James was adept at picking up the intonations in women's voices. He waited for her to continue and frowned when there was nothing forthcoming.

'I don't want you to return to Paris,' he surprised himself by saying, and Jennifer looked at him in astonishment.

'Well, we can't stay here for ever pretending the rest of the world doesn't exist,' she pointed out. She turned back to face the window, resting in the crook of his arm. The moon was big and fat and round and it filled the bedroom with a silvery glow.

James was accustomed to women making demands on his time. It irritated him that she made no attempt to demand anything. Having spent the past few days living purely for the moment, he was now driven to get inside her head and discover what she was thinking. He had just nailed his colours to the mast and told her that he wanted her to quit her job immediately for him, and was her only response to be that they couldn't stay put and block out the rest of the world? As if that were the only logical option to ditching her Paris placement?

'I'm not implying that we should do that,' he said edgily. 'But we're going to have to start thinking about leaving here…and we're going to have to decide what happens with us now.'

'Maybe we should go our separate ways,' Jennifer told him. He might want her to give up her job immediately but that was just him reaching out and taking what he wanted without a scrap of thought for what *she* wanted. She had been a keen observer of his girlfriends down the years. None of them had ever lasted longer than a holiday. He had taken what he wanted from them and discarded them when he thought that it was time to move on.

'You mean that?' He raised himself up and spun her round to look at him because he wanted her undivided attention.

'Look, you're not into long-term relationships—'

'And that's what you want?'

Of course it was! But she knew what would happen next if she were to say that. His pursuit, such as it was, would come to a grinding halt. She might play hard to get, but, really and truly, did she want this to end so abruptly? Eventually, it would, but why shouldn't she enjoy herself for as long as she could and let tomorrow take care of itself? She hated the weakness behind that choice but even more she hated the hypocrisy of pretending that it would be worthwhile to walk away now and become a martyr to her principles.

'Let me finish,' she inserted, picking and choosing her words very carefully. 'We…this…I guess, for me, this is unfinished business…'

'*Unfinished business?*' He flung aside the duvet and strode towards the window to glare outside at the picture-postcard winter scene before swinging around to scowl at her. 'I'm *unfinished business*?'

'Okay, maybe I didn't phrase that quite as well as I should have…'

She sat up and drew her legs up. 'Come back to bed. I…I…' Some truth forced its way out. 'I don't want to go back to Paris either,' she confessed, at which he slowly returned to lie down next to her.

'Then pack it in. Tell them something. Anything. I want you here with me.'

'Yes…it's fun…it would be nice to carry on seeing one another, I guess…' *But for how long?* That was a question that was definitely off the cards. 'I mean, no strings attached, of course…'

He could feel a return of that groundswell of dissatisfaction, the same dissatisfaction that had slammed into him when she had labelled him as *unfinished business*, and he couldn't understand why because what she was saying tuned in perfectly with his own personal philosophy. No strings attached had been his motto for a very long time. And wasn't she, in her own way, his unfinished business as well? Something had been started four years ago and it had now reached fruition.

'I never took you for a *no-strings-attached* kind of girl.'

Jennifer stilled. He knew her so well, but did she want him to ever suspect how much he meant to her? Did she really want to open herself up to being hurt all over again? She couldn't face his pity for a second time.

'It just shows how much you have to learn about me,' she murmured lightly.

'So you'll email your Paris office…bid them a fond adieu…?'

'I'll go and discuss the matter with my boss over there,' she said firmly.

'I don't know how long I can wait before you return. If we're talking in terms of months, then forget it. I'll go over there myself and drag you back to London.'

He propped himself up on one elbow, rested his hand on her stomach and traced the outline of her belly button. Jennifer, caught in the now familiar tide of longing, fought to stay in control.

'Do you always get your own way when it comes to women?' she asked breathlessly, staring straight up at the ceiling and not pushing him away when he dipped his fingers lower to sift the soft, downy hair between her thighs. Before he could start doing even more dramatic things to her body, things that always seemed to wreak havoc with her thought processes, she wriggled onto her side so that their bodies mirrored one another, both of them propped up on their elbows, staring directly into each other's eyes. She didn't want to get hopelessly lost in making love. She wanted to talk, really talk.

'I can't tell a lie...'

'What do they hope for?' she asked in genuine bewilderment. She knew what *she* hoped for, but she was a lost cause and had been from as far back as she could remember. Other women, women he had gone out with for a matter of a few weeks, surely they couldn't all be silly enough to think they could tie him down? Or was he only attracted to women like himself, women who wanted affairs and were happy to part company when the lust bit was exhausted?

'What do you mean?'

'Do they honestly think that you're going to offer them a lasting relationship?'

'How can they?' James said impatiently. 'The women I date always know from the beginning that I'm not interested in walking down the aisle. Why are we having this discussion, anyway? When we both agree that you're going to leave Paris immediately and come back here...'

Jennifer ignored his interruption. 'And they don't mind?'

'I suppose,' James admitted grudgingly, 'there are instances when one of them might have wanted to take things to another level, but, as far as I am concerned, if a woman chooses to go out with me, then she chooses what she's signing up for.' *No-strings-attached fun...* He swept

aside the unsettling memory of how her easy acceptance
of that had thrown him.

'And you've never been tempted?'

'You talk too much,' he growled.

'You'll have to get used to it.'

'You never used to ask so many questions.'

'I never used to ask *any* questions…but then again, we
were never in the place we are now, were we?'

'I've never been tempted.' He lay back and shielded
his face with his arm, then he pulled her against him and
slung his arm around her shoulder so that the tips of his
fingers were brushing her nipple, although his mind appeared to be far away.

'You probably don't remember when my father died,' he
surprised her by saying. 'You would have been…what…
fifteen? It was a pretty terrible time all round. Daisy was
in pieces.'

'I remember. You abandoned your gap year and went
to work. It was tough. I know.'

'They had just lost their figurehead. The employees
were edgy and so was the bank. I'd worked there before,
summer jobs…well, you know that.' He felt her nod against
him and he inhaled deeply. He had always thought it a
myth that confessions were good for the soul, so why was
he telling her this? 'I knew a bit about the accounts but I
was green around the ears. Like it or not, though, I was a
majority shareholder and responsibility fell on my shoulders.'

'And you were still grieving for your dad… How hard
that must have been, James…' Her heart went out to him
because, however mature he might have been for his age,
he had still only been a kid, really, one forced to grow up
very, very quickly.

'It was...very hard. I was in a bad place. I got involved with a woman.'

'You *got involved with a woman*?'

'You say that as though I started growing two heads and five arms,' James said drily. This was new ground for him. This window in his life had always been kept a secret. No one, including his mother, knew about that indiscretion ten or so years ago. He had never been tempted to confide in any of the women he had dated, even though they had all pressed him for details of his personal life as though getting beneath the armour would guarantee a foot through the door.

Jennifer had a moment of feeling special until he continued in the same flat, neutral voice, 'And the reason I'm telling you now, aside from the fact that we go back a long way, is that I want you to understand why I've made the choices that I've made with women.'

Jennifer was still trying to work out which woman he was talking about. She remembered that time quite clearly, although it was many years ago. He had lost the easy banter and the light-hearted teasing and was beginning the transition to the man he would later become. Controlled, single-minded, adept at channelling his incredible intelligence towards a single goal and getting there whatever it took. For the first time he had been around and yet she had hardly seen him.

'I thought you were completely wrapped up with the company,' she said, looking at him. 'When would you have had time to go out socialising? Dad and I nicknamed you The Invisible Man because we knew you were around but we just never saw you.'

'Well, I didn't go out socializing. The socialising came to find *me*.'

'What are you talking about?'

'Anita Hayward was the accounts manager. She looked like something that had just stepped off the cover of a magazine. Long legs, long hair, long lingering looks whenever she came into my father's office where I had set up camp. She struck just the right note between sympathy and a matter-of-fact acceptance that, tragic though the circumstances were, life had to go on. It was a break from seeing the pity in everyone's eyes and hearing the sympathy oozing in their voices. It seemed to be what I needed at that moment in time. She made it her mission to fill me in on everything that was going on in the office. I was sharp enough to know the mechanics of how things worked but I knew nothing about the people and I needed to get them onside. Twenty-minute briefings at the end of the day turned into dinners out.'

'Your mum said that you were working at the company, making sure that loose ends were tied up...but you weren't working...'

'Nope. I was being worked over.'

'What do you mean?'

James had intended to throw her the bare bones. It was more than he had ever thrown anyone else. Now, as he lay flat on his back and stared up at the ceiling, he was reliving a time he had relegated to history.

'I should have been at home. At least, I should have been at home more than I was. Instead, I was being seduced by Anita Hayward of the long red hair and the slanting green eyes.'

'And you still feel guilty...' Jennifer deduced slowly.

'Very good, Sherlock.'

'But no one operates on all cylinders when they're experiencing great stress. We react in different ways. What... what happened...in the end?'

'In the end,' he said drily, 'I discovered that she was

after a promotion. It was as simple as that. I had been used by an ambitious woman who wanted to make sure that she got the top job when the cabinet was reshuffled. And by the way, she had a boyfriend. I caught them in one of the directors' offices when I happened to return to the building after hours because I'd forgotten something. Either the boyfriend was in on the game or else he was just another sap she was using for her own ends. The fact is that, at a crucial time in my life, I took my eye off the ball.'

He turned to her, cupped her breast in his hand and Jennifer covered his hand with hers.

'You use sex as a substitute for talking,' she told him and he smiled crookedly at her.

'And you talk too much.'

'So…because of one unfortunate experience, you decided…what…?'

'I like the way you describe that wrong turn as an unfortunate experience… Well, because of that unfortunate experience, I made a rational decision to steer clear of anything called uncontrolled emotional involvement.'

For Jennifer, the long line of airhead blondes now made a lot of sense. He had fallen in love, or *thought* he had fallen in love, with a woman who was sensitive, intelligent, beautiful and mature, and, for his trouble, he had ended up being manipulated at a time when he had been at his most vulnerable. He had emerged from the experience with the building blocks for a fortress and behind the walls of that fortress he had sealed away any part of him that could be touched. The women he had dated since had been disposable and she would be as well.

Realistically, she might last a bit longer because of their history, because they had slightly more going for them than just sex, but she, like the rest of them, would be disposable.

'What happened to her?' Jennifer asked, and when he replied she could hear the ice in his voice.

'She got the sack. Not immediately, of course, and not directly. There are all sorts of regulations pertaining to employee dismissal. No, she was treated to a series of sideways moves. The vertical line she had manoeuvred towards suddenly flattened out and became horizontal. Removing myself from the equation, she failed to realise that there was no way I could have someone working for me who was capable of deceit. Strangely enough, even after I caught them having sex on the desk, she continued to believe that she could patch things over and pick up where we had left off. When she realised that her career in my company was over, she decided to lay all her cards on the table. Not only had she slept with me to further her career but she was no young girl of twenty-four with a ladder to climb and a sackful of qualifications. She was thirty-three and I later found out that most of her qualifications had been fabricated.'

'I'm sorry,' Jennifer said quietly and he shrugged against her.

'Why? We all need a learning curve in our lives.'

Jennifer, resting against him, thought that she had already had hers except she seemed to have learnt nothing from it. He had once rejected her and she had thought she had learnt to keep away and yet here she was, in his arms and busy repeating the same process, except this time the hole she had dug for herself was a lot deeper.

'And you've told me this because…you want to warn me off getting too involved with you,' she surmised thoughtfully. 'You don't have to worry on that score.'

'Because I'm your unfinished business?'

'I'm sorry that you found that offensive. I'd always wondered…'

'You don't have to explain, Jen. I've wondered too.'

'You have?'

'I'm only human. Of course I have. I had very graphic dreams about you for a long time after that incident.'

'What was I doing in those dreams?'

'When you're back in London and we have the benefit of a bed with a wrought-iron bedstead and some cloth, I'll demonstrate...'

As she had predicted from past experience, the snow stopped abruptly overnight and the temperatures rose sufficiently for the settled snow to start thawing.

They went to sleep that night and by the following evening, the outlines and contours of the fields around the house and cottage were slipping back into focus. His back was still not in top condition but between them they could clear the drive and he disappeared up to the house to get his car, which he drove down to the cottage. There was snow on the roof and the bonnet but it was melting almost as she looked at it.

In the space of a few days, she felt as though her well-ordered life had been turned on its head. She had grown, developed, matured and become an ambitious, successful and single-minded career woman in Paris, but emotionally she now thought that she had been sleepwalking. She hadn't moved on from James, she had just held herself in abeyance until they met again.

He wanted her to quit her job but he had been careful to give her no promises of a future. They would be lovers. He had treated her the same way he had treated all the women he had ever gone out with. Up front announcing his lack of commitment, making sure she didn't get it into her head that long term was part of his vocabulary.

By the time they left the estate, the insurance company had been contacted and she had also spoken to her father

and emailed him a list of things that would need doing
when he returned.

As James drove them away she looked back at the dis-
appearing cottage as though it had been a dream. When
she turned to look ahead, she wondered how she was going
to fare in the real world and, as though sensing her doubts,
James rested his hand over hers and flicked her a side
ways glance.

'I've been thinking. Perhaps I should come with you to
Paris. It's been a while since I had a holiday...'

Jennifer had had time to think about everything. From
her perspective, she had run into her past and discovered
that she had never managed to escape it after all. Locked
away in the cottage, she had found how fast a youthful
crush could turn into hopeless adult love. She had had
no weapons at her disposal powerful enough to protect
her against the man who had stolen her heart a thousand
years ago.

She wasn't, however, stupid. James liked her. He cer
tainly adored her body. That was where the story ended.
He had warned her off looking for anything more than sex
and she had successfully convinced him that they were
both on the same wavelength.

She didn't have enough good sense to walk away from
him but she had enough good sense to know that when the
time came for them to go their separate ways, she wanted
to be able to do so with her head held high.

'Come with me to Paris?' she said now. 'James...Paris
isn't going to be *a holiday*.'

James stifled a surge of irritation. 'I realise you're going
to be working but it wouldn't be beyond the realms of possibility for me to arrange to be in Paris for a week or so.'

Bliss, Jennifer thought. That would be absolute bliss.
Getting back to her little apartment, knowing that she

would be seeing him later. Cooking together and showing him all the little cafés and restaurants where the owners knew her, taking him to that special *boulangerie* that sold the best bread in the city and the markets where they could stock up on fresh fruit and vegetables and tease each other about who could concoct the most edible meal. She could introduce him to her friends and afterwards they could lie in bed and make love and he could tell her what he thought of them in that witty, sharp, amusing way of his... *Bliss.*

The pleasant daydream fell away in pieces. She knew, without a shadow of a doubt, that if she was to take that first step down the road of doing whatever he wanted it would the first step down a very slippery slope.

'You've been out of your office for several days. How on earth would you be able to wangle a week-long trip to Paris?'

A slashing smile of satisfaction curved his lips. 'Because I'm the boss. I call the shots. It's an undeniable perk of the job. Besides, I've always maintained the importance of having good people to whom responsibility can be delegated. I have a queue of people lining up to prove to me how capable they are of covering in my absence.'

'Well, I'm sorry but I don't think it would be a very good idea.'

'Why not?' He slipped his hand between her legs and pushed his knuckles against her and the pressure was so arousing that she began to dampen in her underwear. The past few days had taught her that he was an intensely physical man. He relied on his ability to arouse to make his point and to win his arguments and it would have been so easy to let him have his way.

He returned his hand to the steering wheel. He couldn't keep his hands off her and he knew that she felt the same way about him. There were times when he looked at her and he knew, from the faint blush on her cheeks, that if he reached out and felt her she would be hot and wet for him. So what, he wondered with baffled exasperation, was the problem in capitalising on the time they spent together?

'I feel badly enough about leaving everyone there in the lurch.'

'You're not leaving them *in the lurch*,' James pointed out irritably. 'They understood perfectly the circumstances surrounding your resignation. Your father's getting older... the emergency at the cottage further proof that you will be needed here more and more over time... The fact that there's the offer of a job that might not be on the cards for ever and you owe it to yourself and your father that you take it while it's there... You've offered to see in your successor and train them up. Why would you think that they're being left in the lurch?'

'Because I do.'

'That's insane feminine logic.'

Jennifer clicked her tongue and sighed because he could be so *black and white*.

'From my perspective,' he continued, proving to her how well she knew his thought processes, 'you've acted in the most sensible, practical way possible.'

'Well, I don't want you around distracting me.'

'But you know how much fun a bit of distraction can be...' James murmured, savouring that small admission of weakness from her. They were few and far between. Much to his annoyance.

'I'll be there for two weeks. Maybe three. Not long. Enough time to clear my desk, pack up the things in my apartment I've gathered over the years, go out with friends...'

Which, to his further annoyance, was something else

on his mind. The goodbyes to the old friends…everyone knew about *making love one last time for old times' sake*… He swept aside that ridiculous concern. Hell, she wasn't like that! But he was scowling at the mere hint of any such thing, the mere suggestion in his head that she might be tempted to go to bed with the good friend and ex-lover artist of the fedora and the earring.

Jennifer saw that scowl and smiled because, even though she knew where he stood on matters of the heart, his unrestrained possessiveness still gave her a little quiver of satisfaction. She hugged it to herself and savoured it for a few seconds.

'So let me get this straight,' he gritted. 'You don't want me in Paris and you also don't want either of us to tell our parents about what's going on…' It wasn't cool to behave like a petulant teenager and he forced a tight smile, which he was pretty sure wasn't fooling anyone.

'Well, I explained why I thought it wasn't such a good idea to tell Dad and Daisy,' Jennifer said vaguely. Her father knew her better than anyone else. He would never buy the fiction that she was the sort of girl who would indulge in something passing and insignificant with the guy who had stolen her vulnerable teenage heart. He would immediately know that she was in too deep. There would be questions and speculation and she wouldn't be able to wriggle out of telling him the truth.

'And I explained why I didn't get it.'

'I'm practical.' She began listing the reasons once again while her treacherous mind broke its leash and started imagining how wonderful it would be if she could shout her love out to the whole world. 'We both are…we know that this is just about having fun, so why drag other people into it?' She and James, lovers and in love, building a future together…she and Daisy planning a wedding, nothing too big…just the local church…friends and neighbours… 'It would just make it awkward when the inevitable happened.'

'Nice to know you're planning the demise of what we have before we've even begun.'

'These are *your* rules, James. You don't do involvement.' He couldn't argue with that. She was the perfect woman for him. She challenged him intellectually, which he found he enjoyed, and they were brilliant in bed together. In fact, they couldn't have been more compatible. She also respected his boundaries. There had been no coy insinuations about the importance of commitment, no leading questions that involved long-term planning, no shadow of disappointment when he had told her about his ill-timed disastrous affair with Anita and the consequences of it. Nor had she tried to lecture him on the importance of letting go of the past. In that respect, she ticked all the boxes.

He wondered why he wasn't feeling more pleasantly satisfied.

'Besides—' she thought it a good idea to move on from the commitment angle, just in case he got scared that she was hinting that *she did do commitment* and *preferably with him* '—we've both agreed that we're not each other's type…' Or something like that. The night before, when the conversation had mysteriously returned to Patric, even though he was no longer in her life *in that way*. James seemed obsessed with Patric and she couldn't understand why unless it was to confirm his singular position in her life, with no spectres at the feast. He wanted her in place and at his beck and call, without distractions from anyone, even an ex-lover, although, in return, she knew that he would never give those assurances back to her. The playing field would never be level as far as James went.

'So I'm not trying to sabotage what we have,' she concluded. 'We both know that this is just physical attraction. It'll pass in time and we'll both move on so why involve other people when there's no need?'

'Why indeed?' James grated.

'Let's just have fun. And no complications…'

CHAPTER SEVEN

JAMES glanced at his watch for the third time in ten minutes. She was running late, which was unusual for her, but he didn't mind. For the first time in nearly three and a half months, she had actually suggested meeting up, as opposed to waiting for him to take the lead. She had called him on his mobile and he had immediately booked dinner at an exclusive restaurant where, and this was just one of the upsides of wealth and power, his request for a secluded table at the back was instantly accommodated.

Of course, despite the fact that he had always loathed a woman who tried to insinuate him into a social life he didn't want and engineer arrangements without plenty of prior notice, it annoyed him that Jennifer was so completely the opposite.

She engineered nothing. She was impossible to impress. She declined his gifts. She was irritatingly elusive. Twice she had laughingly turned down his invitations to the theatre because *she was busy* and then failed to come up with an explanation why. Busy doing what? Once she had bailed on him claiming tiredness. Admittedly, he had telephoned her at short notice, in fact at eleven o'clock at night, but after a series of exhaustive meetings the only person he had wanted to see had been her. In fact, he had brought the meetings to a summary conclusion because visions of her lying naked in bed had been too much. He had failed to laugh along when she had told him, yawning, that he couldn't possibly come over because a girl needed her beauty sleep.

She wasn't playing hard to get. Far from it. When they were together, she was everything a man could wish for. She made him laugh, turned him on to the point where he was capable of forgetting everything, argued like a vixen if she didn't agree with something he said and had no qualms in teasing him on the grounds that everyone needed to be taken down a peg or two now and again. She didn't play games. She was up front in everything she did and everything she said. He had had no option but to swallow down his intense irritation when she failed to put him first.

And she never talked about a future. Everything was done on a spur-of-the-moment basis and he had gradually, inexorably and frustratingly come to the conclusion that, however sexy and accommodating she could be, he was a stopgap. When he thought about that for too long, he could feel a slow anger begin to build so he didn't think about it. Instead, he told himself that that was a good thing because stopgaps didn't lead to attachments and attachments, as he had made perfectly clear to her at the beginning of their relationship, were not on the horizon. Clearly they weren't on hers either.

A waiter came to refill his drink, a full-bodied red wine, asked him if there was anything, *anything at all*, they could bring for him while he waited for his companion. The chef, they assured him, would be more than happy to concoct some special delicacies, nothing heavy, perhaps something creative with the excellent fois gras they had only today taken delivery of...

James waved the man aside and turned on his iPad.

He sipped his red wine while lazily scrolling through

the pictures in front of him. Pictures of a house, neatly positioned in one of the leafy London suburbs, within handy commuting distance of the offices. Not a flashy apartment, which Jennifer accused his place of being... no porter sitting at the front behind a marble desk, which she found impersonal...no opulent artificial plants in the foyer, which she exclaimed weren't nearly as good as the real thing and must take for ever to dust, what a waste of someone's time.

A house in the suburbs that was already part of his vast property portfolio, which had last been rented out over a year ago and which had dropped off the radar since then. It couldn't compete with the ultra-modern places more centrally located, which appealed to expensive overseas executives. It had been brought to his attention by one of his people three weeks previously as just one of a batch to be considered for sale. He had pulled it out, seen it personally himself and made his decision on the spot to hang onto it. With some decent refurbishment, it would be perfect, and he had relished the thought of how delighted she would be at being able to move out of her poky shared house to a charming little cottage with a small but well-developed garden, a butcher, a baker and a candlestick maker within walking distance and a busy but distinct village atmosphere. Since then he had sent an expensive team of decorators in and it had been transformed, updated, modernised but retained its period style, which was the only stipulation he had made to the head of the design team. Perfect.

To think that six months earlier he might have sold it! Who said that life wasn't full of happy coincidences?

He sat back and contemplated, with satisfaction, the excitement on her face that he predicted he would see when he told her the good news. Whatever rent she was paying, he would make sure to charge less. In fact, he would happily charge nothing but he doubted she would accept that, given her stubbornness and her pride. It would be a done deal and he would no longer have to make allowances for her friend every time he visited her, tiptoeing just in case Ellie was asleep, making sure not to drink wine that wasn't Jennifer's or open beer that belonged to Ellie's boyfriend. Job done.

He glanced up, saw her hesitating by the door of the restaurant, casting her eyes around for him, and he turned off the computer, leaving it on the table next to him.

God, she was sex on legs. He had told her to don her finery, that the restaurant was one of the top ones in London, and she had. Winter was finally beginning to lose its icy winter edge as spring made itself felt and she was wearing a slim-fitting, figure-hugging dress in deep reds and browns with a pashmina artfully arranged loosely over her shoulders. Her curves seemed to grow more luscious by the day and his body was predictably reacting to the sway of her walk as she spotted him, to the sight of her cleavage, which even the modest neckline of the dress couldn't quite hide because her breasts were so lush and abundant.

For the first time, Jennifer watched James's lazy assessing smile and, instead of feeling thrilled, she felt the knot of tension in her stomach tighten.

How close she had come to cancelling out on this date! What an effort it had been to climb into clothes that had been so horribly inappropriate for her mood!

She had to force a returning smile on her face and by the time she made it to the table, her jaw was aching and her nervous system was in overdrive.

She slipped into the chair facing him, barely aware of the waiter pulling it out for her, and placed her hand over her wine glass, asking instead for a glass of fresh juice.

'You look stunning.' Deep blue eyes roved appreciatively over her. 'I'm going to enjoy taking that dress off you in a couple of hours...'

'I'm...sorry I'm a little late,' Jennifer said weakly, fiddling with the end of the pashmina.

'Traffic!' He threw his hands up in a gesture of frustration at the horrors of getting around London. He was picking up something, an uneasy atmosphere, something he couldn't quite put his finger on.

'Actually, the traffic was fine. I just...left my house later than I expected...'

'Woman's prerogative.'

'I'm never late, James. I hate it.'

'Well, you're here now. At least you haven't bailed on me because your house mate was feeling down and needed a shoulder to cry on.'

Jennifer flushed. Little did he know that her occasional cancellations had been carefully orchestrated. A sense of self-preservation had made her instil a small amount of distance and she was very glad of that now.

She fiddled with her hair, made a few polite noises about the restaurant, told him that there was no need to bring her to such an expensive place, that she was more than happy with cheap and cheerful.

'I've never been out with a woman who hasn't appreciated being taken to somewhere grand.'

'I'm not impressed by what money can buy, James. How many times have I told you that?' She heard the sharp edge in her voice and she watched as he frowned and narrowed his deep blue eyes on her.

'Are we going to have an argument?' He sat back and folded his arms. 'I should warn you that I have no intention of participating.'

Now that he mentioned it, an argument was just what Jennifer wanted, something to release the sick tension that had been building over the past few hours. An argument would be a solid staging post for what had to follow.

'I'm not having an argument with you. I'm saying that I'm not impressed by...*all this*. I mean, it's just one of the things that reveal how different you and I are. Fundamentally.'

'Come again?' James sat forward and this time the navy eyes were sharp. 'I thought you would like to be treated to a meal out somewhere fancy. I hadn't realised that you see it as a direct attack on your moral code and I certainly hadn't thought that I would be accused of...what is it exactly? That you're accusing me of...?'

'I'm not accusing you of anything. I'm just saying that this isn't the sort of place I would choose to eat. Waiters bowing and scraping, food that doesn't look like food—'

'Fine. We'll leave.' He made to stand up and Jennifer tugged him back down.

'Don't be silly.'

'What's going on?'

'Nothing. Nothing's going on. Well...'

'Well...what?'

'I've been thinking...' She drew in a gulp of air and had to fight a sudden attack of giddiness. Did he have to look at her like that? As though he could see straight into her head? Her heart was beating fast, a painful drum roll that added to the vertigo.

'Never a good idea.' His unease was growing by the second. 'My advice to you? Don't think. Just enjoy.'

'You don't know what I've been thinking.'

'I don't need to know. I can see from your face that whatever it is, I won't want to hear.'

'I just want you to know that I stick to what I've said all along, James. You and I aren't suited. We have fun together but, in the long run, we're like oil and water. We just don't have personalities that blend together. I mean, not in the long term.' She stared down at the swirling patterns of her dress.

'I have no idea what you're talking about and if you're going to say something, then I suggest you actually look me in the face when you say it.'

'This…' She looked at him. 'All of this…has been fun, really great and I appreciated every second of it, but I think…I think it might be time we call it a day.'

'I'm not hearing this.' He kept his voice very low and very even. If he gave in to what he was feeling, he thought he might end up doing untold damage to the exquisite, mind-blowingly expensive decor in the restaurant. 'You're breaking up with me. Is that what you're saying?'

'In a manner of speaking.'

'What the hell does *that* mean? I don't know what's going on here, but this is not the place for this conversation. We're going back to my apartment.'

'No!' Jennifer could think of nothing worse. The familiarity…the kitchen where they had prepared meals together reminding her of how much she was going to lose…the coffee table where they had sat only a couple of days ago playing Scrabble…which she had brought from the house with her and which she had forced him to play as a relaxation technique, although that had gone through the window when he had decided that there were other more enjoyable ways of relaxing…the bedroom with the king-sized bed, which she would no longer occupy…

It would all be too much.

James held up both hands in surrender but his eyes were cool and questioning when they rested on her face.

'Look.' She splayed her fingers on the table and stared intently at them. 'There's something I need to tell you but first of all, we need to get this whole relationship straight

We need to admit that it was never going to stay the course. We need to break up.'

James raked his fingers through his hair and found that his hands were shaking. 'Between last night and tonight, you've suddenly decided that we need to *break up*…and you expect me to *go along with you*? I'm not admitting anything of the sort.'

'This isn't how I meant this conversation to be, James. This isn't where I thought I'd find myself, but something's…something's cropped up…'

'What?' With something to focus on, his mind went into free fall. It was a weird sensation, a feeling of utterly and completely losing all self-control. 'You've found someone else. Is that it?' His voice was incredulous. Break up? How long had she been contemplating *that*? Had there been some other man lurking in the background? One of those fictitious sensitive, emotionally savvy guys she had once told him made ideal partner material? He could think of no other reason for her to be sitting opposite him now telling him that *it had been fun but*…

'Don't be crazy. I haven't found anyone else. When would I have had time to go out looking?'

'Are you telling me that you think I've monopolised your life? Is that it? Because I'm perfectly happy to take things at a slower pace.' He could scarcely credit the levels to which he was willing to accommodate her.

Jennifer was sure that he would be. He hadn't emotionally invested. He could always tame his rampant libido until such time as it was no longer rampant.

'No, it's not that.'

'Let me get this straight. For no particular reason, you've suddenly decided that we can't go on. There's no one else on the scene, we've both been having fun and yet it's no longer enough. Am I missing something here? Because it feels as if I am.'

'There's no easy way of telling you this, James, so I'm just going to come right out and say it. I'm pregnant.'

She couldn't look him in the face when she said it so she stared down at her lap instead while the silence thickened around them like treacle.

'You can't be. You're using contraception. I've seen that little packet of pills in the bathroom. Are you telling me that you've been pretending to take them?' At some point, the wires in his brain appeared to have disconnected. In possession of one huge, life-changing fact, he found that he could only fall back on the pointless details around it. 'I can't talk to you here, Jennifer.'

'I'm not going to your apartment.'

'Why the hell not?'

'Because I want to deal with this situation in neutral territory.'

'Your choice of words is astounding.'

'How *else* do you want me to phrase it, James? Shall I start by telling you that I'm sorry? Well, I *am*. And before you even *think* of accusing me of getting pregnant on purpose, then I'm warning you not to go there because that's the *very last thing on earth* I would do.'

'Message received loud and clear!'

'I *have* been on the pill. I can only think that that first time…'

'We used a condom. We were protected. We were *always* protected. This is madness. I can't believe I'm hearing any of this.'

'Because you signed up for a life you could control!'

'It's not going to get either of us anywhere if we start arguing with one another!'

'You're right,' Jennifer whispered. 'And I didn't come

here to argue with you. I'm happy to take the blame. The first time we made love, I used a condom that I'd had for absolutely ages...' *Four years to be precise. How ironic that the condom she had bought to enjoy sex with him all those years ago had become the condom that allowed her to fall pregnant.* 'It may have perished. They can.' Salt water seeping through the foil would do that, she thought, and if not salt water when her bag had dropped into the sea, then an infinitesimal puncture with the sharp edge of a key, or nail clipper or tweezers or any of the hundred and one items she had flung in her bag next to it over the years.

She had gone on the pill the second they had returned to London because he had laughed and told her that he would be a pauper at the rate they went through condoms, little knowing that by then it had been too late.

'I did go on the pill when we got back here so I never noticed that I hardly had any kind of period at all and nothing a couple of weeks ago, so I decided to go and see the doctor just to make sure that I was on the right dosage. Anyway—'

'You're pregnant.' It was finally sinking in. 'You're going to have a baby.'

'I'm sorry.' His face was ashen. 'You're in shock. You must be. I understand that and I'm sorry that I've spoilt the meal but it's been on my mind all day and I just wanted to get it out of the way. And now that I have, I think the sensible thing to do would be for me to leave and for you to take a little time out to adjust to the idea, so...'

He was going to be a father!

'But why didn't I notice?' he asked, dazed.

'We never notice things we aren't expecting. Not really. And I'm not one of those rake-thin types who show every ounce of weight they put on. Apparently someone with a fuller figure can hide a pregnancy for a lot longer.' Part of her wished that he would be open with his displeasure. Instead, he looked like someone who had been punched in the stomach and, instead of reacting, decided to lie on the ground and curl up instead. It wasn't him! That in itself was proof of how thrown he was and of course he would be! She had had a head start in the shock stakes. She had had several hours in which to absorb the news. The accusations would come when it really and truly sank in, the reality, the consequences, the potential to throw his neatly ordered life out of sync for ever. The waiter came and was waved away.

'You're going to have my baby and you greet me with the opening words that you want out of the relationship?'

'We don't *have* a relationship.' Jennifer tensed as she sensed the shift in the atmosphere. He had looked glazed but now his eyes were sharpening and focusing on her. 'We have…had…a passing physical interest in each other. And don't look at me like that. You know that I'm just being honest.' Was he aware of the fleeting pause she allowed, a window in which he could contradict her, tell her that things had changed, that he might not have entered their relationship with a future in mind but had found commitment along the way? The brief silence went unfilled. 'Neither of us counted on this,' she said abruptly.

'You're going to have my baby and the only way you can think of dealing with the problem is by breaking up…'

Jennifer stiffened at his use of the word *problem*.

'It seems the best solution,' she said coolly. 'You didn't ask for this to arise and I'm not going to punish you, or me for that matter, by putting you in a position of having to stand by me whether you like it or not.'

'I don't believe I'm hearing this. We're lovers but have you forgotten that we also happen to be friends?'

She had forgotten neither but how could she explain

that a baby needed more than a couple united by passion? Or even, for that matter, friendship?

'So tell me,' James said with increasing cool, 'how do you see this panning out? Perhaps you'd like me to walk away from you and leave you to get on with it?'

'If that's what you want to do, then I'll accept it.'

'If you really think that that would be an option I would consider, then you don't know me very well, do you?'

Which was why, of course, she had pre-empted any reaction by breaking up with him. She had known that he wouldn't walk away from the situation. She could never have fallen head over heels in love with a man capable of doing that, and that in itself was the problem. James would want involvement. He would want to do the right thing but his heart wouldn't be in it. Any affection he felt for her would eventually wither away under the strain of having to deal with a child he hadn't asked for and being stuck with a woman he had never envisaged as long term.

'We'll have to get married.' Something powerful stirred inside him, something he could scarcely identify.

'And that's exactly why I opened this conversation by telling you that it's over between us,' Jennifer said quietly. 'I know you want to do the right thing, but it wouldn't be fair on either of us to be shackled to each other for the sake of a child.'

They both broke off while the waiter came to take their orders. James didn't bother to consult the menu. He ordered fish and she followed suit, not caring what she ate. Her appetite had deserted her.

'And marriage!' She leaned forward to continue where she had left off. 'I bet you've never given a passing thought to the idea of getting married, have you?'

'That's not the point.'

'It's exactly the point,' Jennifer cried. 'Marriage is

something serious. A commitment between two people who see their lives united for ever.'

'At least that's the romantic interpretation of it.'

'What other interpretation could there possibly be?'

'Something more pragmatic. Think about it. One in every three marriages ends in the divorce courts and all of those bitter, sad, divorced couples probably sat across each other at a dinner table holding hands and waxing lyrical about growing old together.'

'But for two out of those three, the holding hands and waxing lyrical works. They end up together.'

'You're an eternal optimist. Experience has taught me to be a little more cautious. But none of that matters and we could argue about it for the remainder of the evening. The fact is, we're in a situation where there's no choice.'

Jennifer's heart sank. If she didn't love him, maybe it would have been easier to settle for the solution that made sense, but if she married him, she would be torn apart.

'I'm sorry, James,' she said shakily, 'but the answer has to be no. I can't marry you because you think it makes sense. When I get married, I want it to be for all the right reasons. I don't want to settle for a reluctant husband who would rather be with someone else but finds himself stuck with me. How healthy would that be for our child, anyway?'

How could life be suddenly turned on its head in the space of a few short hours? Very easily was the conclusion he was reaching as he looked at her stubborn, closed expression.

Rage at her blinding intransigence rushed through him in a tidal wave. 'And tell me this. How healthy would it be for our child to grow up without both parents there? Because that's something you need to consider! This isn't about you and your romantic notions of fairy-tale endings!'

Jennifer flinched and looked away. 'You're not going to make me change my mind,' she said, gathering all the strength at her disposal.

'No? Then let me provide you with an alternative scenario. Our child grows up in a split family and in due course finds out that both of us could have been there but you wouldn't have it because you were determined to look for Mr Right, who may or may not come along. And if he does coming along…well, I'm telling you right now that he won't be involved in bringing up my child because I'll fight for custody.'

Battle lines had been drawn but Jennifer could scarcely think so far ahead.

'And your father. What do you intend to tell *him*?' This before she had had time to digest his previous statement.

'I haven't thought—'

'Because don't even think about insinuating to your father that I haven't offered to do the decent thing. I intend to make it perfectly clear to my mother and to John that I've proposed to you and that you have in your wisdom decided that the best course of action is to go it alone. We can see what they make of that.'

'I don't want to fall out over this—'

'Then maybe you should have thought about broaching this bombshell in a slightly different way!'

'It wouldn't have made any difference. The result would have been the same and I'm sorry about that. Look, I can't eat any more. I've lost my appetite. I think I should go back home now.' She half stood, swayed and sat back down. In an instant, James was at her side, all thoughts of pursuing his argument forgotten.

Jennifer was barely aware of him settling the bill, leaving a more than generous tip for the waiter, who had sensed an atmosphere and had patiently left them alone. She had her head in her hands.

'Honestly, I'm fine, James,' she protested weakly as soon as they were out of the restaurant.

'How long have these giddy spells been going on?'

'I get them now and again. It's nothing to worry about...' But it was comforting to have his arms around her, supporting her as he hailed a black cab and settled her inside as though she were a piece of porcelain.

'What did the doctor say?'

'I didn't mention them. I was too shocked at finding out I was pregnant!'

'You should go back. Have a complete check-up. What's with these people? Don't they know how to do their jobs?'

'Don't worry. It's nothing!'

For the first time since finding out about the pregnancy, she wondered whether she was making the right decision in turning down his proposal. Whether he loved her or not, he was a source of strength and when would she need that strength more than right now? When she was facing motherhood? He wanted to do the right thing. Was it selfish of her to hold tight to her principles? Or in the big scheme of things, was *he* right? Could his suggestion of a loveless marriage be the right one?

The questions churned around in her head for the duration of the trip back to her house although by the time they got there, the giddiness had disappeared, replaced by utter exhaustion.

'We can talk about this tomorrow,' she told him by the front door and James looked at her in glowering frustration, his hands jammed into his pockets.

'We weren't talking back there. You were dictating terms and I was supposed to listen and obey.'

'It's hard for me too, James, but marriage is a big deal

for me and I want to marry a guy who wants me in his life for all the right reasons.'

'Weren't you happy when we were together?' he asked gruffly and, taken aback by the directness of the question, Jennifer nodded.

'So now that there's a baby, why would that change?'

'Because,' Jennifer said helplessly, 'it's not just about having lots of sex until it fizzles out and we say goodbye to one another and move on.'

'But the having lots of sex is a start.'

'You're so physical, James.' She could feel her body quivering at the hundreds of memories she had of them making love. She would never forget a single one of them. 'The cab driver's going to start getting impatient.'

'Why? It's good money sitting there with the meter running. We still need to talk this one through. In fact, let me get rid of him. I could come in with you. The lights are all off, which means your house mate probably isn't here. We could discuss this in private...'

What he meant was that they would make love. It was the language he spoke most fluently and she knew she couldn't trust herself if they climbed into bed together.

'We both need to think about this.' She placed her hand on his chest to stop him from following her into the house. 'Tomorrow we'll think about the practicalities. And by the way, I would never tell Dad that you weren't taking the responsible attitude, James,' she returned to the insinuation she had never protested.

He nodded, at a loss for anything else to say. What did she mean about right reasons? Wasn't a child a good enough reason for them to be married? It wasn't as though they didn't get along, weren't fantastically suited in bed. He was genuinely bewildered at his failure to convince her.

He wondered whether he should have taken a step back,

led up gently to the notion of getting married. She had stated from the very beginning that she wasn't looking for commitment and yet he had jumped in, feet first, arrogantly assuming that she would fall in line with what he wanted. But how could she fail to see that getting married was the most practical solution to the situation? And what about *them*? Was what they had about to dissolve because a baby on the way had crystallised the fact that she didn't see him as a long-term partner? He felt hollow and angry and impotent.

At any rate, there was nothing to be gained by continuing to push her into the decision he wanted her to take. It was clear that she wasn't about to let him into the house and she looked utterly shattered. For her own good, he knew that he should go and let her get some rest, but he still hesitated because he couldn't think of her walking away from him. It wasn't going to happen. He would make sure of that.

His mind returned to that picture-perfect house, bristling with new furniture, updated to within an inch of its life, perched in its very own garden, a stone's throw from all those quaint village services she had always raved about. He had intended to present it to her with casual indifference, a little something he had pulled out of his portfolio. He would have offered it to her at a laughably low rental and suggested that it would hit the open market if she decided not to take it because of her pride. Faced with that, he had known that she would not have been able to resist.

Well, the house was still there but now it would be his trump card.

The sick feeling of helplessness that had earlier gripped him began to dissipate. He was a man who thought quickly and made decisions at the speed of light. He was a man who found solutions. He had extended the obvious solution and had been knocked back, but now he had another solution up his sleeve and thank God for that. For a few minutes back there, he had not been able to think clearly.

'You're right,' he said heavily. 'Although I don't like leaving you like this. You look as though you're about to collapse.'

'It's been a long day.' For one craven, cowardly moment Jennifer was tempted to open the door for him, let him in so that she could curl up in his arms and fall asleep. She just wanted to hold him close because he made her feel safe.

'Tomorrow, then,' he murmured, badly wanting to touch her but instead pushing himself away from the doorframe. 'If you still want to meet on neutral territory, then we will. If you're agreeable to coming to my apartment, I will get my caterer to prepare something. We can talk about what happens next...take it from there...'

CHAPTER EIGHT

TAKE it from there...yes. Discuss the practicalities...of course. But are you excited...even just a little...?

That was the question Jennifer would really have liked to have asked him. Once she had recovered from the shock of being told that she was pregnant, she had been thrilled at the thought of having a baby, of having *James's* baby. In the space of twenty-four hours, she had managed to wonder what the baby would look like, what sex it would be, whether he or she would attend a single-sex school or a mixed one, what career path he or she would follow, what his or her girlfriends or boyfriends would do for a living and at what age he or she would be married.

She was *excited*.

She didn't think that excitement would feature on James's chart of possible reactions to the news. She thought that the best she could hope for would maybe be *acceptance* and its close relation, *resignation*.

How could he not see that any marriage based on a situation where those two damning words were involved would never be anything more than a marriage of convenience? Destined to eventually fail because the last thing a marriage should ever be was *convenient*?

Nevertheless, that didn't stop Jennifer wondering what it would be like to be married to him. She marvelled, sitting in the back of the chauffeur-driven car he had sent for her, how close she could be to everything she had ever dared hope for while still being so far. She wondered whether his anger and disappointment at what had happened would have gathered steam overnight. Had he lain awake thinking that, thanks to her idiocy, his plans for his life were now lying in ruins at his feet? Without a roomful of unwitting chaperones to keep the full extent of his reactions at bay, would he feel free in the privacy of his own apartment to really let rip when she showed up?

At any rate, they were going to have to reach some sort of agreement with regards to the way forward because she couldn't keep her father in the dark for ever. She was due to visit the following weekend and she intended to break the news then that he would be a grandfather.

With the days getting longer, it was still bright by the time she got to his apartment at a little after six and there was no time to brace herself for the sight of him because he was waiting for her in the marbled foyer as she entered. Fresh from work and still in his suit, although without a jacket and with the sleeves of his white shirt rolled to his elbows and his tie loosely pulled down to allow the top two buttons of his shirt to be undone.

'Oh.' Jennifer came to a dead stop as she was buzzed in. 'Have you just arrived from work? You should have called and asked me to get here a bit later. I wouldn't have minded.' All over again, she felt that powerful sensual tug towards him, as though her body had a will of its own the second she was in his presence.

James frowned. He had grown accustomed to her exuberance. Her awkward formality was a jarring reminder of the situation in which they had now found themselves. He shoved his hands in his pockets and took a few seconds to look at her. She was wearing a stretchy knee-length dress in shades of green and was it his imagination or could he now see evidence of her pregnancy? More rounded curves, breasts that would be substantially bigger than a handful... On cue, he felt himself harden and, given the inappropriateness of the moment, he dealt with that by walking towards her and keeping his eyes firmly focused on her face.

'Don't worry about it. Plans have changed. We won't be heading up to the apartment.'

'Where are we going?'

'Should you be wearing such tight dresses?' He cupped her elbow with his hand and hustled her back towards the front door. 'Now that you're pregnant?' Hell, she looked even sexier than ever. What man wouldn't run into a lamp post trying to catch a backward glance at her luscious body. 'Your breasts are spilling out of the top of that dress!'

'Yes, I've put on some weight.' Jennifer felt herself flush at the thought that he might be turned off at the sight of her increasing size. He was, after all, a man who was primarily concerned with the whole 'body beautiful' rubbish. If he wanted her to hide herself in smocks now, then what on earth was he going to do when she reached the size of a barrage balloon?

'I don't need to get into maternity frocks just yet,' she snapped, watching as the chauffeur hurried to open the passenger door for her. 'Some women *never* buy maternity clothes! Have you seen how unappealing they can be?'

'You won't be one of those women.' He grimaced in distaste at the memory of a certain recent magazine cover that had been lying around his apartment, courtesy of Jennifer. It had featured a semi naked actress, heavily pregnant, in a few shreds of clothing that had done nothing to conceal her enormous belly.

'You can't tell me what I can or can't wear!'

'I just have. Tomorrow we'll go shopping. Get you some looser stuff.'

'Is that one of the *practicalities* you were planning on talking to me about?' She spun to face him as soon as the passenger door had slammed behind him. 'Because if it was, then you can consider it discussed and struck off the list!'

James gritted his teeth in frustration. Not the perfect start to the evening.

In the ensuing silence, Jennifer debated whether she should apologise for overreacting and decided firmly against it.

'Where are we going?' she asked eventually.

'There's something I'd like to show you.'

'Really? But I thought we were going to discuss...how we're going to deal with the situation...'

'Consider what I show you as part of the ongoing conversation on the subject. Were you all right when you got back to your place last night?'

'What do you mean?'

'You felt faint at the restaurant.'

'Oh, yes. Well, that was just my nerves.' She rested her head against the window and looked at him from under her lashes. 'I know you think that I'm being unreasonable, James...'

'This is a debate that can only end up going round in circles, Jennifer. Let's put it on the back burner for the moment and concentrate on a more productive way forward, shall we?' They had cleared the centre of London in record time and were now heading south west. 'Question— when do you intend to break the news to John? I'd like to be there.'

'I don't see why—'

'Is every suggestion I make going to end in a pointless argument?'

'I'm sorry. I don't mean to be difficult.'

'Good. At least we agree on one thing. It's a start!'

'There's no need to be sarcastic, James. I'm trying my best.' She looked away quickly. Honesty forced her to admit to herself that that was hardly the strict truth. So far he had risen admirably to the occasion and she had relentlessly shot him down in flames. Was it his fault that he couldn't supply her with the words that she wanted to hear? He had not once apportioned any blame on her shoulders, even though he must surely be blaming her in his head. He had offered to do the decent thing and was probably baffled by her refusal to even consider the possibility of marriage. He had no intention of leaving her in the lurch even though he doubtless wanted to run as far as his feet could take him to the farthest corner of the earth because fatherhood, for the man who couldn't commit, would have been the final albatross around his neck. His *one hundred per cent innocent* neck.

He wanted to do what was best for the baby growing inside her, *their baby*, and all she could think was that he didn't love her, that she would become a burden, that he would end up hating her. He was thinking of the baby. She, on the other hand, was thinking about herself.

Consumed by a sudden attack of guilt, Jennifer lapsed into nervous silence and watched as they cleared through the busiest part of London, heading out until increasing patches of greenery replaced the unremitting grey of pavements and roads.

She still had no idea where they were heading and was surprised when, eventually, the car weaved through a series of small streets, emerging in front of a house that looked as though it had leapt out of a story book.

'Where are we?' She looked at him with bewilderment and James offered her a ghost of a smile.

Thirty-six hours ago, he thought, this would have been a terrific surprise for her. Now, it was part of his back-up plan.

'We're in one of the leafier parts of London.'

'I didn't think they existed. At least, not like this...' She couldn't take her eyes off the picture-perfect house in front of her. The small front garden was a riot of flowers on the verge of bursting into summer colour. A path led to the front door of the house, which was small but exquisite. A child's painting of a house, perfectly proportioned with massive bay windows on the ground floor, flanking a black door, a chimney minus the smoke, beautiful aged stone awash with wisteria. To one side was a garage and to the other one mature tree, behind which peeped a lawn swerving away towards the back of the house.

'Who lives here?' she asked suspiciously. 'If you had told me that we would be visiting friends of yours, then I might have worn something different.' She was annoyed to discover that she was already thinking about changing her wardrobe, stocking it with baggier, more shapeless garments even though she had protested otherwise.

'It's one of the properties in my private portfolio.' He was already unlocking the front door, pushing it open and standing aside to let her brush past him.

'You never mentioned this!'

'I never saw the need.'

'It's wonderful, James.' Flagstones in the hallway, cream walls recently painted from the looks of it, a deep burnished wooden banister leading up to the first floor. Jennifer tentatively took a few steps forward and then, becoming braver, began exploring the house. It was much bigger on the inside than it looked from the outside.

Downstairs, a range of rooms radiated from the central hallway. There was a small but comfortable sitting room, a dining room, a box room with built in shelves and cupboards that had clearly been used as an office, a separate television room and, of course, the kitchen, which had been extended so that it was easily big enough to fit a generous-sized table as well as furniture. It was a kitchen and conservatory without the division of walls. French doors led out to a perfectly landscaped garden. Whoever had owned the house previously had been a keen gardener with an eye for detail. Various fruit trees lined the perimeter of the garden and between them nestled a bench from which you could look back towards the house and appreciate the abundance of plants and flowers.

'Gosh.' Eyes gleaming, Jennifer turned back to James. 'I can't believe you would ever choose to live where you do when this place could have been an option.'

'It's very country cottage. Why don't you come and see the upstairs? I think you'll like the four-poster bed in the master bedroom. Everything has been done to the highest possible standard while maintaining the period of the place. Did you get a chance to see the Aga in the kitchen? I can't think that there would be many properties in London boasting one of those.' He wondered what on earth someone would do with one of those. He had no idea. It looked like a baffling piece of kitchen equipment, but she had wistfully mentioned them in the past and he had taken mental note. In fact, he had furnished the house with her in mind. He had been surprised at how many details of her likes and dislikes he had gathered and stored over time.

'You sound like an estate agent.' But for the first time since she had broken the news, James could see laughter in her eyes. Where he had failed, the house appeared to be succeeding, and before she could remember that she was fighting him he ushered her up the stairs so that she could gasp and admire the bedrooms, the bathrooms, the walk-in dressing room in the master bedroom.

'So,' he said, once they had returned to the kitchen and taken up position at the wooden kitchen table, wooden because she had previously expressed a dislike for all things chrome and glass, 'what do you think of the place?'

'You know what I think, James. I imagine it's been written all over my face.'

'Good. Because this is one of the practicalities I want to talk to you about. A shared house isn't going to be suitable for a baby. This, on the other hand...' He made a sweeping gesture to encompass the cottage while keeping his deep blue eyes firmly fixed on her face.

He could see the indecision on her face and had to fight down the desire to tell her that she had no choice in the matter. Laying down laws and trying to browbeat her into submission hadn't worked. 'I firmly believe,' he carried on smoothly, just as she was about to say something, 'that children benefit from a more relaxed lifestyle than living in the centre of London can provide for them. Don't you remember how much fun it was for you growing up in the countryside? Granted this is nothing like the countryside but there's a garden, quite a big one by London standards, and all the shops you might need are within walking distance.'

'But don't you have plans for this place? I mean, was it rented out before? I hope you didn't turf out any tenants, James.'

'Your faith in me knows no bounds,' he said drily, knowing that part one of the battle had been won. 'I didn't turf anyone out. You like the place and I think it would be ideal. It's within commuting distance from London. In fact, surprisingly convenient for the underground...which brings me to the small matter of your job.' Which, he could see from the expression on her face, was something she had given no thought to.

'My job…I hadn't really thought…'

'It's going to be awkward.'

'Are you telling me that I'm out of a job?' Jennifer demanded, bristling.

'Far be it from me to tell you anything of the sort. But think about it. You're pregnant. You won't be able to keep it under wraps and sooner or later it's going to emerge that I'm the father. Might not be the most comfortable situation in the world for you…'

'So I leave and do what?'

'Practicality number two. Money. Naturally, if you want to stay on at the company then there's no way I would stand in your way. I have no problem dealing with whispers behind my back and if you think you can deal with that as well, then I'll support you one hundred per cent in staying on.' He allowed a few seconds of silence to follow that statement. It took a strong person to survive the toxicity of office politics. 'At any rate, whether you continue working or not, I intend to open a bank account for you and, just in case you want to argue with me over this, I'm telling you right now that no child of mine will want for anything because you're too proud to accept money from me.'

'I have no objection to you paying for our child, James,' Jennifer muttered awkwardly as she feverishly played in her mind the scenario of her co-workers gossiping behind her back. She could be a genius at her job and would still not be able to fight the rumours that she had got where she was because she had been sleeping with her boss. Pregnant by him would stoke the fires from a slow simmer to a blazing inferno.

'*You* come as part of the deal, Jen,' James said gently. 'I intend to ensure that your bank balance allows you freedom to choose what you want to do. Carry on working for the company, go ahead. Find another job closer to this place, then feel free. Give up work altogether, then I'm one hundred per cent happy with that solution. It's up to you. Of course...' he appeared to mull over his next few words '...I'm jumping the gun here, assuming that you don't have a problem moving out here...'

'It might be better all round to be out of central London,' Jennifer concurred, trying hard not to show her relief at leaving the house. Ellie was free, single and disengaged. She played loud music and entertained her boyfriends with exuberance. It was her house. In between all the other stresses, Jennifer had wondered how a baby would feature in that set-up. She sneaked a glance at the super modern kitchen, the granite work surfaces, which blended so harmoniously with the old-fashioned dresser and the mellow kitchen table with mismatched, charming chairs. She could get a kitten.

'And the job?'

'I'll have to think about that.'

'But not for too long, I hope. Your replacement would have to be found,' he murmured. 'Could take ages...but moving on from there to the thorny subject of our parents...'

'I told you...I'm going to break it to Dad on the weekend.'

'I'd also like my mother to be present...'

'Yes. Of course.' She hadn't actually dwelled on that particular horror waiting round the corner, but, of course, Daisy would have to be present.

'How do you think they're going to take the news?'

'Why are you talking about this,' she said with a hint of desperation. 'I'm just living one day at a time.'

'Which doesn't mean that tomorrow isn't going to come.'

'I know *that*.'

'Do you?'

'Of course I do! I'm not a complete idiot. I know there are going to be lots of complications to sort out along the way but at least we've managed to do something about the first one. I mean, I *had* actually wondered whether sharing Ellie's house was going to be suitable for a baby. And it's a busy road. I've always felt sorry for those women pushing buggies on crowded streets, trying to get them on and off the buses...'

'The cottage is vacant. I'll make sure that you're moved by the end of next week. You won't have to lift a finger.'

Hearing him say that was like heaven to her ears. She didn't want to feel burdensome to a man who didn't love her, but, still, she could feel his strength seep into her and the temptation to close her eyes and lean on him was so great that she felt giddy.

James stood up, walked to the fridge and told her that he had taken the liberty of getting his caterers to prepare a light supper for them.

'Sit,' he ordered, when she automatically began rising to her feet. 'I've got this.'

'I feel like I'm on a roller-coaster ride with someone else manning the controls,' Jennifer mumbled, but halfheartedly, and he glanced across at her with a crooked smile.

'Go with it.'

'But I don't want you to feel that you've got to play the responsible role,' she protested, clinging to her principles by the tips of her fingers. 'You haven't listened to what

I've said. You don't have to *take care of me*. It's enough that you're allowing me to move to this cottage.'

'And you haven't listened to *me*. I intend to be fully involved. I have no intention of letting you play the independent woman, keeping me at a distance while you wait for Mr Right to come along.' Just thinking about that set his teeth on edge. Food ready, James took it to the table in its original containers, which he had stuck in the microwave, and placed two plates and cutlery alongside them.

'We have to get past this…atmosphere…' he gritted, sitting back and waiting as she dished out some of the one-pot dinner for herself. He had had a little time to think about the change in her attitude towards him and he had worked out the reason behind it. Where their relationship had always been one of easy-going friendship, which had developed into something even more so after they had become lovers, the fact of her unexpected pregnancy had thrown up all the downsides to what they had. She could no longer relax with him because she now felt trapped, hemmed in by a situation she couldn't reverse and, in one way or another, stuck with someone she had always planned on moving away from eventually. She wasn't in it through free choice. She was in it through lack of option.

Which didn't mean that he was going to allow himself to be shunted aside so that she could start her search for her knight in shining armour the second their baby was born. No way.

Which, in turn, brought him to the delicate part of the proceedings.

He thoughtfully worked his way through the meal in front of him, half listening as she tried to assure him that there was *no atmosphere*, that she was *just tense, that's all*, that she was very pleased that they were both being *so adult* about everything. In mid-sentence, he cut her short by raising his hand, and Jennifer stuttered to silence.

'Why don't we go and relax in the sitting room?'

'It feels odd…when someone's probably just left this place…'

'Let me dispel that myth,' he drawled, getting to his feet. 'The house was last rented out over ten months ago. It's just been recently refurbished.'

'Has it? Why? Were you going to put it on for rental again?'

James flushed darkly. 'It doesn't matter.'

'So…all this furniture is new?' Jennifer stood up, marvelling that there was not a single thing in the house that she wouldn't have chosen herself.

'Yes, I had my people equip it,' he allowed, omitting the fact that he had personally instructed them in what to buy.

'They couldn't have chosen better.' Jennifer gazed admiringly at the deep, plush sofa in the sitting room, the broad comfortable chairs on either side of it. Every detail took her breath away, from the rich burgundy drapes to the intricate Persian rug covering the polished wooden floor.

She flopped onto the sofa and curled her legs under her. Disturbingly, because she was determined to keep her distance, James sat next to her, then turned, his arms along the back of the sofa and behind her.

'So…'

'So…?' She could feel her heartbeat pick up and a fine film of perspiration break out over her body.

'So I want you to tell me why the atmosphere has changed so fast between us…'

'Well, isn't it obvious?' Jennifer stammered. She blinked rapidly to try and stabilise her nerves, which were suddenly in wild free fall. Two days ago, she would have been in his arms right now, two days ago they would have been making love. Yes, things had changed, but he would still be bemused by her retreat. Without the complication of being emotionally involved, lust, for him, would still be intact.

'Nope.' He inclined his head and continued staring at her.

Jennifer wished that she had some sharp retort to counter that, but she didn't. She was suddenly hot and bothered and flustered and very much aware of his proximity.

'Then it should be...'

'Why is that?' He sighed and raked his fingers through his hair in a gesture that was so familiar that Jennifer felt her heart tug painfully. 'Has pregnancy done something to your hormones? Turned you off sex? Or have you suddenly found that you're no longer attracted to me because you're carrying my baby?'

'No!' The hot denial was out before she had time to think about it and swallow the shaming truth back down. 'I mean...'

'You mean you *are* still attracted to me,' James murmured with satisfaction.

'That's not the point!'

'The point being?'

'The point being that there's more at stake than just the two of us being attracted to each other and *having fun*, no *strings attached*.'

'You say *having fun* as though it's a crime against humanity.'

'Stop confusing me,' Jennifer cried, standing up agitatedly and pacing the sitting room, aware of his deep blue eyes thoughtfully following her. She paused to stand in front of him. She was fired up with a tangle of confusing emotions. She could barely think properly. She wasn't expecting him to reach out and place his hand gently on her stomach. She froze.

'I want to feel it,' James said unevenly. Children had never appeared on his radar but now that he knew that she was carrying his child, he was driven to have tangible evidence of it, wanted to feel the more rounded stomach.

'When will you feel it moving?'

'James, please...'

'I took part in the creation...surely you wouldn't deny me the chance to feel it?' He slipped his hands under her dress and gently tugged it up to expose her stomach. He felt her release her breath on a shudder but she didn't move away. How oblivious had he been? She was by no means big but she was certainly bigger than when they had first become lovers, her stomach smooth and firm but no longer flat. She was wearing little cotton briefs and they were low enough for him to see the shadow of soft, downy hair peeping above the elastic band.

He closed his eyes, faint with an overwhelming surge of intense, driven craving. It was like nothing he had ever felt in his life before. He had had friends who had wittered interminably about the joys of parenthood, who had reliably informed him that having a baby was like nothing on earth. He had always listened politely and promptly shoved the rhapsodies into the waste disposal unit in his head. Now, he wondered...was this what it was all about? This weird feeling that left him shaken and uncharacteristically out of control?

He would savour the moment and not question its origin. He felt her fingers settle into his hair as he shoved the dress farther up so that her bra was just visible.

With a soft tug he pulled her towards him onto the sofa and she fell with a little thud into the squashy cushions.

Jennifer knew that this was not how the evening was

supposed to proceed. She was *vulnerable* and should be *protecting herself.* That certainly did not include letting him pull her dress over her head, which he was now doing, not to mention unhook her bra so that he could ease it off her shoulders to expose breasts that were sensitive and tingling with wanting him to touch them.

Which, of course, he did, but not until he had told her how her body had changed.

He grazed his teeth against her nipples, sending a compulsive shiver rippling through her body. 'How couldn't I have seen the changes to your body?'

'You weren't looking,' Jennifer breathed unevenly. 'Nor was I and, like I've said, we just don't really notice what we're not expecting.' In fact, she had known that she had put on weight, but she had assumed that it was because she had been eating more, enjoying the domestic life with a man who refused to be tamed.

James barely heard her. He was too busy licking and tasting her, circling the stiff buds with his tongue before lavishing his attention on them in turn. She arched up, eyes closed, with her hands clasped behind her back.

His mouth was clamped on one nipple and as he sucked it she twisted and moaned, automatically parting her legs, inviting his hand to cup the throbbing mound between her thighs.

He could feel her dampness seeping through the cotton underwear but he was in no hurry to take off the flimsy garment. Instead, he pressed down and kept up the insistent pressure as he continued to lose himself in her glorious breasts. He liked the way she writhed every time he dipped his fingers deeper into her wetness. How could she hold herself at a distance from him? How could she deny that what they had together was good? Beyond good? He slipped his hand underneath the briefs and she groaned as his searching fingers began stroking her, over and over and over again, rubbing her clitoris until she wanted to pass out with pleasure.

They made love slowly, as though they had all the time in the world, and afterwards she almost dozed off in his arms.

'We shouldn't have done that,' was what she said instead, hating herself for having succumbed and terrified that it would just be the start of a pattern. He would get too close and she would give in because she was weak. She scrambled to push herself away from him but he yanked her back.

'Try and say that with conviction and I might start believing you.'

'I mean it, James. It's not on.'

'That's not what your body spent the past hour telling me.'

'And I don't *want* to let *my body* deal with this situation!' She pushed against him and scrambled around for her clothes, ashamed of herself.

James propped himself up and looked at her as she wriggled into the dress.

'I know you don't,' he agreed gravely, and Jennifer shot him a suspicious look from under her lashes.

'You do?' She looked at him uncertainly.

James sat up, strolled to where his boxers had been tossed, put them on and then turned to look at her.

'You're still attracted to me but you don't want that to get in the way of making what you think is the right decision.'

'Well...yes.' She sat back down, although this time on one of the chairs instead of on the sofa. Her body was as stiff as board and her hands rested primly on her knees as she continued to warily look at him. Fading light made his half-clothed body look as sculpted and as perfect as a classical Greek statue. She thought it would help if he could stick a shirt on.

'And I apologise unreservedly if I took advantage of your weakness and seduced you.'

'Well, you're not entirely to blame...' Jennifer was driven to admit, looking away with a guilty flush.

'Of course you're not going to want to get back into the situation we had, given the circumstances.'

'No-o-o...' Jennifer dragged out that one syllable for as long as she could while she tried to figure out where his speech was going.

'In a matter like this, you simply don't see the value of thinking with your head.'

'It's not *that*—'

'And I won't waste time trying to make you see that this is *just* the time when you *should* be thinking with your head. You don't want to marry me and I accept that.'

'Really? You do?' Why did that hurt so much?

'Why do you sound so surprised?'

'Because you seemed so convinced that getting married was the only option we had. As if we were still living in Victorian times and you had to make an honest woman of me, however unhappy we might both have ended up being!'

James held his cool and continued to look steadily at her. 'Let's just say that I'm willing to make compromises in that area.'

'What sort of compromises?'

'You move in here and I move in with you. No marriage, but I think we should see how it works out, give this a chance for the sake of the baby. If it doesn't work out, then we do the modern thing and walk away from each other.' He flushed darkly and looked away. 'We were happy…before this all blew up,' he said in a rough undertone. 'What's to say that we couldn't be happy again?'

CHAPTER NINE

JAMES didn't realise just how happy life with Jennifer was until he got her panicked call in the middle of a meeting.

When he had suggested that they live together, he had had no idea what he had been letting himself in for. He was a man accustomed to freedom of movement and independence, fundamentally unanswerable to anyone. Of course, he acknowledged that that state of affairs had undergone some change in the weeks after they had become lovers. He had also acknowledged that had she agreed to his original terms they would probably have been married by now, but somehow the fact of marriage had seemed less daunting than the fact of living together.

With a sense of duty no longer in the equation, living together had struck him as more of a commitment, even though he couldn't fathom why.

He had engineered a smooth transition for her from apartment to house. Despite her reassurances that she was as healthy as a horse, waving aside the occasional giddy spell as nothing to worry about, insisting that she continue working until a suitable replacement was found for her position, he made sure that she had as little to do as humanly possible during the actual move. Packing a few personal items into a suitcase was just about all he allowed her to get away with.

Clearing his own apartment had been a far weirder experience. The enormity of what he was doing only struck him when, after two days and a lot of overtime from engineers kitting out an office space in the house, he finally closed the front door on the outside world and joined her in the kitchen for their first meal as…a couple living together.

It had felt like a massive step but he had made sure to conceal any trepidation from her. He knew that she remained wary and hesitant and pregnancy appeared to have made her unpredictable. It happened. He knew. He had surreptitiously bought a pregnancy book and had read it cover to cover. He now felt equipped to start his own advice column.

'James…do you think you could get here?'

'What's wrong?' Few people had his private cell number. He had felt his phone vibrate in his pocket and her name had popped up. Immediately he had silently indicated to the assembled financiers that they should continue with the meeting and he had left the conference room. When she had started working at the little publishing company that he had inherited as part of the much bigger takeover package, Jennifer had never contacted him. She had quit two weeks previously and not once had she called him at work, even though he had repeatedly told her that she was more than welcome to interrupt his working day.

If the tone of her voice hadn't alerted him that something was wrong, the mere fact that she had called would have.

An emotion shifted into gear that he almost couldn't recognise. It was fear.

'I'm bleeding…I'm sure there's nothing to worry about—'

'I'm on my way.'

Jennifer lay back on the sofa with her legs raised and

tried to stay calm. Looking around her, she took in all the small touches she had introduced to the house that had very quickly felt like a home. The vases filled with flowers picked from the garden, the framed photos on the mantelpiece, the ornaments she had picked up from Portobello Market a couple of weekends previously. She wasn't entirely certain that James even noticed them and she hadn't wanted to point them out.

She had been gutted when all talk of marriage had been dropped so quickly. Had he been relieved that that final act of commitment had been avoided? Living together was so different and, of course, she had no one but herself to blame for not grabbing his marriage proposal when it had been on the cards.

Not that she regretted it. She still believed that without love a marriage was nothing more than a sham and yet...

Hadn't he been just the perfect partner ever since they had moved in together? She constantly told him that there was no need for him to treat her as though she could break at any given moment, and yet hadn't she loved every minute of it? Hadn't she begun to hope that the love he didn't feel for her might begin to grow from affection?

And now...

Jennifer didn't want to think that she might lose this baby. She wished that she had paid more attention to those dizzy spells she had been having off and on. If she lost the baby, then what would happen to her and James? It was a question she didn't want to think about because the answer was too agonising to deal with.

She closed her eyes and kept as still as possible but her mind continued to freewheel inside her head, irrespective of her desperation to keep it under control. She had already invested so much love into this unborn baby. How would she cope if anything happened?

She sagged with blessed relief as she heard the sound of James's key being inserted into the door, and he was in the act of removing his jacket as he pushed open the sitting room door and strode towards her, his face grey with worry.

'I shouldn't have bothered you—' She smiled weakly as she snapped out his mobile and began dialling.

'And hurry!'

'Who have you called?'

'The doctor.'

'I panicked. I'm sorry, James. I'm sure all I need is a bit of rest.'

James knelt down next to her and slipped her hand into his. 'You're not a doctor, Jen. You don't know what you need. Gregory is the top guy in London and a personal friend of the family. I asked him whether I should get an ambulance to take you to hospital but he said that he'll give you the once-over first. You scared the hell out of me.'

'I didn't mean to.'

He asked her about her symptoms, detailed questions to which he produced a series of clinical answers, and she smiled when he confessed to the pregnancy book languishing in his briefcase.

'A little knowledge is a dangerous thing, James.'

'Why didn't you tell me sooner that the giddy spells hadn't stopped?'

'I didn't want to worry you. I didn't think that there was anything to worry about...' And besides, she could have added truthfully, she hadn't wanted to rock the boat. She hadn't wanted to face up to anything that might cast a shadow over the picture-perfect life they had been living for the past few weeks. Except uncomfortable questions couldn't be put to bed by ignoring them and they were out of the box now, demanding attention.

'I know you're going to tell me that this isn't the right time to have this conversation, James, but—'

'It's the right time.'

Jennifer's eyes fluttered and she felt her heartbeat quicken.

'You don't know what I'm going to say...'

'I do.' He smiled crookedly at her. 'Do you think I don't know you a bit by now? Whenever you want to broach a delicate topic of conversation, you lick your lips for courage and begin to play with your hair.'

'I didn't think you noticed stuff like that.'

'You'd be surprised what I notice.' *About you.* 'You won't lose this baby.'

'You can't say that and what if I do?' There. It was out. She closed her eyes and calmed herself by taking deep breaths. Deliberately, she stuck her hands by her sides and fidgeted with the baggy tee shirt she was wearing.

'Then the time is right for us to talk about what happens. Before Gregory gets here. Stress isn't good for you and I don't want to stress you out but I need to say something.'

Jennifer looked at him with resignation. She wanted to put her hand over his mouth and hold the words back but he was right. He needed to tell her that their arrangement would not survive a miscarriage. The stress of hearing it would be a great deal less than the stress of lying here pretending that everything was just fine. And if she didn't lose the baby, then it would be good to know the next step forward. She realised that through the happiness and joy of the past few weeks, there had remained a poisonous thread of doubt that things would continue the way they were for ever more. That just wasn't how life worked. Now, she would put a face to those doubtful shadows and, yes, there would be disappointment all round, because their respective parents had accepted the situation and given their full support, but life was full of disappointment, wasn't it?

'I know that sharing this house with me probably wasn't what you had in mind when you realised that you were pregnant. You were only just coming into your own and suddenly...fate decides that it's time for you to have another learning curve...'

'What do you mean *coming into my own*?'

'I mean—' he sighed heavily and raked his fingers through his hair '—you'd led a sheltered life and then you go to Paris and return a changed person. You're sexy as hell and you're on a journey of discovery.'

'I hadn't realised that I was that adventurous.'

'You fell into a relationship with me to fulfil some youthful infatuation but I know you still want to get out there and discover what the world has in store for you.'

'I do?'

'Of course you do. You said as much when you told me that I was unfinished business. Unfinished business comes to an end eventually.' He looked away, his broodingly handsome face flushed. 'I guess I maybe ambushed you when I suggested we live together... You'd already turned down my marriage proposal. I'll admit that there was a certain amount of blackmail involved when I suggested that we live together. How could you turn down marriage *and* turn down the other reasonable alternative on the table without appearing utterly selfish?' He threw her a challenging look.

'It was a good idea,' Jennifer murmured, heart beating fast.

'And it *has* been...hasn't it? Good?'

Jennifer nodded, because it required too much effort to try and work out how much of herself she should give away. Should she tell him that it couldn't have been better

He had been affectionate, supportive, reassuring and, as she had always known, wonderfully funny and entertaining. He had returned from work early so that she could put her feet up while he had cooked. He had put up with Ellie coming round every few days and had only given her the occasional dry look when her best friend had launched into colourful stories about her love life. He had indulged her sudden taste for soaps on television and brought her cups of tea whenever she wanted. She had been spoiled rotten and that was the problem. It had felt like a *real* relationship. But there was no ring on her finger and she was now terrified that if there was no baby to provide the glue that kept them together, it would all come crashing down around her ears. Had she been too greedy in holding out for perfection?

'I'm going to tell you something, Jennifer, and it may shock you but it needs to be said before Gregory gets here.' James looked at her and felt the ground shift under him. He had always been able to predict the outcome of the things he did and the decisions he made. But then, his biggest decisions had always involved deals and business. He had come to realise that, where emotions were involved, there was no such thing as a predictable outcome, which made it a hell of a lot scarier.

Jennifer braced herself for the shock. She reminded herself that it was better to get it all out of the way.

'If you lose this baby—and I don't think for a minute that you will. In fact, you're probably right, there was probably no need to get Gregory over at all, but better safe than sorry—'

'Just say what you have to say,' she told him gently. 'Between the two of us, I'm the only one allowed to babble when I'm nervous.'

James opened his mouth to tell her that he wasn't

nervous, that nerves were a sign of weakness. Except he *was* nervous.

'Whatever the outcome, I want to marry you, Jennifer. Okay, I'll settle for living together. I don't want to rush you into anything and living together at least gives me a shot at persuading you that we can make this work. But I want to persuade you of that whether or not there's a child involved.'

She looked at him in silence for so long that he began to wonder whether he had got it all wrong. The signs had all been there. Hadn't they? He had a talent for interpreting nuances. Had that talent let him down now?

'We've been happy. You said so yourself.' A defensive tone had crept into his voice.

'Very happy,' she finally whispered, which he thought was a start. She could feel tears begin to gather in the corners of her eyes. Pregnancy had sent her emotions all over the place. Now she wondered whether they had interfered with her hearing as well.

'Are you saying that you want us to be married… whatever…?'

'Whatever.'

'But I don't understand why.'

'Because I can't imagine that there could ever come a day when I wouldn't want to wake up with you next to me, or return from work knowing that you'd be waiting for me. I love you, Jennifer, and, even if you don't return the feeling, I wanted to lay my cards on the table—'

'When you say you *love* me…'

'I love you. With lots of strings attached. So many strings that you'd tie yourself up in knots trying to work your way out of them.'

'I love you too.' She tried to hold back the tremulous grin but failed. 'And what strings are you talking about?'

'I'll tell you later.' The consultant had arrived, a very tall, very gaunt middle-aged man with a severe expression that only relaxed into a smile once his examination was completed and he accepted the cup of tea offered to him.

Some slight concern but nothing to worry about. Blood pressure was a little on the high side but nothing that some rest and relaxation wouldn't sort out. The bleeding would stop and, although he could understand her worry, rest assured that it had not been a dramatic bleed. He had examined and listened and everything was in order. And she was in good hands. He had known James since he was born because he had delivered him.

Jennifer smiled and listened, relieved that her panic had been misguided. Her mind was all over the place. Relief that everything was all right. Wonder mixed with disbelief that James had told her that he *loved her*. Had he just said that because he had thought it might calm her? Had he known that that was what she had wanted to hear? She caught his eye and tried to still the nagging doubts from trying to get a foothold.

Everything in that warm glance he had given her made her heart soar but acceptance of the fact that he didn't love her was so deeply embedded that she was cautious of letting herself get wrapped up in silly dreams.

He could read her mind. The second the consultant had left, he settled her comfortably back on the sofa, tucking the cushions around her and tutting when she told him that she wasn't an invalid.

'I'm not sure I can believe you in any matters to do with health when you decided to keep those giddy spells to yourself,' he chided, and Jennifer half sat up and drew him towards her.

'And I'm not sure I can believe what you said before...'

'I could tell that that was playing on your mind.' He

sighed and pulled one of the chairs towards the sofa and sat on it, taking her hand in his. 'And I don't blame you. I know I made it clear from the start that I wasn't into long-term relationships and I had the history to prove it. My life was my work and I couldn't foresee a time when any woman would take precedence over that. I never realised how big a part you played until you left. I had become accustomed to having you there.'

'I know,' Jennifer said ruefully. 'I always felt like the girl in the background you could relax with but never really looked at. I just saw a procession of gorgeous little blondes and it didn't do anything for my confidence levels. And then I got my degree, got that job in Paris…and best of all, you asked me out to dinner. I thought it was a date. A proper date. I thought you'd finally woken up to the fact that I wasn't a kid any more. I was a woman. I was so excited.'

'And then I knocked you back.'

'I should have known that nothing had changed when you ordered cake and ice cream as a surprise, with a sparkler on top.'

'I'd do the same thing now,' James told her with a slow smile that made her toes curl. 'You love cake and ice cream and I love that about you. I didn't knock you back because of how you looked.'

'It felt that way to me,' Jennifer confessed.

'You were on the brink of going places. When you kissed me, I felt like a jaded old cynic taking advantage of someone young and vital and innocent. You had stars in your eyes. I honestly thought that you deserved better, but it was hard. I'd never touched you before. I was so turned on… We should have had all this out in the open a long time ago.'

'I couldn't. You were right about me. I was very innocent and very young. I wasn't mature enough to handle a discussion about it. I just knew that it felt like the ultimate rejection and I ran away.' She sighed and looked at him tenderly. 'I thought I'd built a new life for myself in Paris and, in a way, I had.'

'You're not kidding. I had the shock of my life when I saw you again at the cottage. You weren't the same girl who'd made a sweet pass at me four years before. I couldn't take my eyes off you.'

'Because I had changed my outward appearance…'

'That's what I thought,' James confessed ruefully. 'I wasn't into the business of exploring my motivations. One and one seemed to add up to two and I took it from there. I never stopped to ask myself how it was that you were the most satisfying lover I'd ever had.'

'Was I? Really?' Jennifer shamelessly prodded him encouragingly and he favoured her with one of those brilliant smiles that could literally make her tummy do somersaults.

'You're fishing.'

'I know. But can you blame me? I spent years daydreaming about you and then just when I thought I'd mastered it, we meet again and I discover that I've always been daydreaming about you. When we finally became lovers… it was the most wonderfully perfect thing in the world.' She thought back to the moment the bubble had burst. 'I never thought for a second that I would get pregnant and the really weird thing was that it was the fault of my condom, the condom I'd bought four years ago…'

'To use with me?' James looked at her in astonishment. 'You're kidding.'

'No, I'm not. I hung onto it for so long that it went past its sell-by date. Actually, I think drowning in salt water and being bashed about in my bag can't have helped prolong its useful life.'

'Well, I'll be damned.'

'When I found out, I had to face up to the truth, which was that you found the sex amazing and you liked me because we'd known each other for such a long time, but you didn't *love* me.'

'The whole business of love was something I hadn't got my head around. I just knew that you turned up holding a bombshell in one hand and a Dear John letter in the other and I couldn't seem to find a way of getting through to you. When I proposed to you, I didn't pause to think that you might actually turn me down.'

'If I'd known…'

'Shall I confess something?'

'What?'

'This house was never renovated to be rented or sold on.'

'What do you mean?'

'It came to my attention because it had been out of action for a while. It must have slipped through the net somewhere along the line but, the second I saw it, I knew I wanted it for you and that was long before I found out that you were pregnant. God, I was a fool. I should have known from the very second I started thinking about you and houses in the same breath that I had fallen in love with you. In fact, I was going to tell you about it when you broke the news.'

Pure delight lit up Jennifer's face and she flung her arms around his neck and pulled him towards her.

'I thought when you dropped all talk about getting married that you were relieved to have been let off the hook… Most men would have been if they found themselves landed with an unwanted pregnancy…'

'Relieved to have been let off the hook?' James laughed and stroked her hair. 'All I could think was that you wanted out, you wanted to be free to find this perfect guy of yours and all I could think was that I needed to put a stop to that, needed to show you that *I* was that perfect guy... I knew that the thought of marriage had sent you into a tailspin. You didn't want to marry me and I wasn't going to try and force your hand and risk you pulling back completely.'

'But I *did* want to marry you. You don't know how much. I just didn't want to be married for the wrong reasons. I hated the thought that you would put a ring on my finger because you couldn't see any other way round the situation. I didn't want to be your lifelong obligation.'

'So now I'm asking you to be the lifelong love of my life. Will you marry me...?'

The wedding was a quiet affair, with family and friends, and, after the scare with the pregnancy, baby Emily was born without any fuss at all. She was plump and pink, with a mop of dark hair, and for both Jennifer and James it was love at first sight.

For a commitment-shy guy determined never to be tamed, James was home promptly every evening. It was very important to delegate, he told her—delegation ensured that employees were kept on their toes and it motivated them in their careers, and if he had taken to working from home now and again, then it was simply because modern technology made it so simple, virtually mandatory in fact.

She would have to get used to having him under her feet because, he further informed her, he was tiring of the concrete jungle. It was no place to bring up all the children he planned on them having. It was a cut-throat world and, besides, there was just so much money a man could use in a lifetime and, that being the case, why waste time pursuing more when there were so many other, more rewarding things to do with one's time?

And there was no doubt what those other things were.

Jennifer teased him about the man he had become and she knew that she would spend a lifetime ensuring that the happiness he gave her was returned to him a thousandfold...

* * * * *

LET'S TALK

Romance

For exclusive extracts, competitions
and special offers, find us online:

MILLS & BOON
A ROMANCE FOR EVERY READER

FREE delivery direct to your door

EXCLUSIVE offers every month

SAVE up to 25% on pre-paid subscriptions

SUBSCRIBE AND SAVE

millsandboon.co.uk/Subscribe

MILLS & BOON

THE HEART OF ROMANCE

A ROMANCE FOR EVERY KIND OF READER

MODERN
Prepare to be swept off your feet by sophisticated, sexy and seductive heroes, in some of the world's most glamourous and romantic locations, where power and passion collide.
8 stories per month.

HISTORICAL
Escape with historical heroes from time gone by. Whether your passion is for wicked Regency Rakes, muscled Vikings or rugged Highlanders, awaken the romance of the past.
6 stories per month.

MEDICAL
Set your pulse racing with dedicated, delectable doctors in the high-pressure world of medicine, where emotions run high and passion, comfort and love are the best medicine.
6 stories per month.

True Love
Celebrate true love with tender stories of heartfelt romance, from the rush of falling in love to the joy a new baby can bring, and a focus on the emotional heart of a relationship.
8 stories per month.

Desire
Indulge in secrets and scandal, intense drama and plenty of sizzling hot action with powerful and passionate heroes who have it all: wealth, status, good looks…everything but the right woman.
6 stories per month.

HEROES
Experience all the excitement of a gripping thriller, with an intense romance at its heart. Resourceful, true-to-life women and strong, fearless men face danger and desire - a killer combination!
8 stories per month.

DARE
Sensual love stories featuring smart, sassy heroines you'd want as a best friend, and compelling intense heroes who are worthy of them.
4 stories per month.

To see which titles are coming soon, please visit

millsandboon.co.uk/nextmonth

JOIN US ON SOCIAL MEDIA!

Stay up to date with our latest releases, author news and gossip, special offers and discounts, and all the behind-the-scenes action from Mills & Boon...

 millsandboon

 millsandboonuk

 millsandboon

It might just be true love...